Jonathan Taylor is author of the memoir *Take Me Home: Parkinson's, My Father, Myself* (Granta Books, 2007), and is editor of *Overheard: Stories to Read Aloud* (Salt, 2012). He was born and raised in Stoke-on-Trent, and now lives in Leicestershire with his wife, Maria, and their twin daughters, Miranda and Rosalind. This is his first novel.

ENTERTAINING STRANGERS

JONATHAN TAYLOR

SALT

CROMER

PUBLISHED BY SALT PUBLISHING
South Lodge, Hall Road, Cromer NR27 9JG United Kingdom

© Jonathan Taylor, 2012

First published by Salt Publishing, 2012

Printed and bound in the United Kingdom by Clays Ltd

Typeset in Paperback 9 /12

ISBN 978 1 907773 27 3 paperback

1 3 5 7 9 8 6 4 2

This book is dedicated to S.K., who should not be confounded with any of the characters herein. Nor should the plot be mistaken for a very similar true story.

Be not forgetful to entertain strangers: for thereby some have entertained angels unawares.
—*Hebrews 13, v.2*

For Beans,
Hope you enjoy it!
17.11.12   Very best wishes
and love,
Jonathan

CONTENTS

PRELUDE

PRELUDE

And . . .

    . . . and the fire happened almost seventy-five years ago . . .

    . . . but somewhere, somehow, the city still burns.

    The fire was seventy-five years ago . . .

    . . . but somehow, somewhere, in the back of my mind, the city still burns.

    The fire was seventy-five years ago, one-thousand-six-hundred miles away . . .

    . . . but somehow, lost somewhere in the back of all our minds, it carries on.

    The city still burns . . .

    . . . and the city still burns . . .

    . . . and the city still burns . . .

    . . . and . . .

ACT ONE

1.

. . . and it wasn't till much later I realised what had happened—that I'd fled the burning city of my memory, my dreams, my history, only to be sucked into someone else's. In a very different way, this someone else's burning city was just as unreal, bizarre, disorientating as the one I had left behind, and seemingly forgotten. Where my city was swarming with soldiers, the someone else's city was swarming with ants . . .

I'll explain, or try to.

One exhausting and exhausted night—I found out afterwards it was the year 1997—I'd sat down for a minute on a dog-piss-soaked doorstep in a dog-piss street in a dog-piss town, when the door I was leaning against gave behind me. Not being at my most alert, after the gin I'd scavenged from various bins, I fell backwards into darkness, hitting my head on the door frame. "Fuck," I said. Then, straight away, I shushed myself, praying I hadn't woken anyone up—though, at that moment, I felt unsure that there was anyone in the door or house or world who was wake-uppable.

I got up, and peered inside the doorway. I couldn't see anyone or anything, except a mess of free newspapers and unopened letters. Nothing I saw or heard alerted me to how strange life inside the house was going to turn out. There were no alarm bells, literal or otherwise. So I stepped inside. At least it'd be a bit warmer here, a bit less rainy: that was all I was telling myself—well, apart from the second "Fuck" when I slipped on a tupperware catalogue and skated across the hall. The skating ended when I hit a shoe rack and half a dozen empty wine bottles — masquerading as shoes — fell on top of me. "Fuck," I said — and straight away shushed myself and the bottles, in case someone was about.

Covered in bottles and newspapers, I reckoned I might bed down for the night without anyone noticing, and leave early next morning. I'd felt I was drowning outside in rain and dog piss, but here it was warmer, drier. Even if someone were upstairs, they might not find me — I just had to keep the sound of "Fucks," breaking bottles, head-banging and newspaper-skating to a minimum.

Better still, there in front of me was the sitting room and an old sofa — like the lost memory of a mangy but comfy dog I'd snuggled up to in a different city, a past life. With that half-memory, the sofa suddenly seemed to zoom off to a far horizon, as I stood up and staggered in its direction. I lunged out for it and fell over an unseen coffee table. Piles of books thumped on the floor, half-empty glasses fell and shattered, and one of table legs broke. "Fuck," I shouted, holding my knee and hopping round the room. I stepped in a cold plate of chilli which stuck to my shoe, and hit a TV, knocking it off its stand into the wastepaper bin. "Bastard-shit-bollocks," I said for a change, thinking the mangy dog-sofa was laughing at me, as it zoomed back from the horizon into view. Catching it unawares, I leapt for it.

Having finally attained sofadom, the TV switched itself on and a Hammer Horror started in the wastepaper basket. "Fuck Fuck Fuck," I said — and straight away shushed both myself and the television, by kicking the plate of chilli at it from my shoe. "Fuck," I said, "I hope no one heard those last fucks."

And with that, exhausted, so exhausted, I let myself sink into the dog-like sofa, swallowed by the huge mouth at the back, letting its yawns close round me, letting those mangy dog memories take me back to a different city, a past life ...

"Oh, *hello*."

There was a darker dark in the room. All I could make out was the pom-pommed outline of a long, satin dressing-gown — a woman's dressing-gown worn by a man's voice — two

elements united only insofar as they issued from the same
dark-dark place in the room, and both smelt of cigarettes.

The dressing-gown said, "Oh, *hello*," with a voice like
Radio 4.

I was going to say "Fuck," and "Sorry," and dash past
the dressing-gown into the street—before he or she started
screaming, hitting me, ringing the police. The street suddenly seemed such a long way away: out of the sofa, past the
dressing-gown, over the chilli, round the coffee table and TV,
skating down the hallway. Such a long way: perhaps instead I
might just disappear down the back of the dog-sofa, ingested
forever with the lost coins, sweet wrappers and fluff.

But no, it was no good. Sink as I might, I couldn't get down
far enough for the dressing-gown not to see me, the Radio 4
voice not to find me. Surrendering to the inevitable, I started
prising myself out of the sofa's jaws—when the dressing-gown
suddenly announced: "Ants."

I said: "You what?"

The dressing-gown said: "Ants. They're everywhere, you
know."

I said: "Oh," and looked around me.

"This book, for example—full of them."

I peered through the darkness at the book he or she was
waving, but it looked insect-free to me, so I just said: "Oh."

"Yes, every book I read is full of them. Even when it's not."

"How can a book be full of ants when it's not?"

"Ah, that is the question, that *is* the question, to paraphrase
another ant-ridden book."

"*Hamlet*'s not full of ants."

"Yes it is."

"No it bloody well isn't." I was getting exasperated. Not
being practised in these situations, I wasn't sure what kind
of argument a surprised intruder and the resident of a house
should be having, but this certainly wasn't it.

"There were ants in the first performance, and they've fea-
tured in the play ever since."

"For Christ's sake."

"Look," he or she said, sounding like some walking text-book, "there are a quadrillion ants in the world, which means an average of five ants per square yard (ish). The stage at the Globe Theatre was about a hundred square yards — maybe more, maybe less, no one really knows — so there must have been at least a few hundred on stage, back in 1602. Maybe some of them joined in the final death scene — tragically squashed under-foot as the first Hamlet was poisoned. Theirs was not mere play-acting — they died for their art."

The dressing-gown had built up to a grand peroration in his or her last speech, and now fell silent. He or she seemed to be trying to remember something: "Ah, yes, that's how it goes: 'We'll set thee to school to an ant, to teach thee there's no labouring i'the winter.' Beautiful. Don't know what it means, but it's beautiful."

"Where does that come from?"

"*King Lear*, of course. Odd, really. Ants are normally associated with hard work, but Shakespeare reverses that. He says they know when to take time off, take an ant holiday — in the winter, or when things are crap. And he's right, if you think about it. Not only do ants hibernate when it's cold, there are species called Workerless Ants who don't work at all, just sponge off others. Brilliant — nature's free-loaders. Look at the ants round here. They're all too ready to take time out to go binge drinking."

"What the hell are you going on about?" I asked, still half-trapped in the sofa.

"Whenever I drop some booze on the floor, or sugar, or whatever, they always congregate round it and have a party." The dressing-gown spoke through a yawn: "Quite right too, those ants. I'm going to their school, I can tell you. Why labour i'the winter, when you can drink cheapy booze? And my God, is it winter here, always — even when it's spring it's winter." He opened the curtain and peered at the rain outside. "Look at it. Spring is the new winter. We might as well have some Vermouth. It's all the landlady's got left, bless her."

I wondered whether it would be wiser to leave him or her

and the ants now—to get out of this mad place before it was too late. But the Vermouth, the sofa and my tiredness were telling me otherwise. "Okay," I said.

The dressing-gown stalked out of the room, and returned a few seconds later with two glasses and a bottle. He or she switched on the light and kicked the door shut.

Squinting, I saw him—in the light, I decided it was definitely a 'him'—for the first time. He was tall, pale, skeletally thin with sunken cheeks, mid-thirtiesish, half-shaven—as if he'd got bored and given up—his face the burnt-out ashes of good looks. He moved in a jerky way, lunging towards me one moment, and standing upright, puffing on a cigarette the next.

And, yes, he was definitely wearing a woman's nightie.

"Why are you wearing *that*?" I asked, as he set out the bottle and glasses on the broken coffee table.

"What?"

"That dressing-gown."

"Because I went through 'er upstairs's whole wardrobe, and it was the only one that fitted."

"Yes, but . . ." I gave up. I felt like I'd fallen into a different dimension, a parallel universe, in which the normal rules of logic didn't apply, in which questions never received the right answer. I took the drink and knocked it back.

"More?"

"Okay."

He tipped the bottle unsteadily, his hands trembling; some of it went in my glass, some on my hand, some on the floor.

"Sorry," I said, though it wasn't my fault.

"Never mind," he said, looking at the spillage on the floor, "it's a libation to the ants." He raised his glass to them.

We drank in silence for a few moments. Then he sprang up. "Food?" he asked. "Let me fry the fridge for you."

Without waiting for a response, he disappeared again. From another room, I heard clattering, banging and blaspheming. After a few minutes, I got up from the sofa and wandered in the direction of his well-spoken "Christs."

"Oh, hello again," said the dressing-gown when I found the

kitchen—as if he'd entirely forgotten I existed, his mind taken up with the task in hand.

"Hello."

The task in hand seemed to consist of frying a huge pile of bacon, sausages, eggs, even pies in a wok, with a fag hanging from the corner of his mouth. I sat down at the kitchen table with my Vermouth and watched.

"I love cooking," he said, adding another half block of lard and stirring everything up into a mess.

As soon as everything was black, he tipped the contents of the frying pan onto a plate and brought it over to the table with a bottle of ketchup. He poured himself another glass of Vermouth, lit another fag, and started to pace up and down the kitchen. I started eating. I didn't care if the food were carbon-black, white or neon.

"Ants are good cooks as well, of course," he said.

"Really?" I asked, though I was barely listening by now.

"No, not really, I was lying." He grinned. "But they do prepare their food carefully. They have whole kitchens devoted to the preparation of food in their nests. Some have gardens of fungi, some have farms of aphids that they milk. African driver ants can take weeks to strip their food. Amazing, I saw them on a David Attenborough thingymajig. They can take down whole cows, even human beings, and reduce them to bone." He thought for a moment. "They eat us and we eat them—there are only a few insects you could say that about. You'd have thought the survival of the fittest would break down in cases where both species can eat the other. As regards us eating them, Toasted Leaf-cutter ants are a delicacy in Columbia, I'm told. Australian Aborigines eat honey ants. Never tried them myself. You're lucky to get medium rare steak round here, let alone anything more exotic."

"Oh," I said, finishing off the food, and pushing my plate to the furthest side of the table—to be honest, I didn't really want to be reminded of what I'd just eaten. I burped, stretched and then yawned. Realising that the dressing-gown was waiting for some kind of response to what he'd just said, I yawned again: "Gosh, that's really interesting."

The dressing-gown stubbed his cigarette out on my discarded plate. "Isn't it? Ants — amazing, bloody amazing." He looked down at the plate. "Ah, I see you've enjoyed my cooking. Quite licked it clean." He looked me up and down, perhaps for the first time: "Cleanliness is a virtue next to godliness for the ants, you know. Not only do they clean themselves — by gathering saliva on their legs from their mandibles, and rubbing it over their bodies — they also lick each other clean." I wondered for a moment where this was leading, and tried to remember where the front door was. "Yes, they lick each other clean — a truly cooperative society. Marvellous. And, erm, if you don't mind me saying, not to put too fine a point on it, I was wondering if you might want to cut a leaf out of the ants' book? To be honest, I have seen cleaner ants — again, if you don't mind my saying." He paused, but I obviously looked blank. "Again, not to put too find a point it, you're soaked through and filthy. You look like — I don't know — like someone who's been drowned and burned at the same time, and then come out the other side." He paused. "What I'm asking is: would you like to avail yourself of our facilities?"

"Pardon?"

"Use the bath, darling, use the bath."

"Are you sure you don't mind? Are you sure, me coming out of, well, nowhere and using your bathroom?"

"Not *my* bathroom, darling. The positively Stalinist fixtures of this abode belong entirely to our beloved landlady, otherwise known as 'er upstairs. And anyway, ant colonies often permit visits from other species" — I sensed he was drifting off the topic of bathrooms — "Myrmecophiles, they're called: guests who the ants tolerate for various reasons, like beetles, wasps and caterpillars. Then there are the aphids, of course. The ants tend them, protecting them from predators, in return for getting honeydew from them. It's a harmonious, reciprocal arrangement, what the books call a 'mutualism.'

So if ants can come to such mutual arrangements with their guests, please, feel free."

I didn't feel *entirely* free as I stripped off in the bathroom, wondering—if I were meant to be an aphid—what 'honeydew' I was expected to produce in return for my host's hospitality. Moreoever, the bathroom door wouldn't quite close, and the dressing-gown continued to talk ants at me from the kitchen, as he paced up and down, down and up. I dragged the over-flowing bin to the door to prop it half-shut. Still, despite these minor inconveniences, the near-boiling water felt lovely as it closed over my head, drowning out the ants-tanoi in the next room. It felt so natural to be under the water, as though I'd been here before, as though I were practised in drowning.

When I finally surfaced and opened my eyes, the dressing-gown was peering through the slit in the door. "Don't mind me," he said. "I just brought you a towel and some of our land-lady's pyjamas. I'm afraid they're not as elegant as the negligée I'm wearing. They've got teddies on, though they appear to be Satanic teddies, given their forked tails." He glanced down at the pyjamas, and then at my clothes on the floor. "I suppose, insofar the pyjamas represent what passes for a certain sub-genre of fashion these days, they'll at least be a bit more up-to-date than what you were wearing before. I mean, what 1920s charity shop were you a refugee from? For that matter, can I come too?"

I didn't answer, so he pushed the pyjamas and towel through the gap in the door, and paced away.

I dried myself off (quickly) and put on the Satanic-teddy-bear pyjamas. Back in the kitchen, my host poured both of us another Vermouth, and then chucked the bottle into a bin liner in the corner. "You no longer look like someone who's dropped in from history," he said, glancing up and down at the Satanic teddy bears, "but you do look a fright." Given what he was wearing, I wondered what he thought he looked like.

"We might as well retire, I suppose, now the Vermouth has been completed," he announced—as though the alcohol were some kind of project. "You can have my bed if you like.

I would offer you my landlady's bed, but she may come back any time, you never know. She waits till I least expect it, then pounces, demanding I return all her booze, saucepans and, well, whatever else I may or may not have borrowed. Sometimes, the selfish bitch even demands that I pay something for rent. My God—after all the orgasms I've given her." He pulled a face, though I wasn't sure what the face was meant to represent—his disgust, or his landlady's sexual pleasure. "The point is, darling, that she might be pissed off if she comes back and finds you on her bed. And the same goes for the sofa. So you can have my bed, and I shall avail myself of the comforts of the floor."

I told him he was too kind, and tried to insist that he take the bed, but he "wouldn't hear of it."

His bedroom was on the ground floor, next to the kitchen, and was littered with books, LPs, CDs, music magazines, political magazines, pornographic magazines, half-written letters, credit card bills, shredded credit cards, glasses, mouldering glasses, empty bottles, stains, blankets, blankets with stains, and stains with stains. There were dozens of posters and postcards pinned higgledy-piggledy to the walls. There was even a pistol sellotaped above the bed, with a beautifully-written note underneath:

Exhibit A:
Gun used to murder myself, at approximately 6.45 in the afternoon, on 8th September, 1992, AD.

In a previous world, I might have felt uncomfortable lying underneath a murder weapon, but it was my first bed for a long while—a long while I couldn't remember—and I didn't care. Once in bed, squinting through the lamplight, I asked the dressing-gown if he wanted to share it with me. "I won't do anything to you," I said.

"Is that a threat or a promise?" he asked.

"Whichever you want," I said.

"It doesn't matter," he yawned. "I'm happy on the ground

with my friends the ants. Sometimes I put sugar down to attract them, or I spill Vermouth like this." Through the half-dark, I could seem him tip the remainder of his glass onto the carpet. "A kind of libation to them . . . As I said before, they like to party round the booze." He thought for a moment. "I tell you what. Let's put some music on for them—something they like. What about *Carmen*?"

"Why *Carmen*?" I asked.

"Because ants love *Carmen*."

"How do you know?"

"Because they take part in it."

"Really?" I asked, thinking we were back on old ground, *Hamlet* all over again.

"In the *Tom and Jerry* cartoon version anyway. Jerry marches loads of ants onto the score of *Carmen*—the score that Tom's trying to conduct an orchestra from. Tom thinks ants are notes. He gets confused, and starts conducting the wrong pieces—like 'Yankee Doodle Dandy' and 'Camptown Races,' instead of 'The Toreador's Song.' The ants in question must have been American patriots, and low-brow American patriots at that. Or perhaps they're anarchist ants, subverting *Carmen* just because they can."

"Perhaps," I yawned, taking the CD he'd passed me, and sliding it into the player on the plywood cabinet next to me. The overture started, but seemed strangely far away . . . like the memory of an opera that once was, the energy behind it having ebbed away, the Fate *leitmotif* old news . . . and always somewhere in the orchestra, somewhere in the chorus, some-where in the counterpoint, there were traces of 'Yankee Doodle Dandy' or 'Camptown Races' played by ants, fiddling with their six legs . . .

. . . and I realised I was dozing, when the dressing-gown suddenly coughed and said out loud: "By the way, the name's Edwin. Edwin Prince."

"Oh," I mumbled, "You can call me Jules."

"Nice to meet you."

"Nice to meet you too, Edwin."

... and I felt the ants lullabying me to sleep again, carrying me away on a million million ant backs to a parallel universe, a different time, from which I couldn't escape ... a parallel universe and different time where homeless strangers fell asleep in people's houses to the Fate theme of *Carmen* ... their particular fate being never to leave.

2.

Therefore we find, at the top of each class of animals, the ants, the parrots, and the monkeys, all combining the greatest sociability with the highest development of intelligence.
— Peter Kropotkin, *Mutual Aid*

It could hardly have been six next morning, when a marching rhythm, as if from those million million ant feet, started invading my dreams. I thought I could hear the ants chanting one of the U. S. Marines' Jody calls as they marched. Finally I came to, and the marching feet were pacing feet, and the ants were Edwin in the kitchen, striding to and fro, fro and to, and the Jody call was his mumbling Nietzsche to himself.

Of course, I didn't know it was Nietzsche till I emerged from the bedroom, and headed past Edwin towards the bathroom. Somehow, Edwin was managing to sip the remnants of last night's Vermouth, smoke a fag and read at the same time, despite having only the customary number of hands. When I look back on those early days now, I always remember him like this: striding up and down the kitchen, no doubt walking miles in a space of fourteen square metres, holding aloft Nietzsche or Schopenhauer or (when on holiday from heavy literature) *Housewife Sluts*, chain-smoking, chain-Vermouth-drinking, chain-reading, stopping me halfway towards somewhere to recite aloud some passage or other in stentorian voice, always seeming to lean in towards me, always seeming to invade my body space, always seeming to tower over me — though he could only have been just over six foot. His breath, warmed with Vermouth, coffee and fags would surround me, and his nose would almost touch mine, it was so close. My gaze skewered by that sharp nose, it was hard to look anywhere but straight at him, at his wide eyes, his protruding chin, his yellow teeth, his hollow cheeks. His cheeks were so hollow, his whole body so thin, it seems to me now—looking back—as though his many and recurrent neuroses, anxieties and depressions had, over the years, picked the flesh off his bones, bit by bit. Back then, of course, I didn't know what I know now, and I saw only the physical, not the mental, emaciation; I saw only a bony face lunging towards mine, and a mouth insisting that I hear more from Nietzsche, Schopenhauer, Hegel.

That first morning, he started as he meant to go on, by heading me off at the pass with the book he was brandishing: "Listen to this. Amazing stuff from Nietzsche here"—as if it were the morning news bulletin. Nietzsche News.

"Good morning, Edwin. Isn't it a bit early for Nietzsche?"

"It's never too early for our Friedrich. Listen: there's a passage here where he compares immigrant Chinese to 'industrious ants.' Everyone reads it and thinks he's being racist, Chinese-ist. But people don't notice the next bit, where he says that they might add 'something of Asiatic calm and contemplativeness' to Europe. It's like the *King Lear* stuff I was talking about last night. Ants and Chinese are both industrious and contemplative at the same time. Who could you say that about in the Western world? We have to choose between industry or contemplation—no one's meant to do both, and jobs are usually one or the other. Ants, though, know how to mix a contemplative attitude with industry; they mix laziness and work, in a perfect Zenic balance. In fact, their leisure is the same as their work. Holidaying round a lake of spilt Vermouth is work and pleasure at the same time. Listen to this . . ."

As he was reading, I was nodding and gradually backing away, towards the bathroom. But as I backed up, he advanced—until I was pinned against the bathroom door, in a dead end with Nietzsche. Finally, the door swung open behind me, and I stumbled in and wedged it shut. From just outside, I could still hear the Nietzsche News bulletin going on regardless, like a radio you couldn't switch off.

After washing my hangover under the cold tap, cleaning my teeth with my finger, and swallowing two old paracetamol, I took a deep breath and emerged from the bathroom to a fresh barrage of "Listens," "Hey, this is amazings," and "Did you knows?" I sat at the table and nodded and yawned and yawned and nodded.

Edwin didn't yawn once. He just kept on talking and talking, whilst he burnt me some toast and made me a cup of lukewarm coffee. "Do you want anything in that?" he asked, pointing at the coffee. Something in my head crunched at the suggestion, but he was already topping up the coffee with whisky.

"Okay then."

"I found it hidden at the bottom of the landlady's laundry basket. Gosh, there's no trust in the world . . ."

"Terrible," I said, sipping the coffee, allowing my mind to drift into nowhere, no-time, whilst Edwin chattered on and on.

". . . except, of course, in the ant world. They trust each other, help each other, work together, holiday round Windermeres of booze together. Everyone thinks, just because we misuse the word 'queen,' that ant colonies are strict monarchies. It's human language, not ant language, that's monarchical, aristocratic, hierarchical. There's much more to ants than our limited language gives them credit for. Ant societies are a wonderful example of a benign nature where animals don't compete. Did you know that ants often have a two-part stomach, one half for themselves, one to share with other ants? There's this thing called *trophallaxis*, where each ant regurgitates some of its food to share with everyone else. Ants share their whisky, unlike that bitch upstairs."

"What's her name?" I asked.

"Whose?"

"The bitch upstairs."

"She's not upstairs at the moment. She's been out for days, at Salacious Whatsit's house, no doubt."

"Who's Salacious Whatsit?"

20

"The ratty alien who's friends with the big slobbery baddie in *Space Battles* or *Star Scraps* — or whatever it's called. Can never be bothered to waste brain cells on the names of these low-brow things."

I was feeling dizzy again, whisky-dizzy. "No, I mean, who is Salacious Whatsit outside of *Space Scraps*?"

"'er upstairs's boyfriend, of course. Looks like him."

"I thought you were ..."

"Bonking, darling. Bonking. Not –" he grimaced, "not girlfriend and boyfriend. No, it's just a way of paying the rent, in the currency of orgasm. Don't think it'll last forever, though — then she'll kick me out."

I decided I didn't like the sound of "'er upstairs," or her *Space Scraps* boyfriend, and wanted to leave before they returned. I downed the coffee, and got up.

"Before you go, back to wherever or whenever you came from ..." He rushed out of the room. A moment later, I could hear scrabbling and swearing coming from his bedroom. "Bugger, bugger, bugger, where is it?"

I wandered towards the front door. I'd been in this house long enough, and had a strange feeling that, if I didn't leave now, something indefinable would trap me here for a very long time. I could hear the Fate theme from *Carmen* in my hangover, over and over.

"I've got to go. Thanks for the ..."

"Just a minute!" he called, still throwing things around in his bedroom, "I've got something I want to give you." I wondered what it was: given what he'd said about the rent, money didn't seem likely. Food? More alcohol? Cast-off dressing-gowns?

"Here you are," he said, stepping into the hallway, holding a book. "It's a copy of *Mutual Aid* by Peter Kropotkin. Everything you ever needed to know about ants and politics."

I didn't know what to say. "Very useful" or "Just what I needed" didn't seem to cover it, so I just said, "Cheers."

"Thank you for listening," he said, like a radio programme signing off — Radio Nietzsche, perhaps.

"And thank *you* for everything, the food, the Vermouth, the Bizet." I took his hand and he actually managed eye contact. All of a sudden, I found myself saying: "And . . . and thank you for making me believe again that there are still such things as English gentlemen in the world—a belief I lost a long, long time ago."

For once, for a moment, he didn't say anything—and by the time he opened his mouth, I had turned and left, taking the Kropotkin with me. I thought I would never see him, or an English gentleman, again.

3.

*Strangely enough, they did not run away from the fire. They
had no sooner overcome their terror than they turned and
circled and some kind of force drew them back to their for-
saken homeland. There were many who climbed back onto
the burning log, ran about on it and perished there.*
—Alexander Solzhenitsyn, 'The Bonfire and the Ants'

Drowning in rain, I'd sat down for a minute on a dog-piss-
soaked doorstep in a dog-piss street in a dog-piss town—when
the door I was leaning against gave behind me. Through the
gin cloud in my head, I'd already guessed what door it was. I
hadn't wandered around town trying to find the door again.
Quite the opposite: I had no recollection of the door's number,
of the street's name, of where the street was; and for an unremembered number of days I had done my best not to think of
the door—to wander streets and turn corners which wouldn't
lead me back to that place of ants and Vermouth.

Or at least I thought I had. To be honest, I had no recollection of the past few days, any more than I could recall a past
before that. I assumed I was homeless, but I had no conception of why or how, and whether there had ever been a home
in the first place. Perhaps terrible things had happened to me
before Edwin, sundering me from home, but I had no memory
of them, any more than I had memories of the last bin or the
last half-eaten sandwich. My mind seemed to have misplaced
the past tense somewhere, and was stuck in an ever-recurring now. Sometimes I thought I could hear the past tense

mewing distantly, like a lost pet, but I had no idea where to start looking for it: in a bottle of gin, in Edwin's house in spring 1997, or in a dream of a seventy-five-year-old burning city, a dream I hadn't had yet, a dream which would creep up on me over the next few months, and finally pounce . . .

But I'm getting ahead of myself, jumping into the future, into a future dream of the distant past. Back in spring '97, I had no more grasp of a future tense than I had of the past. I had no idea where I was going, or what was going to happen, when I turned into a certain dog-piss street; I had no intention of sitting on a certain dog-piss doorstep, leaning against a certain front door. But as soon as the door gave behind me, I knew I'd found myself at Edwin's place again, through no volition of my own.

For an irrational moment, it crossed my mind that perhaps there was a reason I was back here — that perhaps I'd been led back here by something or other, or I'd been sent here on some errand. But what was the point of being sent on an errand without knowing what that errand was? And who was I to be sent? And who or what would send me? As soon as I reached the third question, the very idea that I was back for a reason disappeared in a puff of ludicrous abstractions: Destiny, History, Karma . . . Fuck, I thought. I must be losing my mind.

For a long while, I lay on the threshold, half in, half out, staring up at the ceiling, trying to rediscover my mind. The lower half of my body was getting drowned by the rain, whilst my upper half was drying by the hall radiator. Finally, the shadow of a tall man holding a cigarette and glass passed across my upper body:

"Well, *hello* again, stranger," said the shadow.

"Hello, Edwin," I said.

"You just have to listen to this," he said, and bounded back into his bedroom along the corridor. There was no "why are you here again?", "what are you doing down there?", "would you like to come in and dry off your bottom half as well?" — so my bottom half stayed in the rain, and my top half stayed on the mat.

Suddenly, from his bedroom came what sounded like a violin being savaged with a wire brush—no, a dozen violins savaged with a dozen wire brushes—no, a dozen cats shrieking whilst savaging a dozen violins with a dozen wire brushes. "Oh my God," I said, as Edwin's shadow fell over my head again, and the noise got louder and louder. "Oh my God," I said for a second time, for once feeling the need to invoke religion, against this anti-musical curse. "What the fuck is that?"

"Marvellous, isn't it? A masterpiece."

"A fucking mental-piece, you mean. What the fuck is it?"

"It's my stereo."

"Yes, okay, but what's on the stereo?"

"It's the end of the world!" he declared, triumphantly: "Isn't it remarkable, modern technology—you can stage the apocalypse in your own bedroom."

This bedroom apocalypse was getting louder by the second, and I had the strangest feeling that it had somehow broken into the secret garden of my past, and was uprooting all my other musical memories, annihilating long-ago songs from a far-away country. If Edwin didn't switch this horror off soon, I thought, there'd be no music left in my mind or the world. There'd probably be no Edwin either, given that the next-door neighbour was now banging on the wall, shouting muffled obscenities and threats.

"Turn it off, for Christ's sake, Edwin," I pleaded. "It doesn't mix with my gin head, and your neighbour'll kill us if it carries on."

"Everyone's killed by the end of it," said Edwin. "That's the point of the piece. Well, kind of. Only ants survive."

"That's rather, erm, specific, isn't it? It's a piece of music about ants surviving the apocalypse?"

"Yes and no."

"But why ants?"

"Because they're the only survivors of a nuclear holocaust."

"I thought that was cockroaches."

"No, it's ants."

"I was sure it was cockroaches."

"Ants have survived seventy-eight million years longer than human beings already. Do you think they'd be fazed by a geologically insignificant event like a nuclear war?"

"Never really thought about it."

"Exactly. You haven't, but they have — contingency plans for everything are built into their nature. Far more intelligent than human beings, ants. We think just because each one of us has got one hundred billion brain cells, and each one of them have only got 250,000, we're the master race. What nonsense. We forget that, unlike us, ant colonies work collectively, as a superorganism, so it's the total brain cells per nest that counts. The ant nest is one gigantic brain, which can easily eclipse our own. And in some places in the Mediterranean and South America, there are super-colonies — thousands of square miles of ant colonies working together, thinking together. Imagine the combined brain power. Whilst we human beings are stupidly blowing ourselves up, the ants are combining, evolving, collecting our remains to make nests. Brilliant. Even the Bible admits it — that ants are super-intelligent. Even the bloody Bible says they are one of the 'things which are little upon the Earth, but are exceeding wise.'"

As Edwin and the 'music' were both going on (and on), the neighbour's door opened, and a half-dressed man appeared in front of my legs. He ignored me and glared straight at Edwin: "For fuck's sake, will you turn that godforsaken noise down? Some of us are trying to watch telly instead of listening to shit."

Edwin said nothing. His neighbour glared at him for a moment, and then stomped back into his house, slamming the front door. "Gosh," said Edwin, talking as if the man were still there, "keep your string vest on, won't you? I think you'll find it's Krzysztof Penderecki's *Threnody to the Victims of Hiroshima* you've been listening to, not shit, not excrement. Peasant. I think you'll find it's physically impossible for human beings to listen to excrement. Ants, on the contrary, can sense tiny vibrations of the ground through their legs, so they may well be able to 'hear' excretions in that way." No doubt feeling he'd had he final word, Edwin swivelled round and went to turn the stereo off.

"Thank God, thank Christ," I said, still in a religious mood, and glad the apocalypse was over for now.

"You see," said Edwin, returning from his bedroom, "I only listen to apocalyptic music at the moment—well, generally speaking. It's the only music that fits my mood, or fits the world: Wagner's endings, Mahler at his bleakest, Langgaard, Lutoslawski, Stockhausen, Ligeti, Penderecki, Schnittke . . ."

"Who?" I asked.

"Who who?" Edwin asked.

"You what?" I asked.

"Which one of them are you asking 'who?' about?"

I was about to answer: "The one who sounds like a Russian sneeze," but then thought better of it. Instead, I didn't bother to answer at all, in case we got bogged down in another going-nowhere discussion. Edwin paused, hardly registering that I didn't say anything. In the weeks to come, I'd start to wonder if it mattered whether or not I contributed anything to our conversations; in his mind, the script was already written, his responses already prepared, whether I said anything or nothing, or just talked nonsense.

"Never mind," he said, after a short silence. "The point is that these apocalypses soothe my mind—like the kind of relaxing classics you get on Classic FM, or radio stations like that."

"The Penderecki? Relaxing classics?" I almost choked.

"Yes, it calms my mind to think of a human-being-less world with only ants around."

"Or cockroaches."

"Whatever. I need a drink. Had a bit of a Penderecki day, to be frank." He thought for a moment. "No, strike that. Had a bit of a Penderecki life. So it's definitely Vermouth o'clock."

Instead of going back into the house to get one, he stepped over me into the street. "I got my income support through," he explained, "so let's go to the pub."

By the time I got up, he was halfway down the street. I pulled the door to, and followed him—through some dark, Satanic streets, down a flooded alleyway, past a half-lit business of an unspecified nature called *Club Class*, along the towpath of a disused canal, over an abandoned shopping trolley—until we reached The Dying Swan, a pub locked in beery twilight.

We were dripping at the desolate bar, drenched, when another customer turned round on his stool and looked everywhere but at us. He was short, with unbrushed hair and a filthy, grey suit which looked like he'd gone to work one day, and never found his way home. He was twitchy, trembly, nervy, but his face, eyes, mouth were drained of all expression and colour.

"Good evening," Edwin said to him, "good to see you in your customary Dying Swan position as ever. One wouldn't want venerable traditions broken." He indicated me to him, him to me: "Meet my friend and The Dying Swan's resident Poet Laureate. How are you today, my good sir?"

In response, The Dying Swan's resident Poet Laureate intoned:

"The woods decay, the woods decay and fall,
The vapours weep their burthen to the ground
Man comes and tills the field and lies beaneath,
And after many a summer dies the swan . . ."

Despite being drunk to the point of absurdity, the Poet Laureate spoke mournfully, beautifully, with a voice like a thousand funerals.

"Not feeling too good, eh? A bit Tennysonian?" Edwin turned to me and tapped his head—the pot calling the kettle black, I thought. "It's a bad day," Edwin whispered to me, "when he's on the Tennyson," as if it were some kind of drink.

Edwin ordered a couple of "the landlord's cheapest and nastiest" drinks, and one for the poet at the bar, and we retreated to a corner. "What's wrong with that Poet Laureate guy, then?" I whispered.

"Ah, a sad, sad story—so sad, it might even be true. Ages ago, the barman told me he was some genius engineer at the pet food factory—you know, the one by the station. His wife upped and left him and he started drinking, or he started drinking and his wife left him, can't remember which came first—chicken and egg kind of thing. He never recovered, and has drunk himself into idiocy ever since. All that's left is nine-teenth-century poetry. Someone said he was doing an Open University course on poetry when his wife ran off, so his mind kind of, well, got stuck there."

"Bloody awful."

"Isn't it? Always had my suspicions about the Open University."

We drank and drank again and then drank again. Every now and then, the Poet Laureate would turn and not look at us, droning:

"Such such were the joys,
When we all girls & boys
In our youth time were seen,
On the Ecchoing Green."

For some reason, he seemed to think Edwin and I exemplifed the sentiments of the poem.

"Shut the fuck up," someone shouted from a far corner of the pub.

There followed a few minutes of silence, until: "'Such such were the joys . . .'"

"I told you to shut the fucking fuck up," came the shout from the corner. "Can't you see we're trying to watch the footie?"

There followed a few minutes of silence, until: "'. . . When we all girls and boys . . .'"

"For fucking Christ's sake!" In retaliation, the man in the corner turned the volume of the pub television right up, till Chelsea versus Liverpool drowned out the William Blake from the bar.

The Poet Laureate wasn't happy at this moratorium on Blake, and eventually came over to sit with us. He shook his fist at the man in the corner and the TV, expressing his frustration with the words: "'O for a Muse of fire!'"

"Quite," said Edwin, adding a double gin to his pint. "Here's one for a start."

He downed half of it, whilst jeers came from the TV in the corner.

"'O for a Muse of fire!'" said the P. L.

"Hang on a minute," said Edwin, putting his drink down. "Hang on just one cotton-picking minute. That's not the nineteenth century."

"'O for a Muse of fire!'" the Poet Laureate burped.

"That's Shakespeare."

"'O for a Muse of fire!'"

"You're branching out, my friend. Well done, excellent stuff. Real progress," Edwin said, patting the Poet Laureate on the back, and talking as if the latter had been undergoing psychological treatment at his hands (God forbid). "Next stop *Beowulf*. Then it's all the way back to the Greek classics. Let's drink to that."

Someone had obviously scored for either Chelsea or Liverpool, as the crowds on the TV cheered loudly, and there were accompanying grunts from the corner of the pub.

"'O for a Muse of fire!'" shouted the Poet Laureate.

"Apart from the drinks, I don't think you'll find one of them round here, I'm afraid." Edwin paused, and seemed suddenly maudlin. "You know," he said, putting his arm round the P. L., who wriggled under the physical contact, muttering something incomprehensibly un-Shakespearean. Edwin didn't notice. "You know, we're very similar, you and me," he said. "Utterly hopeless. Stuck in the dead ends of high culture, whilst around us all anyone really cares about is playing with balls."

He yawned. "Talking of which, it's my bed time." He got up from the table and looked back at the two of us. For a moment, I thought he might just say "goodbye" to us both, and go—that he'd leave me forever at the table with the Poet Laureate. For a moment, I was in a Limbo where anything might happen, where Edwin might wander back home, where I might wander back to nowhere, no-time — or somewhere, sometime even worse — where the spell might be broken, where the strange world that was coalescing in front of my eyes might disintegrate before it was fully formed. I wouldn't have minded if this had happened — honestly, I wouldn't. I was only trembling because I knew that he might ask me back to the house or he might not — and what he did would decide things once and for all.

There was a long pause.

"Coming?" he asked, yawning again.

4.

The Dying Swan's Poet Laureate thought Edwin meant him too, so he followed us out of the pub and through the rain.

"'O for a Muse of fire!'" he intoned to passers-by.

"Fuck off," the passers-by said back.

"Shakespeare's first draft," commented Edwin. "Not as good." The passers-by glared narrowly at the three of us. "Gosh," muttered Edwin, "anyone would have thought they were offended by my Shakespeare criticism," and we hurried back to the house — over the shopping trolley, along the towpath, past the half-lit business of an unspecified nature, down a flooded alleyway, and around the corners of dark, Satanic streets. I wondered if I'd ever really know the way to the house.

As soon as we were inside, the Poet Laureate somehow conjured up a drink in his hands and sat on the sofa, whilst Edwin lit a cigarette to warm himself. I retrieved a smelly towel and the landlady's teddy-bear pyjamas, which were still on his bedroom floor from the previous week. Drying myself and changing in the bathroom, I could hear "'Ah God, we have no stars! / About our souls in care and cark / Our blackness shuts like prison-bars'" coming from the living room.

Then I heard the front door open and slam, and a high-pitched woman's voice from the hallway. "Fuck," I said, "the landlady," tripping over the towel and hitting my head on the bathroom door.

"What's that noise, Edwin?" I heard from the hallway. The landlady spoke, or rather shouted, in a broad Leicestershire accent. "How many people have you got in here, for Christ's sake?"

"It depends how you calculate it," I heard Edwin answering her from the living room.

"How can it depend on how you calculate it?"

"Are we counting ants, for example?"

"We're counting human fucking beings."

"Ah yes, darling, but what *is* human?"

"For fuck's sake. For fuck's sake. For fuck's sake," she said half a dozen times. "You're so fucking infuriating sometimes. It's fucking obvious—you let strangers come in, they could be anyone, burgulars, murderers, rapists . . ."

". . . or, you know, 'messengers sent from the Spirit World,'" added Edwin in a fake and over-the-top American accent. "Surely that's the sort of thing you believe in, darling, with all your New-Agey *razzmatazz*."

"Don't fucking patronise me. Don't take the piss out of me." From the bathroom floor, I heard her trip over a can. "And fucking hell—on another subject: look at this place. It looks like a fucking squatters' dive, like a fucking paupers' den."

"If you charge extortionate rent, you get paupers."

"I'd hardly say charging you zero pounds is extortionate."

"Charging sex sounds pretty extortionate to me, darling."

"Not the kind of sex I get from you."

After this, I heard her storm into the kitchen, and then try the handle of the bathroom door. She shoved at the door, hitting my head with it again. "Fuck," I said, and then: "Sorry," as I stood up, and opened the door wide for her.

Face to face for a moment, I hardly took her in: all I saw was a near-middle-aged woman with a white face and purply-black hair, wearing a velvet dress, and carrying a handbag over her shoulder in the shape of a coffin. "Mutton dressed as teen-age-Goth-Lamb," Edwin would say later. She looked me and my—or rather, her—teddy-bear pyjamas up and down, shook her head, snorted, and pushed past me into the bathroom.

I wandered back to the living room, where Edwin greeted me with a Vermouth. I sat on the sofa next to the Poet Laureate, whilst Edwin kept pacing up and down the room, drinking, smoking, sweating, shaking and muttering over and over: "I don't do confrontation. I hate confrontation. I don't do confrontation."

"'O for a Muse of fire!'" said P. L.

"Damn right. Damn right. Damn right," muttered Edwin, pacing backwards and forwards, forwards and backwards. "I don't do confrontation. I hate hate hate confrontation. Do you do confrontation? I don't. I hate it. Hate it. Hate it."

From the other room, I heard the bathroom door open and shut, and the clack-clack-clack of the landlady's steps across the kitchen floor. I thought she might come back to the living room for a second slanging match, and I found myself trembling with Edwin. He stopped pacing and looked straight at me for a moment. We both stopped breathing.

And then started again, as her footsteps receded up the stairs to her bedroom.

"What a blessèd relief," said Edwin. "Halle-bloody-julah." He filled up our glasses, and then collapsed in the armchair opposite. "Bloody feminists," he said, raising his glass, "bane of one's life." "Bloody feminists" was one of Edwin's favourite pejorative expressions; in fact, over the next few months, I heard the expression in such a variety of contexts for such a variety of different targets that I came to the conclusion he had no particular politics in mind when he used it; rather, "bloody feminists" was a catch-all insult for any women who annoyed him.

We sat and drank until the Vermouth was finished and my eyes closed themselves. The last thing I heard—as one might expect—was Edwin: "Bloody feminists."

I awoke from Blakean dreams of fire and water and angels into darkness. The Poet Laureate was asleep next to me, glass on his lap, muttering Blake in his dreams. From somewhere else, there was a louder moaning. I squinted through the dark; Edwin wasn't in the armchair. The moaning was coming from somewhere behind me. I wondered if Edwin and the landlady were making up. I wondered if a cat was crying outside. I wondered if someone had been stabbed in their sleep. But no, the moaning was none of these: it was too deep, too monotonous, too insistent. The hairs prickled up on the back on my neck.

I pulled myself off the sofa and stumbled out of the room in the direction of the noise. Through the darkness, over the cans, into the hallway, past the piles of bills: the moans were coming from Edwin's room.

The door was slightly ajar, so I poked my head in. All I could see was a wriggling shadow on the bed — the wriggling shadow of Edwin, moving back and forth like a drunk pendulum, dreams tick-tocking in his head. Maybe he mentally paced up and down, walking miles in his sleep, just as he did in his waking hours. I moved closer to him, and decided he was snoring rather than moaning — waving rather than drowning, you might say — so I wandered into the kitchen and looked in the fridge. There was a bit of old cheese, a tomato, three radishes (for some reason) and an impersonation of ham in a tin. I piled them all up on a piece of bread, and found a jar of marmite to spread on top. I rounded it off with a packet of stale crisps and a second piece of bread. After the unremembered bin meals of the previous week, it tasted like the God of Sandwiches.

As I was finishing it off, the snoring coming from Edwin's room seemed to change back into moaning. This time, I thought I could hear mumbling amongst the moaning too — even the odd bark, as if his dreams were morphing before my ears into something werewolfish. God, I said to my sandwich, just what I fucking need.

I swallowed down the last crust, and wandered back to Edwin's door. For a second time, I poked my head in. He was still penduluming back and forth, forth and back in the bed; but now the snores were whimpers, and occasionally an incoherent word emerged from his werewolf dreams. I stepped into the room and up to the bed. There were tears and sweat on his face. "Are you okay, Edwin?" I whispered, but there was no answer. He carried on rocking, whining like a child, barking like a wolf. Sometimes the indistinguishable words were deep, slow, creaky like those of an old man; sometimes they were surprisingly shrill; sometimes they sounded like commands, sometimes like an argument, sometimes like a list of names and places.

"Are you okay, Edwin?" I asked again, slightly louder. I was worried: I'd heard of people dying in their sleep, and of people dying from being awoken from their sleep. I didn't know what to do.

I reached out to touch him. Immediately, he jumped up at me, eyes wide, with one last bark that I could understand: "Mother!"

5.

When I woke up the next morning, I was momentarily uncertain who I was, where I was, what age I belonged to, whether I was alive or dead—until I gradually remembered I was called Jules, I was lying on a sofa in 1997, and I seemed to be breathing. As these things came back to me, I lay staring at the ceiling for some time. The Poet Laureate had left, and the house seemed peaceful for once. But then the landlady stomped in, so I closed my eyes again and pretended to be asleep. She sat on the edge of the armchair opposite, and switched the television on, munching a piece of toast. Within five minutes, she was gone from the room, and out of the front door.

Edwin poked his head round the door: "Has she left for work? Phew. Bloody feminists, can't abide them."

"How do you know I'm not one?" I asked.

"One what?" he asked, distractedly. I sometimes wondered if he even listened to himself, let alone anyone else.

"A feminist," I said.

In response, he looked me up and down and arched an eyebrow: "Oh come on, darling, look at you. Don't be ridiculous. How can you be one of *them*?" He grinned at me. "Anyway, back to business. Now we're free of feminists and landladies, I can show you something. Got it through the post this morning, but had to hide it while 'er upstairs had her toast."

He vanished for a moment, then reappeared carrying a large package. He placed it on the coffee table, and started ripping off the brown paper. Inside was a box labelled in big black letters: the 'Myrmecoluxe Ant-Farm Starter Kit™.'

"Marvellous, eh?" said Edwin. "Soon the ants in the house will outnumber the feminists ten thousand to one." He was excited, tearing the box open, throwing around the foam packing and bubble-wrap, pulling out the parts inside. There was a plastic tank, a second tank for 'foraging,' some plastic tubing, a bag of coloured sand, some tweezers and a badge, which read: 'Myrmecophiliac.' Edwin pinned it to his lapel, and pulled himself up tall. "Right, all we need now are the residents of our Antropolis."

"Are ants not included?"

"No, but today we'll go on a school trip to find them. What do you say, darling?"

I'd hardly got any pressing engagements, so I said yes. Within seconds, Edwin was raiding the kitchen cupboards for tupperware boxes to trap the ants, as well as old bags of sugar to lure them into the boxes, and trowels to dig them out of their nests. I sat at the table with a coffee, and decided to broach the question I'd wanted to ask him all morning. I'd tried to think of ways of bringing up the subject, but nothing had come to mind: mothers and barking like a werewolf in one's sleep just didn't seem to come up in the normal run of conversation. So out of the blue I just said: "Edwin, who's 'mother'?"

Edwin went on emptying the cupboards, with his back to me. "You what?"

"Who's 'mother'?"

"A woman who gives birth, I suppose. Though I'm sure the feminists would have something to say about that."

"I mean, who's 'mother' to you?"

"The woman who gave birth to me, I suppose," said Edwin. There were no "Why do you asks?" or "What strange questions," of course. He seemed barely to register that someone else was talking, let alone that the someone else might be thinking of something other than ant-farms.

"But who do you call 'mother'?"

"Well, now that's a different question," said Edwin. He carried on throwing things around in the cupboard, but I could almost sense his unseen grin. "Who I *call* 'mother'—that's a very different question. That's most women. There was my ex-wife, for example . . ."

I opened my mouth to interrupt him ("Ex-wife?"), but stopped myself, concerned that the question might lead the conversation down umpteen Edwinian blind alleys. Not that conversation with Edwin was ever anything other than blind alleys, false doorways and upside-down maps.

". . . yes, used to call the ex-wife 'mother.' We had this kind of Oedipal thing going, if you see what I mean."

"For Christ's sake, Sigmund, too much information."

"I wear my unconscious on my sleeve," said Edwin. "Aha! Found it!" I wondered for a moment if he meant his unconscious; but no—he'd found a large sandwich box at the back of one of the cupboards. "Ant heaven," he said, and the 'conversation' about his mother was over before it got anywhere. Nothing ever seemed to get anywhere around here.

"Let's go a-hunting for ants," said Edwin, brandishing a trowel at me.

6.

Once a dream did weave a shade
O'er my angel-guarded bed,
That an emmet lost its way
Where on grass methought I lay.

—William Blake, 'A Dream'

We wandered along the towpath, over the shopping trolley and past The Dying Swan (at which point Edwin visibly hesitated, but the ant urge over-rode the drink urge), across a bridge, past an abandoned factory which was gradually being eaten by nature, past a dozen dog-walkers with angry dogs ("He won't hurt you"), and finally out into the countryside—or, at least, a place where there were more brambles, and the roar of the M1 was softened by distance. We took a footpath which diverged from the canal into a raggedy copse, and started looking round for ants.

Edwin stood for a minute, shifting his weight from one leg to another, umming and ahhing.

"What's the matter?" I asked.

"How does one put this? Not to put too fine a point on it, not to beat around the proverbial bush, in short: do you have any idea how one goes about finding the little buggers?"

"For fuck's sake, Edwin, I thought you'd know."

"Not as such," said Edwin.

"What have we come all this fucking way for then?"

"I'm sure we'll work it out. First thing's first." He pulled out a trowel, a sandwich box and a bag of sugar from the plastic bag he was holding, and handed them all to me. Then he took out another bag of sugar for himself, opened it up, and started sprinkling a bit of it on the ground. "We'll seduce them with sugar, and then follow them back to their nests." He grinned an Edwin grin. "Sounds kind of similar to what I used to do of a Saturday night."

"I don't know what you mean," I said.

"Nor do I," he said, "but it sounded good."

He sprinkled a few small heaps of sugar around the clearing, and we waited.

Nothing happened.

"I tell you what," said Edwin, "let's split up, to use the terms of *Scooby Doo*. That way, we can cover more ground."

So I wandered off, here and there sprinkling a bit of sugar on the ground as I went. After about ten minutes, I found myself in a similar clearing to the first, but no Edwin and no heaps of sugar. No ants either, but I was less worried about that. I'd thought this was a small copse, not a full-blown wood.

I looked one way and the other, and realised I couldn't see which path I'd come from, couldn't see or hear Edwin, and even the sounds of the M1 were coming from an unexpected direction. I didn't know where I was, didn't know the way back to Edwin, let alone the way back 'home' . . . something about an alleyway and a towpath and a shopping trolley and a pub . . . It all seemed so far away, as if I were losing my grip on alleyways, towpaths, trolleys, homes, now, and floating above them, like some kind of ghost, some kind of lost spirit, some kind of fallen angel, and . . .

And then I remembered the piles of sugar I'd left: like Hansel and Gretel, I could follow the trail back with them. I saw the first pile at the far edge of the clearing, followed the path next to it, and was soon with Edwin again, who was triumphantly waving a tupperware box full of earth, sugar and ants: "Got them." He was clearly overjoyed. He took out a magnifying glass from his coat pocket and peered through the lid: "Judging by the grey-black colour, the single-segmented waist and the general hairiness, these are *Lasius niger* workers."

"Is that good?" I asked, wondering if he were making it all up.

"I suppose you'd expect wood ants round here rather than garden *nigers*. But they're very common, get everywhere. They've probably come here to colonise other ants' homes. Ruthless buggers—worse than human beings." He hesitated. "Or perhaps not. Anyway, let's go for a drink with our new friends."

Just for a moment, he brought the box down and looked closely at the futile busyness inside, at the hundreds of ants scurrying nowhere, hitting their heads against the invisible plastic walls; and, ever-so-quietly, I thought I heard him whisper to them: "I'm sorry, chapesses. I'm sorry."

7.

'Learn each small people's genius, policies,
The ant's republic, and the realm of bees;
How those in common all their wealth bestow,
And anarchy without confusion know.'
—Alexander Pope, *An Essay on Man*

After half a dozen drinks outside The Dying Swan (the landlord wouldn't let the ants inside — as Edwin pointed out, he was probably afraid they'd start a war with the ants already there), we wandered back to the house, and Edwin spent the rest of the afternoon setting up the ant-farm in the back-yard.

He started by putting the tupperware box of ants in the fridge: "Cools them off," he said. "They fall asleep in the fridge, so it's easier for them to be transferred into the farm. That's what it says in the instructions, anyway." He'd laid out the instructions — 'How to Establish a Happy Terrarium' — on the kitchen sideboard, and every so often pretended to consult them.

"Terrarium — sounds like a Roman ruin," I said.

"An amphitheatre for ants. The questions is: are we the audience, or is it they whose compound eyes are watching us?"

I told him he sounded like a '50s B-movie, so he told me to sod off, and returned to the instructions. The next job was setting up the nesting tank, which he did in the back-yard, on top of a rusting cast-iron table. He poured in a thin layer of pebbles at the bottom, followed by the coloured sand, almost to the top, followed by a pint of water. Then he patted the sand down with a trowel, and left it to dry for a while. "We'll let the water soak into the sand for an hour or so," he said. "You need the water to soak in because otherwise the ants can't build solid tunnels — especially *Lasius nigers*, who don't build tunnels very well at the best of times. In dry sand, their tunnels might collapse and bury them alive. One wants a farm, not some kind of ant Golgotha." He yawned. "According to the instructions, you're meant to leave the water to soak in overnight, but I don't want to wait that long — and anyway, the ants'll get impatient hanging around in the cold." We wandered into the kitchen to get our drinks, and he lit up. "God, I need a rest. One can work too hard, you know," he said, peering at the ants sleeping in the fridge.

After a good half-hour's rest and two Vermouths, Edwin took the second tank — the foraging tank — into the back-yard, placed it on the garden table, and attached it to the nesting tank with a piece of tubing. He poured some more of the coloured sand in the bottom of this tank, and then went in search of plants, stones and twigs to put on top. He found the stones and twigs in an alleyway, and a couple of small pot-plants in the landlady's bedroom. Shaking them out of their pots, he said: "Perfect," and consigned them to his ant world: "Perfect for me, that is — it's probably hell for plants."

He patted soil from the pots round the plants, stepped back, shook his head, and uprooted the plants and put them in different places, rearranging the stones and twigs in a new pattern. Then he did it again, putting the plants back where they were in the first place. He was so careful about it all, as if he were landscape gardening on a miniature scale: "One wants one's antish friends to be happy in their new environs. It's the least one can do after kidnapping them what must be thousands of ant-miles from home — the equivalent of us waking up in Turkey." Next, he took the cellophane off a long, plastic tube, which had a red bowl at the bottom. "That's why I ordered what they call the 'deluxe' starter-kit, with the foraging tank and this here water reservoir. If one has to play God over beings cleverer than oneself, one may as well try to be a benevolent god—a stupid but benevolent god."

He stuffed some wet cotton wool into the bowl at the tube's base, and then fixed it to the side of foraging tank, so that the bowl would be accessible to the ants when they needed a drink. "I need one too," he said, and wandered back into the kitchen, to pour himself a Vermouth and light up again. "God, this is exhausting. Almost done."

By now, it was late afternoon; finally, Edwin took the tupperware box out of the fridge. Inside, the ants were sleeping in clusters. "Oh dear, probably left them in there a little too long. Never mind, here goes." He opened the box, and laid it in the foraging tank, and then sealed up the lids of both the foraging and nesting tanks. "An insect prison," he said, not grinning. We watched in silence as the minutes and hours ticked away and, one by one, the ants woke up from the cold and started tottering about.

Within three hours or so, the foraging tank was all movement, and Edwin was toasting the ants with Vermouth: "To our masters . . . No, strike that. To our mistresses: they're all female workers, every one of them. God, what a sterile, sexless hell I've created. Instead of what I wanted—the ants outnumbering the feminists ten thousand to one—I've founded a state entirely of feminists."

He took a swig of Vermouth. "Still, it is beautiful," he said, as the twilight closed in around us, and we gradually became transfixed by the fractalic patterns the ants were weaving in their new home. "Like the shape of infinity," murmured Edwin, half to himself.

"What do you mean?" I asked, wondering whether it was a good idea to encourage him.

"The collective patterns they move in resemble the sign for infinity—you know, the lemniscate, the lazy eight, the figure eight lying on its side. It's like that lithograph by Escher, Möbius Strip 2."

"The what by what?"

"M. C. Escher's famous image of ants crawling round the

Möbius strip, the one everyone knows." He always spoke like this — as if you were bound to know what he was talking about. You could end up quite insecure, quite self-conscious about your ignorance if you were exposed to Edwinisms for long periods. I combatted that insecurity by waving everything I didn't know or understand by: move along please, no ignorance to see here, thank you. On this occasion, I just nodded: ah, yes, M. C. Escher's well-known lithograph, of course, how could anyone not know that?

"Escher's lithograph shows the ants crawling round the sign for infinity," continued Edwin, in lecture mode, "but what the image also implies is an analogy between that sign and the body of the ants. Structurally speaking, each ant's individual body, with its thorax joined to its abdomen by a narrow waist, also looks like the symbol of infinity. So the individual body is inscribed with the same pattern in which they're moving collectively — their individual bodies mirror their collective bodies, and vice versa. The individual is just a miniature version of the collective. They are the perfect social mechanism." By this point, he looked almost mesmerised, staring wide-eyed at the tank: "And . . . and watching them like this means that our own eyes become inscribed with their infinite patterns. Ants . . . ants, I tell you, they are our connection with the infinite."

Normally, I'd have put him down as drunk or insane, but the ant-farm had mesmerised me too . . . and there was nothing in my mind apart from the infinite patterns of ant work . . . and there was nothing in my eyes apart from a continuum of ants, moving round and round the lemniscate, surveying, carrying, digging, on and on, forever and ever . . . and I breathed in and out, as the ants flowed round and round . . . and there was an unusual moment of calm in this strange house, in Edwin's chaotic life, in both our vertiginous histories . . . and for once and once only, I felt there was a beautiful order in things.

For once and once only, I understood how Edwin found in the ants a kind of idyllic escape from the ambivalence, complexity and ugliness of human life; and although, at other times, I found elements of the ants' behaviour all too reminiscent of the terrors and lunacies of the human world—and, for that matter, of Edwin's and my lives and histories—for once and once only, I shared Edwin's faith in them . . .

Or, at least, that was until the hypnotic spell was broken by the front door slamming, and two muffled voices in the hall.

"Bugger," said Edwin, taking off his coat and draping it over the ant-farm, "it's 'er upstairs and the boyfriend—Salacious Whatsit."

'Er upstairs's footsteps went straight up the stairs, but, before he followed her, Salacious Whatsit poked his head round the back door to scowl at us in the yard. Edwin and I stood in front of the covered ant-farm, so he wouldn't see it. No one said hello; it didn't seem the done thing.

After Salacious Whatsit's scowl had gone, disappearing upstairs, I turned and whispered to Edwin: "Gosh, he really is a space alien, isn't he?"

"An alien without the laughs," said Edwin, who was trying to light a cigarette with trembling hands. "At least the real-life Salacious Thingymajig has a few giggles with Jobby the Hoot, or whoever his boss is called. No giggles allowed here, thank you." He drew on his cigarette. "She looks like a Hammer Horror, he's space opera incarnate. If they bred, a new Hollywood genre would be born." He shivered. "But let's not think about them breeding. Let's go inside before either of them sees the ant-farm. Salacious Whatsit probably eats creepy-crawlies."

Back in the living room, I took my place on the sofa, and Edwin resumed his normal pacing, smoking, drinking and reading—this time Oswald Spengler's *The Decline of the West*, which seemed to take his mind off his nerves, as he laughed into the Vermouth now and then.

"Amazing," he said. "Spengler equates wars between tribes in Sudan with ant wars. Sudanese wars, he reckons, aren't part of what he classes as human history, so they're as meaningless as wars between ants. He manages to insult ants and the Sudanese at once. Ants and the Sudanese live outside history. Good for ants and the Sudanese, I say. We could all do with living outside history—wish I could. Anyway, that's what Spengler thinks: there are European wars which mean something for history, and then there are antish wars which mean nothing." Whilst Edwin was talking Spengler, a door slammed upstairs. Edwin looked heavenward and said: "I think we're in for one of the latter now."

Two pairs of footsteps stomped down the stairs: clack, clack, clump, clump, clack, clack, down and down, nearer and nearer, like some cheap soundtrack to *The Decline of the West*. I was trembling too by this point—even though I could easily have walked out of the front door and never come back.

The living room door burst open, and there was the landlady in all her Gothic fury—black hair, white make-up, skull necklace—with Salacious Whatsit in tow.

"Listen to this," said Edwin, ready to start the Spengler spiel all over again, in a rather absurd attempt to head the landlady's fury off at the pass: "Amazing . . ."

She stamped her stilleto. "Edwin, I don't want to fucking listen to any of your 'Amazings' today."

"Just this bit . . ."

"No, Edwin, I've done enough listening to you and your fucking books. You and your books'll bloody well listen to me for a change." From the doorway, she waved a bill at him. "Here is a bill from British fucking Telecom, Edwin. British fucking Telecom. Do you know what it's about? Do you?"

"I would imagine the phone, darling."

"Don't you fucking 'darling' me." She was increasingly hysterical, her over-lipsticked mouth contorting into all sorts of shapes. "This bill is for 962 pounds and forty-five pence. That's 962 fucking pounds and forty-something fucking pence."

"Forty-five," corrected Edwin.

She ignored him: "And why is it that much, Edwin? And why?"

Salacious Whatsit repeated: "And why?" under his breath, gurning in the shadows behind her. "And why?"

"Presumably because that's how much we owe?" suggested Edwin helpfully.

"That's how much *you* owe. *You*, not 'we.' And you'll fucking well pay it, Edwin, before we get disconnected."

Deliberately, in his own time, Edwin put Spengler and his glass on the coffee table, and then felt his pockets up and down. "Oh, I'm sorry," he said. "I don't seem to have 962 pounds and forty-five pence on me at the moment. Will you take an IOU?"

"No, I fucking will not take an IO-fucking-U." She stamped her heel again. "For Christ's sake, Edwin. How the fuck did you run up such a bill?" Salacious Whatsit muttered something half-audible about the reason rhyming with banking, and the landlady said: "No, don't answer that question, Edwin. We know already. We fucking know what you've been doing—all those dirty calls."

"How do you know they were dirty?"

"We rang one of the numbers on the bill to see what it was you'd paid so much for."

"Well, I hope you deducted that phone call from my bill."

The landlady tried to say something, but it came out instead as a glare like formic acid.

Salacious Whatsit stepped into the breach: "Don't you think you should be saying sorry, Edwin? Don't you think you should be apologising to your ever-so-patient landlady for using her phone for dirty calls?"

"As I say, how do you know they were dirty? As a matter of fact, I hardly ever got to the dirty bits. The dirty bits were a mirage, a vanishing horizon—after the long intros and warnings, the girls would be so polite, I found it hard (so to speak) to bring up the subject of dirty bits. And the longer we chatted, the harder it was to cut to the chase, as it were. One felt rather embarrassed once one knew that 'Juicy Lucy' was a single mum with two beautiful children, who got through their Asda clothes like you wouldn't believe, and who so wished to holiday somewhere different from Torquay this year, but couldn't understand that their mother was maxed out on her credit card, and so had been forced to take up phone sex as a part-time job."

"Edwin?" said the landlady.

"Yes, darling?"

"Shut the fuck up. Shut the fuck up. Shut the fucking fuck fuck fuck up." She was half-shrieking, scratching her indigo nails down the wall to her right. In the shadows, her boyfriend looked even more Salacious and space opera-ish than normal, a malignant joy screwing up his whole face.

By contrast, Edwin just stood there, with a slight frown, as if he were considering some philosophical ant problem. Finally, he reached down, picked up his Vermouth from the table and ventured a sip.

At that, the landlady raged up to him, and knocked the drink out of his hands. The glass smashed near my feet, but I stayed quiet and still. I didn't want to be noticed.

"Was that necessary, darling?" asked Edwin.

"Stop pretending to be Oscar fucking Wilde," shouted the landlady, "because you're not. You're not Oscar fucking Wilde—you're a fucking idiot."

Edwin looked himself up and down. "Who says I'm not Oscar Wilde—or Oscar 'fucking' Wilde, for that matter? How do you know, darling?"

"Because he fucking well died, I don't know, hundreds of years ago."

"I think you'll find it was only ninety-seven years ago. And anyway, even if he did die a long time ago, you never know what's happened since."

"What the fuck do you mean? What are you going on about?"

"Well, darling, you're the one who believes in reincarnation, transmigration and all that New Agey Jazz."

The landlady rattled her bangles at him: "Edwin, I am not having this conversation. I am not having this fucking mad fucking conversation. You are not Oscar fucking Wilde reincarnated."

"You may have a point. Unlike me, he went in for young lords more than ants, as far as I know." He thought for a moment. "Hmm. Must look that up sometime. Note to self: look up connections between ants and Wilde."

"I don't fucking care about connections between ants and Oscar Wilde. I don't fucking care. And you can say what you like: you seem to think you're Oscar fucking Wilde reincarnated, and can swan around how you want. But you're not and you can't. It's fucking pathetic. You live in 1997, not 17 or 18-whatever, and you're just a fucking con-artist who's taking advantage of—no, *stealing* from his landlady."

"That's a bit strong, isn't it?"

"No it's fucking not. Not paying your rent is stealing, and I could have you chucked out. You didn't even bother filling out your housing benefit forms to pay me that way."

"I'm an anarchist, darling. You can't expect an anarchist to fill in housing benefit forms."

"Last week you told me you were a fascist."

"Same difference, darling. To be an anarchist means you can be any other -ist you feel like. That's the beauty of anarchism. As Kropotkin –"

"I don't give a shit about Krappy-pot-kin. I give a shit about my money. You managed very well to fill in the forms for your dole—just not for my rent. Fucking hell, Edwin. Fucking hell—you do my head in." She took a deep breath, and her tone calmed somewhat: "Listen, Edwin. Listen to me for once. You've got to pay the BT bill, and you've got to start paying the rent properly."

I sneaked a glance at Salacious Whatsit, wondering if he knew about the previous rental arrangement between his girlfriend and Edwin. He was nodding and smirking to himself.

Meanwhile, the landlady was taking more deep breaths. "Listen to me," she kept saying. "Listen to me"—a plea which just underlined its own futility every time it was repeated: Edwin *listen*? "Listen to me, Edwin. We'll do a deal. You get a job ..."

"A job?" he asked. "A job? A job?"—he played with the word in different voices, as if it were a novel but intriguing ant theory: "A job?"

For a few moments, their row seemed to have malfunctioned, stuck in robotic repetition, as she kept saying: "Listen to me," and he: "A job? A job?" In the doorway, Salacious Whatsit kept nodding mechanically too.

"Listen, Edwin. Listen. Listen. I'll pay the BT bill, but you'll pay me back. And you'll get a job and start paying the rent."

Then, in a shush of velvet, she and Salacious Whatsit were gone, leaving Edwin elongating the word "job?" under his breath, till it seemed to fill the room. Only when the front door slammed did he snap out of it.

He turned to me. I thought he was going to tell me how much he hated confrontation, or shout "Bloody feminists" over and again. Instead, he spoke calmly and quietly: "I tell you what I haven't done in ages. I tell you what: to paraphrase Irving Berlin, there may be trouble ahead, but while there's moonlight and music and Vermouth and income support, let's face the music and dance."

Before I could ask "What?," he'd darted out of the room and into his bedroom — from where I heard him scrabbling around, followed by "Got it," and the crackle of an old LP on his stereo. He rushed back into the living room and pulled me off the sofa. From his bedroom, at high volume, came the music. "There's something somewhere I find distasteful about Aram Khachaturian's tub-thumping," said Edwin, as he put one arm round my waist, and took my right hand in his, "but I can never quite put my finger on what that something somewhere is." I murmured something about feeling the same — though for different reasons. Khachaturian's music made me feel uneasy, as if I'd forgotten something dreadfully important, and it was reminding me in a cryptic way. "Never mind," said Edwin, "it was all I could find for present purposes. Let's waltz."

And suddenly-madly-staggeringly-drunkenly, to Khachaturian's waltz from *Masquerade*, and the neighbour's rhythmic three-four banging on the wall, and our own panting breathlessness, we're waltzing around the living room, weaving horizontal 8s amongst the beer cans and broken glass . . .

. . . until the music finishes almost as soon as it began, and it's quiet in the house apart from LP crackles, and Edwin looks down at me for a moment, and then announces, "Good evening," and strides out of the room.

That night, lying on the sofa in the darkness, I decided to get a job too—and it dawned on me that life was gradually ingesting me again: first a sofa to sleep on, then a person who knew me by a name (even if he never used it), then a job. Where would it end?

Finally, I fell asleep to a strange dream—a dream that I was nearly one hundred years old, and had sprouted glorious wings with age; but I couldn't fly, couldn't even move, and a million leaf-cutter ants were sawing my paralysed wings off, tiny piece by tiny piece, and carrying them back to their nest. I awoke with a start, trying to dismiss the nightmare, the wings, the leaf-cutter ants, as nonsense; but the feeling of extreme old age just wouldn't go away.

8.

A couple of nothing-days later, Edwin was purportedly at the job centre (or "labour exchange" as he preferred to call it), and I was purportedly watching adverts about repaying your debts—when the phone rang. This didn't happen often, so I downed my Vermouth and walked twice round the room to clear my head, before answering it.

"Hello?" I said to a receiver held at arm's length. At that moment, I wished the landlady had allowed the phone line to be cut off after all. It could have been anyone at the other end—tax office, benefits office, Juicy Lucy, the past . . .

But no, it wasn't the past—or, at least, not my past. It turned out to be Edwin's mother: "Hello, it's Edwin's mother 'ere." Judging by her voice, she was obviously in some distress ("quivery voices down the blower were always one of her specialities," Edwin remarked later).

"Hello, it's Ed's mother 'ere, looking for 'im at this number I got a 'old of." Unlike her son, she spoke with a broad accent, where *h*-s were dropped, *s*-s were pronounced as *z*-s, *i*-s (as in 'it') pronounced as *ee*-s, *oo*-s (as in 'look') pronounced as *oooo*-s. I hadn't heard the accent before, couldn't place it. Again, later on, Edwin told me that it was a Stoke accent. I asked him how he was so Radio 4 when his mother seemed so very Stoke. "*Seems* is the word," he said, "it's all an act: she thinks she'll get more sympathy with a broad Stoke accent."

Act or not, he explained that, in his early twenties, he had reacted against his mother's accent, and everything associated with it. He'd set about educating himself out of all things

Stoke-on-Trent—out, as he put it, of Stoke accents, Stoke habits, Stoke sexualities, Stoke ways of not-thinking, and ultimately Stoke itself. I asked him why he was so keen to get out of Stoke, and (indeed) get the Stoke out of him. He told me that if I ever went there, I'd understand.

Having visited Stoke since, I can see his point, though I can't help thinking that his compulsive self-education was impelled by something more than mere "de-Stokeification" (as he called it). Education was certainly a form of escapism for Edwin, but there were other things he was escaping from than mere geography, amongst which might be listed social class, history, reality, and other people's minds. All of this became apparent when I went to visit Stoke and his family. In the meantime, he'd often mournfully look about himself, declaring: "Marvellous thing, education, isn't it? I can quote Wordsworth at will, tell one Penderecki piece from another—which is saying something, given that I don't think Penderecki himself can—and look where it's got me. I educated myself out of Stoke and into oblivion."

Back on the phone, Mrs. Prince was trying to get back in touch with oblivion: "Hello, it's Ed's mother 'ere."

"Hello, Mrs. Prince."

"Hello, dear."

Given my Vermouth and her distress, we didn't seem to be getting past hello, so I said it again: "Hello."

Suddenly, not even knowing who I was, she launched the conversation with: "It's 'im, y'know."

"Who's 'im, I mean him?"

"'Im, he's at it again." All of a sudden, she was crying, sobbing all over the phone.

"At what?"

"Hitting me. He's started it again. Bugger won't stop. It hurts, it really does when he gets going. He's not like his brother, not gentle like our Ed."

At that moment, there was a colossal bang from somewhere behind her.

"What the hell . . .?"

"That's 'im too. He's got his air rifles out in the kitchen, and one of them's just gone off. Second time today. He's spent all morning polishing and stroking them, like. He's got three or four of them. Treats them like pet dogs. Oh, I don't know how to cope any more. I don't know how to manage without our Ed. I don't wanna sound like a bloody postcard, but I wish he was here. I always do. He was always me favourite."

"I'm not surprised, Mrs. Prince, if the other shoots your kitchen," the Vermouth said for me. Then I felt bad, and added: "Sorry about it, Mrs. Prince. Your son's out at the moment. I can tell him . . ."

"Tell him I rang and what I said. Tell him his brother is 'itting me again. Tell him he's started on the Armenians again."

"The Armenians?"

"Yeah."

"What's he doing to the Armenians?"

"Oh, 'e's always on about the Armenians, dear. As if there are any of them in Stoke-on-Trent — they haven't even got human beings here yet, from what I can see. But he thinks they're everywhere — under the sink, in the bathroom, living in tip. Probably who he thinks he's shooting in the kitchen. He always used to have it in for them bloody Armenians, just like his granddad, and now he's started on them again. You tell our Edwin that. You tell him the Armenians are back."

"I will, Mrs. Prince," I said.

"And tell him . . . tell him . . ."

"What, Mrs. Prince?"

"Tell him his mother isn't well," she was very insistent. "Tell him she's suffering, like. Got 'igh blood pressure and cholesterol and all sorts. Feels terrible all the time. I don't like to talk about it, especially to strangers, but you know, me legs are covered in varicose veins, like a flipping road atlas — and I get so out of breath chasing after me other son and his guns. It's ridiculous at my age. Everything's gone to wrack and ruin, without our Ed."

"I'm sorry to hear that, Mrs. Prince."

"You just tell our Edwin. You just tell him, my dear."

"I will, Mrs. Prince. I will tell him. You look after yourself."

Suddenly, she was calm, and the tears stopped as abruptly as they'd started: "Thank you, my dear—you're an angel. That's all I wanted. Thank you. Goodbye."

A couple of hours after I put the phone down, Edwin strolled in, and I told him what had happened, about the phone call, about his mother's sobs. I told him about wrack and ruin, the varicose veins, the high blood pressure, the cholesterol. I told him about his brother shooting the kitchen. I told him about the Armenians. I told him his mother said "tell him, tell our Edwin" over and again.

He listened, nodded, and immediately sprang into action—by ringing BT to change our phone number.

ACT TWO

9.

3D Ant Attack: you are a stick man searching for a stick woman in the City of the Ants. The ants have tied up the stick woman somewhere in the labyrinthine ruins, and it is your quest to rescue her and lead her back to safety. When you find her, the chemistry between the two of you is obvious: she is identical to your stick man, but has a skirt, plaits and keeps saying: "Take me away from all this," every time you hold her stick hand. You want to take her away from all this, but the ways are windy and the ants poisonous. You can shoot them or jump on their heads, but they retaliate with formic acid, paralysing both of you to the spot. Then they come at you in swarms of thousands and bite you over and over again. They have numbers on their side—insects always have numbers on their side—and increasingly you feel that escape from the ant labyrinth is an impossible dream. The ants have overrun the city and the stick woman is tired and time is running out and the exit seems a long, long way away . . .

. . . and it all reminds me of a time and place I can't quite recall, a past city from which only my memory escaped, a burning city where my stick self is still wandering, forever trapped with a marauding army, never finding the way out, never reaching a successful 'Game Over' . . .

. . . until I feel I have wasted a thousand lives in that ruined city, and my stick man and stick woman have died a thousand ant-deaths . . .

. . . and finally Edwin's ancient computer gives out.

10.

"Stupid game," said Edwin, who'd been playing *3D Ant Attack* as much as me. "The ants' antennae are all out of proportion, and ants would never behave like that towards humans — they're far too gentlemanly. It almost makes one want to get a job, if this is the best way one can waste one's time" — and off he trotted, back to the Job Centre.

Within a few weeks, both of us had a job: I was distributing free newspapers on street corners, and Edwin was working in a local call centre. He didn't land the job through any "fault" of his own, as he put it; in fact, he admitted that he'd never actually been *in* the Job Centre at all, except to sign on. He'd circled it a few hundred times, weighing up the virtues of Jobs vs. *3D Ant Attack*, but had never got to the point of stepping inside to inspect the vacancy boards. Rather, he'd got the job because the landlady had recommended him to a friend of hers, who worked as a 'team leader' at a call centre, on a premium rate phone line. The company who ran the phone line was called *Encyclodial*, and it was the new employee's job to answer callers' questions on any subject, using a computerised reference library.

"I told my friend you had a lot of experience in premium chatlines," announced the landlady one evening, her pencil eyebrows raised. "I said you had the gift of the gab, and she said 'yes, that's all very well, but talking too much might get in the way of processing the requisite number of customers per hour.' So I said you can think very quickly. But she said that 'thinking wasn't required, because all the information you need is to hand, on the computer.' Then she asked me: 'Does he have a strong accent? You can't run a business like ours with Scousers or Geordies—people just don't trust them, don't believe that they know anything about anything.' So I said no, you don't have a strong accent, and she said 'Okay, you're hired.' You start next Monday. Edwin, listen to me. Fucking listen to me. I've got you this job with a friend. I don't want you ruining my relationship with her. You've got to try and behave"—at which point Edwin saluted the landlady: "Your wish is my commode."

She fixed him again with a glare: "Edwin, I'm not fucking joking here. This is serious. I've got you a job—I more or less did the fucking interview for you—and you better not let me down."

After she'd left, Edwin said, "I think us both getting a job calls for a commiseration—no, sorry, I mean celebration. Let's go to the pub."

The Poet Laureate was in his customary seat in The Dying Swan, wearing his customary grey suit, drinking his customary beer, and muttering something that Edwin told me was Wordsworth:

"Blest the babe
Nursed in his mother's arms, the babe who sleeps
Upon his mother's breast, who when his soul
Claims manifest kindred with an earthly soul,
Does gather passion from his mother's eye."

The P. L. seemed to get stuck on the last line, repeating it over and over again with different intonations. Eventually, Edwin bought him a drink, which I couldn't help feeling was to make him shut up. The P. L., though, carried on talking into his beer, making bubbles with Wordsworth.

Sitting down at a table, Edwin raised his glass. "Since the Poet Laureate over there has brought up the subject, here's to the women in my life, or should we say the *ex*-women in my life. Here's to"—he hesitated, and I thought he was about to say "mother"—"here's to, for example, the ex-wife. If only she could see me now, new job and all. If only she could see the heights to which I have sunk and the lows to which I have risen."

I decided here was an opportunity to ask him about his ex. "Who's the ex-wife?"

"Someone who was once my wife and is now my ex."

I felt like we'd been here before. In fact, all conversations with Edwin felt like *déjà-vu*. "Yes, but . . ."

"Actually, what I've said isn't true. She isn't my ex-wife."

"Who isn't?"

"My wife."

I was getting lost.

"My wife isn't my ex-wife technically, because we never actually got a divorce. Couldn't be bothered."

"Why did she leave you?"

"Because she realised I was gay."

I wasn't surprised to hear this—I'd been much more surprised when I discovered that he'd had a wife, because right from the start I'd thought he was probably gay. Still, to be polite, I said: "I didn't realise you were gay."

"I wasn't."

"Pardon?"

"I wasn't when I was married to the ex-wife-who-isn't-really-an-ex. Then I was straight. Before I met her, I was gay, but I never told her till the end of the marriage. It was a secret, just like it was a secret when I was gay that I was fancying women. Back then, I hid my heterosexuality behind my San Francisco moustache. Most people get outed in the end. But I went from one closet to another—a homosexual pretending not to be straight to a heterosexual pretending not to be gay. Didn't like either scenario, so now I'm firmly an asexual-homo-heterosexual. You might say I used to be bisexual, but now I'm not so sure."

I stayed quiet, confused. The P. L. moaned Wordsworth at the bar.

"Anyway," said Edwin, "we never finished this toast to the not-ex-wife." Our glasses clinked. "May she rest in peace."

I was shocked. "I didn't know she was dead. I'm sorry."

"What are you sorry about?" asked Edwin.

"Your wife, or ex-wife, being dead."

"I never said she was dead."

"Yes, you did. You said: 'May she rest in peace.'"

"That's not saying she's dead."

"Well, is she?"

"What?"

"Dead, for Christ's sake. Dead." I couldn't believe I was losing my temper with someone over the question of whether or not his wife had died. But then Edwin had this knack of provoking aberrant emotions and impossible conversations. "Dead. Dead. Can we get this clear: is she fucking dead?"

Edwin thought for a moment. "In a sense."

"Fucking hell, Edwin. How can someone be dead 'in a sense'?"

Edwin cast his eyes round the pub and its inmates. "I think that is quite obvious."

I was on the point of giving up. Direct questions never got anywhere with Edwin: he seemed incapable of giving a straightforward answer. If this was sometimes infuriating, at least it meant that he himself was unlikely to expect straightforward answers from me. In fact, he had never once asked me any questions about myself to which I might give answers, whether straightforward or bent-sideways, and for that I was relieved. Sometimes it made me wonder if Edwin noticed my existence; for the most part, though, I was grateful for the anonymity provided by his lack of curiosity about anyone but ants. If he'd ever asked me about myself, where I came from, what was my history prior to meeting him, I think my overriding emotion would have been embarrassment, having nothing to tell him. My conscious mind was still stuck in an ever-recurring present tense, unable to recall anything from the near or distant past, and (to be honest) never really thinking about it. In that sense, my own mind was merely a reflection of Edwin's attitude towards me: both implied that I had no past worth enquiring about, no existence beyond the here-and-now.

Edwin was more explicit about the non-existence of his ex-wife: "She is dead in the sense that there is a grave in my mind in which the good parts of her rest in peace."

"Where are the bad parts of her?"

"They're currently sailing around Warwickshire, I believe, with some bloke who lives on a barge. Used to know him myself, millennia ago. He works as a compère, a tour guide for one of those open-top bus tours they have in Stratford. He makes it up on the spot—tells all the American tourists fantastic histories in which Shakespeare shagged William the Conqueror in such-and-such a high-rise, or Henry VIII hid in this boozer during the Civil War. He could charm the pants off Queen Victoria. He gives the punters what they want, and they probably don't care that it's all made-up crap. Talented bastard."

The Poet Laureate had been quiet during the talk of dead or semi-dead ex-wives and their lovers, but now butted in with:

". . . in her web she still delights
To weave the mirror's magic sights,
For often thro' the silent nights
A funeral, with plumes and lights
And music, went to Camelot."

Edwin looked up, beaming, seemingly inspired—and certainly very drunk. "My God. That's right. That's bloody well right," he said, and stepped over to give the P. L. a slap on the back. "You're a genius. You're absolutely right," he said again and again—though in what way P. L. had been "absolutely right" was a bit beyond me. "I'll give the punters what they want too. I'll do it. I'll be like Mr. Open-Top-Bus—no, strike that, better. Whether the callers at this two-bit operation want fact or fiction, history or bull-shit, I'll bloody well give it to them. I'll charm them, startle them with my knowledge and delight them with my Received Pronunciation." He slapped the P. L. on the back again, and the latter burped. "You're absolutely right, my friend."

Edwin turned to me. "This job could be just what I'm looking for. I could be bloody made for it, and it could be the making of me all at once. Long live *Encyclodial*, and long live me. I'll charm the pants off their callers, and be good at something for once in this sodding life."

The barman wandered over. "Same again?" he asked.

11.

And what's more wonderful — big loads that foil
One ant or two to carry quickly, then
A swarm flocks round to help their fellow men.
                                        —John Clare, 'The Ants'

And for a while, Edwin did seem happier. He'd come home in the evening with a smile, telling me and his ant-farm how he'd "charmed the pants" off forty callers that day; how he'd won the record for the longest individual calls three weeks in a row, making loads of cash for the company — and a bit for him too, since he was paid commission per minutes he was on the line; how he'd established a fan-base of callers, who asked specifically for him; how people were ringing up the premium phone line just for a chat "with that pleasantly spoken gentleman who likes ants"; how his posh voice made the more mature female callers go trembly at the knees; how at least one of them had offered to send him her frilly underwear. "You see," said Edwin, "I've got what the other vacuities who work there don't have — the ability to improvise, technically known to us in the chat-line business as 'bull-shitting.' I am *Encyclodial*'s Executive Bull-Shitter Extraordinaire: the others just find the relevant encyclopedic entry, read it off the computer screen, and then try and flog the CDs of the Encyclopedia. But I improvise, embellish, turn it into a story — it's the way I get the punters to stay on the line. Some school-kid rings up to ask about Napoleon III, and I end up telling him the story of margarine, and the part it played in the Franco-Prussian War. Or some student rings up about Henry VIII, and I cast aspersions on Anne Boleyn's relationship with horses. With me, they get information and entertainment in one."

So one afternoon, back from a wet morning of handing out wet papers to wet commuters, I decided to ring Edwin at *Encyclodial* to experience his informative and entertaining spiel for myself. I sat down in the living room with a stale biscuit and a carton of milk, and dialled the number.

I was greeted by a recorded message: "Welcome to *Encyclodial*, the phone-opedia of all human knowledge. If there's a question we can't answer, it's not a question worth asking. Before we continue, please note that this line is charged at £1 a minute. All calls are recorded, and you must have the bill-payer's permission to call this number. Please hold for one of our expert operators to answer your query."

I held. Some synthesized Bach played in the background.

"Please hold."

I held. Some synthesized Vivaldi played in the background. I drank some milk, and then spat it out. It was on the turn.

The Vivaldi stopped mid-phrase.

"Welcome to *Encyclodial*, the phone-opedia of all human knowledge. Your knowledge handler today is Kelly. How may I help?"

"Hi, Kelly. Would it be possible to speak to Edwin?"

Kelly seemed a little put out. "Can't I help with your query?"

"I'm sorry, but I'd like to speak to Edwin."

Kelly snorted, "Whatever," and put me on hold.

"Please hold," came the electronic voice.

I held. Some generalised aspirational piano music played in the background.

Then it was Edwin's voice in its most elevated—no, over-the-top—tone: "Welcome to *Encyclodial*, Edwin here—ready to dazzle you with the wonders of knowledge, thrill you with the delights of history, geography, science or the arts. 'What I want is Facts,' says Charles Dickens's Gradgrind, but what you get with Edwin at *Encyclodial* are facts with sugar on the top." He paused for breath. "How can I help you today, sir or madam?"

I didn't want Edwin to recognise me, so I disguised my voice, raising it half an octave to the pitch of a school-child. I sounded kind of ridiculous, but Edwin didn't seem to notice. "I want to find summit out for me homework with me teacher, Mrs . . . erm . . . Evans," I said.

"And what is that, my young friend? What titbits of human wisdom can I dispense for the delectation of Mrs. Evans?" I hesitated, wondering how a school-child could possibly understand Edwin's patter. "What is the theme of the domestic dissertation you are undertaking for your schoolmistress?"

Stupidly, I hadn't planned what I was going to ask beforehand, so I stammered for a moment or two. I cast my eyes round the room, searching for a subject—preferably one that had nothing to do with ants. On the milk carton in front of me was a cheery cow, so I said: "Cows." At least, I thought, cows were about as far from ants as it was possible to get, and even Edwin wouldn't be able to connect the two.

"Cows," he said back, "– a rather broad subject for a homework topic. Never mind. Cows, cows, cows. Give me a moment, my young friend, whilst I load up the *Encyclodial* entry on cows on my screen. Cows, cows, cows." Whilst the computer was finding the entry, he repeated the word in different voices, as if it were a miniature song: "Cows, cows, cows. Cows, cows, cows. Aha! Cows." He now read from the screen: "Cows: a colloquial term for female cattle. They are a prominent member of the subfamily *Bovinae*, of the family *Bovidae*, of the genus *Bos*. Cattle are defined as even-toed, hooffed, ruminant mammals. They descended from wild cattle, aurochs, which roamed Europe and Africa for thousands of years. These wild cattle were domesticated in Neolithic times, probably about 8,000 BC in the Middle East, from where they were brought into Europe by farmers. Cattle are raised for beef and milk, and breeds have different specialities. The best beef breeds originated in Britain. These include the Hereford and the Scottish Aberdeen Angus. The most familiar breed of milk cow is the familiar black and white Friesian, seen throughout the whole country." He paused. "Though not, of course, in the terraced hell where I live. Cows know better than that." He paused again.

"Go on," I said. "I'm getting it all down."

"Cattle have one stomach — not four, as some people think — with four separate compartments. Cattle are ruminants, which means they repeatedly regurgitate their food and re-chew it as 'cud.' This gives them the ability to consume grass and other foodstuffs which would otherwise be indigestible." With that, Edwin burped, presumably thinking that a school-child would find it amusing: "I could do with a bit of rumination myself." I didn't laugh — couldn't manage it in my fake voice — so he returned to the computer script: "Cattle are grazing animals, and are generally farmed in herds on rangeland. Farmers provide cattle with land, vegetation, medical assistance, washing facilities and hoof care; in return, cattle provide meat, sustenance, hides, leather and milk." Somehow, I sensed Edwin was starting to drift away from the script again. "It's the kind of reciprocal arrangement which is echoed throughout the animal kingdom. Look at the ants."

"Ants?!" I said in my usual voice, and then immediately corrected myself: "Ants? Why ants? What have ants got to do with cows?" I couldn't believe Edwin was going to find a way to wriggle ants into the conversation: "Ants?"

"Ah," said Edwin, "ants, like human farmers, tend tiny creatures called aphids — greenfly to you and me, sometimes known as 'ant cows.' It's the ant version of dairy farming: the ants keep herds of aphids, tending them for their milk."

"Milk?"

"A sugary liquid, aphid honeydew. Aphids feed on sugary sap inside plants. Because there's sugar but not much protein inside the plants, the aphids have to eat lots of sap to get the protein they need. So they overdose on sugar, and have to excrete it as kind of . . . sugary poos." Again, it struck me that Edwin's phone manner was a strange fusion of his customary rhetoric mingled with the odd sop thrown in for his (suppos-

71

edly) school-childish listener. "Ants love these sugary poos. They stroke or 'milk' the aphids with their antennae, and the tickled aphids produce a tiny bubble of honeydew on their posteriors . . . erm . . . bums. The aphids keep the honeydew balanced on their bums, so the ants can lick it off."

"That's very kind of them," I said in my fake voice.

"Indeed. It's an amazing relationship. It seems that aphids' bums have evolved to look like ants' faces, so they're comfortingly familiar, and the ants don't object to licking them. Imagine that with humans and cows."

I didn't know what to say apart from "Yuck."

"It's not 'yuck,' though. It's amazing. Ants and aphids alike have evolved their bum-licking arrangements over millions of years. It's like the effect of human beings on cows — how our Neolithic ancestors domesticated the aurochs to produce the cattle species we know now. And vice versa: no doubt the domestication of cows has affected human evolution as well, even though we haven't noticed." His voice was increasingly excited as he got into his stride: "Evolution isn't all about brutal competition. Different species change each other, come to rely on each other. The ants have come to rely on the honeydew which aphids produce, and the domesticated aphids themselves have evolved differently from so-called 'wild' ones. Wild aphids get rid of the honeydew quickly, whereas domesticated ones keep it balanced on their bums so the ants can feed off them; wild aphids excrete a sticky wax to deter enemies, whereas domesticated ones don't. They don't need to, because that's the ants' job: in return for the honeydew, the ants protect their aphid friends from predators like ladybirds and lacewing flies."

He was building up to a grand conclusion: "Marvellous, amazing: the relationship between ant and aphid is an example of what's called a 'mutualism' — a symbiotic relationship, in which both species help the other. Mutualisms are different from parasitisms, where one partner exploits the other, and often destroys it. Mutualisms are signs of a benign nature — the kind of nature which human beings have forgotten about since bloody Darwin. Not that it's poor old Darwin's fault. It's the fault of the crappy world human beings live in, which values parasitisms more than mutualisms, competitions more than mutual aid ... no, strike that: a crappy world where we're forced into parasitisms — like me and my landlady, for example, or my grandfather and, well, everybody. I tell you, in my whole life, I only know one example of a human mutualism." I caught my breath for a second, thinking he might be about to mention his friendship with me — but no, of course not: "In my whole life, I've only got one friendship which is a kind of mutualism: this guy at the pub who dispenses poetry in return for me buying him beers. I don't know what I'd do without him. You might say he is my aphid, I am his ant, the beers are his sugar sap, the poetry is my honeydew."

Edwin laughed, audibly pleased with his own autobiographical riff. I, on the other hand, wondered what the hell a real school-child would have made of all of it.

He continued, but quieter now: "The ants and aphids live together and help each other. Neolithic farmers were the same with their cows. In traditional farms, animals were allowed to roam where they like, in and out of the house, as if they were part of the family." I wasn't entirely convinced that Edwin's knowledge of traditional husbandry would stand up to scrutiny, but I let it go because, by this point, I was intrigued about where the telephonic monologue was leading. "That was traditional farming. With intensive farming, though, we've got rid of all that, and become parasites, exploiting the animals to disease and death, and giving nothing back."

Edwin was sniffing strangely. "If only we could learn from the ants and the aphids. They know what community is. They know how to help each other. We've turned nature into hell, whilst the ants show it can be heaven. They live in communities where people take care of each other, don't just abandon each other, or crush each other under-foot in senseless competition. Everyone has a natural place, a natural role, and everyone relates to everyone else. They've never heard of loneliness: the children are tended by workers; workers tend one another;

aphids are tended by workers and provide food in return; the queen is tended by everyone and provides eggs in return. It's utopia, the perfect organic community.

"Look at army ants. When they're looking for food away from the colony, they sometimes build a temporary bivouac. The bivouac is actually made of thousands of ants all joined together with their claws and mandibles. The queen and young are protected inside. Amazing: a living home where everyone is physically and spiritually linked to everyone else. Amazing, absolutely amazing. If only human beings were as evolved as the ants, and not self-centred bastards. Perhaps, given another seventy-eight millions years, we'll reach their level of sophistication, and be able to form bivouacs together, instead of living in our crappy terraces a long, long way from anyone — instead of being isolated from mothers and brothers and families and homes — instead of everyone abandoning everyone else. We're such selfish, self-centred bastards. If only we could go to the ants' school, if only, if only," he repeated half a dozen times.

Then, silence. I thought I heard someone crying quietly behind him; but perhaps I was mistaken.

After a long pause, I spoke in my fake voice: "Thank you. You've been very helpful."

"We're here to serve," he said, and I rang off, wondering what on Earth the phone conversation — if you could call it that — had really been about.

12.

12, Festival Street,
Burslem,
Stoke-on-Trent,
April 10th 1997.

Our dearest Ed,

A very happy birthday yestaday off of your old mum—which, by the time you get this letter, wont be yestaday, but quite a few days back. I don't know when I'll get chance to post this to you cos of what's been going on here (like usual). So sorry it's late. You know how it is.

I hope your well, or at least better than what we are. I know I go on bout it, luv, but I cant help it. I'm all on my own, like, with him and his Armenians. Bloody Armenians—I'm sick to death of them. Had an ear-full and life-time of them, what with your granddad and now your brother. Its a sodding good job I've never met any of the boggers, or I'd give them what for. Sometimes I wunder how it all started, and other times I cant give a monkeys.

I know, I know, I'm moaning again. I know you hate it. Sorry. Its hard to think of anything else, when Dr. Jones has just told you that your old hart's a bit on the weak side and youve got high blood pressure and all that. Sometimes, I just sit in me chair with the TV off, listening to the thud, thud, thud of me hart. Dont sound like what it did when I was young and fancy-free. Well, okay, not fancy-free. Not sure life was ever like that, specially when your granddad was around.

But I wont bang on about the past or me ills, nor about how everything here's racked and ruined. You only have to go down street to see that—hole place is falling to bits, lumps of concreet and bricks everywhere. What a shithole, if you pardon me language—I know you dont talk like that these days.

None of that probly makes you want to come and visit. But if, like, you were passing the area any time, and fancied dropping in, your old woman'ld be very happy to see you. She hasnt got much to look forward to, part from hart failure and 'him' hitting her again, so it'd be oppreciated.

Sorry, moaning again.

Love to the birthday boy,

The old woman xxx

13.

"Melodramatic bitch," said Edwin, screwing up the letter. He opened the top of the ant-farm and dropped it inside. "There, she can emotionally blackmail the ants instead. See what they'll make of the 'oh-my-poor-old-dicky-ticker' crap. They'll probably use it to line their nest. Best thing for it."

He stared at the ants' nest for a long while, and then suddenly burst out again: "And you know what annoys me the most?"

"No," I said.

"It's all that bad grammar."

"Oh," I said, "I'm sorry to hear that."

"I'm sorry too. I'm sorry the bitch feels she has to pretend she can't spell or punctuate just to wring out every last drop of emotional blackmail."

"Pretend?"

"Of course," he said, as if I should know. "It's all a put-on. Just like her accent. She's far cleverer than she wants you to think. Scheming bitch. She could use apostrophes quite well if she wanted."

Once again, he turned his attention to the ants' nest, and gradually stopped shaking. "They're so reassuring," he said, crumbling in some old biscuit for them to eat. "They manage their lives, families and social relationships so much better than us, stupid crappy beings that we are."

The ants had made themselves at home in the nesting tank. From the outside, through the perspex, the dead-ends of their tunnels and the sides of some of the chambers were visible. In the early days, Edwin had placed a large flat stone on top of the sand, because (he said) *Lasius nigers* are much happier building nests under rocks than in sand alone. He needn't have worried—the ants seemed to manage their new environment without any further human intervention. Over the weeks, we watched as the ants excavated a whole underground town. Edwin, of course, took on the role of ant commentator, explaining everything the ants did in minute detail.

"You see, over there, yes, there: what they are doing is digging out that tunnel with their mandibles. They chew the sand and mix it with their saliva to form tiny bricks. Then they use those bricks to support the walls and ceilings. The sand they don't want is transported to the surface. They're like miniature JCBs, but much more refined, much more powerful. Each year, ants across the Earth move something like sixteen billion tons of dirt. Amazing. Look at the way they engineer the chambers. The floor slopes inwards to drain off water. They invented drainage tens of millions of years before crappy human beings." Edwin always seemed to take a peculiar comfort in belittling the human race in unfavourable comparisons with ants. "Crappy human beings," he'd say, over and over, mesmerised by the activity in the ant-farm. He could spend hours in front of it, just as most people spend hours in front of television: "Ant TV is miles better, much more enlightening."

Edwin was especially glued to Ant TV when conducting one of his "experiments." He insisted to me (as if I cared) that these experiments were "scientific yet benign." They were designed, he said, to pinpoint means of enhancing the life of the colony, and were by no means born of curiosity for its own sake. "I want to help the ants," said Edwin, "so there'll be no vivisection here, thank you—no grown-up children, otherwise known as scientists, pouring boiling water on ants just to see what happens. My experiments won't hurt, they'll help."

The experiment over which he spent most time was what he called 'A Study in the Musical Appreciation of *Lasius nigers*.' He told me he was aiming to work up the notes from the study into an article for a music journal; though (of course) he never got round to it. The study was inspired by the ants in Tom and Jerry's version of *Carmen*, and, indeed, *Carmen* was his starting-point for the experiment. "On the Tom and Jerry cartoon," explained Edwin, "the ants march to music, and end up creating their own jazzy *Carmen*. Outside of the cartoon, no one realises that ants really are musical creatures. They hear by sensing vibrations through their knees, and they produce a kind of music by what's called stridulation—that's the rubbing of one of their gaster or end segments against another. They use it to call for help if they've been buried in a cave-in; and some leaf-cutters use it to tell friends that they've found a juicy leaf. It's a squeaky noise to human beings, but to the ants it's opera, it's Carmen's 'Habanera.' In my experiment, I want to find out if ants react to the human 'Habanera' like we react to their stridulations. I want to see if it's just squeaky noise to them, or if they're more appreciative of human culture than we are of theirs."

So, one Saturday morning, Edwin opened his bedroom window—which looked out on the back-yard—balanced the speakers from his stereo on the window-sill, turned the volume up full, and blared the 'Habanera' from *Carmen* straight at the ant-farm. "Marvellous," said Edwin, now standing in front of the farm and 'observing' the ants' reaction. "They can't help but be moved by Victoria de los Angeles's soprano."

The ants, though, didn't seem particularly moved, and carried on doing whatever they'd been doing before. When it finished, Edwin tried the 'Habanera' again, and then again, and then once more for good measure. "For my results to be convincing, the observations need to be based on a large enough sample," he explained to the angry neighbour who poked his head over the wall, complaining about *Carmen*-on-a-loop.

"You can stick your observations up your arse," said the neighbour. "I'm on nights."

"Can't you see this is science, darling?" asked Edwin.

"I'll tell you what fucking science is," said the neighbour, red patches bubbling round his face, "science is the impact of my fist coming into collision with your fucking jaw, if that opera shite carries on a minute longer."

So that was the end of the day's science experiment.

Early next morning, however, Edwin was at it again. He lunged towards me, invading my body space as he so often did when he was excited or drunk or both, brandishing the CD of *Carmen*: "When there was a lull at work yesterday afternoon," he said, "I read up on the science of ant hearing, and decided that there was a flaw in our original set-up. We need to fine tune our experimental equipment." Given the red-faced neighbour and his fist, I wasn't entirely comfortable with Edwin's use of the pronoun 'we.' I wasn't sure I wanted to be included in something destined to annoy the neighbour and his fist still further. Edwin, however, was too engrossed in setting up his 'laboratory' to listen to my warnings. "Don't worry," he said, as if I were anxious on a scientific point, not one to do with fists, "I've got it all under control. I realised what we did wrong yesterday. Most scientists think that ants don't pick up sounds in the air—just vibrations in the earth. So what we're going to do today is put speakers on the garden table with the ant-farm. That way, they'll pick up the vibrations through the bottom of the tanks. They'll hear *Carmen* through their legs."

Despite hearing it through their legs, the ants still didn't react in any visible way to the 'Habanera.' Edwin tried it again, whilst I glanced round nervously for the neighbour. There were no signs, though, from either ants or neighbour that they'd registered the music. So Edwin tried the *Carmen* overture. Again, nothing. He stood, shifting his weight from one leg to another, scratching his chin. "Hmm. Perhaps nineteenth-century opera isn't their thing. Let's try some other music. Let's find out what is to their taste."

Firstly, he tried 'The Irony Foundry,' a short orchestral piece by a Soviet composer called Mossolov. I'd never heard of it, but Edwin said that if ants really are just machinic workers, as they are so often portrayed, it should be perfect for them, since the piece conveyed an "heroic yet mechanical ideal of work in a 1920s Soviet iron foundry." Once again, however, the ants had no visible reaction to the music: they just carried on scuttling around, digging, transporting, eating as they had before. Edwin was jubilant. "I told you so!" he said, as if I'd ever dared (or bothered) to contradict him: "I told you so! Their indifference to Soviet machine music proves what I've always said. They're not just the soulless automata we take them to be. There is more to ants than machinery; there is more to ants than Soviet work-ethic. All that crappy 1930s propoganda that compares Soviets to ants is insulting to ants. The ants would have hated Soviet drudgery and machinery—their evident distaste for Mossolov proves it. QED."

I wasn't entirely convinced that anything had been proven or demonstrated, but was too busy keeping an eye out for angry neighbours to worry about it much. Edwin, meanwhile, was already moving onto the next piece of music in his experiment. "We must find out what it is they like," he shouted to me from his bedroom. "They're not Russian Futurist ants, so I think we can assume they're not Socialist Realist ants either. I tell you what, let's try some marching music. If they're not machinic workers, ants are just as often depicted as soldiers in a mini-army. Let's see if the troops'll muster to Elgar." And he put on a record of Elgar's *Pomp and Circumstance* marches at top volume.

Nothing happened. Edwin wondered for a moment if he were seeing the ants moving in a straighter line than normal, but then put it down to the morning's intake of Vermouth. "Nope, nothing. Again, at least it shows what I've always suspected: militaristic metaphors for ants are reductive. It seems that all the images we use to encompass ant-dom are rubbish. Ants aren't machines, ants aren't workers, ants aren't soldiers. Real ants can't be reduced to crappy human comparisons or metaphors." Nevertheless, he seemed a little deflated that none of the metaphors he'd tested had come off.

After a cigarette, he brightened again: "I tell you what. Let's try some Wagner."

"Please, no," I said, thinking we were going to be here for sixteen hours. All of the neighbours would be after us. "Not Wagner."

"Yes, we'll try Wagner. We'll play them the finale of *Götterdämmerung* and see if they enjoy the end of the world. We'll see if they like hearing the destruction of human civilisation. A bit of *Schadenfreude* for ants."

I said I thought that *Götterdämmerung* was about the end of the Gods, the Fall of Valhalla, not the destruction of human civilisation. Edwin waved my objection away as irrelevant: "One and the same thing, especially to ants."

But after half an hour of immolation and apocalypse—whether of Gods or human beings—the ants remained unmoved. From this, Edwin drew the dubious conclusion that ants would take no pleasure in the end of the human race. "Darwinians seem to think all species are in brutal competition with each other, want to exterminate each other. But the ants' attitude to Wagner contradicts that."

Puffing on another cigarette, he drifted off on a Edwinian tangent: "There's a great film from the '50s called *Them*. In it, giant mutant ants . . ." He stopped suddenly, and then went off on a tangent of a tangent; I'd never met anyone before Edwin who could interrupt himself, argue with himself to such a degree, as if he were many voices in one: "Actually, have you noticed that both words 'gi-*ant*' and 'mut-*ant*' end with 'ant'?" I said no, I hadn't noticed; I was still distracted by the neighbour's threats, and kept glancing up at his bedroom window, expecting his red and angry head to poke out any time.

Edwin carried on regardless, discoursing about 'gi-*ants*' and 'mut-*ants*': "It's almost as if language itself is terrified of the possibility of giant, mutant ants. Anyway, where was I?" This was a rhetorical question, so I carried on staring into space, aware that the monologue would continue whether I responded or not. "As I was saying, there's this 1950s film, *Them*. In it, the scientists get terrified that these mut-*ants* will mark the end of the human race's evolutionary dominance, that the gi-*ants* will gradually kill off human civilisation. But you can see from how the ants reacted to Wagner that the scientists in *Them* are wrong. Ants would never want to see the end of human civilisation, whether or not they're blown up to giant size. Ants are content to share the planet with us, and we should learn to live with them. It's like the aphids: ants have evolved to the point that they can live happily with other creatures. We, stupid idiots that we are, have not—look at our neighbour, for example."

Given Edwin's determination to blast out music at full volume, I decided that it wasn't just the neighbour who hadn't evolved to the point of living happily with other creatures. "Edwin, can't we give it a rest?"

He thought for a minute. The ants' lack of reaction to any of the music had disappointed him, and he was on the verge of abandoning the experiment. "At least we've learned a lot from our observations," he said. He pursed his lips. "Okay, we'll just test one more piece on them. We've tried nineteenth-century opera, Soviet machine music, a march and the end of the world. What's left?" He went to rummage in his room, and eventually I heard the crackle of an LP through the speakers.

Some beautiful English-hymnish-folkish string music filled the back-yard, as though our bleak terrace had been invaded by a proliferating garden. I felt the hairs on the back of my neck prickle up. Edwin came back into the yard and stood with me, and we listened and watched the ants.

Perhaps it was the Vermouth I'd been drinking, or perhaps it was two hours of staring at black dots, but suddenly I became convinced that the ants' behaviour *had* changed. They seemed slower, more thoughtful in their movements. The diggers came to the surface and hovered about at the top of the nest; the transporters put down their cargo for a rest; the eaters looked up from their biscuit crumbs. Everything in the nest seemed to have slowed down.

Or, at least, that was until the neighbour's bedroom window opened above us, and a beer can hurtled past my head. The neighbour poked his head out: "Will you shut that fucking noise up once and for all? I'm sick of it and so's my dog. If I have to come down there, you'll fucking regret it."

Edwin went indoors to switch off the music, muttering something about ants appreciating human music more than human beings themselves. The neighbour's head disappeared, and the window banged shut. Edwin came back out into the yard, looking at his watch, and talking in a pseudo-scientific manner: "Experiment discontinued at eleven hundred hours. Results: *Lasius nigers* remained impassive to Bizet, Mossolov, Elgar, Wagner. Conclusions to be drawn: *Lasius nigers* are not an operatic, mechanical, militaristic or apocalyptic race. Further results: *Lasius nigers'* behaviour radically altered when played Ralph Vaughan-Williams's *Fantasia on a Theme of Thomas Tallis*."

"You thought you saw that too?"

"Definitely, certainly, absolutely. The ants' rate of movement decreased markedly during the *Fantasia*. Inferences to be drawn are as follows: *Lasius nigers* enjoy music from the English pastoral tradition. These are English ant-refugees kidnapped to a surburban hell, nostalgic for the loss of their beloved countryside. For them, the music expresses this nostalgia, the nostalgia of exile. Not sure I approve of their taste, but there you are. Thus concludes today's experiment." He leant forwards, pressing his nose against the perspex of the foraging tank—his head no doubt that of a giant (or gi-*ant*) for the ants within—and whispered to them: "You old Rom-*ant*-ics, you. Who'd have guessed—sentimental ants, or should one say, sentim-*ants* . . ."

It was then that we heard the letter-box rattle from the hall, and slap of a letter on the mat. Edwin went to pick up the letter, and brought it back into the yard. Standing in front of the ant-farm, looking at the hand-writing on the envelope, he said, "Shit, it's the mother." Momentarily, I thought he meant the ants' mother, writing to them from the countryside they missed so much. But no: it was the letter from his own mother which, after reading, he screwed up and threw into the ant-farm.

That night, I couldn't sleep — one of the springs in the sofa was trying to sodomise me — so I went to make a sandwich in the kitchen. Sitting at the table, I heard Edwin's bedroom door open quietly. His shadow glided into the corridor, opened the back door and stepped outside, into the yard. A minute or so passed, and his shadow came back in and returned to his bedroom. After another half hour of eating mouldy bread and soft crisps, it happened again: Edwin's bedroom door opened, his shadow glided out into the back-yard, and then came back again.

I got up from the table, and wandered into the yard to see if I could work out what was going on — why Edwin kept going outside at this time of night. At first, it was too dark to see anything. Finally, looking down at the ant-farm, I noticed that the lid of the foraging tank was a bit askew. I was readjusting it, when I saw the screwed-up letter from Edwin's mother. I thought it looked different: it seemed to be in a different place in the tank, and was now more folded than screwed.

I replaced the lid of the tank, and went back to bed, wondering how many more times that night Edwin would visit the back-yard and re-read the letter, awake or asleep.

14.

"I got you a birthday present," I said to Edwin, a few nights later.

Edwin looked surprised.

"Sorry it's late, but I didn't realise it was your birthday till I saw your mum's letter."

"It's not late, as a matter of fact," said Edwin. "Today is my birthday. My mother always got it wrong. I suppose it's my fault, to some extent. I down-played my birthday at home. Always saw it as just another floor in the descending elevator towards the inevitable—towards, that is, the fate of my grand-father, and ultimately death."

"God, Edwin."

"No, not God—towards death, I said. God doesn't figure in it."

I was getting exasperated, which wasn't quite the emotion I'd anticipated on saving three days' earnings to buy Edwin a present. "Do you want this present or not?"

For once, Edwin smiled a genuine smile that wasn't a grin—and I realised he was actually excited at the rare pros-pect of receiving a gift. "Of course I do, darling, just fooling around. Let me see it."

I handed it over: it was small, flat, and wrapped in news-paper. Edwin turned it over, shook it and put it to his ears. He raised his eyebrows. "Doesn't look like much," his face seemed to say.

"Go on, open it," I said.

So he did. Inside, were two pieces of orange card—two

return train tickets to Stoke-on-Trent, booked in advance for the following Saturday. He stared down at them. "I thought we could go and visit your mother," I said.

There was a long silence.

He handed the tickets back to me. "Thank you for your consideration," he said, ever-so-formally—as if he were addressing a company, "but I find that we cannot accept your offer."

Before I could say anything, he swivelled round, and disappeared into his bedroom. After a minute or so, the dulcet tones of Penderecki flooded the hallway.

"Happy birthday," I said to the Penderecki.

For the next couple of days, Edwin listened to Penderecki continuously, scuppering any chances of my bringing up the present again. He'd come home from work with a bag of chips and go straight to his room. The door would slam, and *Threnody to the Victims of Hiroshima* would scream out of his stereo. He'd play it again and again, turning up the volume if I knocked on his door. I couldn't begin to guess what listening to Hiroshima being musically bombed hundreds of times over was doing to his head, but it was certainly jangling my nerves living in a house full of Holocaust.

Eventually, during one of the *Threnody*'s quieter sections, I tried shouting through the door: "Edwin, won't you come out?"

No answer, apart from Penderecki.

"Edwin, won't you come out and talk to me?"

No answer, apart from Penderecki.

"Edwin, for God's sake. For God's fucking sake. I thought you wanted to see your mother. I thought that was what you really wanted. I saw you the other night, going backwards and forwards to the ants' nest, fishing out your mother's letter and putting it back again. I thought you wanted to sort it out with her. I thought it might help you feel happier if you met up. I'm sorry, Edwin, if I got it wrong. I wasn't interfering in your life . . . Okay, I *was* interfering in your life. But Edwin, for God's sake, can't we talk about this?"

No answer, apart from Penderecki.

"Edwin?" I banged on the door. "For fuck's sake, Edwin. For fuck's sake. For fuck's sake, Edwin." I must have banged on the door and repeated "For fuck's sake, Edwin," for two whole *Threnody*s; but when the bomb dropped on Hiroshima for a third time, I gave up and started walking away.

Then I lost my temper, and turned back to kick the door. "For fuck's sake, Edwin. You don't have to go, but you could at least not be a fucking pig about it."

Suddenly, the door opened a crack, and Edwin's head poked out. He was almost grinning: "A *sucking* pig? What on Earth do you mean, darling, 'I don't have to be a sucking pig about it'?"

"No, a *fucking* pig. A *fucking* pig. Fucking. Fucking," I corrected him.

"Oh, I see," he said. "That's more like it. I wondered for a moment what you were going on about." He looked me up and down. "I thought it was some weird kind of insult or curse from wherever it is you hark from." And with that misunderstanding cleared up, he shut the door again, and returned to his Penderecki.

I returned to my shouting: "You *are* being a fucking and sucking pig. You are."

No answer.

"Very well, then. I'll fucking go on my own. Now I've got these crappy tickets, I'll go. I've never been to Stoke-on-Trent. I'll have my own fucking day out, my own holiday, and you can stew here in your Penderecki juices, you . . . sucking pig."

Whilst I was shouting these culinary insults, the front door opened, and the landlady walked in. She squinted at me as if I were rather strange, and then went straight upstairs.

I kicked Edwin's door once more for good measure. If I were strange, I thought, he and this insane world were partly to blame.

15.

The morning after next, I left the house for the station. I didn't really want to go, but once I'd said I would, I felt compelled to; and, anyway, I had no urge to hang around the house, waiting for Edwin to emerge from his Penderecki.

So I had some stale toast, said goodbye to the ants, and walked to the station, through some dark, Satanic streets, down a flooded alleyway, past a Siberia of abandoned trucks, and finally onto the platform. The train clunked into the station and clunked out again, with me on board. A huge man grunted at my ticket, telling it to change at Derby station.

At Derby, I bought a paper, and stared at something about an upcoming general election. I handed the paper to a tramp: because of my new job, I was more comfortable giving away newspapers than reading them myself. I never felt any connection with the headlines, never felt that they bore any relation to my life. From somewhere — I don't know where or how — I seemed to understand most of the references, knew most of the names and places on an intellectual level; but there were random gaps I couldn't explain, and, on a personal, emotional level, I somehow felt that I was living a different history to people around me. My headlines, names, places, even dates were different to theirs. So, instead of reading the paper, to wile away the time, I bought a can of beer, and sat watching nervous men creep into the massage parlour opposite the station.

After an hour or so, it was time for the connection to Stoke-on-Trent. The train clunked into the station, and clunked out, with me on it. Once again, a huge man grunted at my ticket, telling it that Stoke was "the stop after the one after the one after next." I settled down with my ticket and can, and watched the greys and browns roll past.

Soon, the greys and browns of the countryside merged into the greys and browns of the city. The train came to a halt at Longton, where no one got on or off, and which looked like the stop before the end of the world. And then, finally, we were there, and the train emptied onto the platform.

Once outside the station, I stood for a while, staring at a statue of eighteenth-century ceramics manufacturer, Josiah Wedgwood. He had a pot in one hand, and someone had put a can of lager in the other. It looked like he was weighing up alternatives: go into pottery, or get drunk? Which was it to be?

Since this was a kind of holiday, I chose the latter, and went to have a couple of pints in a nearby pub. After an hour of the landlord telling me all the places I had to visit whilst in Stoke, and an hour of my repeating that I couldn't afford any of them, I left with instructions on how to get to Burslem, in the north of the city.

I was told to walk past Josiah Wedgwood — who was still weighing up his options — till I got to a main road. From there, I could catch a number 21, which would take me to Burslem Market Place. After that, the landlord was a bit hazy, and told me to ask again. Given the morning's beers, I was also a bit hazy, and wandered around for a while, lost in terraced streets. I kept circling back to Josiah Wedgwood, and he kept pointing me in a different direction.

Just when I was starting to think that Stoke was a ruined maze of terraces and Josiah Wedgwoods, I struck off in a different direction and found the main road and the bus stop. The bus came, and I was soon trundling through a larger maze of terraces, ring roads, pound shops, concrete, dereliction and rubble, amongst which I started to miss Josiah Wedgwood. I found it hard to imagine Edwin growing up here; but then, I found it hard to imagine Edwin growing up anywhere. He was as much out of place back home, as he would have been here — as he would have been any place, any time. My annoyance with him for not coming was ebbing away, and I was feeling sorry for him once again, perhaps because I empathised with that feeling of displacement: I too always felt out of place, out of time. "Bloody Edwin. Bloody, bloody Edwin," I muttered to myself, trying to cling onto my frustration.

Then the driver shouted: "Market Place, Burslem," and I got off.

Following the driver's directions, I walked down Scotia Road, and turned into the inaptly named Zion Street. Crossing onto a Hobson Street, where everything, even the sky, seemed brown, I continued down until I reached a right turn into Festival Street. The numbers counted down from 122, and the houses seemed to count down with them — from well-kept town houses to boarded-up terraces with sofas growing into lawns. Number 12 was near the end. It was a semi-detached ex-council house, set back from the road. The lawn was uncut and the curtains still drawn at half-past-midday. I stood in front of the house for a long time. At first, I had no urge to knock. I had come to see Edwin's family home because I couldn't afford any of the other Stoke sights; and now I had seen it, I could go.

But I didn't go. I walked up to the front door and pushed the dead bell. I pushed it again, and knocked at the same time. The curtain to my left twitched. A bedroom window upstairs slammed shut. Next door's cat shrieked.

I knocked again. Through the frosted window in the door, I could see a silhouetted shape moving. The shape came towards the door, unlocked it from the inside, and opened it. For a second, I blinked at the shape in front of me, which was that of a young man, who looked too big for the corridor in which he stood. His hair was unwashed, and the lower half of his face grubby, unshaven — I couldn't see the upper half, because his straggly hair hung over his eyes. He wore a baggy cardigan; perhaps if it had been a woman's nightie, I would have recognised the family resemblance with Edwin more readily. As it was, I didn't think anything — as if the young man's blankness on finding me at the front door had been transmitted straight into my mind too. He didn't look at me on answering the door, didn't ask who I was, what I wanted; he just grunted, and turned back down the hallway. By the time I could take him in, by the time I managed "Excuse me," he'd already shuffled off, through a doorway at the other end of the hall.

I hovered on the threshold for a minute, staring into an empty corridor. Again, if I hadn't been transfixed by the young man's blankness, I might have wondered whether leaving front doors open ran in the family. But instead, I just stood there, staring into nothing, waiting for something to come out of nothing.

Eventually, a door to the left of the hallway opened, and a middle-aged woman peered at me with an uncertain manner. Everything about her was uncertain: she had silver hair, which seemed uncertain whether it was the result of bleaching or ageing; her jeans and scarf were faded, and seemed unsure whether they originated in the 1960s, '70s, '80s or '90s; and from moment to moment, her mouth wavered between different expressions, ages, decades. There was a long pause.

"Hello?" she asked, in the broad accent I remembered from the phone call, and now recognised as Potteries.

"Hello," I said.

"Hello," she said. We'd been in this hello loop before. Then she blurted out: "We never buy anything, you know." I wondered whether she meant from door-to-door salespeople, or more generally.

"I'm not selling anything. I'm visiting."

"We never 'ave visitors," she said, "not since 1995." She seemed on the verge of chasing me away, slamming the door in my face, but couldn't quite bring herself to do anything so decisive.

"Don't shut the door, Mrs. Prince." I tried to think of an excuse for why I was here: "I was just passing the area on, erm, business, so thought I'd drop by. I'm a friend of your son's. You might remember: a while back, you spoke to me on the phone about him."

Her eyes narrowed: "Which son?"

"Edwin, of course. Edwin."

And that was the magic word. Immediately, she stepped into the hallway, opened the front door as far as it would go, and almost pulled me inside. Then she shut the door behind me, to keep me there. She never once asked my name; to her, my name was "Edwin's friend," and that was enough—enough for her to grab a total stranger by the elbow, drag them into the house, and propel them through the door from which she'd first appeared.

Inside was a chaotic living room, carpeted with make-up, once-new dresses, old magazines, the faces of has-been celebrities of the '60s and '70s, and wallpapered with dress patterns, lists of things to do, and family photos, mixed indiscriminately with more photos of celebrities. I felt surrounded by faces.

"Please," she said, ushering me through the labyrinth of magazines and celebrity smiles, "please, sit down. Can I get you a cup of tea, dear?"

"Yes, please."

She thought for a moment. "Oh, silly me, we don't 'ave any tea at the mo'. Can I get you summit else?"

"What do you have?"

She stared into space, moving her lips, as if listing a myriad of possibilities to herself. When, though, she finally spoke out loud, these multiple possibilities boiled down to: "Gin?"

"Yes, that's fine, Mrs. Prince."

"Gin and tonic for two," she said, and stepped over to a dilapidated drinks cabinet in the corner of the room. Whilst she was preparing the drinks, I stared at the dust and photos on the mantelpiece in front of me. As far as I could see from where I was sitting, most of the photos were defaced or damaged in some way: there were smashed frames, black holes where heads should have been, and whole figures cut out from family line-ups. Hanging above them all was a huge photo of an elderly man's gaunt face, shot from below his Stalinesque moustache. The face was looking into the far distance—or, at least, the face would have been looking into the distance if its eyes weren't charred holes and shattered glass.

Returning with the drinks, Mrs. Prince followed my stare: "That was 'im. That was 'im in his prime."

"Who?"

"Edwin's grandfather, me father, of course." Of course, she seemed to say, how silly of you to have to ask. She'd lived with the photo for so long, she couldn't conceive of anyone not recognising the person in it, eyes or no eyes.

I took the drink she offered. We both stared at the photo some more. "If you don't mind my asking, Mrs. Prince, what happened to your father's eyes?"

She frowned. "I'd forgotten about that, dear." Forgotten, I wondered? How could you forget the most striking aspect of the picture? "Yes, I'd forgotten that. I spose you get used to it and don't notice it after a bit. 'He can't see us so we don't see him,' Ed's brother said once."

"How did it happen?"

"How did what happen, my dear?" asked Mrs. Prince. It began to dawn on me where Edwin's propensity for circular conversations came from.

"How come the picture is, well, blind?"

"Oh, that," she said, staring down at her drink and swirling it round and round. She still didn't answer my question. "Nice gin this."

"What happened to your father on the photo?" I asked again.

She looked up, suddenly flaring with anger. "Ed's brother 'appened to it, that's what. Him and his darling air rifles 'appened to it. What do I have to put up with in this bloody 'ouse? All me photos of me father used for target practice. I know he was a mean old git, but he was me father, after all's said and done and done and said. The poor bogger's dead and buried, twenty odd years back, and no one deserves to have their eyes shot out after they're dead."

I finished the gin, put down my glass, and got up to have

a closer look. I lifted the photo off the wall, and peered behind — and there, sure enough, were two small holes where the air-rifle pellets had ended up, after passing straight through the grandfather's eyes. Replacing the portrait, I looked more closely at the other photos on the mantlepiece: every one which included Edwin's grandfather had bullet holes instead of eyes.

I sat back down. "It's a bit disturbing, isn't it, Mrs. Prince?" I asked, starting to worry about being under the same roof as this eye-sniper.

"You're telling me," she said. "You're bloody well telling me. For Christ's sake, what do I have to put up with? For Christ's sake, my dear." She sank into an armchair, shaking her head. I wondered if it were me who had pissed her off, but was reassured when she poured both herself and me another gin and tonic. I was as disorientated by her manner as I'd been on first meeting Edwin. Like him, she didn't seem to have any conception of 'normal' ways of talking to a stranger, beyond the offer of tea (which she didn't have anyway). There was none of the customary self-censorship: as soon as I met her, she bombarded me with emotions and memories, as though I had known her father, her sons, and herself for years, and would understand.

Her tone changed, quietened for a minute or two: "Having said that, at least it means me father doesn't have to see all those 'orrible things any more."

"What 'orrible . . . horrible things?"

"I dunno," she said, and the conversation seemed to have turned into a dead-end. I hesitated for a few seconds, starting to wonder if it was the gin or conversation which was confusing me.

I stumbled towards a question: "Mrs. Prince, you said that your father doesn't have to see horrible things any more?"

"That's right," she said.

"Well, if you don't mind my asking, what horrible things?"

"I dunno," she said. There was another pause, another looming dead-end — until she added, in a dreamy, disinterested way: "Oh, I dunno what 'orrible things. He'd never talk about them. He never talked about anything, did our father. But he was in the navy for years, in the 1920s and '30s and whatever. When I asked him about it when I was a kid, he'd say he'd seen worse things than anything what you can imagine. He was prob'ly trying to scare me cos I was a right so-and-so back then. The only thing he ever did tell me was a list of the places he'd been to—and funny, that's what frightened me the most, that list. Like a list of dead people, that's what I thought as a kid. I think it's why I've never been anywhere—you know, travelled anywhere—except here, in crappy Stoke. The old man made me a bit scared of having me own list, if you see what I mean."

She grinned, and I glimpsed Edwin in her grin: "Actually, you know summit? I realised as I got older that his list changed a bit each time he said it—some places dropping off, some places added. So I reckon he was probably making loads of it up. Lying old bogger: was probably stuck in Liverpool or some dive like that most of the time." The grin drooped suddenly, and she murmured into her drink: "Though there was this one very foreign place I reckon he had been to. I only heard it on the list once, and then he shut up, and wouldn't mention it again. He looked kind of 'orrified when he'd said it, like he shouldn't have. Like he didn't want to think about it. I got out a map once, to look where it was, but couldn't find it anywhere."

"Where was it?" I asked, sitting forwards.

"Dunno, can't quite get it right in me head—something like Smurfit or Smelly or Snooky, one of them foreign names."

All of a sudden, I realised she was peering at me over her glass, squinting at me as if I were far away, on a distant horizon: "Are you okay? You look a bit . . . odd."

"Can you smell something?" I asked.

"What?" she asked.

"Something like smoke? And . . . can you hear something like crackling?"

She put her glass down, and sprang out of her chair: "Oh God, oh God, p'raps it's him—me son—burning stuff in the kitchen again. Shitty shitty shit." She dashed out of the room, swearing to herself.

A minute or so later, she came back in, more slowly. As she sat back down, she looked at me with narrowed eyes, and, locked in that hard, analytical gaze, I couldn't help remembering what Edwin had said—that she was far cleverer, far more perceptive than she pretended to be. The gaze was only momentary, and the hardness melted from her eyes, as she resumed her drink: "No, nothing. Perhaps it's all in yer 'ead, my dear. Perhaps you're hearing or smelling things."

"Maybe I am," I said.

"Where were we, anyways?" she asked. She seemed genuinely to have forgotten what we were talking about.

"We were talking about your father." This prompted no response. "Your father. On the photo."

She latched onto the word 'photo,' ignoring the reference to her father, perhaps tired of the subject: "That's right, the photo. The bloody photo, for Christ's sake," she said, spilling gin everywhere in sudden fury, "it does me blood pressure no good at all. And look what he's done to me other photos. I gave up replacing them after a while—there weren't no point. I had some lovely ones of our Ed, from when he was younger. But as soon as I put them up, *he*"—she indicated behind her with her thumb—"*he* takes them down and cuts Ed out of them." I peered at the holes in some of the photos on the mantlepiece, and, sure enough, many were Edwin-shaped.

"Why does he do that?"

"I dunno. I dunno, except sometimes, I've sneaked up to his room when he's out back cleaning his rifles. The cut-outs of Ed are spread all over his bed and the floor, next to books of famous composers and a magnifying glass." Her voice dropped, and she leant over to whisper to me: "You know what I reckon's going on?"

"I have no idea, Mrs. Prince," I said, honestly.

"D'you wanna know?"

"I suppose so," though I wasn't quite sure.

"Well, when they're all spread out, he always puts the

Ed-cut-outs next to photos in the books. These photos are all of the same guy. They're all of a composer called 'Aroom Catchy-tunian,' or summit foreign like that. It's him. In me son's mind, he's the one that's to blame for everything bad these days: Aroom Catchy-tunian."

"Aram Khachaturian?" I asked, trying to work out if she were smiling at her own deliberate mistake. It must have been deliberate, because the name kept changing throughout the rest of the conversation — from Catchy-tunian to Kitsch-etonian to Catch-the-coldian — until I too started feeling disorientated, even disturbed, by this name-changing, shape-shifting bogeyman.

"Whatever the name is — I don't know about these kinds of people meself, or their kinds of music. I was into the Stones when I was young. And now, I quite like watching a video Ed got me once of Chinese opera. Have you ever seen Chinese opera?"

"No, Mrs. Prince," I said, trying to will her back onto the subject of Edwin's brother. I poured her another gin and tonic, and asked: "No, I haven't, Mrs. Prince, but I have heard of . . . Aram Khachaturian. What were you saying about him?"

"The point is, see, that, before he came back to his room, I was looking at these books of his, and I noticed that this Catchery-tulunian-whoever bloke is Armenian. It all adds up, like."

"Does it?" I asked.

"Of course. He reckons that Ed is really this Catchy-thingian, in some strange way or other — he reckons that our Ed is an Armenian composer. It all adds up, logical like."

I wasn't sure what form of logic or mathematics she was referring to; but I thought a few more gin and tonics would help me work it out, so I poured us both another. A creak to my right made me jump. I thought the door moved slightly, and a shadow changed in the gap between door and frame.

Edwin's mother's eyes were wide, and she was clinging on to my sleeve. "He's prob'ly listening to us now. I hardly dare say the word 'Armenian' these days, in case he hears. But actually, it's better if he's down 'ere listening to us, cos it means he's not upstairs. Somehow, that's worse. I reckon he sits up there for hours with that magnifying glass, comparing cut-outs of them both, trying to detect tell-tale similarities—for hours, I tell you, and all I can hear is rustling and muttering." She relaxed a bit, and let go of my sleeve. "I know that's what he's doing up there cos he used to do it before, a while back, with the drummer from Supergrass. He used to think the drummer was Ed too. That wasn't so bad, though, as mixing Ed up with this composer bloke: Danny Goffey (or our Ed) didn't seem to be Armenian—so the two stupidities didn't get all mixed up in his 'ead. And, anyway, me son quite liked Supergrass's first album. He said that Goffey's (or our Ed's) backing vocals added something to the band's songs. That meant he could just about put up with Ed 'lying' about what kind of music he was into. Just about, though he looked pretty pissed off with Supergrass at the time. They're not my thing, of course, not '60s enough. What do you think of them?"

"Who?"

"Supergrass."

"I don't really think anything of them, Mrs. Prince."

"Ah, you're like him, our Ed—you like the classical stuff. I could tell as soon as you came in the house you were one of *them*—one of them classic-al-is-ists, like."

"Actually, I'm not really . . ."

"Yes, dear, I knew it. I knew that these days our Ed would have friends who know stuff and listen to culture. Not like his mother, or—when he was alive—his granddad. He was an ignorant old bogger, y'know. He hated music in general, and the classical stuff in particular, banned it from his 'ouse—said it was 'all Armenian to him.' I think it reminded him of those 'orrible things from his past, somehow or other." She thought for a moment, her head to one side. "Y'know, p'raps that's why me boys got into this classicalist music—cos their granddad hated it so much." She said this as if the thought had never crossed her mind before. It had clearly been a long time since she talked to anyone, and during that time, she probably hadn't thought about anything but day-to-day survival. So all conversation topics, all thoughts, seemed new, fresh. Now, for example, it was gradually dawning on her that she hadn't seen her first-born for years, and that he had a different life elsewhere: "He's got his life and his classicalist, culture-ist friends like you, a long way away from his '6os mother, mad brother and dead bogger of a granddad. No wonder he don't want anything to do with us." She was building up to tears, so I decided to keep the conversation moving, to avoid any pauses which might be used for crying.

"You were saying, Mrs. Prince, about Supergrass's drummer?"

"That was ages ago, the stuff about the drummer. Soon fizzled out — something to do with the brown cap he wore on one of their songs, and Ed never wearing a cap. Now instead it's all Catchy-tunian-this, Catchy-tunian-that. God, poor old Catchery-tunian — from what I read in me son's books, he wasn't even very good. All I know about him is that he wrote the theme tune to one of me dad's favourite sailing programmes on the telly. Can't remember the name of it, and it's not the sort of thing that'd even, like, register with me son. He misses all the important stuff. I mean, for a start, he seems to have missed the kinda basic thing that this Catcher-looney-tunian-whatever bloke died ages ago. But apparently here he is, nearly twenty years later, wand'ring round the crappy Midlands, trying to escape from a nutty brother." She took a deep breath, threatening tears again. "Me poor boys. They're both lost to me and each other. It's real shitty, this life, real shitty."

Now it was too late, and she was crying. I would have handed her a handkerchief if I had one; but I didn't so I couldn't.

After a minute, the crying died down, and she stared at the carpet for some time. "Bloody, bloody 'ell, no wonder he hates our Ed so much, if he thinks Ed's an Armenian. No wonder he runs away or gets angry whenever he thinks Ed might come home. Not that our Ed has been home for, well, years, to see his poor old mum. But who can blame him when we're wracked and ruined like this? Shitty, shitty life."

"I'm sure Edwin will come and visit soon, Mrs. Prince," I said. "He's just . . . caught up with a few things at the moment."

"Caught up with avoiding us," she said, slurring her words slightly. "Caught up with avoiding his family and bloody Armenians. He don't care if the woman who raised him is riddled with illnesses, like bloody bullet-holes. He don't care. God, no one bloody cares, dear, no one bloody well cares."

I felt tears rising into my eyes now. There was something overwhelming, something hypnotic about this woman and her heart-on-the-sleeve misery which I couldn't define afterwards, post-gin, but which, at the time, made me squeeze her hand — made me want to fall to the floor and put my head in her lap and help her in everything and anything, as long as she would be my mother too. I suddenly recalled the Book of Ruth — my favourite bit of the Old Testament as a child — and I wanted to repeat Ruth's words to her mother-in-law, Naomi: 'Intreat me not to leave thee, or to return from following after thee: for whither thou goest, I will go; and where thou lodgest, I will lodge: thy people shall be my people, and thy God my God. Where thou diest, will I die, and there will I be buried.'

Of course, I didn't make this declaration; and, afterwards, the Biblical mood passed with the gin, and I felt slightly ashamed of my emotion, unable to explain to myself the effect of this strange woman, except in terms of alcohol.

Not that, back then, that stopped me pouring another drink, whilst she wailed on: "No one cares that I've got a thirty-two-year-old son who I have to watch all the time in case he does something stupid, who I have to support with some crappy allowance, who I have to cook and clean and tidy for" — I stopped myself glancing round the room at this point, in case she felt contradicted — "who I have to get up when he can't be bothered to get up, who I even have to wash when he can't be bothered to wash — can you imagine that? — whose idiocies and paranoias and crap I have to bloody well share, who I have to follow when he goes out, who follows me whenever I go out, who . . ."

"Can't he be, erm, treated, Mrs. Prince?" I asked, interrupting the endless string of "whos." "You know, if you don't mind my asking, what's the doctor done?"

"The doctor, dear?"

"Yes, the doctor. Has the doctor said anything or done anything?"

"Oh, we don't see no doctor. Me father hated them, said they were all Armenians. Still, I spose we *could* see a doctor," she frowned, as if the thought of medical treatment had never struck her before, "sometime."

The door to my right creaked again, and she jumped. "God, look at the time," she said, glancing at a clock on the mantle-piece, which was showing the wrong time — whether too early or too late, I couldn't tell. "He's probably wondering where his dinner is. He'll be unsettled as it is, what with visitors and all. I'll have to get his dinner, make sure it's bang on five-thirty, or he'll go mad. You don't want to see him mad. He hits me, you know, hits me right in the eye. I know one day he'll use those rifles on me if he doesn't get his dinner on time, or something stupid like . . ."

The door creaked again. She stopped mid-sentence, and sprang out of her chair. "Right, dinner. Would you like some, dear?"

"No, I should be going."

She looked genuinely crestfallen.

"I'm sorry," I said, "I've got a long way to go." My bladder was jabbing me, with numerous gin and tonics. "But before, can I use your bathroom?"

She directed me up the stairs, across the landing and to the first door on the right. I locked myself in and sat on the toilet. The window was open, and I felt the fresh air on the back of my neck. It was cool in here, and the coolness made me realise how over-heated and over-ginned my head was — in fact, how over-heated and over-ginned the whole house was. I got up and splashed some cold water on my face, staring in the mirror for a few minutes; I wondered if I could climb out of the bathroom window and down the drainpipe, rather than returning to the stifling atmosphere downstairs. I wanted to leave this living melodrama, escape from this "soap-opera house," as Edwin would call it later on.

But no, I did the 'sensible' thing. I unlocked the bathroom door and stepped out onto the landing. To my right, one of the bedroom doors was open—it had been closed when I'd first come upstairs—and the relative darkness within made me curious. I tapped on the door; there was no answer. I poked my head round the door and murmured: "Hello?" Still no answer. I stepped inside.

Given the single bed and men's underpants lying everywhere, the room presumably belonged to Edwin's brother. It was small and dark—the curtains were drawn—and full of anachronisms from boyhood: there were toys which had never been put back in their boxes, toys which had never been taken out of their boxes, clothes which would no longer have fitted, posters of long-forgotten bands. Scattered amongst the débris were LPs, CDs, musical scores and photocopies. I sat down to flick through one photocopied score, which lay open on the bed, and which was covered in coloured underlinings, circlings and spirallings.

Then, I felt someone's breath on the back of my neck and a whispering in my ear: "They were playing his music on the radio. They were playing his music on the radio. They were playing his music on the radio," the whisperer kept echoing. I wondered if anyone in this family ever greeted a stranger in a conventional way; but I was beginning to forget what the conventions were.

"Oh," I said.

"Don't you get it? Get it? Get it? Getitgetitgetitgetitgetit? They were playing his music on the radio."

"I get it," I said, lying.

"They were playing his music on the radio—broadcasting *that* harmony to everyone. It was on every channel. I detuned the station and tuned another one, but it was still there. *That* harmony."

"What harmony?" I asked, not turning round, not even moving when I felt the whisperer's spit on my earlobe.

"*That* harmony, of course. The harmony that keeps chasing me. Just when I think I've got away—just when I think I've turned a corner—just when the music seems to have escaped from it—it comes back. At first I thought it wouldn't get out—I thought it was safely contained, in *his* music."

"Whose music?"

"*His*, of course." From behind me, the whisperer pointed at the now-familiar name at the top of the score on the bed. "His, his, his, his," he hissed again and again. "*His* music—I thought it was safe, but the harmony started to leak out from the edges of his scores. That terrible Armenian sound started to infiltrate other people's music, and it's now got into everything—I can hear it in Cher, for Christ's sake. Cher, for Christ's sake. I daren't switch the radio or television on. It chases me everywhere: I hear it in the street, in the humming of the heating, or when someone turns a tap on. Not many other people notice, of course—I suppose because they don't have *my* musical ear. They're not trained to hear it. And the sound assumes so many different disguises. It's slippery, shape-changing: that's how it gets by without detection. Sometimes, it's a flattened third added to a major chord. Sometimes, it's an added seventh, flattened or natural, hidden in the bass pedal. Sometimes, it's implied horizontally in the melodic phrase, rather than vertically in the chord. Do you see? Do you understand?"

If I'd been in the right frame of mind, I might have told the whisperer that he sounded like a talking textbook with a complex; and I might have been been surprised by this—surprised that the whisperer was so well-spoken, so intelligent, given what I'd heard about him from other people. But I wasn't in the right frame of mind, wasn't able to be surprised about anything. Ever more insistent, the whisperer's whisper seemed to surround me, and I felt trapped in his world, unable to dis-associate myself from it; I felt I was losing sight or hearing of any world outside this one—and the likelihood that the whisperer had rehearsed this whisper to himself a thousand times before made the feeling more, not less, intense, because it was as if I were over-hearing someone else's thoughts, being subsumed into someone else's mind. For a little while, the whisperer's whisper seemed to be everything there was in the world: "The harmony is carnivorous, cannibalistic, parasitic," it continued, repeating the last three words half a dozen times, like a refrain. "The harmony eats proper music from within. It's a parasite. Other people don't realise how dangerous the situation is. But we do" — mesmerised, I hardly noticed the shift to "we" — "We do. We've understood the real meaning of *his* words. We've understood what the Armenian *really* meant, when he made that famous speech about harmony."

"What famous speech?" I asked, trembling in anticipation, as though the answer were of life-and-death importance.

"*That* speech, of course: the one he made in England, when he almost gave the game away. The speech when he crowed to his audience that Armenians hear chords differently, because of their folk music. You remember, you must remember, the whole world knows about it -" here, he bent down, and reached out for one of the books on the floor. In the corner of my eye, I glimpsed his arm — pale, unexpectedly muscular, as if he'd been in training for some kind of war — and a mop of dark, sweat-ridden hair. So close to me, I could almost feel as well as see his whole body trembling, flexing with excitement, as he scooped up a book, flicking backwards and forwards through the pages.

"Here it is. Here it is. Here it is," he said, standing up again. From behind me, he reached round and thrust the open book in my face, as though threatening me with a dangerous weapon. He pointed at the text with a shaking hand: "Look here. Here. You can see it in his own words. For Armenians, he says here, a tonic chord needs an added seventh for it to sound right, natural. That's what he says — his own words! Armenians hear normal, tonic chords as dissonances. What we hear as consonance, *they* hear as as discord. Our beauty is their ugliness, our nature is their unnature. In his very own words, here, look, he admits an antithesis between our harmony and theirs. And yet . . . and yet, despite saying this, he carries on composing his music, music which insidiously poisons our harmonies with theirs—music which pretends to be Western, which uses Western instruments, but which makes us hear the un-Western as Western, our abnormal as normal, our dissonance as consonance.

"For Christ's sake, isn't it obvious?" he asked, seeming to shake his listener into commonsense: "In some of his chords, natural and flattened thirds co-exist, undermining our sense of the difference between major and minor—destroying the very basis of European harmony. The very basis! It's a trap, a trap, a trap, atrapatrapatrapatrap..." He paused, took a deep breath, changed tack. "Look. Haven't you noticed the similarity between the words, 'harmony' and 'Armenian'? It's all part of the plan, to make us unconsciously associate *them* with harmony. But their music isn't ours—it's all a poisoned trap ... It's poisoning our music, destroying our sense of harmony from within. *He* was in on it. *He* admitted it. *He* was their secret weapon." The whisperer repeated these sentences seven or eight times, as if they clinched his point—as if they were hard evidence. "*He* was in on it. *He* admitted it. *He* was their secret weapon ...

"After all, he performed his music in forty-two countries around the world. Imagine that: forty-two countries, many of them in the West, where he poured his poison into our ears, and made our own harmonies come to seem disharmonies, our own music unmusical. I tell you, his music is a conduit between theirs and ours, Armenian and European, East and West. Look at the Second Symphony, the third movement, where he layers the Armenian folk-song 'Vorskan Akhper' on top of that cornerstone of Western music, the *Dies Irae*. Cunning, cunning bastard: by mixing the two, the symphony destroys our sense of our own music. 'I hunger to bring my Armenian heritage out into the mainstream'—they are his words. His words—he admitted it. He admitted he wanted to pollute the Western mainstream with Armenian culture."

At this point, he suddenly rushed to the bedroom window, climbed onto the sill, and swept open the curtains with a flourish: "Look! Look!" he whispered, as loudly as it is possible to whisper, jabbing a finger towards the street below—where a flat-capped man was walking a scraggy dog, which now started howling. "But more importantly: listen! Listen!" The whisperer's back was to me, and he was silhouetted against the light, as his whisper reached a climax: "Listen and look down there: our culture, our very essence is being undermined, and no one understands—no one is doing anything about it! They're just walking dogs, for Christ's sake! But it'll sneak up on them! It'll catch up with them! And finally, finally, finally, I tell you, we ... we ... we will become Armenianised!"

For a moment, the ludicrousness of the whisperer's peroration broke the mesmeric spell; the whisperer's mother's words came back to me ("God, poor Catchy-tunian—the bloke died ages ago, and wasn't even very good"), and I had to cough to cover up a laugh.

The whisperer didn't notice my cough-laugh; and I decided it was time to creep away, before he got even more worked up. I turned to leave, but he leapt down from the window-sill, and came up behind me again, almost pinning me forwards onto the bed, whispering, whispering in my ear:

"Listen. We've got to resist the Armenianisation. Somehow, we've got to ethnically cleanse our harmonies. We've got to reclaim them for ourselves, before it's too late. It might already be too late. But we can at least try." He pointed again at the score on the bed. "And one way I've been trying is to rewrite the Armenian's own music, purging it of the Armenianisms, filling it with common chords and Western harmonies. I've been going through the godforsaken 'Sabre Dance,' expunging all those Armenian harmonies, sevenths, chords which are both major and minor at the same time. What do you think of what I've done so far? What do you think?"

I was no musicologist—could hardly read music, and didn't remember what my father had once taught me—but the score seemed to me just a mess. "Interesting," I said.

"It's not 'interesting,'" insisted the whisperer. "It's not 'interesting,' it's vital work. Vital. Vital. Vitalvitalvitalvital. Even other people have started realising how vital it is. I heard someone on ITN talking about what I was doing with the 'Sabre Dance' the other day. The news is finally spreading that we have to find some way of cleansing music.

"But no one quite understands how sensitive the situation is. What if *he* saw the news? What if *he* hears about what I'm doing, and comes back to Stoke? He's been here before, poking around, checking up on what I'm doing. I get scared about what he'll do to me next time — or what I'll have to do to him.

"Or perhaps he'll send someone else in his place." The whisper was suddenly full of suspicion: "You. You. You're not one of them, are you?"

"One of whom?" I asked, trembling again.

"*Them*."

"You mean Armenians?"

"Yes, *them*."

I didn't know what to say, so I chose: "No."

The suspicion evaporated from the whisperer's whisper — and it struck me that, for someone so paranoid, he was peculiarly trusting: "That's all right then. But you understand, don't you? I can't be too careful. Not at this early stage. No one understands how hard the task ahead is going to be to rid our harmonies of *them*. No one understands. The harmonies, they get everywhere. You can hear them lurking in the most unsuspecting places. They get into extractor fans, the buzzing of telegraph lines, lamp-posts. I've heard them in my sleep, sucking out my European mind, replacing it with Eastern ways of feeling. If you listen carefully enough, you'll hear them in our dawn chorus, in the whooshing of sewers." There was a pause, as if he were listening to the sewers now.

Then: "That's the thing with Armenians — cunning bastards. You can never be too careful. Take *him*, for example. In encyclopedias, he's been pretending to be dead for twenty years. All of them, cunning bastards. My grandpa knew how it was. He'd always tell us to watch out round corners, or treading on joins in the pavement, because *they* might be there — waiting for you. But even he didn't get it, didn't understand the full extent of what was going on. He didn't crack the code like me, didn't understand that they can lurk in the corners of music as well. I worked it out. I cracked the code. I worked it out ..."

From downstairs, the clanking of water-pipes interrupted him. The whisperer's mother had probably just turned on a hot tap.

"There it is—the harmony! There it is!" the whisperer said, triumphant. "You must be able to hear it now!"

Before I had time to tell him that all I could hear was an ageing hot water system, he was scrabbling through papers on the floor. "God help us," he said. He uncovered something long, half brown, half black, and ran out of the room in a blur. Behind me, I heard his feet pounding on the stairs, two at a time.

Wondering what the hell was going to happen—what the hell he was going to do—I turned and dashed after him, but he was gone by the time I reached the stairs. A few steps down, I heard a shriek from below, a clatter of something falling to the floor, and what may or may not have been a gunshot.

I know I should immediately have leapt down the rest of the stairs, to find out if anyone was hurt, if anyone needed help, if something terrible had happened. I know I should have done that, but I didn't. Instead, for a few seconds, I stopped on a tiny landing, which was like an island, halfway down the stairs. I could hear raised voices, things being chucked around, the clank of water-pipes; but, from my island, all these sounds seemed strangely distant. I suddenly felt like I had lived in this house for years, and had heard the shrieks, the breakages, the gunshots a hundred times before: the melodrama had become wallpaper, and the angst had become the boy who cried wolf.

And gradually, I realised I was staring at a small, black and white photo of a young and rather sullen lad from long ago. There were various dusty photos dotted around the wall above the landing, but it was this one which caught my eye. The lad, who couldn't have been more than eighteen or nineteen, was dressed in an old-fashioned sailor's uniform. He had evidently been distracted at the moment the picture was taken, for he was looking intently at something to his left. His eyes were wide and white, his hair black, his moustache a sketch, a prototype. Behind him, the photo had faded, but he might have been on a harbour of some sort—there were ropes, tramlines, and what could have been the hull of a ship in the distance. Where there might have been a tell-tale ship's funnel, the photo was too damaged to make anything out: the photo had clearly been folded many years before, and had gone white around the fold, like a scar running through the sky, through the boat and across the lad's chest.

I cannot tell you what made me do it, but slowly, carefully, I reached across and unhooked the picture from the wall. I turned it over, and bent back the four metal clips which held it together. Lifting off the hardboard backing, I slipped the photo out of the frame. On the back were some scribbles: '1922' and a place name which had been scribbled out. Carefully, I put the photo into my pocket. Then I reassembled the frame—now empty but for dust—and hung it back in its original place.

Straight away, the voices from downstairs seemed louder again, and I was back in spring 1997, in Festival Street, Stoke-on-Trent. I decided it was time to go and find out what had happened.

At the bottom of the stairs, I followed the voices into the kitchen. There they were: mother and son, kneeling on the floor amidst smashed plates, cutlery, McDonald's cartons, spilt cat litter and discarded air rifle, her arms encircling him, his head buried in her bosom, his sobbing muffled by her breasts, his tears soaking into her top. I hadn't expected this at all: I'd expected him to be towering over her with his rifle, or her cowering in a corner whilst he ran amok. But no, by the time I reached them, he was the one cowering, sobbing, whilst she held him forcefully to her.

Neither son nor mother seemed to notice me; I felt that I was intruding, but didn't know how to get away, what apology to make.

"There, there, don't worry yerself, darling, don't worry," she was murmuring, stroking the back of his head.

"I thought," he moaned, "I thought . . ."

"It don't matter what you thought," she said. "Just remember what we always talk about."

"What do we always talk about, mother?"

"You know. The Rules. Our rules."

"Yes, I know them," he whimpered, seeming scared of what was coming. His voice was different to that of the whisperer upstairs—that had been the whisper of a man, whilst this was more like the whimper of a boy. I wondered for a moment if they were the same person; after all, I had seen the face of neither upstairs's whisperer nor downstairs's whimperer. "Yes, mother, honestly, I do remember them."

"Are you sure?"

"Yes, mother," he hesitated. "Honestly, I do. You won't make me say them, will you?"

"I think you've got to after what you've just gone and done. You've wrecked and ruined dinner and upset your poor old mother. You don't understand what I have to go through with you."

"Yes, I do, mother. Honestly. Honestlyhonestlyhonestly."

"No you don't—if you did, you wouldn't never run downstairs with one of your rifles, breaking everything, shouting and screaming."

"I'm sorry, mother, I promise . . ."

"It doesn't matter to you that I do everything for you, wash you, cook your dinners, tidy your room, look after you. You have to make life even more difficult for your poor old mum, by upsetting her, over and over again. The 'ouse is wrecked and ruined, and me blood pressure's through the roof. And when I'm dead and gone, then you'll have to manage yerself."

"Mother, please don't say things like that. Please don't. I promise. I promise I'll not hurt you again. Please. Please, mother. Please. I'll repeat The Rules if that's what you want."

"Okay then, you do that."

"I will, mother. I'll repeat The Rules to you if it makes you happier, if it makes you well"—and he proceeded to recite The Rules into her bosom: "I promise not to leave the house without asking you; I promise to go only where you say I can go; I promise always to come home afterwards; I promise not to see anything you say isn't really there; I promise not to hear anything you say you can't hear; I promise not to speak to anyone you don't want me to speak to; I promise not to shoot my air rifles in the house; I promise only to love you."

"That's better," she said, squeezing him even more tightly. "That's me son. He's come back to his mother."

"He has, mother, he has."

I looked down at them both on the floor, and I realised I could have been in his place, if I had succumbed to the gin-laden desire which had overwhelmed me earlier—the desire to drop to my knees and declare with Ruth: 'Intreat me not to leave thee, or to return from following after thee . . .'

"I'm leaving," I announced, suddenly. I didn't know who was Ruth, who was Naomi any more. I just knew it was time to leave this strange place, this formidable woman, this chaotic son.

Edwin's mother looked at me, over her son's shoulder. I think she'd forgotten I existed. "You what?"

"I've got to go . . . train to catch."

"Oh," she said, and she looked sad again. Still, she never moved from the floor, and nor did her son. "I 'ope we'll see you again sometime? I know it's a bit weird round here, like, but you're the first guest we've had for ages. It was lovely meeting you, my dear—you've been an angel to put up with us."

"It was . . . lovely meeting you too, Mrs. Prince." I thought for a moment, and then grabbed an unopened bill from the side-board, found a pen swimming in some old gravy, and scrawled down our address and new phone number. "Look, here's our number. Perhaps you could come and visit us, me and Edwin, sometime?"

She seemed bewildered by the suggestion. "Yes . . . yes . . . I spose I could. Although, p'raps not tomorrow, cos . . ."

"I didn't mean tomorrow," I said. "I meant, well, sometime soon."

"Sometime soon? Yeah, I spose I could . . . though I'd have

to sort out the newspapers, and this back door doesn't lock very well, and then there's the cat shitting everywhere all the time . . ."

I glanced at my watch. "Goodbye, Mrs. Prince. Nice to meet you and your son. Perhaps see you again" — and I left, before she could worry any more about the practicalities of another meeting.

Once outside, in the fresh, cold air, I felt tears running down my face. Waiting at the bus stop, an old man asked me if I was all right. And I answered: "It's not me. It's not me. It's not me."

16.

The journey back to Edwin took me through the latter stages
of drunkenness, a gin-haunted sleep, an instant hangover and
Derby station. By the time I reached 'home,' the afternoon's
events seemed a lifetime away. Thank God.

I let myself in the house. Edwin's bedroom door was ajar
(for the first time that week), and terrifying discords were
blaring into the hallway. Back to normal, I thought. I wandered down the corridor, and peered into his room. It was
empty, and the music was coming from outside. Through the
bedroom window, I could see the stereo speakers were back
on the garden table with the ants. "Come and listen to this,"
shouted a voice from the yard.

I stepped round to the back door, which was already open.
"Come and listen to this," repeated Edwin. He was sitting next
to the ant-farm on a tatty deckchair—as though the yard were
a beach—wearing one of the landlady's ball gowns. It was
black silk, with red taffeta thrills, and a low-cut front, showing
off his chest hair. He saw me looking him up and down. "It's
all in the worst possible taste, to misquote the great Kenny
Everett," he said, crossing and uncrossing his legs, "but I'd
run out of dirty clothes." He was obviously drunk: he had a
pint glass of sherry in one hand, as well as a cigarette in the
other, and a remote control on his lap. He put down the glass,
and picked up the remote, pointing it at the bedroom window.
The CD rewound squeakily for a moment. Then he pressed
play.

There was quiet, until the stereo unleashed a torrent of

swirling orchestral noise around us ... then the noise waltzed away into the distance ... then a discord pounced and caught us in its claws ... then there was a never-ending screech from a high trumpet ... and then the discord again, and I thought we'd never get away ...

Then it faded ... and Edwin rewound the CD and played it again. Even the ants looked distressed, scurrying round and round in circles in the foraging tank.

"I had this dream last night," said Edwin, as the dissonance pounced again. "It was about a chord—this very discord we're listening to, in fact." The hairs on the back of my neck prickled up, as I was struck with a feeling of *déjà-vu*. For a second, it wasn't just Edwin's voice I was hearing, but also his brother's, whispering in two-part counterpoint about pernicious harmonies, concords and discords. At this point, I only felt the intertwining of their voices as an uncanny sensation; later on—much later—I'd come to understand the nature of this musical overlap, this strange parallelism.

But I'm jumping ahead of my story. Back then, as I say, I was just unsettled by the coincidental mirroring of the two brothers' voices, their shared subject-matter: "You see," continued Edwin, "last night I dreamt that my mother was stuck in this discord for eternity."

"What on Earth is it?"

"It's a bit from Mahler, his Tenth Symphony—and the discord is some distant and dissonant variant of F-sharp minor which sounds like all the notes are being played at once. That's what it says in the sleeve notes, anyway. Unlike my looney-tunes brother, I can't read music, so I don't know anything about a distant and dissonant variant of F-sharp minor." He yawned. "God, my brother used to go on and on and on about chords and harmonies and stuff. You got the impression the peasant didn't actually like the music he was dissecting."

I could hardly believe my ears: after a week of barricaded doors, after weeks of refusing to talk about his family, here he was, sitting in a deckchair, sipping sherry, and referring dispassionately to his brother and mother as if they were the most everyday of subjects. I'd expected all sorts of things on my return from Stoke: anger, silence, or just carrying on as 'normal,' purposely covering up the obvious fact of my trip with endless ant-talk and copious amounts of Vermouth. What I hadn't expected was this apparent openness, this sudden smuggling of his mother and brother into his conversation as if they'd been there all along. But then, it almost goes without saying that Edwin never behaved as I expected, even on days when he wore a dress.

The discord came to an end a second time, and Edwin rewound the CD and re-started it, much to the ants' annoyance. The dissonances seemed to surround, encase us all. It was probably just the after-effects of the afternoon's gin, but I felt strangely paranoid that the orchestra was somehow shrieking about us, in gruesome F-sharp minor.

Edwin continued, oblivious as ever to what I, the ants or anyone else were feeling or thinking: "I might not know what a variant of F-sharp minor is, but what I do know is that it's bloody terrifying, and that I had this weird nightmare that my mother had been petrified, Mahlerified, in it. Tonight, I've been listening to the CD over and over to see how that would feel."

"And how does it feel?"

"Pretty horrid."

He took a puff of his cigarette. The music was winding down from the dissonance, fading away, trying desperately to sound tuneful. Before he could rewind it again, I snatched away the remote control. My hangover had returned full force, and neither my head nor the ants could bear another replay.

"If you listen to the rest of the music," said Edwin, "if you listen to the soothing, stringy bit that comes after the dissonant section, and winds down to the end of the movement, it's as if the music itself can't quite escape from the discord, is trapped in it, like my mother in the dream. Just when you think the music's turned a corner and become beautiful again, there's that bastard discord, quieter now, but still haunting everything." He sighed, melodramatically: "A bit like the twentieth century in general. Started off with discord, and we never quite got away. God, when will this awful century end?" He paused, and then turned to me, with cheery bathos: "Fancy a drink?"

I went and got myself a beaker, into which he poured the remains of the cheap sherry. Edwin lifted his glass and said: "A toast. To my nutty family."

I raised my glass and took a sip.

"Despite the twentieth century," I said, "you're looking chipper."

"One can't be miserable all the time, darling, however hard one tries." He looked away and frowned at something. "Talking of which, how is my brother? Who does he think I am now?"

I told him his brother had moved on from thinking he was the drummer in Supergrass to a reincarnated Aram Khachaturian.

"Ah," said Edwin proudly, "I'm going up in the world: low-brow to middle-brow. Next step Mozart, then I can die happy."

ACT THREE

17.

Winter is come and gone,
But grief returns with the revolving year;
The airs and streams renew their joyous tone;
The ants, the bees, the swallows reappear.
                    —Percy Bysshe Shelley, *Adonaïs*

"It's raining ants!" shouted Edwin, one afternoon. "It's bloody raining ants!"

He'd burst into the front room, where I was asleep on the sofa, and was pulling at my blanket. I grabbed it back and covered my head. "Bollocks," I said.

"It's not bollocks! It's not raining bollocks! It's ants! It's raining bloody ants, I tell you!" He was euphoric, as if it were the Second Coming or something. I, on the other hand, had only just got back from a wet morning of distributing free newspapers, and wanted my afternoon snooze.

"Bollocks," I said again. "Ants don't rain. Go away."

"But they do! They do!" he shouted. "I'll show you! I'll prove it to you!"—and, with an evangelical strength, he wrenched the blanket off me, pulled me to my feet and propelled me into the hallway and out of the front door.

I was about to tell him to fuck off and sod off and roast in hell, when I saw what he meant: outside, it really did look like the sky was crying ants, and the pavement and road and cars and window ledges and my hair and hands were covered in hundreds of thousands of tiny black tears.

"We live in Biblical times!" declared Edwin, jubilantly,

throwing his arms wide. "It's an Old Testament plague on all of our houses!"

At that moment, the next-door neighbour emerged from his house, looked into the sky, down at the ground, and then straight at us. "Speak for youself," he said to Edwin. "Seems more like a plague on weirdos to me." He turned to me: "For Christ's sake. Can't you shut this fucking madman up?"

I didn't know what to say, but Edwin looked down at the neighbour's feet and spoke in his most imperious voice: "Please can you watch where you tread with those thick boots of yours? They've already prematurely ended the lives of two dozen of *our* fellow creatures." He laid heavy stress on 'our,' subtly implying that the ants were related to us but not the neighbour. No doubt in Edwin's mind, this was a devastating insult—the idea that we shared a common biological, evolutionary and cultural fellowship with the ants, whilst the neighbour was a member of a species with nothing in common with them, seemingly beyond the ant pale. The insult, though, was lost on the neighbour, who just grunted: "I'm off to vote in the election for anyone who'll ban fucking weirdos from out the country"—and off he stomped, deliberately stamping on as many ants as he could.

"Witness the thick boots of genocide," pronounced Edwin to his back. "May your house be smited by the Lord with plagues of ants forever and ever. Amen." That was probably the closest I ever heard Edwin get to prayer.

"Shut up and don't be stupid," I hissed. "You'll get us both punched."

"Actually, darling, you're right. I was stupid," he said.

"Really?" I couldn't believe Edwin would ever admit he'd been stupid.

"Yes, stupid, really. I shouldn't have prayed for eternal plagues of ants on his house—that'd be a blessing, not a curse. I should've prayed for, I don't know, cockroaches or some vulgar, lower-class insects instead. This is too glorious a phenomenon to waste on the lumpen proletariat." For the second

JONATHAN TAYLOR

time, he spread his arms wide and looked up at the swirling, swarming ants above him. "Isn't it wonderful? Amazing?"

Ants rained down on him as he waltzed out into the middle of the street, tearing open his shirt and declaiming:

"I have walk'd about the streets,
Submitting me unto the perilous night,
And, thus unbraced, Casca, as you see,
Have bared my bosom to the thunder-stone;
And when the cross blue lightning seem'd to open
The breast of heaven, I did present myself
Even in the aim and very flash of it."

Momentarily, Edwin and the world around him seemed quite Shakespearean, quite awe-inspiring. But then a car arced past him, hooting its horn. He ignored it, and instead lunged in my direction, grinning: "'I . . . have bared my bosom to the thunder-stone': that's Cassius that is, in *Julius Caesar*" — and I couldn't help thinking that he'd been teaching himself the speech beforehand, in case some relevant dramatic occasion arose.

And the occasion certainly seemed dramatic, at least at the time: there were swarms of flying ants in the sky above Edwin's head, and armies of winged and unwinged ants at his feet, picking their way through the wreckage of a million ant corpses — friends and family crushed by cars and thick boots. "Isn't it amazing?" Edwin kept saying, not bothered by the ants crawling all over him, looking for a home in his mouth or down his trousers. "It's like something off Arthur C. Clarke's *Mysterious World* — but unlike most of the stuff he talked about, it's real, natural. The natural is always more fantastical than the supernatural."

"If it's natural, what on Earth is it?" Normally, I wouldn't encourage Edwin to lecture me about anything ant-related (or anything else, for that matter); but it was such a bizarre experience that I wanted some explanation.

"It's the mating flight," Edwin said, skipping back onto the pavement, suddenly two inches from my face. "It's perfectly natural: ants everywhere do it once or twice a Summer after rain." He frowned, looking down at his watch. "The only weird thing is that 1st of May is a bit early — perhaps they were bored with all this rubbish on the telly about a crappy election. Oh, and the other weird thing is that they'd come here, to do their mating in this sexless shithole."

"What is a mating flight then?" I asked, frustrated that he was getting distracted (as normal) from what had originally been a simple question demanding a simple answer.

"What happens, you see, is that all the local male and queen ants get together to have a huge orgy in the sky. God, those ants, they know how to live. They fly off at the same time from different nests, and have the orgy-to-end-all-orgies in huge swarms. In fact, it really is the orgy-to-end-all-orgies for the men, because they crash to the ground and die after they've, erm, delivered their cargo of sperm. The queens, after getting their oats, land somewhere, tear off their own wings, and then burrow down in the earth to start a new colony with their ferti-lised eggs. Sometimes, they move into an old colony and take it over."

It wasn't until over eight weeks later, in early July, that we realised this had happened with Edwin's ant-farm. On the morning of the mating flights, Edwin had been in a hurry; after feeding the ants, he hadn't put the lid on properly, and one of the fertilised queens from the swarm must have crept inside to lay her eggs. We only noticed — or, to be exact, Edwin only noticed and pointed it out to me — when the queen's eggs hatched and new *Lasius niger* workers were seen dashing around the foraging tank.

A few weeks before this happened, though, Edwin had suspected something was afoot when he'd found a couple of murdered workers on the surface of the nesting tank, and had tried to institute a 'Whodunnit'-style investigation into the crimes. None of the ants had been receptive to interroga-tion, so he'd gone on to collect forensic evidence, both from the murder scene, and inside the nesting tank itself. Taking a straw, he'd pushed it into the sand; then, he'd placed a magnifying glass on top of the straw and tried to peer down it, in an attempt to see what was happening inside the many chambers and tunnels. All he achieved were a few collapsed tunnels and some buried-alive ants; but, just for a moment, he did get a glimpse at what looked like an underground nursery of larvae. "I must be seeing things," he said. "An all-female colony can't reproduce without men like me."

"Or queens," I said.

He squinted at me, and then smiled: "Exactly — an all-female worker colony can't reproduce without men or, indeed, queens like me."

Of course, what Edwin didn't know at that point was that there was now a queen in the colony. Although we never actually saw her — she was esconced somewhere deep inside the nest, laying eggs, scheming schemes — it became clear she was there when, a few weeks later, the new worker ants started appearing in the foraging tank. I wouldn't have noticed they were new, but Edwin claimed to recognise 'his' ants individually. And anyway, the new brood were smaller than the others, and the foraging tank seemed busier than before.

"Look at them scurrying around, obeying queenie's orders," he sneered. "It's the same old story — yesterday's anarchistic commune, yesterday's idealism, yesterday's freedom is today's establishment, monarchy, tyranny." He turned to me, suddenly wistful. "Utopia never lasts long," he said.

18.

Back on May 1st and the afternoon of the mating flight, I was standing in the hallway, trying to shake the ants out of my hair, when the doorway darkened, and I looked up to see a silhouette the size of a bouncer standing there.

"Good afternoon," said the silhouette. "Gosh, it's nice to be finally here." The silhouette had a very feminine, lispy voice for that of a bouncer.

"Good afternoon," I said.

The silhouette put down two huge suitcases it had been holding, and seemed slightly—though only slightly—smaller for doing so.

"Is Eddy in?" asked the silhouette.

I suddenly understood how Edwin's mother had felt, finding me at her door: I wasn't used to visitors either.

"Yes, I think he's out the back. Shall I say who's calling?"

"Tell him it's the ex-wife," she said. "That'll put the wind in his sails."

I turned and headed down the hallway to the back door. I pushed it open, and there was Edwin, pacing backwards and forwards, smoking, drinking and reading *The World as Will and Idea* by Arthur Schopenhauer. Of course, I didn't know and (quite frankly) didn't care that it was *The World as Will and Idea* by Arthur Schopenhauer; I just wanted to tell Edwin that his ex-wife was at the door. But I only got as far as: "Edwin, your ex-wife . . ." before he'd lunged at me with his usual harangue: "Listen to this. Amazing stuff. It's from Schopenhauer. He's talking about how all nature is at strife . . ."

"Edwin, I've got something to tell . . ."

"Yes, yes, darling, but you've got to hear this first." I half-wondered if he'd already guessed what my message was, and was deliberately avoiding it, burying his head in the Schopenhauerian sand. "Just listen, I think this is amazing—even if I also think it's wrong. Schopenhauer reckons that all animals in the world, from the smallest to the largest, are trying to destroy all the others, so that they can occupy every bit of time and space. All species, all families, all selves are at war. In that sense, he's a bit like an extreme Darwin, I suppose. But no, he's even more extreme than that. He talks about how the bull-dog ant from Australia—by which he no doubt means the *Myrmecia* genus—actually fights itself when it's cut in half. The head bites its own tail, and the tail stings its own head, because they don't recognise each other any more. The science is dubious, of course; but for Schopenhauer it demontrates that everything in nature is at war with everything else, even within the same organism, even within the self. My brain would eat my feet if it could. Isn't that an incredible idea, even if one doesn't necessarily agree?"

"Yes, but what's even more incredible is that your ex-wife is . . ."

"My ex-wife is certainly a good example of total warfare in nature. Bitch. She'd chew my head off if she could. And I'd do the same. Schopenhauer's right, at least when it comes to humans—though I couldn't possibly agree with him when it comes to ants."

". . . in the hallway," I said.

"Who's in the hallway? Schopenhauer? Gosh, what an honour." By this point, I couldn't help thinking that his obtuseness was rather disingenuous, a way of postponing the inevitable.

"No, not Schopenhauer, *she*. *She* is. The ex-wife. Here. Now."

For a second, he stared at me, apparently bewildered at the jump back from Schopenhauer World to reality. In Schopenhauer World, ants and exes ate each other. In Edwinian reality, Edwin suddenly beamed, threw down his cigarette, and pushed past me into the hallway, laughing, crying, and wailing: "I've missed you, I've missed you, darling, I've missed you so much, I knew you'd come back to me, I've missed you so very much." In a moment, his ex-wife had her arms round him, and he was sobbing into her formidable bosom. I saw her properly now for the first time: she was a large, rounded woman, full of circles, in her chest, her hips, her eyes, her black hair—much larger than Edwin, who seemed two-dimensional by comparison; she was also visibly older than him, maybe by twenty years.

"I've missed you so very very much," he kept wailing.

"I've missed you too, Eddy," she said, though more calmly than him.

"Everything will be all right now, won't it? Won't it? Won't it?" he asked through sniffles, like a child.

"I hope so," she said.

"I knew you'd come back. I knew it." For the second time that day, he was hysterical, ecstatic. "You know, I was just this moment talking about you." He appealed to me: "Wasn't I? Wasn't I just talking about her?"

I nodded, wondering if he wanted me to recap the conversation we'd been having for her benefit. I decided probably not.

For the rest of the day, I absented myself, thinking that the reunited couple needed time alone. I found my way to The Dying Swan—through some Satanic streets, down a flooded alleyway, past a business of an unspecified nature called *Club Class*, along the towpath of a disused canal, over an abandoned shopping trolley—where the Poet Laureate was slumped in a corner, horizontal, his head almost touching the seat, murmuring Shakespeare to himself. Instead of "'O for a Muse of fire!,'" he seemed stuck on the first four syllables today: "'O for a Muse . . .,'" "'O for a . . .,'" "'O for . . .,'" "'O . . .'" I wondered if his quotations would get shorter and shorter till nothing was left.

Whilst he droned on, I saluted him, and then turned away, staring out of the brown window at the canal outside. On the opposite bank, water rats were having a fight.

God, I felt depressed, and I didn't know why. Certainly, the Poet Laureate and the water rats didn't help; but that wasn't it, that wasn't it at all. Something was wrong, or going wrong, or had gone wrong, or would go wrong. I wasn't sure which, perhaps because I wasn't always sure what tense I really belonged to, present, distant past, future . . . or perhaps because I was dozing off, hallucinating, living a strange, long-ago dream which always recurred when I was down, a dream that the Poet Laureate had reached the end of his quotation, and was repeating "'fire'" over and over again, a dream that there were water rats and rubbish and dogs and body parts bobbing in reddened water around me, a dream that there were boats on a wavering horizon in front, boats I couldn't quite reach, boats in the future tense, in the future-conditional-impossible tense, boats and silhouettes and screams and . . .

I jerked awake at a thud and scream and splash from outside the pub: it seemed that a barge had been trawling its way through the rubbish-laden canal, and one of its crew had hit his head on the low bridge. He'd toppled off into the water, but was soon at the side, pulling himself out. Shaking himself off, he'd run after the barge, which hadn't bothered to stop for him . . .

. . . and, as though reminded of something from that long-ago dream, as though the dream wouldn't let me go, I again felt uncertain what time I belonged to, present, past, future . . . and the dream dyed the canal orange and red, and the canal no longer reflected a pub, but a distant, silhoutted promenade, and there was a roaring and a shrieking and Caruso singing the 'Flower Song' from *Carmen* . . .

. . . and when I jerked awake for a second time, the Poet Laureate was sitting by my side, for once staring straight at me. He was breathing quickly, and, in his cross-eyed way, seemed transfixed, even terrified — as if he too had glimpsed the long-ago dream, its oranges and reds flaming in my eyes. Eventually, I shook my head, shaking the dream and his gaze away.

As I got up to leave, the P. L. suddenly regained the fluency he'd been lacking all afternoon, and declared: "'We walk about, amid the destinies of our world-existence, encompassed by dim but ever present Memories of a Destiny more vast—very distant in the bygone time, and infinitely awful.'"

"Yes," I said, "that's right, that's absolutely right," and wandered home.

Back at the house, I'd expected Edwin and his ex-wife to be noisily locked in his room, eating a romantic meal, or cuddling happily on the sofa.

Instead, they were sitting on separate armchairs at either end of the living room, she upright, arms crossed and scowling, he a few inches from the television, watching intently. They were clearly in the middle of an argument.

"Would you mind leaving us alone for a few minutes?" asked the ex-wife. "We're just in the middle of a . . . discussion."

I was turning to leave, when Edwin said, without looking up: "Don't go. Come and sit down and watch this. Amazing stuff."

I didn't know what to do, so I hovered in the doorway, neither in nor out.

"Would you mind leaving us alone?" repeated the ex-wife politely, "just for a minute or two."

"Yes," said Edwin, before I could say anything, "my friend would mind, and wants to watch this."

I hovered some more, looking between the two of them. "Anyone fancy a drink?" I asked.

"No," they both barked in unison.

"I do," I said, and wandered off to the kitchen. It was best to leave them to it, I thought; and, given their conflicting demands, I decided it was safer to do what the ex-wife wanted—she was obviously tougher than him, and possessed that formidable bosom.

I took as long as I could in the kitchen, pouring a Vermouth, downing it, pouring another one, making myself a crisp sandwich, even going so far as sweeping the never-swept floor, emptying the never-emptied bin, peeling the mould off the never-cleaned table. Finally, faced with a choice between investigating the never-opened bread bin, and returning to the living room with my crisp sandwich, I chose the latter.

Big mistake: the ex-wife was still scowling at Edwin, he staring sullenly at the TV. I sat down at one end of the sofa, and took a bite out of my sandwich. The crunching seemed terribly loud. The ex-wife tutted, and Edwin pointed the remote at the television to turn up the volume.

"For Christ's sake, Eddy, isn't that loud enough?"

"I can't hear over the scowling," he said.

"Don't you mean crunching?"

"No, I mean what I said. Your scowling and frowning and frowling and scowning. It's bloody deafening."

"I'm only scowling because I want to watch the News and you won't let me."

"You can watch it after this is over."

"But it's a video, Eddy. You can see it any time."

I glanced at the television. The video Edwin was watching was a recording of an old and rather sensationalist documentary called *Ant Wars: Insect Invaders*. Actually, I knew it was *Ant Wars* even before I looked, because it was the only video he owned; in fact, it was the only video the old Betamax recorder would play since it had become jammed inside. Because the machine was on its last legs, every twenty seconds or so, the ants on the screen would jerk, as if they had a twitch or insect epilepsy. Simultaneously, the voice of the documentary's narrator would shift up an octave, spontaneously changing genders for a moment.

"For God's sake, Eddy. The video doesn't even work properly," said his ex-wife. "Please, please, please, can't we just watch the News?"

"I've told you," said Edwin, like a sulky teenager, "after *Ant War*'s finished."

"Don't you know there's an election on?"

"So what?"

"What do you mean, 'so what?' Don't you want to see what the election news is?"

"There's no such thing as election news. As wiser anarchists have said before me, it doesn't matter who the people vote for, because the government always gets in."

The ex-wife stamped her foot. "God, Eddy, don't you take any interest in current affairs?"

"This *is* current affairs," said Edwin, waving the remote at the TV and *Ant Wars*. "This is going on right now, somewhere in the world. And why should we be so arrogant as to believe that some crappy election in a backwater shithole of a country is more important than the life-and-death struggles of the small of the world?"

The ex stood up. "Right, I've had enough. I'm off for a bath. When I get back, I expect *Ant Wars* to have finished, and the election news to be on." With that, she stormed out of the room, slamming the door behind her.

Edwin turned to me. "Bloody feminists," he said.

"But I thought you were pleased she'd come to visit," I said, confused. "Bloody hell, you certainly looked pleased earlier, in the hallway."

Edwin snorted. "That was an act, of course. You don't think I'm really that wet, do you? I knew all along why the bitch had really turned up again."

"Why?"

"Because Mr. Open-Top-Bus, her current squeeze, kicked her off his barge. And because I owe her money."

"What for?"

"Oh, something about supporting me during some degree or other I half-did once — can't really remember."

"How can you forget something like that?"

"Some of us aren't obsessed with money," he said grandly, not quite answering my question, which was about forgetting degrees, not money. "But she's an old hippy-feminist-social-ist, and they're always the worst — all they think about is cash,

cash, cash. Money-driven bitch. Give me a Tory businessman any time. Much more honest."

Immediately, the door burst open, and there was the ex-wife, in a towel which looked the size of a flannel on her. By her side were her two suitcases.

"Look," she said, "I know what you're doing behind my back. I know you're slagging me off. And I'm not going to put up with it. I'm going. I should never have come back in the first place."

I was about to suggest that she might want to put on a larger towel before leaving the house, when Edwin cut me short. He shouted "No!," rushed past me, and fell to his knees in front of her, grabbing her legs. He was sobbing again, whining "No, don't go, don't go, dontgodontgodontgodontgo," over and over. I could hardly believe this heap of sentiment was the same as the Edwin of *Ant Wars* — the Edwin who, only a minute ago, had been calling her a "money-driven bitch." Or perhaps I could believe it: Edwin was nothing if not inconsistent.

Finally, he looked up at her, "I'm sorry, I'm sorry, I'll do anything. But please don't go. I tell you what, I'll throw away *Ant Wars* and you can watch the election for ever and ever and ever. But please don't leave me now you've come back."

She pulled him up to his feet, put her arms and, indeed, bosom round him, and stroked his hair, murmuring, "Eddy, it's all right, Eddy. It's all right. I won't go. I won't leave you. And I don't want the News any more either. Let's just go to bed and forget *Ant Wars* and elections ever happened. We're both over-wrought. It's been an emotional day. Tomorrow'll be better. You'll see." And, arm in arm, dragging a battered suitcase each, they disappeared back along the corridor to his bedroom, looking all the world like some Hollywood romantic comedy gone wrong.

19.

"... tell you about the ants whose beautiful house was knocked down by a giant called Tom, and he thought they didn't mind because he couldn't hear them cry, or see them use their pocket-handkerchiefs."
—George Eliot, *Middlemarch*

After Edwin and his ex had gone, I settled down on the sofa to watch the last few minutes of *Ant Wars*. Although I'd seen it a dozen times before, and had been rather overloaded with ants of late, I thought it might provide an antidote to the sickly sight of Edwin sobbing into his ex-wife's almost-bare bosom.

There was no sickly sentiment in *Ant Wars*: it was a sensationalist, violent documentary, which portrayed ants as a brutal and militaristic race. For that reason, I couldn't quite understand Edwin's predilection for it. His addiction to *Ant Wars* — and, for that matter, to the computer game *3D Ant Attack* — hardly seemed to tally with his utopian view of ant society as an escape from the savagery of humanity. Why would someone who found in ant society a model of a perfect community also be drawn to such ant-horrors? To this day, I don't know the answer to that question. Perhaps, as an anarchist, Edwin was joyfully inconsistent in his likes and dislikes, his philosophies and theories. Or perhaps *Ant Wars* and *3D Ant Attack* were the only ant-video and ant-game available to him, so he had to settle for them in lieu of anything better. Or perhaps his exaltation of ant society over human stupidity concealed a neurotic terror that the former might not be so different to the latter—that ant society might not be as idyllic as he wanted to think—and, in his self-destructive way, he toyed with this terror through these darker portrayals of the ant-world. It wasn't till much later, when self-destruction overtook him, that I realised how crucial it was for him and his well-being to cling on to an idealised view of ant society and behaviour.

That realisation came later; in the meantime, I merely wanted to cling onto the militaristic horror of *Ant Wars*, because I thought it might negate what I'd just had the misfortune to witness: the sentimental horror of Edwin sob-sob-sobbing onto his semi-naked ex-wife. But I was wrong, and soon I found myself sobbing, this time at the plight of a nest of black pavement ants:

> ... *an idyllic community*, the American voice-over commentated, *on a patch of wasteland near a busy sidewalk in a busy city. A city within a city: a city of pavement ants, going about their daily business, eating, sleeping, tending larvae, collecting materials for the nest . . . Little do they know that disaster is lurking round the corner, ready to pounce at any moment.*
>
> *Look at this keen worker: she's scouting new territory, a long way from home. In spring, pavement ants like her often try to conquer new land, attacking other pavement-ant colonies, engaging in bloody battles.*
>
> *But today, the unseen enemy is of a different order, and she has bitten off more than she can chew. Today, there are red army ants nearby, and they are not happy.*
>
> *And why aren't they happy? Because our unsuspecting pavement ant has blundered too near their military base. Ants mark their territory with a pheromone, but our pavement ant seems not to have noticed, or to have foolishly ignored the army ants' chemical trail. Nomadic army ants are always on the move, so they are hard to keep track of. They pose a constant and terrible threat to humble home-makers like our pavement ant.*

And look, now they have pounced on her. There are five of them, and only one of her, and she is a third of their size—roughly one eighth of an inch. She hardly stands a chance, though she's not taking it lying down. Notice how she has stretched her legs beneath her, as if she were on stilts—that's her way of pretending to be bigger than she is.

But that won't daunt these hoodlums from the wrong side of the tracks. They have a deadly sting, filled with enzymes which dissolve the enemy's tissues. They can liquefy everything in their path, from pavement ants like this one to much larger animals. Some of them have sickle-shaped mandibles with which they slice their enemy to pieces.

Fights don't last long in the face of this kind of weaponry. Our pavement ant has had her legs cut from under her, and she will soon be a liquid lunch for one of the army ants.

Some of the other pavement ants have arrived on the scene to witness the butchery. A few of them engage the enemy, whilst others run off to alert their colony. Most species have an early warning system, using mandibular glands or even glands in their rectums to leave odour trails to and from the developing battlefield. Here, you can see the pavement ants relaying the message to their comrades by interlocking antennae, and by moving their abdomens backwards and forwards, like some kind of war-dance.

On both sides now, ants are flocking to the scene of battle. From a small skirmish over property, full-scale war has broken out. And this is a fight to the death for the two colonies: here, you can see the smaller pavement ants mobbing one army ant, pulling her legs in different directions till she topples over, ripping at her abdomen with their mandibles, stinging her with their acids. And over here, the army ants are piled on top of one another, surging forwards in organised formation, turning the enemy to liquid underneath them.

The battle lasts for two hours, but inevitably the weaker side are beaten back and back, until the army ants are at the gates of the city. Inside, there is a peculiar stillness for a moment, as the queen and all the innocents hold their breath.

Then, enemy soldiers seal up the entrances, and hordes of army ants march in, victorious. Fighting breaks out in the underground tunnels and chambers, as the pavement ants retreat deeper and deeper into their nest; but it is too late, and they are mutilated, poisoned, massacred in their own homes. Their children — the white larvae — are carried off to be eaten later. Like ant vampires, the army ants will bite through their skins and suck out the blood-like substance inside.

Meanwhile, the underground city is cleared, and only the victorious army ants can be seen, stalking the dark corridors, searching for enemy stragglers who are still in hiding . . .

And all the while, just a hundred yards away on the sidewalk, humans rush by, on their way to work, on their way to parties or concerts, oblivious that an epic life-and-death drama has been taking place nearby. So near, yet so far: the people on the sidewalk are visible from the ants' nest, and perhaps some of the pavement ants looked up and thought their gigantic friends might come to their aid. But no, that is not the way with Nature, where these mini-apocalypses happen every day, and other species hardly notice — till it is their turn. So no one was there to help the pavement ants, as their homes were ransacked, their queens butchered, their children stolen. That is Nature's way . . .

I don't know why this ludicrously hyperbolic conclusion to the documentary brought tears to my eyes; it wasn't, or wasn't just, to do with the massacre of the pavement ants. Rather, there was something pathetic about the way the camera followed dozens of defeated ants, as they escaped the nest and fled towards gigantic human legs on the sidewalk. Almost none of them reached the giant legs — they drowned in puddles, or were picked off by marauding army ants *en route* — and those

that did were crushed under-foot anyway, by heedless commuters.

Something about this scene reminded me of . . . of something that I couldn't be reminded of, that I couldn't remember,
that happened whole lives before I met Edwin . . . but that
somehow was still happening, in an old photo in my pocket, a
dream I had in a pub, a lost chamber of my memory . . .

It didn't make any sense, so I wiped my eyes, pulled the
blanket over my head and settled down to sleep. Maybe
Edwin's ex was right: it had been an emotional day, and I was
just over-wrought.

But it wasn't over yet.

20.

"Are you asleep or not?" someone with a broad Leicestershire accent whispered in my ear.

"Yes," I said.

"Good," the someone whispered again, not bothered by the sleepy ambiguity of my answer. "Can I get under the blanket with you or not?"

"Yes," I said.

As before, only I seemed unsure what my answer meant, and I felt the someone lift up the cover and crawl in. It was a tight squeeze: I was facing the back of the sofa, and the someone moulded him or herself to me, arms round me, legs behind mine.

He or she was trembling and — like everyone else today — seemed to be crying or near crying.

"What's the matter?" I asked. What I really wanted to ask was: "Who is this?," but that question seemed rude, and rather belated, given that I was now sharing my 'bed' with whoever it was.

"It's nothing," answered the someone.

"Okay," I yawned, and started dozing off.

I woke up with a start a few seconds later, when the someone blurted out: "It's just that . . . just that . . . he's left me. He's fucking left me. He doesn't want anything to do with me any more. He found out about the fucking business with me and Edwin."

With a shock, I realised that the someone was the landlady,

although any of the alternatives would have been a bit of a shock too: Edwin, his ex, Salacious Whatsit, one of the ants . . .

"He's left me," the landlady was crying, presumably referring to Salacious Whatsit. It seemed he had found out about her previous 'rental arrangement' with Edwin, and wasn't best pleased. "I thought he knew me and Ed had a bit of fun now and then, and didn't care. After all, he often buggers off with some gothy trollop or other. Bastard. Fucking bastard."

I tried to stifle a yawn. It had been a long day.

The landlady started crying again. "I'm disturbing you, aren't I? I'm sorry, I didn't know where else to go. I don't want to be on my own, and Edwin seems to have a whale in bed with him. I just want . . . I just want to share the sofa with you and be warm. But honestly, you can tell me if I'm disturbing you. Am I disturbing you? Am I? Or not?"

"Yes, I mean no," I murmured. And I was being honest: her whispering, her soft arms, her warm legs weren't disturbing me any more. Instead, they were lulling me away to sleep—the first sleep for sometime which was free of fire, of drowning, of unreachable boats and faces, of photos of boys on quays, and, above all, of ants.

21.

For the next few weeks, my sleep remained free of these things, as my dreams and, indeed, the house in general attained a strange kind of equilibrium — a repetitive, clockwork equilibrium, in which everything seemed to swing backwards and forwards, forwards and backwards, like a perfectly-balanced pendulum. Every night, the landlady would tiptoe down from her bedroom, and creep under the blanket with me, and we would sleep dreamless sleeps. Every morning, she would be gone, and if I bumped into her in the kitchen, she'd hardly acknowledge my existence. Every evening, Edwin and his ex would fall out, and she would appear with two packed suitcases, promising to leave forever. Every night, they would make up, to the sound of creaking bed springs, backwards and forwards, forwards and backwards.

And every morning, Edwin would be pacing, up and down, down and up the kitchen floor, reading and smoking and smoking and reading. But he wasn't reading Schopenhauer any longer: he'd gone back to what he called "more positive views of ant society," in the works of Peter Kropotkin, H. G. Wells and others.

Under the influence of his ex, he and his ants also seemed to be listening to more "positive" music, if one can call it that. Rather than limiting himself to apocalypses and Pendereckis, he started enjoying a more varied repertoire. The house was filled with Bach, Haydn, Mozart, and dissonances were only ever in passing, only ever on their way to concords. I couldn't help but feel this was healthy, that this would do Edwin good—that even if he were not happy in himself, at least he might be happy-by-proxy, through the beautiful and reassuring music which surrounded him.

But then, one day, I found him in the back-yard, listening to Haydn's *Sinfonia Concertante* in floods of tears. God, I thought, haven't we had enough crying recently?

"What's the matter with you?" I asked.

"It's this piece of music," he said.

"I thought it was rather, erm, jolly, pretty, happy."

"No, it's heart-breaking, darling, heart-breaking."

"Heart-breaking? This?"

He thought for a moment. "Perhaps it's just me then. I've listened to so much apocalypse in my time, I hear it everywhere now, in the least likely of places. It has a kind of feeding frenzy on everything I listen to, tearing even the most innocent, the most jolly music to pieces."

"Oh, for God's sake, Eddy, stop being so pretentious," shouted his ex-wife from the kitchen.

"I'm not being pretentious. It's true. I for one can't listen to Haydn without also hearing all the shit that's happened in history since. That makes it sound as dissonant and apocalyptic as Penderecki—or more so. At least, it does to me."

His ex poked her head round the back door. "Eddy, shut up, will you?"

"Yes, darling," he said.

"You don't do small-talk, do you, Eddy?"

"No, darling," he said.

"You don't bloody well talk like normal people, do you? You don't talk about the bloody weather, or ask the time, let alone gossip about which celeb is wearing the best dresses, or who's shagging who."

"No, darling," he said.

"You just do ants or philosophy or apocalypses or apocalyptic-philosophical-ants, and there's nothing in between. For God's sake, Eddy, can't you learn how to talk properly, un-miserably?"

"Yes, darling," he said.

Her head disappeared, as she stomped back to the kitchen.

Edwin shuffled in his chair for a minute or two, grinding his teeth, drumming his fingers — until he couldn't resist any longer, and he shouted: "Darling?"

The ex's head reappeared round the back door.

"Yes?"

"Nothing," he said to her face. But as soon as she turned her back in a huff, he whispered very loudly: "Who *is* shagging whom, then? Who, for example, have you been shagging of late, belovèd wife of mine?"

She turned round again, pulled herself up to her considerable height and glared at him.

"Well, that's small-talk, isn't it?" he asked. "That's what you wanted, isn't it? Isn't it, darling?"

And, inevitably, a row ensued, followed by her packing her cases, followed by a reconciliation — to be followed the next day by another row, another bout of packing, another reconciliation — and so on and so forth, day after day, week after week. No doubt it was Edwin who usually provoked these rows. Even though he claimed he "hated confrontation," he also invited it, whether by casting aspersions on his ex-wife's past conduct, or through his sullenness towards her. He couldn't seem to help himself, as if he were trapped in a game of 'Chicken' with his emotions and his ex. Within hours of a reconciliation, he'd descend into another sulk, grunting at her from the armchair in front of the TV, telling her to be quiet in case he missed a bit of *Ant Wars* — which he knew off by heart anyway. Finally, she would storm off, accusing him of taking her for granted, and he would bitch about her behind her back, and she would turn up with her suitcases packed, and he would burst into tears, and they would disappear into the bedroom. "I'll never be sulky or shitty or miserable with you again," he'd promise, till the next day, and the next, and the next.

But if he himself always reverted to his daily sulk, the world around him did seem to brighten for a while. There was Haydn on the stereo; there was Kropotkin instead of Schopenhauer as bedtime reading; there were flowers in vases; there was fruit juice, as well as Vermouth, to drink; there was fresh air, drawn curtains, clean underwear on the washing line. Once or twice, even Edwin admitted that things were looking up: "It's more or less the first time I've ever managed to hold down a job and an ex-wife simultaneously," he said.

"'Hold down' an ex-wife?" I asked.

"You know what I mean." He yawned. "It's a bit tiring too, doing both at the same time. Reminds me, though, of when she and I first met. Back then, just for a few days, I almost had both her and a job at the same time. They sort of overlapped. I was living in Coventry, for my sins, and was working in this dead-end bookshop."

"Doesn't sound that bad—working in a bookshop."

"Ah, no, it wasn't your musty-dusty-sliding-ladders-against-high-shelves-and-illustrated-first-editions-of-George-Eliot kind of bookshop. Remember this was Coventry, for God's sake. This bookshop was your pile-em-high-sell-em-cheap-four-Dickens-for-the-price-of-one shop. You must've seen the kind of place: where skipfuls of £1 Dickens share tables with heaps of pencils with fluffy caterpillars on the top, and job-lots of bootleg *Jurassic Park* toys. Thousands of *Classics to Relax By* and *Classics to Bathe By* CDs mixed with chocolate Shakespeare characters and novelty *Lord of the Key-rings*. God, what a barren ant-heap of rubbish it was." He frowned at his own words, and then corrected himself: "No, not ant-heap. That's insulting to ants and, indeed, ant-heaps, which are highly structured places—unlike this capitalist hole of a so-called bookshop.

"You know, all the time I was there, there was this white scrawl on the windows, announcing: 'Last Few Days.' I tell you, it was always the Last Few Days in that place. Every day, half a dozen customers would come up to me at the till and ask: 'Are you shutting down then?,' and I'd say: 'No,' and they'd say: 'But it says Last Few Days on the window,' and I'd say: 'But isn't it always the Last Few Days when it comes to Western capitalism? Isn't Western capitalism always threatening to end horribly, but never quite gets there?' The customers'd give me a funny look, and bugger off."

Edwin stared wistfully into space. "If you think about it, perhaps that's where I got my apocalypse fixation from—working in a place where it was always the Last Few Days. But I tell you what—it wasn't half a boring apocalypse, the hundred or so Last Few Days I spent there. All I did was press plastic numbers on a till and lug piles of cut-price writers, composers and philosophers backwards and forwards. God, it was so dull. Since then, I still can't listen to Mendelssohn's *Midsummer Night's Dream* without coming out in a sweat."

"Why?" I said, fighting the urge to drift off into dreamy space.

"Because they played it constantly—every bloody hour of every bloody day, over and over. Like that, it was more like *Music to Slash Your Wrists By* or *Music to Drown By* than anything else. You'd have thought it a bizarre soundtrack to the Last Few Days. Somehow, though, Mendelssohn seemed just as apt as Penderecki or Mahler: the world ending not with a bang but with a Hee-Haw." I frowned, puzzled. "You know—the braying bit in the Overture, where Bottom gets turned into a donkey."

"Oh, I see," I said, wondering how the conversation (if it could be called that) had got onto donkeys. Whilst Edwin was talking, if one dared lose concentration and drift off into space for a split second– as, frankly, it was all too easy to do—one never knew where one would land on return. A conversation about bookshops might morph into one about donkeys, ex-wives might turn into ants.

"You were telling me how you met your ex-wife."

"I was, wasn't I? It's all too easy to drift off topic, though, when one's talking about her. Bitch." Here, his use of the word "bitch" sounded almost affectionate; and he immediately continued his reminiscences: "Where was I? Ah yes, I was working in the bookshop. But not for long. Finally, the bastards sacked me, and it really was my Last Few Days."

"Why did they sack you?"

"For talking to the customers too much. And, well, for scaring them with the end of Western capitalism. Turned out one of the people I'd been chatting to was the company's Managing Director, working *incognito*. Miserable bastard said I was 'alienating buyers.' Seems like all the jobs I ever have are scuppered that way . . ."

"Not this one," I said, "not the one you've got now."

"That, darling, remains to be seen," he said, in his most fatalistic voice. "I seem cursed to be always misunderstood, like Cassandra."

"Like the woman in *Only Fools and Horses*?"

"You know exactly who I mean — the woman in Greek myths, Cassandra, whose prophecies were always true but never believed." I couldn't quite see the connection. "Don't you see?" he said. "Like me, her bosses never saw what a great job she was doing. The MD at the bookshop, for one, couldn't see I wasn't alienating customers. I was attracting them. Some of them would come in just to talk to me about the decline of Western capitalism — including my future-ex-wife-to-be."

He looked down at his Vermouth: "You see, back then, she didn't mind my lack of small-talk, being political herself, as a young-revolutionary-hippy-socialist-feminist" — given her age now, I wasn't convinced by one part of Edwin's nostalgic description of her; but the compound nouns were coming too thick and fast for me to question them. Perhaps there was something about his complex relationship with his ex-wife which lent itself to these compound nouns — compound nouns which continued to litter his speech: "Back then, she went for all my so-called 'apocalyptic-philosophical-ants.' Back then, we had apocalypses in common. They made a good pick-up line for a hippy-socialist-feminist."

"I thought that was what you didn't like about her?" He frowned questioningly at me. "The other day, you were bitching about her hippy-socialist-feminist side."

"I never claimed to be consistent, darling, did I? God, I'd be a crap anarchist if I was. Whatever I feel about it now, back in those halcyon days, I-the-anarchist was turned on by her hippy-socialist-feminism. I'd never met a feminist like her, so I put on all my best charms to pick her up.

"The pick-up was clinched one day when she came in to chat, and I said I couldn't talk. She asked why, and I said because the shop was sacking me for talking. She said 'well, fuck the capitalist bastards, then. You can come home with me as my nude cleaner.' She was sexy and outspoken back then. She didn't have to ask me twice. Straight away, I ditched the company sweatshirt and scarpered with her. It was all so different back then. Back then ... back then ... back then ..."

I'd noticed this in Edwin recently—a proneness to nostalgia (albeit of a peculiar kind), which I hadn't heard from him before. No doubt it bespoke a more settled frame of mind on his part, though I never heard him talk like this to anyone else, and certainly not the ex-wife, despite her being one of the main subjects of his nostalgia. With her, the past was only ever prelude to a row. Perhaps if he'd talked to her about their past like he did with me, things might have ended better for them.

Then again, perhaps not.

22.

And, of course, the ex-wife's version of the past was different—irreconcilably different—to Edwin's. This became clear to me a couple of weeks later, when she told me her version of how she and Edwin first met.

I was sitting in the back-yard with them both, drinking cheap plonk, when Edwin got up, announced that he was going to cook his "speciality" for tea, and strode into the kitchen. I couldn't begin to imagine what Edwin's "speciality" was, but I was instantly struck with prophetic indigestion, and burped.

"You know, that is the first thing Eddy ever said to me," said the ex-wife.

I looked around to see if anyone else was here apart from the two of us, because I was surprised she was talking directly to me. We normally spoke through Edwin or, when alone, sat in silence. I wasn't sure why: perhaps she thought I was some kind of threat; or perhaps I was easy to ignore when Edwin was around. For that matter, everyone was easy to ignore when Edwin was around.

Certain that this time she was speaking to me, I asked: "What was the first thing Edwin said to you?"

"A burp."

This hardly squared with Edwin's version of events, whereby she was charmed with his sophisticated conversation about the decline of Western capitalism. When I recounted her version to him later on, all he could do was grunt and say: "God, women are so bathetic."

Certainly, her story lacked his version's nostalgia or

romance: "Yes, a burp. He was in a crappy job in one of those shops that sell remaindered rubbish. He was standing at the till, looking like death, pretending he wasn't drinking hair of the dog from a flask he'd got hidden somewhere. I went up to him to buy some cheap copies of *Pride and Prejudice*, for the women's literature class I was taking. He hid the flask, wiped his sleeve over his mouth and then burped at me.

"His supervisor heard and shouted at him across the store: 'Don't burp at the bloody customers, Edwin!' He smiled sheepishly, said 'sorry,' and put Jane Austen through the till. Then the supervisor shouted at him again: 'When you've stopped burping at the bloody customers, can you get your arse over here and help shift some of these crappy CDs?' He smiled at me again, handed me my stuff in a bag, and then went over to 'help' his supervisor. They were lifting huge piles of CDs, carrying them from one end of the shop to the other. Well, the supervisor was, anyway. Eddy could only manage five or so at the time, which he kept dropping, much to the annoyance of his apoplectic boss. It was pathetic, but I kept watching Eddy for ages. He seemed out of place, and I felt sorry for him—it was like his hound-dog eyes were almost begging me to 'take him away from all this.'

"I thought he looked like the perfect antidote to the male pigs we'd studied in class, and two previous ex-husbands. And when he finally got the nerve up to talk to me, he seemed intelligent. I felt like the Wife of Bath, finally falling in love with a scholar.

"When he first moved in, he used to clean the house wearing nothing but a frilly apron. I did wonder about him—whether he was, you know, 100% hetero. He thinks it never crossed my mind back then, but it did, especially when we went to visit his mother for the first time, after we'd got married."

"You met his mother?"

"Oh yes." She pulled a face, and leant forwards to spit out a whisper: "What a ghastly woman. We fell in hate on sight. She was the first nail in mine and Eddy's coffin. Of course, Eddy being Eddy, he didn't even notice me and her didn't get on, stuck in his own Eddy-world. But it was clear to me that she didn't want me round, and she kept dropping hints about past male 'friends.' It didn't take Einstein to put two and two together from all her hints, and work out that my suspicions about him and his frilly apron were true. Nor did it take Einstein to work out that she preferred it when he was gay, so she could troop about with a man on either arm. Bitch. Bitch from hell."

Rather taken aback by the ex's rancour, I sat back and sipped my wine, wondering what on Earth I could say in response.

Thankfully, the awkward silence was cut short by the phone ringing from the living room. I jumped up and ran to get it. Normally, I wouldn't have bothered, but it was a bit of a relief to get away.

I picked up the receiver: "Hello?"

I was greeted by a voice which crackled like dry leaves: "Hello, is there a Ms. Prince there?"

"Do you mean Mr. Edwin Prince?"

"No, I mean Ms. Prince."

"Oh," I said. I hadn't expected this. "Yes, a Ms. Prince is here. Who can I say wants her?"

"You can say her *lover* wants her. Her *lover*. Her *lover*. Got that?"

"I've got that," I said, as if I'd noted it down.

"Her *lover* is on the phone, the guy who she makes love to, understand? — the guy she screws, who screws her. And he wants her back. Her fucking *lover* is on the phone, and he'll win her back. Got that?" he asked. I could only assume it was 'Mr. Open-Top-Bus,' the ex-wife's boyfriend from Warwickshire. Previously, Edwin had told me that this man "could charm the pants off Queen Victoria." Quite what he was like in his day job as compère on a tour bus, I don't know, but on the phone he had all the charm of Old Man Steptoe.

"Got it," I said.

"Her *lover* is on the phone, and he'll whip your arse, you frilly-apron-wearing gay-boy. Yeah, that's right, I've heard

150

all about you, gay-boy. I'll whip your arse — or perhaps not. Perhaps I won't whip your arse, because you might like that, mightn't you?"

"I'm sorry, I think you're talking to the wrong person. My name is Jules. Would you like me to get Edwin for you?"

"Don't pretend, gay-boy. I know it's you, you fucking homo. You've got just the kind of homo's voice I knew you'd have — could be a girl's or a boy's or a tranny's or ... anyone's. Fucking creepy, that's what it is. So I know it's you, you fucking tranny, and if you don't hand *her* back to me, I'll come round there and shove a hot poker up your gay-boy arse."

"That's all very well," I said, "but I'm afraid you really are talking to the wrong person. If you wait a moment ..."

"You think I'm fucking stupid, don't you? You think you're so fucking clever, cleverer than anyone else. But it makes no difference, because you're gay and I'm fucking your wife — and fucking your wife like you could never dream of fucking her."

"Charmed, I'm sure," I said, and put down the phone.

It rang again a few seconds later.

"Hello?" I asked.

"Please can I speak to Ms. Prince?" the voice asked politely, as though nothing had happened.

"Yes, of course," I said, and went to tell the ex-wife who was on the phone.

On the way, Edwin grabbed my elbow and stared straight at me. "Is it him?" he asked. "Is it Mr. Open-Top-Bus?"

I nodded.

"Don't tell her," he whispered. "We can change the phone number again."

I shook my head and pulled away.

"Please," he whispered.

I shook my head again, and stepped into the back-yard. "There's someone on the phone for you," I said to her. Even now, I'm unsure whether or not I did the right thing.

23.

"You won't go back to him, will you?" Edwin asked his ex-wife, over and over again. It was as incessant as a child locked in a room: "You won't go back to him, will you? Will you? Will you?"

"Eddy, just leave it alone," she said.

"But you won't, will you? You won't go back to him? Please say you won't. Please say you won't go back, you won't go back to him. Please say you won't. Pleasepleasepleaseplease."

"Eddy, just leave it," she said.

"How can I leave it? How can I? How can I leave it, when you might leave me? I need to know. I only want to know. You can be honest. If you're going back to him, you can tell me. As long as I know, I'll be okay, I can take it. I just need to know. Tell me. Tell me. Tell me. Tellmetellmetellmetellmetellme. Tell me."

"For Christ's sake, Eddy. Shut up. Or I *will* leave you."

He put his hands over his ears. "Don't say that, don't say things like that, don't say that, I don't want to hear it, I don't, I don't, dontdontdontdontdont."

The "don'ts" went on for days, until she snapped: "Shut up. Shut up. Shut the fuck up, Eddy. Shut the fucking fuck up. If you carry on, I will leave you. I will. If you carry on saying 'don't say things like that,' 'don't go,' 'don't leave me,' I will. I tell you, I fucking will. So SHUT THE FUCK UP."

"Okay," he said, and for a while it seemed that he had "shut the fuck up."

But really all that had happened was that the "don'ts" and "won'ts" and "pleases," the insistence and incessant questions, were diffused into everyday conversations about cooking, tea, digestive biscuits: "Do you like the digestives I bought from the shop? Do you like them? Or do you prefer the Rich Tea? Do the digestives go as well with coffee? Do they taste okay? Do you like them? Do you? Do you?"

"Yes," she said.

"You could say it like you mean it. You could. You could say it like you mean it. You obviously don't like them. You don't like the digestives, do you? Do you? I should have bought chocolate ones, shouldn't I? Shouldn't I? You'd have preferred them to the digestives."

"These are fine," she said.

"You don't mean that. You don't mean it. You want chocolate digestives, not plain. You don't like my digestives, do you? I prefer them plain, but you'd prefer chocolate on them. Am I right? Am I right? Am I right?"

"Shut up, Eddy," she said.

"You don't answer my questions. You don't. You're not honest about the biscuits. You won't tell me what you really think. Tell me what you think of the plain digestives. Be honest. Tell me. Tell me. Tellmetellmetellmetellmetellme."

"Shut up," she said.

"But you won't answer. You won't tell me what you really think of the digestives. Would you prefer chocolate ones? Or perhaps you'd prefer Morning Coffee, or Jammy Dodgers, or Fig Rolls?"

"Well, okay, we'll have Fig Rolls next time," she said.

"I knew it. I knew it. Knewitknewitknewit. I knew you'd want bloody Fig bloody Rolls. I knew you'd want the ones I think are disgusting — just to get at me. Just to get at me. Bloody Fig Rolls. I tell you what, I wish I'd never gone to the shop to get you digestives now, all the trouble they've caused." He snatched the plate of digestives away from her. "I'll have those back. I'll have them back. You can go and buy your own."

"Okay, I will," she said.

"Oh, you will, will you? You will — you'll go out to the shop for Fig bloody Rolls, and next time I'll see either you or the biscuits will be in three years time. Well, you might as well go now. Go for your biscuits now. Go now."

In the end, after hours, days of this, she snapped again: "Why shouldn't I? Why shouldn't I go to the shop for my own biscuits? Why shouldn't I? It's not as if you've taken me out once to get biscuits—or anything else, for that matter. You've not taken me out a single time since I got here. Has it ever crossed your mind I might want to go out and buy my own fucking biscuits? Has it ever crossed your agoraphobic mind that I might want to see a world outside these walls and your fucking ant-farm? Has it ever crossed your mind I might want to see people other than you and your little chum here?"

Exhausted, she slumped back into her chair, and a seething silence descended on us all. I wanted to leave the room, but didn't dare move.

After a few minutes, Edwin spoke up in his meekest of voices: "Okay . . . okay . . . okay, darling." He seemed to be feeling towards some grand plan, some Great Idea: "Okay . . . what if . . . what if, darling, what if we . . . instead of going out—I mean, there's nothing out there to go out for, is there?—so instead of going out, what if we invited some people here? We could have a dinner party, yes, a dinner party, and I could cook my speciality."

She seemed placated by the idea, though she wasn't ready to forgive Edwin yet. "Give me back the digestives," she said, "and I'll think about it."

He handed over the plate of digestives, and she sat, munching and thinking.

"Who would you invite?" she asked, "I mean, apart from Jules here, and your landlady?"

He rolled his eyes at me, stumped by the question. It was obviously the flaw in his plan. Terrified that she might erupt again, I made a suggestion: "What about people from work?"

Edwin nodded. "Ah, yes, exactly who I was thinking of. I'll ask the boss and some of my work colleagues. I'll tell them I'm cooking my speciality. They'll all want to come. It'll be like the golden olden days, darling, when we were famous for our entertaining."

Judging by her frown, I guessed that the ex-wife couldn't quite recall the "golden olden days" to which Edwin referred. No matter, she was won over by his enthusiasm, and they began making lists of possible dates, of people to invite, of wine and food to serve. Or, at least, she began making these lists: Edwin seemed to spend most of his time on one particular list — the list of after-dinner biscuits to buy. Fig Rolls didn't appear on it.

24.

So certainly if a man meditate much upon the universal
frame of nature, the Earth with men upon it … will not seem
much other than an ant-hill, whereas some carry corn, and
some carry their young, and some go empty, and all to and
fro a little heap of dust.

—Francis Bacon, *The Advancement of Learning*

Whether it was because of the lack of Fig Rolls, or because
Edwin was threatening everyone with his "speciality," the
list of guests got shorter and shorter, as one after another
claimed a previous engagement. In the end, only myself, the
landlady, and Edwin's boss were left, besides Edwin and his
ex-wife. Still, the ex remained determinedly optimistic about
the dinner party, and she hoovered, dusted, polished and
cleaned the house almost out of existence in the run-up to
the event; I began to wonder if the house would stay upright
when purged of its customary filth. But I needn't have worried,
because the filth was never gone for long—none of the ex's
compulsive cleaning stopped Edwin leaving cigarette butts,
empty bottles, cans, LPs or copies of Kropotkin all over the
place. Sometimes, she'd have a go at him about it, and I'd
come across him hovering in the hallway, carrying armfuls of
butts, bottles, cans, Kropotkins. Half an hour later, I'd find the
same armfuls hidden in one of the kitchen cupboards, or down
the back of the fridge. He seemed constitutionally incapable
of putting things back where they belonged. "To tidy away,"
he said once, "is to replicate on a miniature scale what Hitler

did with the Jews, the Young Turks with the Armenians, and what the Yugoslavs are doing now to each other. Hence the term ethnic *cleansing*. Cleansing, cleaning, tidying—all these things are forms of genocide."

"God, Eddy," his ex snorted, shaking a feather duster, "you're the only person I know who'd justify laziness with the Holocaust."

Still, however lazy he was for most of the time, when it came to the day of the dinner party, he esconced himself in the kitchen with one can of mushy peas, two packets of mince, five bottles of wine, four cookbooks, five CDs, six cans of plum tomatoes and more pulses than I'd seen in my life—or, at least, in this life. "It's my speciality," shouted Edwin over one of the CDs, swigging from one of the bottles of wine, and pouring the rest into a pan. "It's chilli, but with a special ingredient."

"What's that?"

"Mushy peas!" he declared, brandishing the tin. He poured the contents into the pan, and then added another half a bottle of red wine. "Genius, eh?"

Edwin's "genius" made my stomach turn over, so I took the bottle of wine from him and started swigging myself. By the time the one guest from outside the house was due to arrive, we were both as drunk as the chilli.

There were five of us sitting round the kitchen table: myself; the landlady, dressed in all her velvet finery; Edwin, in a black polo-neck and polka-dot cravat; Edwin's ex-wife, in a red top and waistcoat; and Edwin's boss, dressed in a neat, black suit. The boss seemed a small woman—particularly when sat next to Edwin's ex-wife—with tiny, precise hands, one of which was delicately pushing a fork round and round her plate. I watched, drunkenly mesmerised by half a dozen kidney beans going round in circles.

Meanwhile, the ex-wife was asking her: "How's the phone-a-cyclopedia business?"

"It's slow," Edwin's boss answered. "Not so good at the

moment. My directors are getting a bit itchy, looking for savings or innovations."

"Why's that?" asked the ex-wife, who was smiling for once. She was clearly enjoying the opportunity for "small-talk" afforded by the meal. Edwin, on the contrary, was not. In the corner of my eye, I could see him squirming on his chair, waiting for an opportunity to interrupt and redirect the conversation onto more Edwinian topics. I think he found it hard to listen to conversations which didn't depend on his existence in some way—hence his dislike of small-talk, or (to be specific) small-talk which wasn't about himself or ants. On this occasion, he squirmed, he yawned, he stretched, he sighed, but his ex and boss ignored him and carried on.

"Why's business not so good?" asked the ex.

"The internet seems to be taking over everything," said the boss. "The Knowledge Industry is evolving, and I think the directors are worried that *Encyclodial*'s days might be numbered. Punters aren't going to call a premium-rate phone line if they can get the answers they want by pressing a few buttons on a computer."

"So is the business going down?"

"Not necessarily. I've told the directors—we've got to diversify, move forwards and adapt or we'll die."

I thought I heard Edwin snigger, but when I looked at him, he was beating his chest: "Smoker's cough," he explained.

"As I was saying, we've got to diversify to move the business forwards. If it's the law of vanishing returns with the phone line, we need to find other strategies to make up for it." She stabbed a kidney bean on her plate. "I've been given the job of spear-heading these initiatives."

"Well done you," said the ex. "It's good to see a woman in the workplace being recognised for her gifts." The landlady and I nodded and smiled politely. Edwin was looking for something he'd dropped under the table.

"I'm very excited by the opportunity."

"What are you planning to do?" asked the ex.

"For a start, I reckon we need to embrace the information age, rather than fight against it. We need to use the new technology to our advantage. So we're going to develop our website, and push a subscription to that through the phone lines." She peered at Edwin, who'd resurfaced from under the table. "I'm going to put in place a new pay and reward system for our phone operators. Instead of being rewarded for the amount of call-time, operators are going to be encouraged to sell subscriptions to the website, CD ROMs and even computer quizzes based on *Encyclodial*'s gigantic Fact Pool. That way, we'll be at the proactive forefront of the new technologies, rather than reacting against them."

Edwin saw his chance to burst into the conversation, and slurred: "Technologies, eh, technol-ol-ogies, what are they all about? What are they all for?" He was very drunk.

His ex turned to him, "I don't know, Eddy, but I'm sure you're about to enlighten us."

"I will. I'll tell you what they're all about—sex and death, death and sex. That's all, nothing more, nothing less."

"I see," said his ex. The boss was staring at Edwin, her nose wrinkled, her eyebrows almost joined—looking like someone confronted by an alien, gabbling an unknown language. The landlady gripped my leg under the table, and squeezed it ever more tightly as the conversation progressed, or rather degenerated.

"I'm sure you do see, darling," Edwin retorted, glancing sideways at his ex, eyelids heavy with alcohol: "I'm sure you do see. You know all about sex and death, don't you, darling?"

"I don't know what you mean," said his ex. Nor did anyone else round the table.

Edwin snorted with laughter, and almost knocked over a glass onto his boss. With her free hand, the landlady grabbed it and steadied it at the last moment. "Nor do I, darling. I don't know what I mean either. But I will tell you something."

"What? What will you tell us, Eddy?"

"I will tell you what I was telling you before—about technol-o-lurgies. Techno . . . techno . . . they're all about sex and death, every one. Eros and Thanatos, Thanatos and Eros. At base, all techno-no-logies are a way of blowing more people up, or shagging them." He spluttered wine: "Or, for that matter, both at once."

"Darling, please."

"No, it's true. It's true, I tell you. Look at the modern computer—developed during the Second World War. The Second World War! And look at this internet thingymajigy-majig—from what I hear, ninety-five percent of it is porn, and the rest is a knocking shop. Sex and death, Eros and Thanatos: and no doubt your Freudians would say that at bottom they're the same thing." With that, he winked pointedly at his ex-wife, as if to imply that she somehow exemplified the union of Eros and Thanatos.

"Charming," she said, folding her arms.

She and Edwin stared fixedly at each other for a few seconds; then he seemed to forget what they were doing, what he'd been talking about, and reached for the wine to pour himself and his boss another glass. Inevitably, he missed the glass and hit the table-cloth. His boss pulled her chair sharply backwards, so the wine didn't splash her suit. Too late: Edwin kept pouring, and wine swamped the table and the boss's lap. Putting the bottle back on the table, he leant forwards, squint-ing at her trousers, trying to focus on them: "Oh dear dear me," he slurred, "looks like you've made a mess. You'll have to slip into something more comfortable. I've got some lovely frocks you can borrow if you want to come to my room."

Meanwhile, the landlady had leapt up from the table to grab some toilet paper, which she now handed to the boss. Leaning over me to mop up some of the mess on the table, she mur-mured in my ear: "For fuck's sake, Jules, take him away for a bit—before both his boss and wife give him the sack."

I got up and told Edwin that we were going to adjourn to the living room. Curiously docile all of a sudden, he took my hand and I led him out of the kitchen.

Once in the lounge, he produced two huge cigars from his breast pocket, lit them with a trembling hand, and handed one to me. He sat back in the armchair with a glass in one hand, his cigar in the other, looking all the world like an aristocrat relaxing after a successful dinner party. He appeared drunkenly pleased with himself, satisfied that he'd behaved like some Wildean wit, who had entertained everyone at dinner with his sparkling banter. "Sex and death, death and sex, that's all techno-lol-lology is," he kept saying, stumbling over words of more than one syllable.

"Oh," I said, feeling like I had run out of things to say to him—in fact, feeling like I had run out of things to say to him forever. No doubt I was drunk too, but I felt tired of his voice, tired of endlessly being told things, maybe even tired of never being asked anything myself. After all this time, I still felt that I might walk out of the front door, and he'd never notice I'd gone, except insofar as he'd have to find a new echoing chamber for his thoughts and opinions. That was why I was so surprised by the direction our 'conversation' took over the next few minutes.

At present, however, I even began wondering if I amounted to anything as significant as an echoing chamber, given that Edwin was holding forth from his armchair regardless of whether or not I was listening: "You see," he was slurring, "it's all about sex and death. The same goes for evo-lol-lution: look at the ants. All of their evo-lol-lution-er-ary innovations, from ant bivouacs to pheromones, to leaf-cutting to detachable wings, all boil down to sex and death."

I considered interrupting to ask how (for example) the cutting of leaves for nesting and eating equated with his overarching theory; but I decided I couldn't be bothered. Arguing over the theory's contradictions, omissions and exceptions would almost certainly be a waste of energy, considering the amount Edwin had drunk.

"Sex and death, death and sex: that's what it's all about, even in ant techno-lologies—even in evolutionary technologies that we as human beings can only dream of. Only dream of. Look at trap-jaw ants: they can snap their jaws shut in less than one-thousandth of a second. Now that's what I call technology. Look at leaf-cutter ants. Amazing. Some of them can dig tunnels five-hundred feet long. Imagine how long that is in proportion to their bodies, and then think about how much fuss there was when human beings dug something as crappy as the Channel Tunnel."

Edwin paused dramatically, expecting (as ever) a stunned gasp, or some other expression of awe at ant ingenuity; but, to be honest, I was all out of awe after so many months, and I just said "Oh," and yawned.

He squinted at me from across the room — or, at least, squinted at the wall six inches to my left, where he seemed to think one of me was sitting. "Is that all you can say?" he asked.

"What do you mean?"

"I mean, is that all you can say: 'Oh'? Can't you argue with me? Can't we engage in vigorous debate?"

I was surprised at this question: in general, I would have said that vigorous debate, involving argument, negotiation and, above all, *listening* to other people's opinions, was one of the forms of social interaction of which Edwin was least capable; so I didn't know how to answer.

Before I'd thought of anything to say, Edwin had slumped back into his chair, a morose look on his face. Puffing on his cigar, he muttered: "Vigorous intellectual debate: there's something one doesn't get much of round here. All one gets round here is your philistinish taciturny and the Poet Laureate's nineteenth-century poetry. Bloody typical: the only friend with any culture for thousands of miles, and he's got autism or something, and can't hold down a proper conversation, can't debate or discuss anything — hardly even notices you're there."

Irritated, I was tempted to remark that this was one autistic pot calling another kettle black; but even under the influence of a dozen glasses of wine, I knew it was futile to answer back, to argue with someone who couldn't argue, to tell someone who didn't listen that, well, they didn't listen. It was all too easy to run such a non-argument in my head: "Edwin, you don't listen," "Pardon?," "You don't listen to anyone," "You what?," "You never listen to what other people have to say," "Don't be silly—I listen to Nietzsche, Schopenhauer, Penderecki, don't I?," "But that's not the point," "What's not the point? Listen to this—amazing stuff on ants from Francis Bacon . . ."

Sometimes I felt that the only creatures with whom he knew how to interact were his ants. At least he knew them all by name; at least he seemed aware of their needs and desires, in the form of sugar and water and leaves.

"Oh God, what would I do without the ants?" asked Edwin, in a melodramatic tenor, waving his cigar in the general direction of the ant-farm. "What would I do without my ants, the only intelligent life-forms I know? Why am I surrounded by autistics and feminists, for Christ's sake? What the hell is the point of this godforsaken, culture-forsaken wasteland I don't call home?" Having built up to a climax, he raised his palms upwards, like some suffering Job questioning his God; I half-expected him to burst into scripture—scripture I suddenly remembered from a childhood I'd thought beyond recall: 'Oh that my grief were thoroughly weighed, and my calamity laid in the balances together! For now it would be heavier than the sand of the sea,' and 'Behold, I cry out of wrong, but I am not heard: I cry aloud, but there is no judgement,' and 'Where shall wisdom be found? . . . where is the place of understanding?'

Instead, the East Midlands Job in front of me just burped and screwed up his face, glaring at me. From the kitchen came the sound of raised female voices and laughter. This was the final straw for Edwin. He stubbed out his cigar and leapt to his feet, gesticulating wildly and shouting: "Aren't you at least pleased you're not in there, with *them*—with those bloody *feminists*?" Laying great stress on *"feminists,"* as if it were the worst insult in the world, he strode over to the open doorway, directing his invective towards the kitchen: "Aren't you glad you're not in there, cackling with those harridan feminists? Wouldn't you rather be in here talking about ants and intelligent stuff, than in the kitchen, discussing, I don't know, curtains and chintz and vaginas?" The voices and laughter in the kitchen died down for a few seconds, and then started up again, as though nothing had happened. Edwin turned back to me, waiting for an answer: "Well? Which is to be? Kitchen feminism or living-room ants? Eh? Eh? Eh?"

With each "Eh?," Edwin leaned in closer towards me, his sharp nose pinning me down, and I suddenly felt on the spot, faced with a bizarre choice which would somehow decide everything henceforward. In choosing between "kitchen feminism or living-room ants," I felt like I was somehow being asked to commit myself forever, in everything from friendship to politics to gender. But I didn't want to commit myself forever; so I looked down at the floor, and answered, quite honestly: "I don't fucking know." I really didn't know which room, kitchen or lounge, sounded less enticing in terms of the conversation on offer. Perhaps the hallway, with its old newspapers and tin cans, would at least have been quiet. "I just don't know."

"What do you mean, you don't know? What kind of friend are you? Ungrateful sod: why do I waste my intellect on you?" In his drunken fury, he seemed caught on a roundabout of rhetorical questions, unable to get off: "For Christ's sake, what is the point? What is the point of even talking to you? Why do I bother, when you never say anything, never answer anything, never tell me anything? Why do you make me talk all the time, instead of you?" His questions were becoming increasingly disorientating, as they whirled round and round. I'd always thought it was because he talked so much that I hadn't told him anything about myself; but here he was, claiming precisely the opposite: that it was because I never told him anything that he talked so much. Even now, looking back on this strange, one-sided row, I don't know if he had a point, or if it was drunken nonsense.

He'd paused, expecting some kind of response to his rhetorical questions — I have no idea what. But I was still revolving what he'd just said in my mind, so I didn't answer — and my silence sent him into a rage of which I hadn't thought him capable: "Why won't you answer? Why won't you ever answer? You know what, you answer so little that I don't even know what questions to ask in the first sodding place. For Christ's sake. Most people complain of their sodding friends that 'it's always me me me' with them—but with you it's always 'you you you,' and me is nowhere, nothing. Tell me: why is it always you, you, you, never me? Why don't you say anything? Where did you come from? Who the hell are you anyway?"

These final two questions came as a shock, and I had no idea what to say. I suppose I should have expected such questions to come up at some point; and I might well have expected them from anyone except Edwin. No, that's not quite true. I would have expected them from anyone except Edwin and myself. Back then, I seemed incapable of asking myself about the past, where I had come from, who I was before I'd sat down on a random doorstep somewhere in the Midlands, somewhere in 1997. The past was a foreign country, and my memory was pathologically xenophobic.

I'd unfairly thought Edwin was the same. Unwilling for the most part to deal with his own past, he could hardly be expected to express interest in anyone else's. Incapable of interrogating his own motives and memories, I'd assumed he would never want to know mine. It seemed I had underestimated him.

Or perhaps not: as soon as he'd asked the questions "Where did you come from? Who the hell are you?," he turned on his heels, strode out of the living room and out of the house, slamming the front door behind him. It seemed the questions really had been rhetorical, and he wasn't going to wait for answers. I don't think Edwin was ever willing to wait for answers to questions, or solutions to problems.

The landlady poked her head round the doorway, and asked me another question I couldn't answer: "Where's he fucking raced off to now?"

"I don't know," I said once again. I was beginning to feel like I didn't know anything in the world.

"Fucking hell," she hissed, stamping her stiletto through the carpet; it got stuck between the damp floor boards for a moment, and she had to wrench it out. "Fucking hell," she shouted, rubbing her heel, "fucking hell, Edwin, that hurt, and it's your fucking fault. You're behaving like a fucking idiot, as ever. Fucking hell, Edwin, you really know how to fuck people off." In his absence, she directed her invective at me, as if I were his stand-in or understudy. She took a deep breath and sighed her exasperation away. Her tone softened, and she addressed me-as-me (rather than me-as-Edwin): "Jules, you better go after him, check he's okay. We don't want him drowning in the fucking canal and blaming us. Stupid fucking annoying idiot—just the sort of thing he'd do to spite us. Go and find him, will you, Jules?"

"Okay," I said, and ran out of the house.

I followed Edwin through some dark, Satanic streets, down a flooded alleyway, past a half-lit business of an unspecified nature called *Club Class*, along the towpath of a disused canal, over an abandoned shopping trolley—until I reached The Dying Swan. I caught up with him on the doorstep; he looked me up and down, raised an eyebrow, and then stepped inside.

As ever, the Poet Laureate was mumbling to himself at the bar. We sat on stools either side of him, and he glanced furtively between us, one to the other, over the rim of his glass. He didn't say anything.

"Aren't you going to give us some poetry?" asked Edwin, apparently still stuck in a whirl of questions. The P. L. carried on drinking, his neck seeming to shrink into his body. His eyes were wide, and I wondered if he were trembling.

"Don't worry, it's only me," said Edwin, putting his arm round the P. L.'s shoulders. As soon as Edwin touched him, the P. L. jumped up, spilling his drink and flooding the bar and my lap with beer. He backed away, shaking his head furiously, saying: "No no no no no," over and over again.

Edwin said, "Look, I'm sorry," but it was too late, and the Poet Laureate retreated to a far corner of the pub, where he sat, twitching and muttering Keats to himself: "'no—guess? more princely you must be—/ Than to make guesses at me. 'Tis enough / I'm sorry I can hear no more.'"

"Bloody Keats," said Edwin, to no one in particular. He

turned to the barman: "I'm a fugitive from a dinner-party and half a dozen squawking harridans—and I need a drink to wash away the feminism. No: strike that. I need four dozen drinks." Finding, though, that he didn't have enough money for four dozen drinks, he settled for three doubles for himself, a pint for me, and a replacement pint for the P. L. With uncharacteristic sensitivity—though perhaps I'm being unfair again—he took the P. L.'s pint over to where the latter was sitting, placed it quietly in front of him, and then went to sit on a different table. In that way, for half an hour, we all sat separately, not looking at one another, just drinking.

"What's wrong with you lot?" asked the barman.

I shrugged my shoulders, and said for the umpteenth time that night, "I don't know."

Finally, it was closing time. Edwin ordered us all one last double, and the three of us left together, though still not speaking. The P. L. was drunker than I'd ever seen him, so rather than letting him fall in the canal, I upturned the abandoned shopping trolley, and bundled him into it. I pushed him along the towpath of the canal, whilst he and Edwin duetted in an atonal version of the 'Alabama Song' from *Mahogany*.

"Oh, show me the way to the next whiskey bar,
Oh, don't ask why, oh, don't ask why . . ."

"I didn't know you couldn't sing," commented Edwin before the second verse, "as well as knowing all that poetry. You're brim-full of culture, my friend."

"Oh, show me the way to the next little girl,
Oh, don't ask why, oh, don't ask why . . ."

By this point in the 'Alabama Song,' we'd reached the end of the towpath of the disused canal—and from there we wandered past the half-lit business of an unspecified nature called *Club Class*, and then down the flooded alleyway, through dark, Satanic streets, and then home . . . or, at least, the Poet Laureate and I did. Edwin never got as far as the alleyway, the dark, Satanic streets, let alone home. Instead, he came to a halt outside the half-lit business of an unspecified nature called *Club Class*, and peered in through the bars at the window. His singing drifted into humming (at the lines 'I tell you we must die, I tell you we must die'), then umming and ahh-ing, and finally speaking: "Always wondered what it is they sell here," he said, more or less to himself. He hadn't quite decided whether or not he was talking to me yet.

Still, I decided to assume he was addressing me, so I answered: "The place looks dubious to me."

"Could be anything: the sign on the door just says 'Welcome to *Club Class*' and 'Open' and 'Please Enter,' as if everyone knows what the place is for except ourselves. This whole wasteland of a town is in on the secret but us. We are exiles from *Club Class*."

He was starting to get carried away again, and I thought it time to drag him away: "Come on, Edwin, let's go home. It's getting cold, and the guests — well, guest — she's probably wondering where the hell we've got to."

"I don't give two hoots about any of them, and I'm not sure I want to go home." He was pouting like a little boy. "I want to stay here. I want to be let in on the secret of *Club Class*. I want . . ."

"For Christ's sake, Edwin. Let's go home."

He stuck his lower lip out. "No no no. I'm staying here. You can't make me go home. I don't want to go home. I don't want home. I want here." Suddenly, it seemed to me that the drink had shaved twenty-five years off him, and had turned me into his mother. I could see us now — him-at-ten-or-so-years-old and me-as-his-mother — arguing outside some fallen-down bookshop in Stoke-on-Trent, he stamping his foot, me trying to drag him away by the sleeve. He'd be decked out in the most flamboyant 1970s fashions (cravat, flowery shirt, spandex trousers), which I'd made for him by cutting up old husbands' clothes; I (she) would look almost the same as that day in Stoke, but with hair more peroxide than silver, and scarf brighter, more sure of the decade from which it originated. We'd have seemed out of place, out of time in Stoke, which somehow appeared never to have left the 1950s, never to have caught up with my scarf or his cravat. People would have stared at us, because of his screaming: "I don't want to go home! I never want to go home! I hate it there!" I would tell him to "shutupshutupshutup," and perhaps order him recite The Rules—or an earlier, Edwinian version of them: "I promise not to leave the house without asking you; I promise to go only where you say I can go; I promise always to come home afterwards; I promise not to speak to anyone, especially girls, who you don't want me to speak to; I promise not to waste all my time reading books, or listening to records; I promise not to go on endlessly about ants; I promise only to love you." But it would have been too late, and he would have pulled away from my hand, and darted inside the bookshop, and I'd have panicked, thinking he might never come out again—always that nagging fear at the back of my mind, a fear born of my own abandonment of him, some years before.

Back in July 1997, I-as-me didn't yet know about that abandonment—but somehow I must have sensed it, for I said to Edwin: "You might never come out again," in a melodramatic tone not unlike his mother's.

He snorted at me like a horse. "Don't be ridiculous."

"Honestly, you don't know what kind of place this is. It could be a front for anything—fucking gangsters or drugs or anything."

"Well, I am going to find out," he declared, pulling himself up to his full height—as if he were about to conquer a mountain or run a marathon: "I, Edwin Prince, am going to uncover what dubious merchandise this anonymous emporium peddles, and, in short, get some of it."

"How the fuck are you going to do that, if you don't know what you're asking for?"

"I'm going to open that door, walk inside with a confident air, place a twenty-pound note on the reception desk, and say: 'One, please.'"

The ludicrousness of the situation overcame us both for a moment, and we had to avoid each other's gaze in order not to burst out laughing, and hence undermine our mutual aggravation. Even the P. L.—who was still in the trolley—seemed to have registered something in the outside world, and looked like he was suppressing a giggle. His mouth wobbled, and he muttered something incomprehensible.

Maybe it would have been better for all of us if we had given in, and had burst out laughing. Things might have turned out differently, something might have been saved. As it was, the moment was lost, and there was no going back to laughter.

Edwin turned to open the door, and I couldn't help myself—like his mother once more, I grabbed hold of his sleeve and tried to stop him: "Edwin, what about your wife? What about the people back home?"

"In the words of Shakespeare's Coriolanus, sod them all."

"Charming."

"And sod you too."

With that, he opened the door and disappeared inside.

"'O for a Muse of fire!'" said the Poet Laureate to no one.

"Fuck," I said. "Fuck fuck fuck fuck fuck."

Back at the house—down the flooded alleyway, through dark, Satanic streets—the Poet Laureate took his leave on the doorstep, climbing out of the trolley, and pushing it homeward. His singing receded with the rattle of the trolley's wheels:

"Oh, moon of Alabama
We now must say goodbye
We've lost our dear old mama
And must have whiskey, oh, you know why."

Listening to the P. L.'s singing accompanied by trolley wheels, rather than by Edwin, I couldn't help thinking his baritone would have been haunting, if it hadn't been cracked by alcohol and some long-ago trauma. It might have helped too if he'd been able to remember tunes as well as words.

I turned back to the front door, and let myself in. The house was quiet and the lights were off. It was cold, and somehow felt like everyone in the world was dead except me — or perhaps it was the other way round, perhaps it had always been the other way round.

It felt like that until I was half-asleep on the sofa, and a familiar arm drifted round me.

"Where's Edwin?" the landlady whispered.

From my half-dreams, I could hear someone singing "I don't know, I don't know, I don't know, I don't know," to the tune of the 'Alabama Song.'

25.

Dear Edwin,

By the time you read this letter, I will be gone.

I can't live with you and your bloody ants any longer.

You behaved atrociously at the dinner party last night, and it was the final straw. When you didn't come home, I realised I didn't care any longer. I didn't care a Fig Roll that you were probably in a ditch, or in a ditch with some slag, or man, or whatever it is you're into these days. I didn't fucking care. So I've decided I'm going back to Stratford and the barge.

I don't know why I ever decided it was worth us trying again in the first place. I was foolish, and you owed me money. At least I learned my lesson that I'll never see that again.

And I probably won't ever see you again. It's no use. I can't pretend you don't piss me off to the power of ten thousand. If I stayed, one of us would have a nervous breakdown. If I go, at least I know it's not going to be me.

You shouldn't be upset. It's your fucking fault after all.

No more love and kisses,

Your Very Ex.

P.S. The reason I began the letter with 'By the time you read this letter, I will be gone' is because I thought it would piss you off if I ended us with a cliché. God, you think you're so unconventional, so original, but I've seen loads of you on films and

TV, usually played by Richard E. Grant or Marvin the Paranoid
Android.

P.P.S. And you're an idiot there as well.

P.P.P.S. You can stick your ants up your arse. I'm sick of
them.

P.P.P.P.S. I'm so fucking angry I could go on and on with
the 'P.S.s' forever.

P.P.P.P.P.S. But instead, I'm just going to go and let you fill
in all of the P.S.s for yourself. Goodbye, Ed. Goodbye. Goodbye.
Goodfuckingbye.

26.

The 'Dear John' letter was lying open on the kitchen table when I got back from work the next morning. After skimming it, I rushed into Edwin's bedroom, worried he might have done something stupid—well, something more stupid than normal.

I found him on his back on the floor, hand on his forehead, Haydn's *London Symphony* blaring all round him. When he shouted "Turn it off!" as soon as I stepped into the room, I couldn't help thinking he'd been lying there for some time, waiting for me to come back from work, preparing his performance. "Turn it off! Turn it off! I can't bear it!"

I stepped over to the stereo and switched off the CD.

Edwin uncovered his eyes and looked up at me from the floor. "I will never listen to that again," he announced.

"Why not?" I asked. "I rather prefer it to your Pendereckis and Schnittkes."

"Preferences, likes and dislikes are beside the point," said Edwin. "They're not what music's about. Next thing you'll be telling me is that it's about enjoyment."

"What the hell is it about, then?" Once again, Edwin had surprised me by the turn of the conversation. Yes, he seemed distraught; but there was no mention of his ex-wife leaving him. Instead—and perhaps characteristically—he expressed his angst through a dialogue about musical aesthetics. No doubt he had that in common with his brother: in both cases, mental anguish seemed strangely to be refracted through the prism of music. But whereas Edwin's brother was in earnest, it was always difficult to know how seriously to take Edwin's pronouncements, particularly when they were so over-blown, rhetorical as now.

"Music, good music," he continued in this vein, "is totally distinterested in whether we like it or not. It's totally independent of our enjoyment. It just *is* — our pleasure or pain are irrelevancies, mere side-effects. Music is indifferent to human beings, and who can blame it? As Schopenhauer says somewhere, 'music . . . is entirely independent . . . of the phenomenal world, ignores it altogether, could to a certain extent exist if there were no world at all.'" Again, I couldn't help thinking that Edwin had rehearsed this speech beforehand, though I had no idea where it was leading. "Like ants," he continued, "music is an alien civilisation which seems cruelly indifferent as to whether we humans live or die."

"Edwin, you're talking crap." Any sympathy I had left for him now his wife had gone was evaporating, boiled dry by his inability to talk in anything but philosophical abstractions, objective generalities. "For God's sake," I wanted to shout at him, shake him, "for God's sake, Edwin, your ex-wife has left you again, and you're quoting Schopenhauer. For once, can't you resist this compulsive urge to philosophise, generalise, objectify, abstractify everything that happens to you, everything that you feel? Living here with you, I'm beginning to forget how people normally talk about themselves and their lives." But I didn't shake him or tell him these things, because, after his outburst the previous evening, I knew what his answer would be. He would say — quite rightly — that I was one to talk about not talking; that at least he had the philosophical abstractions with which to express himself. I had nothing, said nothing, expressed nothing. No doubt in this sense my frustration with Edwin was hypocritical, and I was sorry for it. Still, I couldn't help it, and said again: "Edwin, honestly, you're talking crap."

"No I'm not. Look at Auschwitz: the orchestra played Mozart *Serenades* whilst thousands of people went up in smoke. The music carried on regardless."

"I think you're missing the point of that example," I said . . .

. . . but then, from a long way away . . . as though from a vanishing horizon at the back of my mind . . . one-thousand, six-hundred miles and many, many years ago . . . like some ancient, faraway tinnitus . . . I thought I could hear 78 r.p.m. crackles of Caruso singing *Carmen*, Mendelssohn's *Midsummer Night's Dream* . . . all mixed up with an old woman's crackly voice, whimpering some forgotten Eastern folk-song . . . amidst other kinds of crackles, fiercer kinds . . .

"What's wrong with you?" asked Edwin, peering at me from his place on the floor. "You just kind of . . . stopped."

"Sorry," I said. "It was nothing, just an odd turn." But I was worried: these "odd turns" were becoming more frequent, and were starting to happen in the presence of other people. Something somewhere at the back of my mind was calling me back, and I didn't want to go. At least, not yet.

"I wondered where you'd gone for a second," said Edwin. "You were miles away — as distant as the music I'm talking about. Anyway," he said, gradually remembering his place in his own script, "where was I? Yes, music, a cruel and beautiful art. And the more beautiful, the more perfect, the more cruel, or, at least, the more cruelly indifferent. When it comes to music, there's a direct correlation between the beauty of music and its indifference to the world of human beings. Bach, Mozart, Haydn, early Beethoven: these wrote the cruellest music because the most beautiful, the most perfect."

"I'd have said Penderecki was pretty cruel, at least on the ears," I said.

"Nonsense," snorted Edwin, "Penderecki's music is much less cruel because the dissonance, the chaos, the shrieks and howls reflect more closely our real world. Don't you see? Cruelty in this case is indifference: Penderecki's music seems less indifferent, more rooted in the real life of this crappy century of ours. Mozart's and Haydn's music, on the other hand, is utterly alien. It belongs to a better civilisation; it refuses to share in our traumas; it makes us realise our inadequacies, how shitty the human race has become. It taunts us."

"That's not indifference," I said.

"Okay, it *seems* to taunt us; but actually it's wholly indifferent to us. I tell you: Bach, Mozart, Haydn, and, in a lesser way, all those who copied them in the nineteenth century—you know, like Mendelssohn, Schubert, Brahms—they wrote the truly dissonant music, because the beauty of their music jars most discordantly with the horrors of life in the twentieth century."

With that, he sprang to his feet and began scrabbling around the room for something. For someone who had just been dumped, he seemed very energetic, even enthusiastic, in his speech and movements. Paradoxically, he was often at his brightest when indulging his pessimism about the human race to the utmost. Here was another correlation which somehow—I'm not quite sure how—tied in with his claim that the beauty of music was directly proportional to its cruel indifference: the more pessimistic Edwin's rhetoric, the more pleased he appeared to be.

Of course, I assumed he only appeared pleased, and that, underneath it all, he was feeling crushed by his ex-wife's departure. But when he produced two dustbin liners from behind his bed, and started bundling armfuls of CDs and LPs into them, there was a hyperactive fervour about his actions which made me wonder how miserable he actually was. He darted about the room in a cloud of dust, dirty clothes, magazines and books, uncovering and collecting dozens of records from the floor, from bookshelves, from behind dead pot-plants, and shoving them into the bin liners. He worked with all the speed of someone packing up home before the arrival of a marauding army, or great fire ... except that there was a crazy joy about his actions, which was underlined when he finished and stood in front of me, holding two bin liners full of CDs and LPs, laughing and panting from his efforts. I peered at his face, trying to detect tell-tale signs of anguish.

Looking back now, I wonder if I was wrong to think that the crazy joy hid a deeper misery. Rather, the joy and the misery were one and the same for Edwin: just as he took a certain pleasure in his pessimism about humanity, he also gained a strange kind of frenzied joy from his own misery. Edwin suffered from a form of self-*Schadenfreude*, taking masochistic pleasure from his own pain. At his most miserable, he was simultaneously at his most ecstatic; for him, the two ends of the emotional spectrum curved round and met.

Now, abandoned for a second time by his wife, isolated from his family, hungover, he was jubilant. "I tell you what we are going to do," he declared. "We are going to disavow this too-beautiful music till such a time that the human race is worthy of it. Bach, Haydn, Mozart, even Mendelssohn, Bizet, Brahms: they're too good for our present moment in history. They have no point of connection with our shitty world. Instead, they just serve to remind us how far we've fallen. All that stuff about harmony, balance, beauty, brotherhood, heroism, humanity—these things belong to another, better universe. So we're going to dump them. We're going to dump them till such a time that the human race is worthy of eating the crumbs from Bach's table. It might be centuries, it might never happen. But this beautiful music has no home in our world right now. So it has to be dumped." There was a peculiar insistence on the word "dumped" throughout his speech.

He handed me one of the dustbin liners—which I immediately dropped, it was so heavy—and he stalked out of the room, with the other one slung over his shoulder. "Follow me," he called, " and bring the bin liner. We're going out." I heard him open the back-door and step into the yard. I tried slinging the dustbin liner over my shoulder, but it was too heavy. "Just a minute," I called back. I was sure Edwin had given me the heavier sack to carry.

Putting the sack back on the floor, I opened it up to see if there was anything I could take out to make it lighter. Perhaps I could hide some of the CDs and LPs somewhere so I didn't have to carry them all; and anyway, I rather liked some of this music, and thought it would be a terrible waste if Edwin was just going to dump it all.

Whilst Edwin was gone, I rummaged around inside, bringing out CD after CD that I liked, or liked the look of: Mozart's

Flute and Harp Concerto, Handel's *Greatest Hits*, Strauss's *Blue Danube and Other Waltzes*, Saint-Saëns's *Organ Symphony*. I stuffed them in every pocket I could find in my jacket and trousers. I guessed that Edwin himself had never even listened to some of these CDs, having bought or borrowed them by the bag-full, from his ex-wife, friends, charity shops. But I didn't want to see them dumped prematurely, and decided to rescue as many as I could.

All too soon, before I'd had time to save more than a dozen CDs, I heard the back-door slam, and Edwin was back in the hall. I suddenly felt guilty — though uncertain what I was feeling guilty about — and was red in the face when he reappeared at the bedroom door. "What are you doing?" he asked.

"Nothing," I said. "Nothing at all. Nothing whatsoever."

"Well then, come along. We've got work to do. Bring the bin liner, and take this." He handed me a rusting spade he'd obviously retrieved from the back-yard. "Let's go."

He turned on his heels, strode down the hallway and out of the front door; and I huffed and puffed and grumbled after him, lugging spade and heavy bin liner — knowing full well that he'd never notice how much I was struggling with the load.

"Hurry up," he said. As he stalked down the dark, Satanic streets, and I tagged along behind, I felt like some over-burdened retainer to a forgotten aristocrat: "Come along."

We turned down the flooded alleyway, strode past *Club Class* (at which point Edwin looked determinedly ahead), and along the towpath of the disused canal. Here, we stopped, and put down the bin liners. "This'll do," said Edwin.

"What for?" I asked.

"I'll show you." And, before I could stop him, he had upturned the bin liner and emptied its contents — of Bachs, Handels, Haydns, Mozarts, Beethovens, Mendelssohns, Bizets, Schuberts and the rest — into the canal. He grabbed the other bin liner and emptied that in too. Hundreds of CDs and LPs floated and sank and drifted and eddied and tangled with stagnant waters, weeds, poisoned fish, water rats, oil, filth. Edwin stood there for minutes on end, watching, as though expecting something to happen. Gradually, his shoulders drooped, and the resolute tautness of the last hour drained from his posture. He looked crestfallen. I squeezed his elbow, but he shook me off.

"No, it's not *that*," he said. "It's not *that*. It's *that* –" here he pointed at the records in the canal, "they've not gone away. They've just stagnated."

It was then that I understood why he seemed so disappointed: he'd pictured some kind of Viking-burial-at-sea for his records, as they sailed off into the distance and burst into flames with the sunset. In lieu of a nearby ocean, he'd thrown them into a disused and stagnant canal, and the effect hadn't lived up to his Viking expectations. Nothing ever quite lived up to Edwin's expectations, Viking or otherwise.

"I'm sorry," I said, not quite sure what I was sorry for.

He sighed. "Never mind," he said, in his most resigned and doleful tone of voice. "Never mind. At least this way nature can enjoy the records." He pointed to the other side of the canal with a stick he'd picked up. "I explored that bank a while back, and found a large *Formica rufa* nest—wood ants to you. Hopefully, some of the records will drift over there, and the ants will shred them and use Bach and Mozart to repair their nest. Ant civilisation is far more worthy of this music than human so-called 'civilisation.' Ant civilisation can appreciate harmony, balance, beauty, brotherhood, heroism, and even humanity far more than we can. Ant civ . . ."

All of a sudden, an over-tanned, orange face appeared above the parapet of the bridge, thirty yards to our left. "Oi!" the orange face yelled. "Oi! You there!"

Edwin turned round—ever-so-slowly—and called back: "Are you addressing us, by any chance, darling?"

"Don't you 'darling' me," shouted the orange face. "What the hell do you think you're doing with that canal?"

"I am filling it with high culture," declared Edwin, "and it is suitably grateful, unlike the human race."

"Bollocks," said the face. "You're filling it with shit, and you're full of it as well. We have a term down at the council for filling canals with shit."

"Enlightenment?"

"You what?"

"Enlightenment? Is that your term?"

The face looked confused for a second, and then continued: "No. Fly-tipping. Do you hear me? Fly-tipping." He was now striding across the bridge in our direction. "We can give you an on-the-spot fine for fly-tipping of five hundred quid."

"I see," said Edwin. The mention of money, and the possibility of losing it were enough to galvanise him into action. Coolly, he turned round, pulled the spade out of the ground, handed it to me, and then said (rather incongruously): "Farewell and adieu, my fair Spanish ladies." With that, he ran off, leaving me with a spade and an angry council worker. I smiled at the angry council worker, who was now close, and getting closer, and then ran off myself—down the towpath, past where the shopping trolley used to be, and then into the back door of The Dying Swan, where I thought Edwin was probably hiding.

He was at the bar, already ordering drinks for himself. I was annoyed at him for leaving me, but there was no point saying anything: he was too taken up with his own world of emotions to understand that there might be other people's worlds out there.

The barman looked up at me whilst pulling Edwin's pint. "Been digging?" he asked.

I'd almost forgotten about the spade I was holding. "No, not really." I turned to Edwin. "Why am I carrying a spade?"

Edwin shrugged his shoulders. "Not sure really."

I pushed the handle towards him: "For fuck's sake, Edwin. You can carry it then."

He looked down at the handle, but didn't take it. "I suppose when we left I had some vague notion that I might bury myself alive with my records—you know, like some latter-day Tutankhámun, waiting for a Howard Carter of a better age to rediscover us. It was a toss-up between burying myself alive or burying my records at 'sea.' By the time we'd lugged the stuff to the canal, I was knackered, so I chose the latter."

Both the landlord and I smiled weakly. But there was no expression on Edwin's face to suggest whether or not he was joking, whether or not he was really considering burying himself alive. Given what happened a couple of months later, I'm still not sure how 'funny' he was trying to be.

The landlord rolled his eyes, and went to serve another customer—the Poet Laureate, in fact, who had just appeared next to Edwin.

"'O for a Muse of . . .'"

". . . fire, yeah, we know," said the landlord. "What do you want?"

The P. L. pointed at one of the beers, and soon we were all sitting at a table in the corner. There was a long silence, until Edwin said: "Bitch."

I waited for him to elaborate, but he just said: "Bitch" again, and then stopped.

The Poet Laureate looked up from his beer, in my general direction:

"Stay near me—do not take thy flight!
A little longer stay in sight!
Much converse do I find in Thee,
Historian of my Infancy."

"What's Wordsworth got to do with anything? In fact, what's Wordsworth got to do with anything ever?" asked Edwin.

"'Float near me; do not yet depart! / Dead times revive in thee,'" said the P. L., apparently in answer to Edwin's questions—though somehow I felt the words applied to me as well.

"Bitch," said Edwin to his beer, "Bitch bitch bitch. Bitchbitchbitchbitchbitch. She went and left me for a second time. A second bloody time. My ex-wife is now doubly ex. An ex-ex: you'd have thought that'd work like a double negative. But it doesn't feel like that at all. Not at all."

He stared down at the table, his eyes seeming to hang low in his face, and for a moment I thought he was going to cry; but sometimes, when he was at his most depressed, Edwin seemed rather to cry with words—they flowed from him like so much salt-water, in a kind of generalised misery. When he was as miserable as this, he talked and talked, though not necessarily about the issue at hand. Instead, all of his miseries seemed to roll into one, and he'd talk about something unexpected, something apparently unconnected with what was happening. In this sense, Edwin's mind seemed like a house with faulty wiring: flick a light switch, and a tap started running; turn on the shower and the radio blared out; bring up one trauma, and his mind suddenly flashed back to a different one.

So now, after no more than a dozen sentences about his wife leaving him, he started talking and talking and talking about something else: his memories of his grandfather. The moment for the conversation I'd expected to have with him about his ex-wife was gone. I'd thought he might cry—and I might tell him that I'd lost all sympathy for him—and he'd ask how I could be so cruel when his fickle wife had left him for a Tour Guide—and I'd answer what did he expect, after last night?—and he'd ask me what about last night?—and I'd say he could hardly expect his wife to stay 'faithful' to him after he'd got drunk and visited a massage parlour—and he'd get angry and snap back, well, yes, but she didn't know about that, and anyway, who was to say that *Club Class* was a massage parlour, he'd never told me what went on in there and never would, as far as I was concerned it could be anything, a branch of the Freemasons or a high-class cattery—and finally the Poet Laureate would quote something more or less inappropriate, and we'd all lapse into unresolved silence. But this conversation never happened, and instead Edwin suddenly started talking about his grandfather.

"He was a mean old bugger," said Edwin, curiously recycling the language I'd heard from his mother a while back, "him and his Stalin moustache. God, I hated that moustache—he used to brush it every morning like some kind of facial pet."

I wondered why Edwin was telling me this; I don't suppose he knew himself.

"I tell you, he was a mean old bugger. But he had a wicked sense of humour—and I mean 'wicked-wicked,' not 'wicked-ha-ha-isn't-that-funny.' I didn't get it when I was three, and I don't think my brother ever did. I suppose it came from when he was in the Navy. He was a young and impressionable rating, it was just after the First World War, and I think he went everywhere and saw everything: the Baltic, the US, Canada, Japan, Sri Lanka, North Africa, and somewhere in Turkey he talked about even less than the other places he didn't talk about—if you see what I mean." At this point, Edwin paused and shook his head, unable to resist an Edwinian generalisation: "Everyone goes on these days about how travel is good for you. What a load of rubbish. Travel—*real* travel, where you see what *really* goes on in the world—is as bad for your mental health as history." He grinned and returned to his beer, quiet for a moment. The grin gradually disappeared. "No doubt my grandfather'd seen some awful stuff, but he didn't have to bring it back with him to Stoke."

"I thought you said he didn't talk about it?"

"He didn't, but he brought it back in other ways—in his supposed sense of humour, for instance. Him and my grandmother—who I never met—had separate bedrooms, which he used to call their 'trenches.' She was the Hun, he the Allies. He used to say that only once did the two sides come together in no-man's-land, 'to play football,' so to speak—and that was when my mother was conceived. Otherwise, their marriage was all barbed wire. Of course, I didn't realise when I was a kid that he'd never actually been in the First World War—that he was a bit too young—and that it was all some kind of joke to him. Christ, he used to tell this joke to a five-year-old: no wonder I can't get the hang of married life.

"He used to 'joke' that the only thing that ever cured his life-long impotence was shelling, and that he'd had to imagine he was shelling his wife to get it up. He used to tell me that my mother, his daughter, wasn't much better than the whores in Saigon, and that he got less for his money. He used to tell me that my mother dressed me like a sodomite, and that they knew what to do with sodomites in Her Majesty's Royal Navy. I looked up 'sodomites' in the dictionary, and next time he said it, I asked him what made them such experts about sodomites in the Navy?

"I was a cheeky bugger back then, but he never hit me, or even seemed to register what I said. He just stared at me with those unmoving eyes of his, and carried on as if I hadn't said anything—carried on swearing at the TV, at the radio, at my mother, at the gangs of teenagers on his street corner, at the Asian shopkeeper down the road, at all Asian shopkeepers, at his canary—who probably bore the brunt of my grandfather's unhappiness after his wife's death. He used to tell me that he'd fed the canary, bit by bit, my grandmother after her death. He said that my grandmother had liked the blasted canary so much more than him, it was a way of getting back at both of them.

"For a long and stupid while, I believed everything he said. I believed it when he told me that I shouldn't hold my spoon in the wrong way, shouldn't run on the lawn, shouldn't step on the cracks in pavements, because these shadowy people called 'Armenians' were always lurking round the next corner, lying in wait for me to slip up in some way. He never told me what they would do to me—just that they were waiting for me, somewhere in the shadows, in the corners of the street, in the corners of his eyes.

"The mean old bugger never smiled when he told us these things, his eyes never flickered, so I was never sure what was a joke and what wasn't. As I say, I don't think my brother ever worked out what to believe and what to laugh at." Edwin took a sip of his beer. "Not that any of it was exactly what you might call 'hilarious,'" he added, "and I think my grandfather knew that. After all, he never laughed once. Even he didn't seem entirely sure which were jokes and which weren't, especially when it came to the stuff about Armenians. Sometimes I caught him looking over his own shoulder when I stepped on pavement cracks."

There was a long pause, and I wondered if Edwin had finished. I hadn't heard any of this before, unlike most of his stories, so I had no idea where the memory started or ended.

All of a sudden, he resumed the memory, and I realised it was far from over: "No, his eyes never flickered. On Sunday afternoons, I'd sneak downstairs, and there he was, glaring straight at the TV or a wall or the canary. I'd sit on the stairs, staring at him staring at something or nothing. He could do it for hours. He was the stillest man I've ever met. It didn't matter what he was staring at — it could be a vase of flowers or a documentary about genocide — he'd never move, never blink. I suppose once you've seen what he'd seen in the Navy, you never need to blink again. Once you've seen the worst, you can stare anything out."

The Poet Laureate seemed to be shifting uncomfortably in his chair. I wondered if he were bored. He was mumbling something vaguely Tennysonian. Edwin took no notice, and continued his story regardless — he wasn't really talking to anyone in particular, and at the best of times never made many concessions to his audience.

"You may ask why I spent so much time with the mean old bugger, given what I've said about him." As he spoke, he seemed to sink into his chair, as if sinking into the memory: "You may ask that."

I thought this was some kind of prompt, so I said: "Okay, why did you spend so much time with the mean old bugger?"

Edwin spoke more quietly now: "Because I had no choice. Because my mother married another man — my brother's father. Because my mother got pregnant with my brother, and decided she couldn't cope at the same time with a new husband, a new son, depression and me. So she decided I was the one of those things which could go, and shipped me off round the corner to my grandfather and the canary. Between three and seven, I was just a visitor at Festival Street, and I saw more of the canary than my own mother. Bitch. Bitch. Bitch. Bitchbitchbitchbitchbitchbitchbitch."

There seemed no end to the "bitches," and I wondered if they could have gone on forever, if I hadn't put a hand on Edwin's arm. He shook his head and pursed his lips. "Bitch," he said one more time, like a full-stop. He was hunched forwards in his chair, and looked up at some point above my head. "Of course, I don't even know what the real 'becauses' of the matter are. I've never talked about it with her, and I'm not sure I want to. All I know is that, between three and seven, my own mother sent me away.

"Then she got divorced again, and I came back. But she still couldn't cope with both me and my brother at the same time, so this time—like a bloody musical clock—the other one was sent away. This time, it was my brother who was packed off for a year or two to my grandfather's. Poor bloke, it's fairly obvious he never recovered."

Edwin pulled himself up from his slumped position, looked out of the window, and gritted his teeth, as if he were posing for some Socialist Realist statue. "I, on the other hand, *did* recover," he pronounced. I must have pulled a sceptical face, because Edwin's shoulders slumped a bit again, and he added: "Well, you know, insofar as madness and sanity are relative values, and you can rate one kind of madness against another, I don't think I'm *quite* as mad as other members of my family." My face must still have looked sceptical, because Edwin added again: "Okay, at least I don't think there are Armenians lurking in the sewers in Stoke-on-Trent."

I shrugged my shoulders to concede the point, and Edwin continued: "I have no idea, of course, and (to be honest) little interest in where all the Armenians-in-sewers-and-round-corners stuff came from. Perhaps it was some kind of racism my grandfather inherited from his father; or perhaps, for some reason, the Armenians were generalised bogeymen in the 1920s; or perhaps he went to Armenia and something happened to him when he was in the Navy. Then again, that would have been a bit difficult, given that Armenia is landlocked.

Nope, I've no idea why our family is scared of Armenians, and frankly I don't care. I don't care. I really don't give two hoots."

He took a big swig of his beer, to underline how few hoots he gave the matter. "Sod the lot of them," he said, and clinked glasses with the Poet Laureate, who was grinning and nodding inanely. "Sod them all." He drank the rest of his beer in one, and went off to the bar for more.

When he returned, he carried on with his story as if he'd never stopped, as if he were somehow always in the middle of it: ". . . yes, that was it: towards the end of my time with him, I reckon my granddad was starting to lose his marbles—well, he started losing even the few he had left, becoming totally marble-less. He was furious more and more of the time, used to forget things, and used to bawl at the canary (who was now dead and stuffed) no end. God, that canary went through hell alive, and probably thought she'd escaped when she finally died. The afterlife must have been a real disappointment: nailed to the same cage and bawled at by the same madman for eternity."

Edwin looked away, into space or the past or both, and spoke more slowly than normal: "Living with him was an eternity. How did I know at three, four, five, six that this wasn't forever—that I'd ever go back to live with my mother? How did I know that my grandfather wasn't immortal and wouldn't outlast me like he'd outlasted his wife and the canary? I imagined myself stuffed in a cage with him bawling at me for years to come. No doubt that's how my poor brother felt too, when he was shipped off to my grandfather's after me. And he got the worse deal, because by then my grandfather was totally marble-less, I can tell you.

"Still, it was my grandfather's dwindling marble collection that saved me, because I witnessed it happening. My poor kid brother just bore the consequences of my grandfather's last illness; but I saw him on the wane. In the last year I lived with him, I watched him become weaker, his glare less focussed, his moustache less brushed. More than anything, I saw him looking over his own shoulder whenever he threatened me with Armenians. So I started stepping on the pavement cracks on purpose, holding my spoon in the wrong way on purpose, running on the lawn on purpose—just to see him worried, just to piss him off."

Edwin laughed a forced laugh. "Kids are cruel sods, don't you think?" I didn't say anything, and he carried on: "Old people think they can out-cruel kids, but it's the kids who always get the last laugh, when oldness starts to take its horrid toll. Kids win by default.

"My brother wasn't with my grandfather at the right time, wasn't there long enough, wasn't clever enough to win out, to realise that the unrestrained anger was a front for this strange well of terror underneath." Edwin whispered this last line like an apprentice Vincent Price; and, not for the first time, I wondered how far the whole memory was true, and how far it was shaped by Edwin's capacity for Hammer-Horrorish self-dramatisation.

Now, he'd obviously had enough of family matters for one day, and decided to round off the story with a hasty, yet confessional coda: "What I regret most, I think, is that I didn't give my brother the key, didn't tell him about the grandpa-secret. Perhaps if I had done, things would have turned out better for him."

"What was the grandpa-secret?" I asked.

"I have no idea," said Edwin. Suddenly relaxed, he sat back in his chair with his beer and put his feet up, pretending the story was over.

I knew, though, that what he really wanted was for me to pursue the subject, so I asked: "If you don't know what the grandpa-secret was, how could you tell it to your brother?"

"I didn't say 'tell it *to* him,' I said 'tell him *about* it.' There's a world of difference."

"What do you mean?"

"I could tell him it existed, not what it was. I could tell him that there was this terror underneath everything which you could play on—by stepping on pavement cracks and running on 'Keep-Off-the-Grass'-lawns. I could tell him to try what I did once, when I was doing some crappy Geography home-work, and asked granddad to list all of the ports he'd visited in the Navy. He thought for a bit, and then reeled them off, like he was ordered to do a roll-call by a commanding officer: 'London, Liverpool, Manchester via the Ship Canal, Bristol, Portsmouth, Southampton, Douglas, Havre, Marseilles, Esjberg, Helsinki, Reykjavik, Halifax, Colombo, Hong Kong, Istanbul, Saigon, Freetown, Lagos, Port Said, Alexandria, Sydney, Cape Town, Nagasaki, Odesa, Smyr . . .' — and there he stopped and wouldn't go on, and just glared at the wall. His face was suddenly . . . suddenly . . ."

Edwin glanced at me for a second and said: "Yes, that's right. His face was exactly like that, like yours is now, all bits and pieces — like the mouth was trying to run away from the nose, the eyes trying to pop out of the head, but all held together by sheer force of will. Yes, exactly like yours is now. What a good impression — how did you know?"

I didn't, couldn't answer, because otherwise my mouth would have run away, and the pressure behind my eyes become too much to bear. Edwin frowned at me for a second; and then lost interest again in anything but his own memory. He continued with his story, and that gave me time to regain control of my face, to disentangle it from my own faraway half-memories: "When he'd got as far as 'Smyr . . .' in his list, nothing I could say would induce him to carry on, or even to take notice of me. So naturally I wondered where 'Smyr' was. I looked it up in a school atlas, and the only port I could find with those letters was 'Smyrna,' an old name for Izmir in Turkey. I took the atlas back to him, showed it to him, and said: 'Is that where you meant, grandpa? Smyrna?' He didn't answer, but suddenly stopped staring in front of him, and glanced behind him, and then shut his eyes — which, to be honest, I don't think I'd ever seen him do before. His eyes always seemed open, awake or asleep.

"Looking back on it, I think he was already very ill by then" — here Edwin tapped the side of his forehead — "and I suppose I should have felt sorry for him. But he was a mean old

bugger, and kids *are* cruel. So –" and here Edwin paused and
lowered his voice, still a little ashamed of his childish behaviour: "So . . . I used to creep into my grandfather's bedroom
late at night when I guessed he was asleep (even though he'd
often still have his eyes open in the dark). I'd tip-toe up to
his bed—all the while expecting his eyes to move and mouth
to shout, but they never did. And then I'd whisper: 'Smyrna-
smyrna-smyrna-smyrna-smyrna-smyrna' in his ears, over and
over again, just to give him bad dreams about the grandpa-
secret, whatever it was. I didn't care if he looked even more
haggard than normal at breakfast; I was a kid and felt he
deserved everything he got, the old bug . . ."

Out of the blue, out of nowhere, the Poet Laureate suddenly stopped shuffling, looked straight at me with the widest
of wide eyes, pointed with a trembling hand, and bust forth in
his most Gielgudian voice:

"O for a Muse of fire, that would ascend
The brightest heaven of invention,
A kingdom for a stage, princes to act
And monarchs to behold the swelling scene!
Then should the warlike Harry, like himself,
Assume the port of Mars; and at this heels,
Leash'd in like hounds, should famine, sword and fire
Crouch for employment. But pardon, gentles all,
The flat unraised spirits that have dared
On this unworthy scaffold to bring forth
So great an object: can this cockpit hold
The vasty fields of France? or may we cram
Within this wooden O the very casques
That did affright the air at Agincourt?
O, pardon! since a crooked figure may
Attest in little place a million;
And let us, ciphers to this great accompt,
On your imaginary forces work . . .
For 'tis your thoughts that now must deck our kings,
Carry them here and there; jumping o'er times,

Turning the accomplishment of many years
Into an hour-glass . . ."

Terrified that the Poet Laureate had somehow turned over the
hour-glass with his speech, that we were jumping back o'er
times to a port of Mars, of famine, sword and fire, that I was
attesting in this little place for a million, that I was a cipher to
some great accompt that was about to be revealed—terrified
by all of these things and more, I jumped up from my seat,
sending drinks flying, overturning the table, and dropping on
the floor all of the CDs that I'd hidden in my coat pockets.

Edwin looked at the CDs swimming in spilt beer, looked
up at me, and then looked back down at the CDs. He raised an
eyebrow. Then he picked them up, one after another, reading
their titles out loud, shaking the beer off them, wiping them
over with his handkerchief, and handing them back to me.

When he was polishing the last CD, I tried to say: "Look, I'm
sorry, but I thought I'd save . . ."

He breathed out of his nose and shook his head: "You
thought you'd save some of the records?"

I nodded.

"You thought you'd save some of the records?" he repeated
the question, as if I hadn't answered it. "You thought you'd
save some of the records?" He seemed incredulous, and could
only find an answer to his own question by shaking his head.
"God, you thought you'd save some of the records behind your
friend's back—and you chose Handel's *Greatest Hits*, Mozart's
Flute and Harp Concerto, Strauss's waltzes, Saint-Saëns's god-
awful *Organ Symphony*? You know, you had the choice to
recover anything from the ruins of our degenerate age, anything—Beethoven's *Ninth*, Handel's *Messiah* for God's sake,
Mozart's good stuff, Bach's anything—and you chose this, you
chose Saint-Saëns's sodding *Organ Symphony*?" He waved the
last CD at me. "You chose *this*?"

"I like the tunes," I said—and immediately afterwards
regretted saying it.

He almost laughed, but didn't: "You like the tunes? You like the sodding tunes? What a philistine you are. You might as well say you prefer nursery rhymes to Bach, TV theme tunes to Haydn. You might as well have saved, I don't know, Supergrass or the Spice Girls. Haven't you learnt anything from living with me?"

"How fucking patronising you are," I said, annoyed both at him and myself. On the one hand, I was angry at myself because he'd been telling me memories which he'd never revealed before; he'd been talking to me, more or less honestly, about his family and childhood; and I'd gone and betrayed him, let him down for the sake of Saint-Saëns. On the other hand, I was angry at him because the 'betrayal' would surely have seemed a drop in the ocean to anyone else — surely? But here I was, worried that the row was going to spiral out of control, that I might not have anywhere to live within a few minutes. So I breathed in the tears and the anger, and murmured: "Look, I said I was sorry . . ."

It was too late. He wasn't listening any more. He got up, and tossed the last CD over to me. His face was full of disdain: "Go and enjoy it. Go and fill ya boots with your Saint-Saëns and your Johann Strauss and your nice tunes, Jules. Jules" — and he took his coat and was gone.

It wasn't the disdain in his face and voice that affected me the most; it was that he'd called me by name. Never once had he called me 'Jules' in all the months I'd known him. In fact, when I came to think about it, I don't think I'd ever heard him use anyone's proper name. People didn't exist as names to Edwin, and I'd often wondered what he'd do if someone knocked at the door and asked to see 'Jules': would he look stumped? Would he have any idea who 'Jules' was?

But it turned out he did know who 'Jules' was; it turned out he did know my name, and had saved it up till now to use it. And instead of being pleased that he recognised me, I was distraught. In that moment, when he finally used my name, a spell was broken — and I felt that the house, our friendship, our enmeshed histories, everything would collapse around us, brick by brick, memory by memory. All that would be left would be the Poet Laureate, muttering: "'... into an hour glass ... into an hour glass ... into an hour glass,'" over and over again.

ACT FOUR

27.

I remember ... I remembered ...

Or perhaps I imagined it.

But let's say for now I remembered; and that this remembering was my first sustained remembering, the first time my mind properly regained a past tense ...

... and yet this first time wasn't *my* past tense, wasn't *my* remembering: rather, I remembered *his* remembering.

That is to say, I remember remembering his remembering ...

That is to say, I don't know how to say it, how to explain it; but at some point, during that strange, Limbo time after our row about Saint-Saëns — a time when I hardly saw Edwin at all, when I seemed to be losing contact with the people and present around me — I remember one of his memories seeping into me ...

No, that's not what happened. I remember one day remembering something for him ...

No, I'm not sure I even remember first remembering — I just remember the memory being there, as if it had always been there, and one day I just turned round and noticed it.

The memory — his memory — may not be a memory at all. It may well be a figment of my imagination. It's too neat, too pat; so perhaps my memory invented it to fill a void, to understand things which couldn't be understood.

All I know is that one day it came to me: a memory, a vision of a past which wasn't my own. One day, I found myself remembering for someone else, remembering by proxy. No doubt it's probably nonsense, but one day, I found myself dreaming a dream . . .

. . . a memory-dream of a young Edwin, pre-pubescent, pre-ants (though not for long), post-separation from his mother — that separation expressing itself in a certain wideness of the eyes, a tautness of the cheek bones from which his latter-day sunkenness would develop, an inability to maintain eye contact with anything but toys — sitting on a green carpet in a living room full of photos and saggy Christmas streamers, facing an even younger brother, pre-paranoia, pre-sibling-misrecognition, post-maternal-separation, his back to me (an invisible observer), and to his grandfather, who is asleep with his eyes open in the far corner, muttering obscenities to himself, his moustache fluttering with each laboured exhalation, each flutter, each exhalation counting down to the last, which will be within the year, but not yet, not in this memory-dream, where he is just staringly asleep, not staringly dead, taking advantage of the quiet whilst his squawking daughter, the boys' mother, is out — perhaps at the sales, perhaps at the hairdresser's — unaware as of yet that Haydn's *Sinfonia Concertante* is stealing from the radio (quietly, ever-so-quietly, so as not to wake him), because, even at this early stage, both grandsons feel drawn to an art-form which they have to smuggle into their lives, waiting for mothers to be out, grandfathers asleep, before they nod to each other, tiptoe over to the radio, and turn it on with the volume down — and then ceremoniously open a Christmas present they have given each other, which happens to be an Airfix model of an ant's exoskeleton . . .

The Christmas present is now in a hundred tiny plastic pieces, scattered betweeen them, the brother having methodically pressed them all out, one by one, whilst Edwin is engrossed in reading the instructions out loud, as if it were a story or philosophical tract; and then he looks over the top of the leaflet at what his brother has been doing, and swears at him, and asks him how it's going to be possible to follow instructions like 'Press out foreleg labelled A9 and glue with

Humbrol Poly Cement to thorax G4,' when all the legs and thorax sections have already been pressed out and mixed up, along with everything else, and the plastic frames, which include the parts' designations, discarded.

But it is possible, because the two brothers spend the next half-hour sorting out the parts, the legs, the thorax, antennae, abdomen, petiole, compound eyes, head and so on, and carefully, oh so carefully, glueing each tiny part together. They don't say much, if anything, they don't look at each other, and they don't overtly smile — their concentration being itself a kind of shared smile — but in this rare, motherless and grandfatherless half-hour, their hands perform a joyful Airfix *pas de quatre* to Haydn, virtuosic in its elegant choreography of sorting, assembling, exchanging, glueing, A9-ing to G4-ing, R3-ing to E6-ing . . .

. . . until the ant is almost complete, only its head needing to be fixed to the thorax . . .

. . . when the front door slams, and the mother has returned with new hair or nearly new dress, and grandfather wakes up with a grunt (that sounds something like "Sm . . . yr . . . Smyr . . ."), and a twitching moustache, and hears the Haydn, and splutters: "Turn that bloody Armenian racket off! Get it off! Now!"

And Edwin stands up, hands on hips, and says, "No, turn it off yourself" — and the mother comes in to the living room, and tells him not to talk to his grandfather like that, or she'll make him recite The Rules, whilst the brother, docile, defeated, slumps over to the old radio and takes out the plug . . .

. . . and the Airfix ant is cleared away, never to be completed, forever headless in its forgotten box.

28.

In the days and weeks after the ex-wife's departure and the ensuing row about Saint-Saëns, I didn't see much of Edwin. We didn't go to The Dying Swan together; we no longer watched *Ant Wars* or played *3D Ant Attack* in the front room; and, believe it or not, I found myself missing his recitations from Schopenhauer, Nietzsche, Spengler. Some days, I even wondered if he were neglecting his beloved ant-farm, when I came home from work to find the water reservoir empty. I'd fill it up and sprinkle sugar into the foraging tank to keep the ants going, at least until their neglectful God remembered their existence once more.

Over the weeks, I gradually became unsure of *his* existence. Witnessing his presence only second-hand—his shadow darting through his bedroom door, his fish-and-chip leftovers in the kitchen sink, his dirty socks in the bathroom—I began wondering if he were a bizarre figment of my imagination. At weekends, he never seemed to leave his bedroom, or even draw the curtains to let the light in—and I wondered if he'd become as photophobic as a queen ant. During the week, he did manage to leave his room, but I still never saw him. By the time I got back from a morning of handing out newspapers full of nothing, he'd already left for *Encyclodial*; and when he returned from work in the evenings, he would head straight for his room and listen to Karlheinz Stockhausen or Olivier Messaien or Luciano Berio or Penderecki or, if we were lucky, Stravinsky's *Rite of Spring*, all at top volume. "God help us," the landlady would whisper to me when we passed in the corridor, or on the rarer and rarer occasions when she came downstairs to sleep next to me on the sofa.

For weeks, all of us, myself, Edwin, the landlady seemed to be living in separate worlds and times under the same roof—worlds and times which only touched at the edges, in corridors, on sofas, through overheard music. Everyone and everything seemed to be receding from everyone and everything else; everyone and everything seemed increasingly unreal, even translucent, to everyone and everything else; and sometimes I had the peculiar feeling that, one day, Edwin and I would pass in the hallway, and he would walk straight through me, me through him, no longer able to hear or see each other.

I had the same feeling with the Poet Laureate, to whom I handed a free newspaper one day, and who looked down at it, and then at me, as though we were messengers from another planet, or another age. Perhaps what stunned him was just the shock of seeing me out of the usual context, away from The Dying Swan; but at the time I felt disconcerted by his seeming inability to recognise me. I said, "Hello, it's me," and he didn't reply. Instead, he just carried on staring at me, his mouth opening and closing, his nose reddening. After a couple of minutes of staring, opening, closing and reddening, I said, "Goodbye," and moved away to a different street corner. There was nothing else I could think of doing.

Nor was there anything I could think of doing to get Edwin to notice me. One morning, I bought him a bottle of Vermouth by way of an apologetic present. I left it on the kitchen table for when he returned from work. But he never came into the front room to thank me for it, or offer me a glass. My only evidence that he had found the bottle, and maybe appreciated the present, was that it was slightly emptier each time I went into the kitchen during the next couple of days.

Then the bottle was finished, and when I found it in the bin, I felt even more bereft than before, having lost one of my last points of contact with Edwin's world. Now, I actually began to wonder if we'd ever see each other again—condemned to haunt each other forever, like ghosts who were always in different rooms, just round corners, out of sight. Our tiny terraced house seemed to fold outwards in unknown dimensions, so it was possible for three ghosts to occupy the same space simultaneously, yet never cross paths.

As well as being isolated from one another, all three of us seemed quarantined from the outside world, an invisible red cross daubed on our door. I sometimes went all day without speaking to anyone — without a single "thank you" for the free newspapers I handed out — and I was sure Edwin too was unhappy at work, talking only to disembodied people on the phone. As for the landlady, she hardly left the house — in fact, hardly left the bathroom, spending hours in hot baths, still recovering from her break-up with Salacious Whatsit. I would go in afterwards, and find crystals, smelly candles, steam and Lavender bubble-bath everywhere. Secretly, I'd lie down under the warm bubbles, with my clothes on or off — it didn't matter. It had been two or three weeks since I'd last felt the landlady's arms round me on the sofa; but her body had just lain here, in these bubbles, as part of this warmth, so it was a good second-best. In this way, I'd try to reassure myself that someone else still existed in the world, or that I did.

It was no good. I could no longer quite persuade myself that I belonged to the time and place refracted and fragmented through the bubbles. As the heaps of foam crackled and fizzed and dissolved around me, so did the world of the landlady, Edwin, the Poet Laureate, the ex-wife, Edwin's mother and brother — until I would be stuck in a kind of Limbo between people, worlds, times, tenses. I'd lived entirely in the present tense for some months, but now the present seemed to be breaking up around me, and it turned out that the past tense had been lurking underneath all the time, like dirty bathwater . . . or dirty water of some kind or other . . . and for a moment, the sides of the bath — like the house — would fold outwards and the bottom of the bath would fall away beneath me, and I'd go under into weedy, quiet blackness, and I wouldn't know which way was up, and I'd try to find up in all the wrong directions, and then, when I'd almost given up hope, I'd finally find it, and I'd resurface and salty water would explode from my mouth and chest, and the horizon would be full of waves, swinging from side to side, and I'd open my mouth to shout for help, but the fiery horizon would swing again, and the shouting would be swallowed by a wave as I'd go under, and, for a second time, I'd lose the sense of up, and I'd think I'd probably lost it forever, and . . .

29.

... and for this second time, just this second time and no others, the landlady would hear the shouts and run downstairs and into the bathroom, to find me flailing in a few inches of lukewarm water, and she'd slap me and drag me out of the bath and lie me down on the floor and slap me again for good measure and I'd think she had a bloody strong slap and that her skull rings were in danger of drawing blood and she'd say, "Fuck fuck fuck fuck fuck, Jules, what the fucking fuck was all that about? Why the fuck did you want to do that, scare the fucking life out of me? Are you on fucking drugs? Are you having some kind of fucking fit? Or are you some kind of fucking lunatic?," and I'd spit out in bubbles that I didn't know the answer to any of those questions ...

... and she'd take me by the hand and dry me off and give me a change of clothes, and that afternoon, for the first time in many weeks, we'd share a bottle of wine and not talk about what had happened, and then we'd fall asleep together on the sofa ...

... until we'd wake up to Edwin returning from the late shift at *Encyclodial*, and his slamming the front door, slamming the kitchen door, slamming the fridge door and slamming his bedroom door ... and then, through the living-room wall, we would hear Penderecki's musical depiction of 'Little Boy' slamming down on Hiroshima, again and again and again ...

"What the fucking hell is his head like, listening to that on a loop?" the landlady would whisper, pressing herself close, hiding herself against me.

"Thankfully, I don't think any of us can have any idea," I'd whisper back.

And we'd listen for a while, waiting for the music to stop, waiting for him to fall asleep—at which point other noises would fill the silence: Edwin's mumblings of "Mother" in his sleep, the tiny janglings of the landlady's bangles and piercings, and the faint cracklings of a fire, which, like a strange form of tinnitus, had been haunting me since lying among the dissolving bubbles . . . no, that's not right, before then—I can't recall when I first started hearing it . . . far, far, away, as though on the distant horizon of every other sound.

"Can you hear it?" I'd ask the landlady.

"What?"

"*That*—a kind of crackling noise."

And she'd jump up and go and check that the gas was off in the kitchen. Coming back, she'd whisper: "No, there's nothing."

And I'd whisper: "Oh," and shrug my shoulders, trying to believe her, trying to believe it was nothing.

"Honestly, it's nothing. Probably just Edwin snoring and muttering in his sleep."

"Oh," I'd say again, knowing that we were heading back to more familiar territory: Edwin.

"He used to keep me awake all the time with his fucking night noises," the landlady would whisper, "and I don't mean sex noises either. He was all grunts, snores, mutterings, 'mother-mother-mother,' 'Armenians-Armenians-Armenians,' and hour-long hums from I-don't-know-what-fucking-boring-operas. I used to have to kick him out of bed, and he'd just roll onto the fucking floor and carry on snoring and humming there. Fuck, I've even heard him talking ants in his sleep."

Despite the "fucks," she'd whisper all this in a peculiarly nostalgic tone, like a mother reminiscing about a prodigal son. Her tone would surprise me, and I'd whisper in the quietest whisper possible—as though I would rather she didn't hear, and so wouldn't answer—"You actually rather care for Edwin, don't you?" I'd hold my breath for the answer, not sure what kind of answer I was afraid of.

She'd snort, and whisper back: "He's the most fucking frustrating fucking idiot-fuckwit I've ever come across. He fucking does my head in, that's what he does."

I'd take this answer as a yes, and everything would seem quiet for a moment—except for the incessant crackling noise, which would seem a little closer, as if eventually it might swallow up everything in the foreground, and the landlady's world would recede to nowhere. For now, though, the crackling would be just that bit louder, and the landlady's arms that bit colder.

Not that she would notice, and she'd carry on: "No doubt about it, he's fucking annoying, and to some extent deserves everything he gets. But," and here she'd hesitate, seemingly reluctant to admit the "but" into consciousness: "But . . . well, I have to admit that I'm a bit worried about him. There he is in there, on his fucking lonesome, not talking to anyone but himself. I mean, imagine that: only having yourself to talk to in the world, and that self being Edwin. God. Then, on top of that, everything outside that Edwin-self seems to be going wrong too. Okay, it's mostly his fucking fault, but . . . well, as I say, I can't help worrying about someone whose ex-wife has left him, who seems to have fallen out with all his friends—if he had many in the first place—and whose job is going down the drain."

"His job?"

"I think so. As far as I can get anything out of my friend, his boss, he's making a right fucking hash of the job at *Encyclodial*. Except that . . ." Again, she would hesitate, as her long-held sense of frustration with Edwin struggled with her anxiety for him: "Except that . . . well, except that it sounds to me like half a dozen of one and six of the fucking other. You know what I mean? The impression I get from hints I've picked up is that it's not just him who's making a hash of his job—that it might be more than just his fault for once. But then I might be wrong." In the darkness, through the crackling, I would hear her grinding her teeth: "You see, Jules, this is how it is with Edwin. This is how it always is. He's so fucking frustrating — everything about him is frustrating, even when things might not be entirely his fault. Even when he might be the victim, it's fucking frustrating because you know he just loves being the fucking victim. Somehow he seems to carry frustration with him, like a fucking pet that's always sniffing around."

With a few more "fuckings," and grindings of teeth, she would settle down, her head back on the sofa — only to bob up, and start hissing again a minute or so later: "And you know what's most fucking frustrating? You never know who or what's to blame. Edwin does such a good fucking impression of a victim, you never know if he really is one or not. Take *Encyclodial*: who knows if it's him or his boss or the company who's making the fucking hash of things. Who knows if it's Edwin or the fucking world that's to blame? Fucking fucking hell."

Again, she would settle down, her head next to mine — until I'd be drifting off to sleep a few seconds later, and she'd whisper: "You know what I'd like to do?"

"No," I'd answer, heavy with sleep.

"I'd like to go into his room now, wake him up, and ask him about *Encyclodial* — ask him what's happening there, and what's happening in his head. Of course, you'd never get the truth from Edwin. But like I say, the problem at the moment is that he's got no one else to tell his fucking lies to."

Then there would be silence for a minute or two, and I'd try and recapture sleep, but tiny, insistent sounds — the metallic click-click-click of the landlady's nose-rings as she nervously rubbed them together, the distant crackling of a fire — would keep me awake. I'd know that she hadn't finished, that there was something else, something she thought was important, that she wanted to say, that her eyes were still open, that she was still thinking, thinking, thinking in the dark; and I'd wait, willing her to get on with it, because her thinking and her nose-rings were getting in the way of much-needed sleep. Nonetheless,

whole minutes would go by, lulling me to sleep, and I'd jump
when she'd finally hiss: "You know what he needs?"

"No," I'd yawn.

"You know what he *really* needs?"

"No," I'd yawn.

"It doesn't matter," she'd say. "You obviously want to
sleep."

"Just tell me."

"Okay, I'll tell you what he needs, and what he doesn't have
at the moment. He needs someone to watch over him."

"Who? You?"

"No, I don't meant like that. I mean a guardian angel, or
something. That's what Edwin needs, someone to watch over
him. He needs a guardian angel. A guardian angel. A guardian angel," and she'd repeat the phrase a dozen times in a
quieter and quieter voice, like a dream, a mantra, an incanta-
tion — though to me it would sound more like a pantomime
conjuring trick, and I'd have to stifle a giggle. I'd feel bad about
the giggle, but the problem was that I'd been prepared and
prejudiced in advance by Edwin's derisory comments about
the landlady's "so-called 'beliefs' in everything from crystals
to Feng Shui to séances to black masses to Glastonbury to
guardian angels to the healing power of skunk. She's the sort
of stupid person like Prince Charles who thinks that belief is
a good thing in itself, non-belief inherently cynical and spoil-
sportish. Like loads of people nowadays, she seems to think it's
possible to believe in everything at the same time. This is the
crappy 1990s, end of the millennium and all that rubbish, so
belief in anything and everything is trendy. But what it all boils
down to is a kind of bargain-basement, everything-must-go,
buy-one-get-one-free, cheapo-Supermarket, sub-Christian-
sub-Jungian-sub-Buddhist-New-Age-neuro-linguistic-cos-
mic-nebulous-spiritualist mishmash that confuses even her.
Bloody feminists." I wasn't sure how the last label related to
the rest of his tirade, but it all seemed to amount to the same
mumbo-jumbo for Edwin.

By the time the landlady had started trusting me enough

to talk about her beliefs — by the time she finally admitted me into what Edwin called her "inner sanctum of inanity," which she kept hidden from non-believers in case of ridicule — I couldn't take her seriously. All I could do was pray that she wouldn't notice my tensing with suppressed laughter. I'd feel terrible about the laughter, but I couldn't help it after Edwin's parody of her New Ageism — it would feel as if I were being ventriloquised by Edwin, who was throwing his laughter into me from the next room.

The landlady wouldn't notice the laughter, and would rub my shoulder blades, saying how tense I was all of a sudden, and how I could do with a Reiki massage, or something of that sort. Then she'd return to the subject of Edwin and guardian angels: "Yes, that's what Edwin needs. I don't know if he's ever had someone like that in real life."

I'd say nothing, and tense again. She'd pull away slightly and sound hurt. "You don't believe me, do you?" she'd ask.

"I believe *you*," I'd say, "but I think it's hard to believe in guardian angels when you live in the East Midlands."

"You're laughing at me," she'd say, "just like Edwin."

"No I'm not," I'd lie.

But it would be too late, and she would have moved away from me — or as far away as was possible on a small sofa. There'd be silence for a minute, and then she'd stand up. I'd think she was leaving me, but she'd say: "Wait there. I'll show you something."

She'd pad quickly away, up the stairs to her bedroom. By the time she'd return to the living room, I would be dozing off again, or at least, would be until she switched on the light. "Look at this," she'd say, perched on the edge of the sofa, holding out a magazine called *Questions of Spirit*, "if you don't believe me, look at page forty-five."

I'd take the magazine, turn to page forty-five, and my eyes would gradually focus on a page of letters to 'Harmony Chimes, Ph.D, Spiritual Agony Aunt.' The landlady would point a trembling finger at a short letter in one corner:

Dear Dr. Harmony,

I am worried about a friend of mine who is also my tenant. He has recently split up with his wife for a second time, and has stopped talking to anyone. Some days, he doesn't even see anyone, locking himself in his room for hours on end. I don't know how to help him. He is an Arian, so is very independent-minded, and wouldn't listen to me. What should I do?

Signed, A Concerned Landlady

In response, Dr. Harmony Chimes had written the following:

Dear A Concerned Landlady,

How lucky this Arian is, to have a friend like yourself. Despite your friendship and kindness, however, Arians are often prone to depression, at which times they will put up barriers between themselves and those they love, and who care for them.

What your friend needs is someone who can break through these barriers — someone special. Everyone has this someone special, a spirit who watches over them, who can reopen their hearts to life. You need to have faith, and believe that that someone special will always appear when most needed.

Your job as landlady and friend is to make sure your house is open and welcoming to this someone special, however and whenever he or she appears. I'd recommend keeping one of my hand-made Guiding Light™ beeswax candles lit every night in a window, to guide your friend's angel to his side. You can order a set of these candles, all of which feature an original illustration by Michelangelo, by sending a cheque for £24.99 (inc. p&p), made payable to Harmony Chimes, to the normal address.

My angelic blessings on you and your friend,
H. C.

When I'd read the column, the landlady would nod and smile,

as if vindicated. She'd take the magazine back up stairs—so Edwin wouldn't find it—and then return to the living room, switching off the lights, and settling back down on the sofa: "You see?" she'd say. "You see? It's not just me who thinks that a guardian angel is what he needs. Harmony Chimes thinks so too, and she's the expert. She's got a Ph.D."

I wouldn't say anything, not wanting to offend her or upset her good mood.

"Look," she'd say quietly, confidently, "you may sneer, but it's not just Harmony either: lots of people have believed in guardian angels throughout history. The idea goes all the way back to really old times, even to Ancient Greek philosophers like—what're their names?—oh yes, Plato and, erm, Python-goras. I've read all about it." Suddenly, her tone would be transformed into something unfamiliar, almost childish; gone would be the swearing, and she'd sound like a five-year-old enthusing about a pet subject—not unlike Edwin and his ants. They were both, in their different ways, walking repositories of pseudo-knowledge: "It's not just 'New Age tosh,' as Edwin seems to think. Guardian angels're much older than that, and everyone who's anyone in the past has believed in them. I've read all about it." She'd keep saying "I've read all about it," perhaps to emphasise that her pet subject was based on the same authority—that is, reading—as Edwin's. She clearly felt undermined by his educated scoffing, and would attempt to defend her own beliefs by recourse to Edwinian methods—by playing him at his own game: "I've read all about it, see. I'm not as ignorant as Edwin thinks, and nor is what I believe in."

"I'm sorry, I'm not laughing at you. I don't think you're ignorant," I'd say, feeling guilty again.

"Even if you did think *I* was ignorant, you mightn't think that the Bible was—and there are guardian angels in there, like Saint Michael. And Jesus, he says that children have angels who take care of them. I read that there's some Saint Jerome or other too, who reckoned that sin drives away your guardian angel"—here, her voice would revert for a moment to her ordinary adult one, as though in a kind of footnote to what she was saying—"and that might make things tricky for Edwin, given the tonnes of sin he's shovelled in his lifetime." She'd pause for a second, and then her tone would be childishly enthusiastic again: "Still, not everyone has to agree with Saint Jerome, so Edwin might be okay. There're lots of other guardian angels in other religions too—they don't have to be Christian. I've read all about it. There's Zoroastrianism, where something called the 'fravashi' is the home spirit of the soul; there's Hinduism, where everyone's got loads of 'devas'; and belief in angels continued all the way up to the twentieth century: the great Aleister Crowley reckoned that everyone's got a Holy Guardian Angel, which is an ideal self, or something like that. Then there're psychoanalysts, who think that guardian angels might be archetypes from the collective unconscious—kind of like messengers, I spose. And best of all, there's my favourite film, *It's a Wonderful Life*—you know, where the angel Clarence Odbody appears to Jimmy Stewart to show him how crap the world would be without him."

The landlady's list of past advocates for guardian angels—from Plato to Christ to Crowley to Jimmy Stewart—might have seemed a little miscellaneous; but I'd guess a lot of her information had come from one of the many paranormal encyclopedias she kept in her room (*From the Apocalypse to Zones of Disturbance: The Pocket Dictionary of the Spirit World*). Or perhaps she'd called *Encyclodial* about the subject. Given what Edwin had said about the misinformation and jumble that was *Encyclodial*, and my own experience of calling him, this seemed quite likely. "Encyclopedias," Edwin had declared once, "are ant-heaps of knowledge without the ants." When I'd asked him what he meant, he'd looked a bit unsure for a moment—I don't think he'd expected to have to explain himself—but then he'd brightened, and had answered: "Well, they're full of empty corridors going nowhere." He'd yawned, and put on his most Marvin-the-Paranoid-Android-from-*Hitchhiker's-Guide-to-the-Galaxy* voice: "Life's a bit like that, don't you think?"

Certainly, I was beginning to think that Edwin's life was like that: a labyrinth of empty corridors with no escape route; so when the landlady mentioned *It's A Wonderful Life*, I couldn't help wondering (out loud) what would happen if Edwin had never been born — what difference it would make to the world.

"It'd make a big fucking difference, I'd have thought, to the world of those ants in my yard," the landlady would say. "Their whole city would never have existed if it weren't for Edwin — just like in the film, where all those people in Bedford Falls wouldn't have houses without Jimmy Stewart's *Building and Loan* company." She'd hesitate, and then add: "And I'd have thought Edwin never existing'd make a big fucking difference to you and me as well."

She wouldn't say what kind of difference; but in the silence which followed, I'd bite my tongue and feel dreadful. "I'm sorry," I'd say to the Edwin in my mind, "what a horrid thing to think." A sudden feeling of desolation would open out inside me, as I'd realise that it was probably me, not Edwin, who wouldn't be missed by the world if I were not here. I'd not even be sure if I'd miss myself.

"I'm sorry," I'd say out loud. "You're right — we'd miss him."

"Problem is, though, there's no one here to show him that. He doesn't have a Clarence Odbody." Then she'd purr ("Hmmm") for a minute, as though working out some complex mathematical formula — until: "But you never know what's really going on, do you?"

"No," I'd say, unsure what I was saying "No" to.

"No, you don't. You never know: perhaps he does have a Clarence somewhere, and he doesn't know yet. Perhaps his Clarence doesn't even know."

"What do you mean?"

"What I mean is, Edwin might have a Clarence who's going to help him, or who is helping him right as we speak, but neither of them know about it. The whole history of Clarences shows that they don't have to come with wings or halos or stuff like that. There's nothing about angels having wings in the Bible, you know. They might just look like one of us. I read this quote the other day — a writer bloke called George Eliot, he says something like: 'the angels come to visit us, and we only know them when they are gone.' They might just seem like ordinary people, who melt into whatever time and place where they appear. They might once have *been* ordinary people, and are just visitors from a different age."

Here, she'd drift off on an Edwin-like tangent, and I'd drift into an uneasy doze, lulled by her Leicestershire accent—as she'd debate (with herself) the idea that angels might come from the past, as opposed to some heavenly region. As far as I'd follow her ramblings from my doze, she'd seem to be saying that guardian angels might be messengers from trau-matic moments in the past of the person being visited—or that person's family's past—come back to heal old wounds. She'd mutter something about the father in the musical *Car-ousel* being a good example; but her explanation would be erased by a mini-sleep. By the time I'd jerk awake, she would have moved on from the father in *Carousel* to wondering how he might fit in with other notions of guardian angels—from psychoanalysts, for example: "It's like what Carlos Jung might say"—she'd pronounce the 'J' in 'Jung' as an English 'J'—"the angel might be a kind of embodiment of something terrible in the collective unconscious of a town or family or whatever. And because it's all unconscious, the something terrible in the past might be something the person who's being visited doesn't know about."

I'd almost hear the landlady frowning, as she worked her theories out: "Having said all that, I don't know if it applies to Clarence in *It's A Wonderful Life*. Perhaps it does, perhaps it doesn't. The point is that he comes from the past. He belongs in a different age, when people drank hot toddy."

"Hot toddy?"

"That's what he orders at this really rough bar in Bedford Falls. Of course, they don't know what he's talking about, and think he's some kind of freak. But he's just bumbling around, working things out. He makes mistakes, like all of us. After all, I read that guardian angels are the lowest of the nine orders of angels, so they're much closer to us humans than, say,

214

Cherubims or Seraphims or whatever. The point is, anyway, they themselves might feel closer to us than higher angels — they might feel like ordinary people, and not know what they've come 'down' for. I read all about it: the word angel comes from Latin or Greek (can't remember which) for 'messenger.' But perhaps angels don't always know what message they've come down to give. Perhaps ... perhaps ..." — here, she'd seem to be feeling her way, girlishly excited by a new theory, unaware of her own naïvité — "perhaps they don't even know they've come down from somewhere else — or some time else — just now and then nagged by something calling beyond themselves, tiny little signs which set them apart."

By this time, I'd be tired and upset with myself, and the landlady's enthusiastic babble would be starting to grate; and I wouldn't be able to stop myself rising to the bait, trying to point out her illogic: "Look, if these people don't even know they're, erm, 'Clarences,' how do they set about 'Clarencing' at all? How can a guardian angel be a guardian angel if he or she doesn't even know he or she is a guardian angel, for God's sake? The angel might get it all wrong."

"That's the point," she'd say, as if vindicated. "That's my point: guardian angels aren't, like, necessarily perfect. They make mistakes, get things wrong, bumble along more or less unaware of what they're doing. Look at Clarence in *It's A Wonderful Life*." She'd talk about her favourite film as if it were absolute proof, as if it were reality; so tough, so worldly on the outside, yet on the inside, she seemed as full of sentimentality and wishful fluff as a Hollywood movie.

I, on the contrary, would now feel full of desolation, brimfull of a bleak kind of nothingness, which I couldn't shake off even in sleep. In my mind, in my sleep, I would envy the landlady's beliefs at the same time as deriding them. In my mind, in my sleep, I'd want to believe in angels too. But in my mind, in my sleep, in my dreams, whenever I'd try to conjure up the face of an angel, all that appeared was the face of an elderly man with a bushy moustache and bullet holes for eyes ...

... And I'd wake up in a sweat, overtaken by an irrational

terror that angels, devils and human beings had all got mixed up, and that it would take forever to separate them out again ...

... And I'd wake up in a sweat, overtaken by those terrible lines from Corinthians: 'for Satan himself is transformed into an angel of light' ...

... And finally I'd wake up properly, uncertain where I was, what year it was, what tense I was living in, whether I was human, angel, or devil.

30.

A phone call, sometime late August, full of dropped *h*-s and *i*-s pronounced as *ee*-s:

"'ello, dear?"

"Hello?"

"Is that our Ed?"

"No."

"His ex-wife?"

"No."

"Good job, couldn't stand the bitch. Who is this then?"

"It's Jules — don't you remember? We met a few months ago."

"Bogger, didn't realise it was that long ago, or that short. Somehow it seems like both at same time."

"I suppose it does."

"When you visited, you left our Ed's phone number. I know I should of used it before now. But, like, well, it's been mad here."

"I can imagine. It's been a bit mad here too, Mrs. Prince."

"Has it, dear?"

"Yes."

"In what way?"

"Well . . ."

"Cos if it's been madder than normal, that might be one sign."

"One sign of what?"

"One sign that 'e's hanging round, sniffing up trouble."

"Who's 'e, I mean 'he'?"

"Me son."

"Edwin?"

"No, t'other one. He got hold of the phone number and address you left. I'd hid it in me underwear drawer. Me son must've gone through it—dirty bogger. Prob'ly thought the flipping Armenians were in there, trying the suspenders on."

"Oh," I said, unsure whether she was joking or not.

"Yeah, you might well say 'Oh.' It's bad, bad, bad news."

"What, having Armenians in your underwear drawer?"

"No, silly. This isn't no laughing matter. Bad news is 'im having our Ed's address. He might be over there now, my dear. He might do anything."

"Anything?"

"Anything. He's capable of anything, y'know."

At this point, she shot off on an unstoppable tangent, as a way of illustrating that her second son was capable of anything. A few weeks ago, she said, they'd had a rare trip into the city, to the Potteries Shopping Centre. He'd slouched after her, from pound shop to pound shop, cheap clothes shop to cheap clothes shop, whilst she'd chattered away, half to him, half to herself: "D'you reckon this'll go with me 'air?" and "What d'you think of this celebrity mag—hardly recognise any of them these days?" and "D'you think the cat'll take to this 'ere value litter?" He'd said nothing in reply to these semi-rhetorical questions, just glancing from side to side with narrowed eyes, scrutinising every tiny movement, listening to every tiny sound around him.

And then, after one "Do you think this is still me size?" question, she'd looked behind her, and found him gone. Immediately, she'd felt her old agoraphobia turn the shopping centre into a vertiginous ziggurat of corridors, mirrors, escalators, car parks, which was far too vast for her ever to find him—so she'd slumped down on a chair in the shop, and a polite assistant had asked what was wrong, and brought her a cup of sugary tea ("Strangers can be dead kind, don't you think?" she asked me on the phone, sounding all the world like some Potteries Blanche DuBois. "Though a quick gin and tonic might've helped better").

Revived, she'd thanked the stranger, and staggered out of the shop, making her way slowly round and round the ziggurat. She'd felt doomed never to find her son, forever wandering down corridors, going up and down escalators, every movement reflected in dozens of mirrors.

But then she'd heard some piano playing, and the murmuring of a crowd. She'd turned a corner, and there he was, sitting at a white grand piano on a café terrace, surrounded by two dozen onlookers. Normally, the piano was reserved for some maestro of muzak playing Carpenters medleys, whilst people shopped and dined; but Edwin's brother had been playing a very different kind of medley—a frenetic one made up of Bach interrupted by Beethoven interrupted by Haydn interrupted by Mendelssohn. "The tunes, they all sounded kinda, like, wrong, if you know what I mean," said his mother to me; and I think I did know, or at least could guess: I think they'd all represented his experiments in rescoring. That is, he'd been hammering out a medley of Bach, Beethoven, Haydn and Mendelssohn purged of any harmonies he classified as Armenian—of all those chords he thought had somehow retrospectively polluted their music.

And the result? The result had been musical nonsense. The result had been that the audience milling round him—seeing his greasy hair, his exaggerated tub-thumping, his over-earnest frown, and hearing this chopped-up, castrated musical mish-mash—were laughing, thinking they were witnessing a comic piano-murderer, deliberately misplaying the classics. Where Edwin's brother had thought he was smoothing the music out, purging it of so-called 'Armenian' discords, all the audience had heard was a different kind of dissonance; all the audience and Edwin's mother had heard was that something was comically "wrong" with what he was playing.

For a few minutes, he'd unwittingly transformed a corner of the Potteries Shopping Centre into theatre—a theatre in which the audience had itself participated: toddlers had danced and tumbled to unintentional discords; teenagers had twirled each other round to contorted cadences; hurrying husbands had ground to a halt and laughed; shorter people at the back had stood on chairs.

When Edwin's mother had pushed her way through the toddlers, teenagers and husbands, she'd touched her son on the shoulder, and he'd stopped in the middle of a phrase. Then the audience had burst into applause for this musical comedian: "Better than the usual tripe they play here," one of the onlookers had said. "I 'ate the Carpenters anyway," said another. "Dead funny, like Les bloody Dawson," said a third.

And not just like Les bloody Dawson, I thought: also like his brother, like Edwin. It suddenly struck me, with some force, how similar were these half-brothers who avoided each other, who thought of each other as enemies. It suddenly struck me how much they had in common, and I wondered why something so obvious hadn't crossed my mind before. Both were obsessed with so-called 'high culture' in the form of classical music, an obsession which no doubt originated as a guilty reaction against their grandfather's suspicion, even detestation of it; both brothers seemed to feel that this music, which was part of their very selves, was threatened in some way—whether by grandfathers or guilt, Armenians or the twentieth-century, history or their own nightmares—and hence that it needed saving, either by rescoring, or storing away for the future in a disused canal; and both brothers heard these threats within the music itself, like a shadow cast across the harmonies—Edwin's brother hearing Armenian chords everywhere, Edwin finding heart-breaking dissonance in Haydn, a kind of consonance in Penderecki. Strangely enough, Edwin seemed independently to be enacting his brother's delusions: whilst his brother was terrified of Armenian harmonies eventually overturning a Western sense of concord versus discord, Edwin was already there, claiming to hear concord as dissonance, and vice versa: "Bach, Mozart, Haydn," I remembered him saying in one of his most high-flown, manic moments, "wrote the truly dissonant music, because the beauty of their music jars most discordantly with the horrors of modern life."

By contrast, the onlookers who had listened to Edwin's brother's rendition of Bach, Mozart, Haydn were not yet there, hearing jarring discords where the pianist thought he had ethnically cleansed the music of all alien harmonies. Their shopping-centre hearing had reversed his reversal, hearing what he thought of as concordant as deliberately and comically discordant.

All of this struck me whilst Edwin's mother was concluding her shopping-centre anecdote on the phone, and it felt like a revelation from beyond myself—after all, what did I know of harmonies, apart from what I half-remembered my half-remembered father telling me? It felt like I was being shown a musical X-Ray of the whole situation, the whole sibling relationship, the whole bizarre mess, by someone or something else.

God knows who or what that someone or something else was. It wasn't—or at least didn't seem to be—Edwin's mother, whose main conclusion from the anecdote was: "I tell you what, we won't be going out again in a hurry. Bloody scary, that's what it was. It just goes to show how 'es capable of anything. I mean, he still thinks our Ed is that Catchy-tullulah bloke. Bloody hell. I told him over and over—I told him: don't go nowhere without my say-so. Don't go nowhere I don't say you can. Always come home after you've been wherever it is I know you're going to. Don't see nothing I can't see. Don't hear nothing I can't hear . . . and so on. But the other day, the bogger got cross and hit me again. Next thing I knew, I was on the kitchen floor, and he was out the door and down the street, breaking all the flipping Rules at once. And what's worse, I think he took one of his air rifles with him, the one he keeps in a kind of sheath-thingy, so it looks like a snooker cue."

"And he's not been home since?"

"No. So I was just ringing up our Ed to tell him to watch out."

"I'll pass on the message if you like, Mrs. Prince."

"Thanks for that, dear — you're an angel." There was a pause, and I wondered if the phone call was over. Then she burst out in anger: "God, what a bogger of a world this is. A bogger. I mean, you never know who might be behind you, with something or other disguised as a snooker cue. It bloody well makes you think, don't it?"

"Think what, Mrs. Prince?"

"Well, think that maybe me son has got a point, when he reckons that the world is after him. Armenians or no bloody Armenians, that's how it feels sometimes."

"I'm sorry to hear that, Mrs. Prince."

"Yeah, I'm sorry too, love. Shit — here I am at my age with high blood pressure and cholesterol through the roof, using my last breaths to chase after two sons gone AWOL, bailiffs round every other day, varicose veins up to my armpits ... God, my world's a catalogue of crap, that's what it is — all wrack and ruin, ruin and bloody wrack, and no Ed to show for it."

"I'll leave a message for Edwin to give you a ring, if that helps, Mrs. Prince."

"Nothing helps, love. I'm sick of all of the crap, sick of what I have to put up with. And you know what I'd like to know?"

"No, what's that, Mrs. Prince?"

"I'd like to know why I — no, why my family — no, why anyone — deserves all this crap. No one should have to go through what we've been through. Or ... or ... perhaps everyone should. Then at least the world'd be fair."

31.

The result of this was like breaking open an ants' nest. Temporary stupefaction, much running about and a few hardy souls spitting acid at the invaders.
—Sir John de Robeck, Smyrna, 1919

After Edwin's mother had put down the phone, I sat for a minute on the sofa, holding the receiver at arm's length, whilst a disembodied voice told me over and over again: "The phone is off the hook. Please replace the receiver. The phone is off the hook. Please replace the receiver. The phone . . ."

Eventually, I replaced the receiver as requested, and then picked it up again, and dialled. After a couple of rings, another electronic voice started talking to me: "Welcome to *Encyclodial*, the phone-opedia of all human knowledge. From neutrinos to the Big Bang, there's no question too small or big for *Encyclodial*. Before we continue, please note that this line is charged at £1 a minute. All calls are recorded, and you must have the bill-payer's permission. Please hold for one of our team of expert knowledge handlers to answer your query."

I held. Mozart's *Flute and Harp Concerto*, arranged for electric xylophone, played in the background.

"Please hold."

I held.

"All of our knowledge handlers are currently busy, but they will answer your call as soon as possible. In the meantime, have you considered a subscription to *Encyclodial*'s website, www.encyclopediaphile.com? At only £5 a month, it's a must for all factfinders everywhere. Ask your knowledge handler for more details, and you'll soon have the world at your fingertips."

Some synthesized Beethoven with a beat played in the background.

The Beethoven stopped mid-phrase.

"Welcome to *Encyclodial*, dah-da-dah, *et cetera, et cetera*. What do you want to know?" It was Edwin. I was going to tell him it was me, that his mother had rung, that I wished we could make up, that everything was going to be okay. But when I heard his voice — when I heard how different he sounded to the last time I'd called *Encyclodial* — I changed my mind. There was none of the Radio 4 charm of the earlier phone call; his voice conveyed none of that animated pleasure he usually displayed when dispensing his superior wisdom to lesser mortals. Instead, his voice was tired, curiously monotonal and, for the first time, I wondered if I could detect the merest hint of Stoke amidst the Queen's English — like the charred ruins of an ancient city glimpsed in the foundations of a new one.

"I want to know about a city," I said. It was the first thing that came into my head. I wasn't thinking; I'd been thrown by the change in his phone manner — thrown from talking to him about his mother, our friendship, the truth, into an abstract question and the fake, school-childish voice I'd assumed in the previous phone call to *Encyclodial*. I immediately regretted it, but by then it was too late, the decision taken, the question about "a city" asked.

"Can you be more specific? Or do you want to know about the Idea of the City in general?"

"I want to know about a city called Smyrna," I said. Again, it was the first city that popped into my head — there was no other reason for me to choose it. No other reason at all. "Tell me about Smyrna for my homework."

There was the slightest hesitation at the other end of the phone: "Smyrn . . . Smyrna?" Then Edwin returned to his former disinterested tone: "Okay, Smyrna it is." A tapping of computer keys was followed by: "Right. Do you mean Smyrna

Georgia, Smyrna Tennessee, New Smyrna Beach Florida, or the-city-which-used-to-be-known-as-Smyrna-but-is-now-known-as-Izmir-in-Turkey?"

"The latter, I think," I said.

"Well, I hope you're sure, for your homework's sake," said Edwin. For a moment, he sounded more like his old self. In the next breath, though, he reverted to the monotone, and was clearly reading out a pre-prepared spiel that wasn't his own: "Before I continue, did you know that *Encyclodial* produces a series of electronic resources which may be of interest to you and/or your school?"

"No, I . . ."

"The electronic resources on offer include *Encyclops 2.0*, an interactive package of CD ROM encyclopedias, *Ask-o-pedia*, a multiple-choice general knowledge quiz for all the family, and *The Cool Britannia Triv-o-phile*, a CD ROM devoted to all your favourite films, celebrities and TV sitcoms. All major computer systems are supported by these products, and you get your money back if you are not fully satisfied. Payment plans are available." The lack of enthusiasm in Edwin's voice was palpable, and I found it hard to believe he had managed to sell any of the products he was meant to be touting.

They were no use to me, anyway. "No thanks," I said. "I don't have a computer."

In response, Edwin muttered something under his breath, which might have been "Never mind," but was more likely "Don't blame you" or "Balls to that." There was some more tapping on a keyboard, and then he started reading off the screen: "Smyrna: old name for modern Izmir, a port city in Turkey, lying on the Aegean coast of the region of Anatolia (now Anadolu). Population in 1990 was approximately 1,760,000, the third most populous city of Turkey. It is one of the seven churches of Asia mentioned in the Book of Revelations, and has arguably had a rather apocalyptic history. Its origins date back four millennia, but it was probably founded by Ionian Greek settlers in 1,000 BC. Smyrna's large natural harbour, the fifty-kilometre-long Gulf of Smyrna, made it an obvious site as a trading port. There are various competing theories from Greeks and Turks as to why the name 'Smyrna' was chosen for the city. One of these connects the name of the city with the ancient Greek word for 'myrrh,' symbol of death and resurrection." Edwin paused. "Are you getting all this down?"

"Yes," I said, a little surprised by his question. He never usually worried about whether or not his listener was listening; I guessed he'd been ordered by the management to punctuate his telephonic patter with at least the odd gesture towards his audience — towards, that is, the kind of two-way conversational interaction which didn't come naturally to him.

Interaction done, he carried on with his spiel: "Excavations have shown that, by the eighth century BC, Smyrna was enclosed by city walls. This is taken as one of the earliest signs of the classical world after the collapse of Mycenaean civilisation. Around this time, Homer is said to have lived and worked in the area. By the seventh century BC, 'Old Smyrna' was already rich and powerful; but between 610 BC and 545 BC, it was sacked by two sets of invaders, first from the Lydian Empire and then from Persia. These were the first of Smyrna's many s . . . sackings." He hesitated for a moment on the word "sackings," as if he'd suddenly developed a stammer, and the word stuck in his throat. Once he'd negotiated the word, though, he carried on with his usual fluency: "The city regained prominence after Alexander the Great's series of conquests, in 300 BC. It was rebuilt on a different site, round the slopes of Mount Pagus, otherwise known as Kadifekale. In 133 BC, Smyrna became a Roman city and, during the heyday of the Roman Empire, the city flourished." Edwin paused again. "Are you still with me?"

"Yes, I'm still with you. Thank you for asking."

"No trouble at all," said Edwin, interaction ticked off for a second time. The interaction was certainly no more than a gesture. I don't think he'd have noticed if I'd said: "No, I don't understand a word you're saying." Either way, he'd have carried on regardless: "Smyrna's prosperity during the Roman

era was interrupted by an earthquake, in 178 AD, which flattened the whole city. Once again, the city had to be rebuilt
from scratch; and it managed to regain its status and wealth
with the help of Roman builders, architects and funds.

"When the Roman Empire started to decline, the city's for-
tunes declined with it. As part of the Byzantine Empire, Smyrna's importance dwindled with the decrease in trade between
Asia Minor, Anatolia and the West. Between 1076 and 1402 AD,
the city was conquered, reconquered and occupied (sometimes simultaneously) by various different powers, including
the Byzantine Empire, Turks, Genoese and Ottomans. In 1084,
for example, the Seljuk Turks destroyed the city, as did the
Persians in 1130. In 1402, the city was levelled to the ground
once more and its citizens massacred by Tamerlaine and his
Mongol forces." Edwin paused, and then — sounding like
some kind of robot, or rather robot-with-irony — said: "If you
would like to know more about Tamerlaine, say 'yes' now."

"No thanks," I said.

"Thank you for your response," said Edwin, as mechanical
as before. I'd never heard him talk like this, without enthusiasm, without personality. Even when he used to read out Schopenhauer or Nietzsche to me, they would somehow sound like
Edwin. But now, on the phone, I couldn't find Edwin in anything he said. He was just reading off the screen, asking me
scripted questions, obeying the rules.

He carried on reading: "Eventually, Smyrna was retaken by
the Ottomans, and officially became part of Aydin province of
the Ottoman Empire in 1426. From the seventeenth century
onwards, Smyrna grew to be one of the most powerful trading
ports in the Ottoman Empire — despite successive disasters,
including a plague in 1676, an earthquake in 1688, a fire in
1743, another plague in 1812, and another fire in 1845."

"Gosh," I murmured, "no wonder the city was mentioned
in Revelations."

"In the nineteenth century, the population of Smyrna
became increasingly heterogenous, including powerful
traders from Western Europe, Americans, as well as Arme-

nians, Jews and Greeks. In the early twentieth century, the population of Smyrna was half a million, the majority of which were Christians, outnumbering the Muslims by more than two to one. There were approximately 210,000 Greeks in Smyrna in 1912, as well as over 20,000 Armenians, Levantines, Europeans, Americans, Jews and others.

"During the First World War, as you may know, Turkey was allied with Germany. This was the time of mass deportations: in 1915, across the whole of Turkey, Armenians were targeted for persecution, ostensibly because they were seen as Fifth Columnists within the Turkish state. They were rounded up in villages and towns, and forced on long and deadly marches into the Turkish interior. Many were shot en-route, or died of exhaustion, beatings and starvation. Figures are disputed, but it is generally reckoned that between 1,000,000 and 1,500,000 Armenians died during this time." Edwin doled out out this information like a BBC news-reader, clipped, disinterested, almost arch. "If you would like more information on the Armenian Genocide (note: term disputed), please say 'Yes' now."

I didn't want any more information about the subject dispensed in such an unemotional tone of voice, so I said: "No."

I heard Edwin strike a computer key. "Thank you for your answer. I will now continue on the subject of Smyrna. During the deportations, Smyrna remained relatively untouched, partly because of its even-handed governor, and partly because of its cosmopolitan connections. After the First World War and Turkey's defeat by the Allies, however, the city's balanced cosmopolitanism became increasingly unstable. Whilst the old Ottoman Empire was falling to pieces—with major parts of it occupied by the British, the Italians and other powers—Greek troops landed in Smyrna, having been given the go-ahead by the British. From the 5th of May 1919 until 1922, the Greek army occupied Smyrna, causing widespread unrest on their first entry into the city, and destabilising the uneasy equilibrium between different races.

"Subsequently, in a disastrous military campaign, the Greek army attempted to take control of large swathes of Anatolia. The Greeks, under their premier Eleftherios Venizelos, dreamt of reconstituting a Greater Greece, a new Byzantine Empire, by carving up what remained of the Ottoman Empire. However, the Greek army fatally overreached itself in pursuit of this so-called Great Idea, or *Megali* Idea, and was eventually pushed back by resurgent Turkish Nationalists. The Nationalists demanded 'Turkey for the Turks,' and were led by their charismatic leader, Mustafa Kemal—alternatively known as Atatürk. If you . . ."

"No thank you," I said, pre-empting Edwin's question, "I don't want to know anything about Atatürk—or anything more than I already do."

"Fine," said Edwin. He sounded slightly annoyed, as if my interruption had interfered with the smooth running of his speech and computer. Nonetheless, he resumed the story of Smyrna: "Defeated, the Greek army fled in disarray, and the Turks re-took Anatolia and, on the 9th of September 1922, re-entered Smyrna." He paused, and his voice quietened—the first evidence in the whole speech of dramatic interpretation on his part, the first tiny glimpse of Edwin in the encylopedia: "No one quite knows or agrees what happened next. The Turkish army tried to reassure the citizens that they were safe; but rumours of rapes, deportations and massacres, first in the Armenian quarter, spread quickly. By the 13th of September 1922, the city was ablaze. Some Turkish sources blame Armenians for the fire; other Turkish sources blame the Greek army who had, after all, burnt many towns and villages to the ground during their chaotic retreat from Anatolia; but the majority of Western sources attribute the fire to the victorious Turkish Nationalists, given eyewitness accounts and the circumstantial evidence that it was the Armenian and Greek quarters which bore the brunt of the conflagration. The Turkish Nationalists wanted revenge for Greek atrocities, and Smyrna purged of its minorities—and a fire was an efficient way of achieving these aims.

"From the 9th of September on, the two-mile-long quay-side gradually filled up with up to half-a-million refugees — including Armenians, Greeks and Westerners — who were soon trapped between the fire on one side, the Turkish army to the north and south, and the harbour in front of them. There were numerous Allied commercial and naval ships in the harbour — American, British, Italian, Japanese — but few of them did anything to help. The Americans and British were under strict orders to evacuate their own citizens, but otherwise to remain neutral. So they stood by whilst the city burned and the people burned, screamed, drowned."

At this point, I was beginning to wonder if Edwin wasn't improvising — or if I was hearing things — or if *Encyclodial* had taken on a life of its own, describing things I didn't want described, remembering things I didn't want remembered. I felt strangely detached from the present, and the encylopedia's past tense was drowning me, bit by bit, until eventually . . .

"Eventually, just after midnight on the 14th of September, the British command in Smyrna had a change of heart, and the ships in the harbour started taking on refugees. Between that point and the beginning of October, Smyrna was emptied of its remaining Armenians and Greeks. It's rumoured that up to 100,000 people died in Smyrna, and maybe 100,000 more Christian males were deported into the interior. This act of ethnic cleansing ultimately led, in 1923, to the infamous Treaty of Lausanne, and the population exchange between Turkey and Greece. According to the treaty, almost all the remaining population of Muslims in Greece were sent to Turkey, and almost all Christians in Turkey to Greece. Thereafter, the city of Smyrna was rebuilt as part of the new Turkish Republic, and thereafter . . ."

"How can you say 'thereafter'?" I asked, without thinking. I was suddenly shouting, and I didn't understand why, or what I was shouting about. Somehow, I felt that I was being shouted through, not that I was doing the shouting: "There can't be a 'thereafter,' not after that. Surely there can't be. How can you say 'thereafter'? How can you say it?"

"Because that's what it says on my computer screen," said Edwin.

"I don't give a fuck what it says on your computer screen," I retorted. I'd totally forgotten about speaking in character — the fictional school-child was gone, and I wasn't sure what had replaced it. Spluttering anger, perhaps. The past, perhaps. Horror at the computer's insistence on 'thereafters,' perhaps. "There can't be any 'thereafters,' not after what you've been talking about. It's the apocalypse — the end of 'thereafters.'"

"I'm afraid not, or at least not according to the computer," said Edwin. He paused, and then carried on in a whisper: "Look, I'm sorry. I really am. But I've been bollocked over and over again about this kind of thing."

"What kind of thing?" For a moment, I wondered if he meant he'd somehow been 'bollocked' over and over again for the Great Fire of Smyrna.

"I've been bollocked for, you know, departing from the script. Not doing what the computer tells me, not saying what it tells me to say. Once upon a time, you see, I used to have lots of callers. I was *Encyclodial*'s Executive Bull-Shitter Extraordinaire. People would ring *Encyclodial* not for facts but for my voice. Women would listen to my smooth, R. P. accent and offer me their knickers. I held the record for the longest calls three weeks in a row — and was rewarded for it.

"That was back then" — he spoke about it as if it were many years ago — "before everything changed, before everything went wrong, and they stopped valuing bull-shit . . . or, rather, stopped valuing my kind of bull-shit. Instead of rewarding length of calls, you see, now they reward number of calls. I can't work that fast — I want to chat to the people who call. I want to expand on what the computer tells me. I mean, what's the point of fact without interpretation?"

He paused, so I said: "I don't know."

"Exactly. But the idiots here don't seem to realise that. They don't seem to understand the *human* dimension of the business. They don't understand that people ring up for a chat with a human being, not just for so-called factual information. Now, if I were running the place, I'd encourage interaction between callers and phone operators." He'd got carried away, and was raising his voice. He seemed now to be expounding his views not only to me, but to the call-centre as a whole: "God, if some lonely middle-aged women want phone sex with the operators, why the hell not? What's wrong with mixing phone sex with facts? I mean, it makes them money after all, at £1-an-extortionate-minute." I thought I heard a half-hearted cheer from some of his fellow male phone operators in the background, though I might have been mistaken. He seemed to rise to his (real or imagined) audience: "I demand the right to have phone sex with my callers!"

I wondered if he'd realised it was me on the other end of the phone, or if he still thought he were talking to a school-child, and phone sex was an appropriate subject for a young caller. Edwin was, frankly, never very good at self-censorship, or adapting his conversation for different audiences — or, indeed, for anyone but himself. At this moment, I think he'd got so carried away, he'd lost any conception of his caller as an individual, and was now delivering a speech to everyone and no one at the same time.

The speech continued: "But no, these Gradgrinds don't value anything apart from facts — facts without sex, facts without frills, facts without a spoonful of sugar to help the bloody medicine go down. Instead, these Gradgrinds value their operators according to how many CD ROMs they've sold, how many subscriptions to the godforsaken internet site, how many callers they've bored to tears, or, in your case, how many callers they've beaten black and blue with 'thereafter' after 'thereafter' after 'thereafter.' God help us, there must be more to knowledge than . . ."

Just then, Edwin's voice was cut off. There was a bleep, and an electronic voice intoned: "Sorry, we are currently experiencing a technical problem. *Encyclodial* apologises for any inconvenience this may cause. We will reconnect you as soon as we can. In the meantime, did you know a monthly subscription to our website will give you access to *Encyclodial*'s unmatched Fact Pool at the click of a mouse?"

I put the phone down, and then realised I'd never passed on the message to Edwin about his brother. I tried calling *Encyclodial* again, but—after the usual preliminaries and tinned Vivaldis—I was put through to a different operator, who insisted that Mr. Edwin Prince "was currently indisposed and unavailable to take calls. Can I help at all?"

"No," I said, "I'm not sure anyone can."

32.

*"I could see men coming nearer and nearer and even the fall
of the men in the front line, leaving it indented and broken,
and the final onslaught with bayonets. Thus the ants take
their exercises around the small yellow mounds of their
nests."*

—Mustafa Kemal, quoted in Patrick Kinross,
Atatürk: The Rebirth of a Nation

I didn't see Edwin again until about 9.30 on the morning of
Monday the 1st of September. And I shouldn't have seen him
then: he should have been in work, and I should have been too
busy handing out the morning's free newspapers.

But the papers had already gone. As usual, I'd been standing in one corner of the marketplace, with the pile of newspapers next to me and a few in my hand. By nine o'clock, the
pile had disappeared, and the rest had been snatched from my
hand by grim-looking people stalking past me. No one smiled,
said "hello," or "thank you." The whole town seemed strangely
silent: no one was talking to anyone else, let alone me. I began
to feel I was transparent, almost invisible. Without anyone to
talk to, without Edwin to half-notice me, without proper memories I could readily recall, I had this peculiar sensation that
I was fading away—fading into a Limbo where no one would
know me, or even see me. Everyone, everything, everywhere
felt empty, and I was lonelier than I had ever been before.

Or perhaps as lonely . . . as lonely as once upon another time
and place which suddenly flashed back to me: darkness for

hiding, a crack of light through which a city winks, my fingers holding open the crack, crushed by the stone slab above, soil and oak and hopefully nothing else against my knees below, a carving knife in my other hand, letting go of the stone slab and the light and the city, crouching in blackness, holding my hair in a ponytail behind me, sawing through it with the carving knife, strand by strand, clump by clump, lying down amongst the dirt and hair and moss, and falling asleep for the last time, waking up every now and then to hear distant shrieks, boot-steps, and cries of "*Korkma! Korkma!* Don't be afraid!,'" and finally waking to the sound of stone grinding against stone, glimpsing a crack of near-dawn from outside as the slab is pulled away, and it's not me that's moving it this time, and the silhouette of a face is peering down at me, and I'm afraid . . .

. . . and someone from another time was asking me a question: "Are you all right down there?"

. . . and I found myself back in 1997, lying face down, drooling onto the last remaining copy of the newspaper. I lifted my head off the pavement, and focussed on the page in front of me. There was a photograph of a blonde woman in a blue dress, with a headline: 'TOO GOOD FOR THIS WORLD.' Gradually, the smaller print came into focus, and I took in the rest of the front page. It seemed that some princess had died in a car crash, and lots of people were upset about it. I wondered if I'd heard the woman's name before. I couldn't recall Edwin ever mentioning her—and most of my conscious memories revolved around him. As ever, I felt strangely disconnected from the world of the newspaper, and this feeling of disconnection had intensified over the last few months. Bit by bit, I was losing touch with the present world; bit by bit, now seemed to be crumbling, falling into the sea of history.

Still, seeing the article in front of me, I couldn't help but feel sorry for now, for 1997 and its grief. I couldn't help but feel sorry for the blonde princess, and for all the people who missed her. I wondered if her death was why everyone had been so unfriendly this morning, and why all the newspapers had been snapped up.

"Are you okay down there?" asked the voice above me again. When I didn't answer, the voice started speaking to a few other people who'd gathered round me: "I just came over to get the last newspaper and bang, the person giving them out was on the floor, fitting or something. It wasn't anything I did. It wasn't me, was it?"

I pulled myself onto all-fours and was about to answer, when, beyond the huddle of people round me, about fifty yards away, I thought I glimpsed a familiar pair of over-worn trousers and scuffed shoes. I scrambled to my feet, and shook off the helping hands and "Are you all rights?"

"God," said the first voice, turning away, "there's no helping some people."

In passing, as I staggered through the small crowd of onlookers, I wondered if I agreed. Perhaps there was no helping some people; but I still felt compelled to follow the familiar pair of over-worn trousers I'd glimpsed across the square. At that moment, pushing past concerned faces, ducking past restraining arms, and then darting across the road, I felt I would have followed that pair of over-worn trousers, those scuffed shoes, to the end of the world, or the end of time.

But now, on the other side of the road, I could no longer see the trousers or shoes. I stopped and caught my breath and glanced around: no, the trousers weren't where they had been, nor where I thought they should be, given the direction they'd been heading. I turned 360 degrees. There seemed to be trousers, shoes and faces everywhere: but none of them belonged to *him*.

I ran a few yards forward, and stopped again. Still no sign. I darted into a couple of men's clothes shops — no sign, and a bit of a long-shot anyway, considering the state of his trousers. I stood outside a woman's clothes shop, thought, well, you never know with *him*, then decided against it. I crossed the road a couple of times, and retraced my steps. Still no sign. I'd lost him.

As I was about to give up, I saw the trousers again in the

corner of my eye. They were disappearing round a corner, up a pedestrianised side-street.

I chased across the road one last time, narrowly missed knocking over a woman and her pushchair, and turned onto the side-street. A hundred yards or so ahead of me, I saw the trousers, the shoes, and now the blue, threadbare jumper all disappear round another corner, to the right.

Why was he here? Why wasn't he in work? These are the questions which should have been racing through my head. But I don't remember anything racing through my head, only the irresistible and inexplicable compulsion to follow him, like a recurring tune or harmony that won't go away. And gradually, added to this was the peculiar sensation that I was no longer sure who was following whom—who was being followed, who was doing the following. Certainly, there he was in front of me, darting round corners, glancing behind him, picking up speed; certainly, there I was behind him, doing the same. But for some reason I started to feel that he was also behind me, stalking me, ready to pounce—and perhaps behind him was me again, and then behind that second me a third him, and so on and so forth *ad infinitum*. I found myself glancing over my shoulder, hiding in doorways, trying desperately not to be spotted by Edwins in front or behind.

The Edwin in front crossed another road, strode round the bingo hall, turned a corner, headed past a greengrocer's, some traffic lights and a sex-shop for transvestites. He walked more and more quickly, as if he too sensed that he was being followed. Out of breath, I hid for a moment in the doorway of the sex-shop and watched him go, down the road, past some boarded-up flats, over the canal. I glanced behind me, and saw a shape disappear into a greengrocer's. For a second, the greengrocer's, traffic lights and sequined basques in the sex-shop window all swirled round me, and I wondered if I were finally going mad.

I crept out of the doorway. I could see Edwin in the distance, turning left into our street. Now I ran. I sprinted down the road, past the boarded-up flats, over the canal. I turned into our street, and could see him in the distance, fumbling with keys in front of our doorway. He found the right key, unlocked the door and opened it—and, just as he was going inside, he turned to look in my direction.

For some reason, I didn't want him to see me—I can't explain why, any more than I can explain why I followed him that day—so I ducked into an alleyway and waited in the dark. "Fuck," I said.

The next thing I knew, the dark lurched forwards and hit me in the head. I heard a crack, the dark spun round, and mud and grit were in my mouth, up my nose, against my right eye. There was something heavy and wet on the left side of my head, pressing me into the mud. "Fuck," I said.

The heavy and wet something lifted, and was replaced by a leathery hand, and a voice, whispering, whispering in my ear:

"You said you weren't one of *them*. You said so. You said you weren't one of *them*. You said so. You saidsosaidsosaidso." The hand pressed down harder, and the mud oozed into my mouth. "You said so. You said you weren't one of *them*."

"One of whom?" I gurgled into mud and blood, though I have no idea if it was intelligible.

"One of *them*."

"Them who?" I wanted to shout. "Which fucking 'them' do you mean?" My head spinning and bloody, I felt dizzied with 'thems'—there'd been so many 'thems' in the recent and distant past, I felt I were drowning not just in mud, but also in pronouns: there'd been 'thems' which were 1950s B-movies, 'thems' which were giant ants, 'thems' which were the women in Edwin's life, unremembered 'thems' which were marauding soldiers in a burning city, thems, thems, thems. "Which of the 'thems' is it this time?"

"*Them. Them.* I asked you, and you said you weren't one of them. I remember. It was before—I can't remember how long ago. But I do remember asking you. You were in my home in Stoke, and I asked you if you were one of them. And you said no."

The hand pressed down on my head harder. I tried to shut

238

my right eye to protect it, but the pressure was too much. I didn't know what to do or what to say, so I just gurgled: "Fuck. Fuck. Fuck. I'm sorry."

"Sorry? Sorry? Sorrysorrysorrysorrysorrysorry? What good does that do? What bloody good is 'sorry'? You told me you weren't one of them, and I trusted you. I told you what I knew. Look how I'm repaid. I saw you in *his* house. I saw you come and go in *his* house. Just now, I saw you following *him*."

"Who?" I asked, rather stupidly. I suppose I half-wondered who the whisperer thought I'd been following—Edwin, the drummer from Supergrass, or Aram Catchy-tunian.

"You know who. *Him. Him.*" It seemed he could no longer bring himself to say the arch-villain's name—stressed pronouns were horror enough: "*Him*."

"Him who?"

"*Him.* The Armenian. The One. The Fifth Columnist of our music."

"But fucking hell you've got it wrong," I spluttered through the mud. "It's not *him*, not now. It's your brother, Edwin."

There was a pause, and I wondered if what I'd said had thrown him a bit. The pressure on my head lessened, and I wriggled my head slightly to one side so I could shut my right eye. Open or shut, it still hurt. For a moment, I desperately tried to imagine the near future, when my eye wouldn't hurt any more, when a hand wasn't pushing my head into the mud, when there wasn't this desperate whispering in my ear; but I couldn't manage it: since that first night when I met Edwin, my mind had misplaced past and future tenses, and now, here in the alleyway, the present rode roughshod over everything.

"This is now," I said. "This is fucking 1997. How can *he* be around now?"

"What do you mean?" the whisperer snapped.

"I mean—how can *he* be around now, when he's been dead for nineteen years? Fucking hell. He'd be ninety-four, not Edwin's age. I know Edwin looks haggard, but this is fucking ridiculous."

"Don't laugh at me. Don't laugh at me. Don't laugh at me,"

the whisperer whispered over and over. "Please don't laugh at me."

"I'm not fucking laughing. I'm not. How can I fucking laugh when I've been fucking head-butted by the wall? Look, he's dead. Dead. Dead. Ring fucking *Encyclodial* and they'll tell you. May the 1st 1978, he died. I looked it up myself. How can he be around now, in 1997, let alone round here?"

"Don't you believe in reincarnation, transmigration, reanimation?" His tone was incredulous, as if he could hardly believe that anyone could be so naïve *not* to believe in reincarnation, transmigration, reanimation.

And, with my face pressed down in the dirt, with a ringing head and bleeding eyelid, I thought he had a point. The first time I'd met him, his insidious whisper had mesmerised me for a few minutes; now, though, after everything that had happened, after all the lunacies, depressions, hallucinations, I'd lost the ability to know whether I was mesmerised or not, and just thought, well, you never know, he might be talking sense. After all, why was belief in reincarnation any more absurd than a belief in guardian angels, or, for that matter, the evolutionary supremacy of ants? Everyone seemed to have their own explanation for what was going on: Edwin explained the world through ants, the landlady through guardian angels and scented candles, the newspapers through the face of a dead princess. With my face in the mud, none of these explanations seemed any more or less ridiculous than the idea that Aram Catchy-tunian was alive and well, and was roaming around the East Midlands, plotting the downfall of Western culture. In fact, nothing seemed ridiculous or far-fetched any more. No one in this world seemed to have a rational explanation for anything—and I'd been surrounded by ants, guardian angels, candles, newspapers and Armenian harmonies for so long that I'd lost sight of what rationalism was, what rational explanations might consist of . . . And, for a second, reincarnated guardian ants with beautiful blonde hair, singing strangely harmonised versions of Elton John songs, swarmed in front of my eyes, and everything and everywhere was on fire, fire, fire . . .

. . . until I realised I was concussed, and the whisperer who was holding me down was waiting for an answer to his question. "I don't know if I believe in reincarnation or not," I said. At that point in time, I really didn't know.

"The evidence is in front of your eyes and your ears. *His* biographers say he and his music will live forever. And listen to this. Get this. Listen to this." He sounded just like Edwin, when he was reading from a book: "Listen to Vazgen I, the Armenian Patriarch. Vazgen said that *his* 'music . . . has lighted the whole world with its rays and glorified the creative genius of the Armenian people.' God help us — it tells you everything you need to know. Everything. And . . . and listen to this too. Bloody Vazgen said that, for what *he* — that's *he*, not Vazgen — did for Armenian music, he 'shall live forever.'"

"That's just a fucking expression," I said.

"No it's not. No it's not. Nononono. Don't be naïve. It's a curse. *He* and his music take on different forms, but they're always here, always around. Listen," the whisperer hissed, "listen. You only have to listen and you'll hear." I listened, and only heard the rain, and our breathing. "Listen, and you'll realise he's everywhere. Look how many people have come after, carrying on his work. There're hundreds of them, poisoning our music and pouring that poison down our ears: Alan Hovhaness, Alexander Arutiunian, Loris Tjeknavorian, Alexander Adjemian, Arno Babadzhanian, Edvard Mirzoyan, Avet Terterian, -ian after -ian after -ian after -ian. And these -ians, they're so brazen about what they're doing nowadays. They've got cocky: look at that last one I said, Terterian. He openly poisons our beautiful orchestras with his horrid Eastern instruments — he poisons the symphony, that amazing thing we've inherited from Beethoven, with the *duduk* and the *zurna*. God, why can't anyone else see or hear what's in front of their noses, their ears? Are people stupid? Are they stupid? Stupidstupidstupidstupidstupid?" He was desperate, to the point of tears. He took a deep breath, and bent down closer to me, so that I could feel his whisper blowing across my left ear.

"They thought *I* was stupid once. They thought I was going to be one of their Western flunkies. They'd got it all planned out: I was going to their Royal Northern College of Music, where I was going to play, maybe even compose, their bastardised music for them. They were forcing me into it. I didn't see it at the time. I didn't see how they were pulling the strings behind the scenes until it was nearly too late. I didn't see that the college had been infiltrated. I'd have ended up their mouthpiece if I'd gone.

"Thankfully, thankfully, thank God and my grandfather, I realised what was going on at the last moment. I understood."

"How was that?" I asked, with the intention of distracting him from his current urge to crush my face into the ground. "How did you come to understand?"

Distraction seemed to work, as the pressure on my face lessened somewhat, and his whisper became less aggressive: "Do you *really* want to know?" he asked.

"Yes please," I said into the mud.

"Well then, I'll tell you." I don't suppose anyone had given his delusions the time of day before, and, as far as one could tell from the tone of his whisper, he was rather pleased. The whisper seemed transformed into that of a much younger man, as if he were nostalgically regressing to an earlier self: "When I was very young, I loved playing the classical guitar and piano, you see — though more and more I had to settle for the guitar, cos we didn't have a piano in the house. I used to make up my own tunes too on the guitar. Back then, I was young and stupid — as stupid as everyone else — and I liked playing what I'd made up to my mother and kids at school. They'd always applaud me, and for a while that made me feel good.

"Only my granddad understood the danger. Only he got it — he banned me from playing when he was around. He said he hated the noise, that he was glad he was more or less tone deaf, that it all sounded Armenian to him. He said that if I carried on, no doubt the bloody Armenians would come and deport me. One day, he even grabbed my guitar off me and put his foot right through it. My mother was furious and I cried and called him a bastard—but now I know he did it for my own good. He did. He did it for my own good. He did. He diddiddiddiddid . . . I realised that too late for me to thank him—he was dead by then."

At this point, the whisperer came to a stop. Desperate to keep him distracted from crushing my face, I snatched for a question: "By when?"

"When I understood, of course—when I understood what he meant by stamping on my guitar, and what it would mean if I ended up in college, in Manchester, away from mother. The moment of revelation."

"When was that?" I asked, expecting some dramatic answer, given the extended preamble.

"Well," he said, "I was in the bath at the time."

I stifled the laughter by swallowing some more mud. This was getting ridiculous: I was being told a bath-time story by a musical mugger. "Really?" I said with a straight face—or, rather, a half-crushed face.

"Yes, really. I was supposed to be giving a school concert that night. Mother said I needed to scrub myself up for it, and a bath might help nerves. After a few minutes, the bathwater got a bit cold, so I turned on the hot tap. That was when I heard it."

"Heard what?"

"*It. It. It.* The chordal progression. It was in the tap, in the hot-water system, in the pipes. You only had to listen carefully enough, and there it was, hidden amongst the overtones, the hissing, the clanking. The secret was to turn the hot tap slowly enough, and you heard the Armenian scale, in a series of tetratones—three ascending tones followed by a semitone. Turn the tap again, and the last note was repeated, as part of a higher tetratone—three ascending tones followed by a semitone—and so on and so forth. It would have gone on forever if the tap hadn't stuck on A-flat."

"I see," I said, fairly bewildered.

"It's not a matter of seeing—it's a matter of hearing. Stupid people don't listen. They don't hear what's all around them—they concentrate too much on seeing, not hearing. They keep watch for enemies at their doors, attacking their homes; but they don't realise the enemy has already arrived, not through sight but through sound. People have to listen, listen, listen, listenlistenlistenlistenlisten –" he seemed to get stuck on the word for a moment, and then took a deep breath and carried on: "People just have to listen carefully enough, and they'll hear how it's got into their homes—tetratones in the water tanks, sevenths in their kettles, minor and major chords co-existing in phone conversations, Beethoven symphonies on the radio which have been subtly reharmonised, vandalised, Armenianised . . ."

I'd had enough of this: with my head throbbing and bleeding, I was not in the mood to discuss complex points of musicology. I wanted to get away, I wanted to get away now—and my mind seized at the first strategy for escape that presented itself. Interrupting Edwin's brother's stream of consciousness, I said: "Homes? The enemy is in our fucking homes?"

"Yes," he said, "yes, obviously." He sounded puzzled—whether by the stupidity of my question, or by the interruption from a voice outside his head, I wasn't sure.

"Are you certain about that?" I asked. "Are you sure it's got to that stage?"

"Absolutely," he said, clearly wondering where the conversation was leading. He was so used to living in a monologue, any kind of interrogation from the outside world must have seemed disconcerting, even upsetting.

"I don't want to upset you. I'm just worried that the situation really is that fucking bad."

"Definitely that bad. No doubt about it."

I tutted, sighed, and would have shaken my head in a disconsolate way if he wasn't holding it down. "Terrible," I said.

"Terrible," he said. His grip on the side of my head lessened once again.

"Fucking terrible," I said, trying to think what to say next to break out of the cycle of "terribles." We sounded more like two *Daily Mail* readers discussing the death of a princess, than an attacker and his victim. Still, at least we'd moved on from musicology. "For Christ's sake," I said.

His grip hardened again: "For Christ's sake, what?"

"For Christ's sake, don't you see? What about *your* home?"

"My home?"

"Is your home safe?"

"No one's home is safe, of course. Of course. Ofcourseofcourseofcourseof . . ."

"Then shouldn't you be there, protecting it . . . protecting your mother?"

His grip lessened. There was a pause. I could hear, feel his breathing in, out, in, out: "Protecting my . . . home?"

"And your mother."

Another pause. "My . . . mother." His grip lessened one last time.

Another pause.

And I realised there was no grip on the side of my face any longer—the remaining pressure was only soreness, not someone's hand. And I realised there was no whisper in my ear any longer—only the sound of traffic, the buzzing of flies, a kettle distantly boiling, none of which sounded remotely Armenian. The whisperer was gone, up the alleyway, onto the street, and heading back to his home in Stoke, where his mother might be in imminent danger from Armenians.

No longer in imminent danger myself, I pulled myself upright, by holding onto a loose drainpipe on the alley wall. I stood still for a minute or two, trying not to cry, pushing the tears back with a thousand swear-words. I moved my jaw from side to side—it wasn't broken. I could stand, I could still see out of both eyes, the blood and dirt would wash away, the ringing head would eventually stop. I kept telling my tears: things could have been a lot worse. Things could have been a lot worse if the whisperer had clung onto his initial conviction that I was "one of *them*." Things could have got a lot worse if he hadn't mislaid the beginning of our 'conversation' in the heat of his paranoia.

Things can always get a lot worse, I thought, rightly or wrongly.

33.

I staggered back to the house, let myself in, and sat down in the living room. The curtains were drawn, and it wasn't till a couple of minutes had passed that I realised the silhouette sitting on the chair opposite was Edwin.

"You look like shit," he said.

"Thank you," I said, dabbing the cut above my eye with a tissue I'd found down the back of the sofa. Edwin prised himself out of his chair, and handed me the bottle of Vermouth from which he'd been drinking, as if it were a bandage or cure-all.

I took a swig, and there was a silence, as I realised he wasn't going to ask what had happened to me. Sometimes, I wondered if he really believed in anything happening to anyone beyond his gaze—and actually, living with him, there'd been times when I too had found myself disbelieving in a world beyond these four walls. So instead of his asking me, I asked him: "What happened to you? Why are you back at this time of day?"

"Been s . . . sacked," he said, hesitating over the word.

"What?"

"You know, sacked, fired." He thought for a minute. "God, sacked and fired: makes me sound like a city."

I wondered if this were a cryptic reference to our earlier *Encyclodial* conversation; but I couldn't make out his facial expression in the dark, and still didn't know if he'd recognised my voice during the phone call or not. So I didn't say anything in response, apart from: "Oh."

There was another long silence.

"Do you want to go to the pub?" I asked. He nodded, and followed me out of the house, uncharacteristically docile. I think if I'd asked him to go to an abattoir, the past, or even his family home, he'd have followed me then. As ever, I missed the opportunity, allowing one of the last moments when I could have helped him to pass me by; and instead we headed for a final time to the pub: through the darkening, Satanic streets, down a flooded alleyway where there was blood mixed in the dirt, past the half-lit *Club Class*, where a hard-looking woman winked at Edwin from the doorway, along the towpath of a disused canal on which floated dozens of mouldering records, Bachs-gone-green, past the place where there was once a shopping trolley—until we reached The Dying Swan.

At the bar, the Swan's landlord glanced up and said to me: "You look like shit."

"Thank you."

"You don't look much better," the landlord said to Edwin.

"Thank you," said Edwin. "I didn't come here for make-over advice."

The landlord went back to pulling pints, and grinned to himself: "I tell you what, though."

"What?"

"I tell you what. There's someone who doesn't."

"Who doesn't what?"

"Look like shit."

"Who's that?"

"A friend of yours. I think you'll be pleasantly surprised." He nodded in the general direction of someone behind us, and grinned again.

We looked round, and there was The Dying Swan's Poet Laureate—but not as we had known him. His hair was still greasy, but was carefully combed across his bald patch; his shirt was still grey with dirt, but he wore a purple tie over it; his left hand was still trembling, but it was holding the right hand of a woman, to which it was communicating the tremble. My gaze took in his hair, his tie, the joined hands, and then followed the woman's arm upwards till it met her smile. The smile was framed by a mass of curls, and a round face which might have recently retired from long service in the Girl Guides.

"Hello," the smile said, in a brisk voice. I felt I was on parade and had been ordered into line. A left hand shot out and grabbed mine.

"Hello," I said, whilst my hand was pumped up and down. I glanced at Edwin—his gaze was slightly behind mine, still travelling up the arm towards the smile.

"Hello," the smile said to Edwin, grabbing his hand.

Edwin coughed, out of breath—the exertion of the hand-shake seemed to have tired him out for the day.

"He's told me lots about you," said the smile, whilst the Poet Laureate nodded and stared everywhere but at us. I assumed that the "he" to whom the smile referred was the Poet Laureate, though I couldn't imagine how he had managed to talk about Edwin and I in nineteenth-century verse.

"Has he really?" I asked. Edwin, for once, seemed dumb-struck, so I felt compelled to say something, anything.

"Yes," said the smile, "though he hasn't seen you round for a while. He wanted, I think, to show me off." She guffawed, so I laughed as well. "I mean, what's the point of a 'trophy girl-friend' if you can't show her to your friends?"

"Nothing at all, I suppose," I said. The Poet Laureate who, till this point, had been nodding, now started shaking his head, still not looking at us. He looked sad for a moment, gen-uinely sorry that he hadn't had a chance to exhibit his 'trophy girlfriend' before now. The smile had used the term ironically, gesturing with her free hand towards her dumpy body, the grubby trenchcoat she was wearing, the walking boots on her feet; but I realised with a jolt that the Poet Laureate believed it—he really did believe he was holding hands with a trophy girlfriend. I felt like hugging them, but I wasn't sure what their reaction would be.

I wish I had, because the next thing I knew, they were leaving: "We'd better be off," the smile said. "Tomorrow's a long day."

"Why's that?"

The smile smiled at the Poet Laureate and then back at us. "Because we're leaving tomorrow."

"For good?" I asked, though I knew the answer before it came.

She nodded. "For good. We're going to Jura. Do you know it? We both need a change, and Jura seems like an obvious choice. We don't know anything or anyone there."

She didn't give me a chance to interrogate the reasons for Jura's 'obviousness' as a choice. Instead, she grabbed my hand, pumped it again, and then grabbed Edwin's and pumped that too. She held his hand a bit longer, and looked up at him. I hardly noticed it at the time, but in retrospect I can't help thinking she saw and understood more in Edwin's face than she let on. "You know," she said, "perhaps you could do with a Jura yourself."

"Perhaps I could," he said, "though I have no idea where to find it." Those were the first and only words he said to her.

There was a silence, and she turned to go. "Come along," she said to the Poet Laureate. He looked directly at us, and spoke very slowly, as if it were a huge effort: "I . . . love . . . her." Then, his explanation over, he turned and left with his trophy girlfriend.

As the door closed on them, I thought about those parting words — "I . . . love . . . her" — and wondered if I'd finally heard him say something which wasn't a quotation. I wondered if he'd finally broken out of the poetic-traumatic loop in which his mind had been stuck; or if "I . . . love . . . her" was itself just another quotation from a million million poems.

I couldn't decide — and, when I next turned to Edwin, I wondered if he'd caught the quotation loop like a cold from the Poet Laureate, for he was mumbling something to himself, over and over again: " 'My friends forsake me like a memory lost . . . My friends forsake me like a memory lost . . . My friends forsake me like a memory lost . . . And . . . And . . . And e'en the dearest — that I loved the best — / Are strange — nay, rather stranger than the rest.' "

34.

Saturday 13th September 1997

To whom it may or may not concern,

Regarding the death of Edwin Prince and his ants

I, the aforementioned Edwin Prince, have hereby decided it is high time to quit this sterile promontory of a world, and exchange it for whatever sterile promontory comes next. "A change is good as a rest," as my mother used to crow—though when the last time she changed anything is beyond me. God, for her, Cliff Richard is still a nice young boy going on holiday, I'm still gay, and my grandfather's still hunched in the corner of his lounge, muttering obscenities at the canary.

In fact, sometimes I feel like that too — not about Cliff Richard, or being gay, but about my grandfather. I hear his voice sometimes, mumbling about Armenians and crap in the corner of my head. I'd like to think the mess we're in is all his fault. I'd like to think that. I'd like to think the self-murder of Edwin Prince (i.e. myself) is his fault. It seems peculiar to me that no one writes Whodunnits about suicides — after all, surely detective-novel readers know by now that he who is found wielding the knife, gun, or (in my case) Nippon is usually the reddest and herringest of all red herrings? Behind that red herring stands the murderer, or, more likely, just another red herring.

For that matter, I'm sure my grandfather is just another red herring, however much I'd like to blame him. I'm sure he had a grandfather-herring muttering in the corner as well, and that grandfather-herring had a grandfather-herring before him, and so on and so forth. No doubt Edwin Prince's suicide is my grandfather's fault—but no more than it is my mother's fault, my brother's fault, the ex-wife's fault, bloody *Encyclodial*'s fault, the feminists' fault, or the fault of those two strangers with whom I share my humble abode. My grandfather was Stalin in disguise, my mother is emotional blackmail incarnate, my brother is a looney-tune, my ex-wife has left me again, my boss has sacked me, my housemates aren't speaking to me, and my one real friend has abandoned me for Jura. It is all these people's fault—and more. Everything is always everyone's fault. The answer to all Whodunnits is potentially that of *Murder on the Orient Express*: everyone is red herring and murderer at the same time.

Do you not feel that sometimes, whoever you are reading this? Do you not experience that vertiginous sensation that every little thing one does, every little decision one makes—answering or not answering the telephone, feeding or not feeding one's ant colony, committing or not committing suicide—is the fault of everyone else, near and far, past and present? This final swig of Vermouth I'm taking now—and now—and now—is equally your fault, whoever you are, and the fault of someone thousands of miles away, hundreds of years ago. Everyone's to blame.

I'd thought the ants were different. I'd believed what John Clare, William Blake, Peter Kropotkin said about them—that they have renounced the Hobbesian war of all against all, that they are white-not-red-in-tooth-and-claw, that rather than murder each other, they spring 'with warm affection to each other's aid,' to quote some minor poet or other.

But then, this morning, when I was cleaning out some detritus from my ant-farm, I found two ant legs on the surface, and it was clear that an ant murder had been committed. I have sellotaped the two legs to the bottom of this letter as evidence, in case a post-mortem investigation is deemed necessary. I think it likely—though I am not entirely certain—that these two legs belonged to the queen: after all, they look slightly longer, and rather more elegant than those of the worker ants. I have, however, never laid eyes on Her Majesty, so cannot positively identify the body. My working hypothesis is that a number of revolutionaries dragged her to the surface, cruelly exposing Her Poor Photophobic Majesty to the light of day, and then they beat her and ate her (for some reason leaving two legs intact).

Now, you might say: well, of course there are deaths in ant colonies. Of course there are casualties in all societies. You might say: there have been at least two previous murders in your ant-farm. Why should you be surprised, why is this any different from those previous murders, except insofar as it is regicide? Are you suddenly turned monarchist that you worry so over the death of a queen, wailing 'God Save Her' whilst sobbing uncontrollably?

I answer no: I remain the *ant*-i-monarchist-neo-anarchist-élitist-etcetera-etceteraist you may or may not have come to love. It is not the victim's queenliness, but her status as a stranger that I mourn. It is not the regicide—or even, for that matter, the possible matricide of the case—but the stranger-cide which I deplore. Here lies a stranger who was once welcomed, now murdered, dismembered and (probably) devoured. I believe that the other ants were hungry, and the first thing they did was turn on the one resident who looked slightly different to themselves (and who had a bit more meat on her).

Okay, okay, I know what you'll say—that it's my fault, that I should have fed them more often. Of late, I've been a little remiss in that respect, and no doubt the ants felt aggrieved by their miniature famine. Despite this omission on my part, however, I'm still justified, I think, in feeling an acute disappointment at their un-anterly-behaviour. At the first sign of hardship in their community, they did what human beings in all their stupidity would have done—found a scapegoat. I'd expected more of them—ingenious escape, communal self-sacrifice, the revolutionary overthrow of their capricious human master (i.e. myself). But not this. Anything but this failure of imagination, this reversion to their lowest human-like instincts.

Maybe (I hope) an ant colony in the outside world would have behaved differently; maybe, with its human master and its manmade environment, my ant colony was poisoned from the start by human motives, human ways of not-thinking, human banalities. Whatever the case, it is clear that the community has failed the test, so I have decided to terminate it, as well as myself. In a sense, the community itself already made that decision, when it devoured its own queen. Together, my ant-farm and I have made our suicide pact, and there is nothing you could say to dissuade us.

As an aside, it's worth pointing out that—whether you believe it or not—ants do commit suicide. They do fall on their tiny swords, and they are capable of suicide pacts. Brazilian ants called *Forelius pusillus* are a case in point. Every night, these ants seal up their nests with sand, to protect them from enemies—even when there aren't any enemies in sight. A few of the colony commit selfless ant-*hara-kiri* by staying outside the nest overnight to finish the job, and ensure that the defences are as strong as possible. By next morning, they're dead of cold.

Then there are the soldier ants *Camponotus saundersi*, who die not from cold, but from their own poison. They are the suicide bombers of the ant world. When their colonies are invaded, they blow up their own bodies, spraying poison everywhere. Amazing, absolutely amazing.

If only my own colony had proved so amazing under duress. But no, it was not to be. Love them as I do, I think it's time we all bid farewell. So, without further ado, without further chit-chat, here is the end of my letter, the end of the ant-farm, and the end of Edwin Prince.

By the by, did you know that some ants sense the end before it comes? Ants have their prophets too—ant-Cassandras who know when the hour of doom is approaching. Worker ants in some species have intimations of their own mortality, and will take on more dangerous jobs outside the nest as death approaches.

So perhaps my worker ants already sense the oncoming apocalypse, their megadeath-by-Nippon-Ant-Killer. I have left a small pot of it in a corner of their nest. They will taste it, carry it home, and subsequently pass it on to the rest of the colony, through *trophallaxis* and mutual cleaning. In this way, it is the ants' mutuality, their selfless community spirit, which will be their undoing. The poison will be spread through sharing, not through egotism or hatred or war. Suicide as selflessness: I see a certain poetry in that.

Soon enough, though, the poetry will be over, and it will be time to say farewell to this vale of tears — so farewell, goodbye, *au revoir, salut, auf wiedersehen, ciao, vale, addio, adiós, ate mais tarde, do widzenia, do svidanja, xaatrak, yia, Allaha ismarladik, ts'tesutyun, menak parov* . . .

Yours,

Mr. Edwin Prince, B.A. (fail), originally of Stoke-on-Trent (for his sins), thereafter of the East Midlands, now looking forward to reincarnation as an ant or (at the very least) oblivion.

35.

I found the letter a couple of hours after it had been written.

I'd been at work all morning — the newspaper was trialling an ill-fated Saturday edition — and had arrived home exhausted by shouting out headlines, and trying to force free papers on laden shoppers. Perhaps they'd had their fill of dead princesses and grief.

I'd had my fill of them as well, and just wanted to collapse on the sofa. First, though, I wandered into the kitchen to fill the kettle, and into the bathroom whilst it boiled. I sat down on the toilet — and it was then that I saw the shit. It was plastered over the walls, on the shower curtain, in the bath.

When I'd seen the shit, I heard the music. It was so quiet, muffled, that I hadn't noticed it before. But it came to my attention because it had stopped for a second, and was starting over again from the Overture — the Overture, that is, to Mendelssohn's *Midsummer Night's Dream*.

That was the moment I knew something was wrong. I sprang up from the toilet, ran out of the bathroom and through the kitchen, and banged on Edwin's door.

No answer.

I tried the handle. It was locked from the inside and I didn't have the right key.

I banged on the door again.

No answer.

I unlocked and opened the back door. In the yard, above the ant-farm, Edwin's window was open a crack. Carefully, I moved the nesting tank to one side of the garden table. Inside, a crowd of ants were huddled round a small dish, whilst other ants scurried towards and away from it. The dish was full of a transparent, viscous liquid.

I didn't know what the liquid was at that point, and didn't give it much thought. Instead, I hoisted myself up onto the edge of the table, prised open Edwin's window, and climbed through the gap, down into his bedroom.

Edwin was lying in foetal position on the bedroom floor. Ranged around him were four empty bottles of Vermouth, a bottle of gin, his suicide note, a pornographic magazine, and ten empty tubes of Nippon Ant Killer Liquid. Before I read the note, I picked up one of the tubes and read the small print on the back very, very slowly:

Nippon Ant Killer Liquid

This 30 ml tube contains 5.5% w/w disodium tetraborate (borax). Controls common black ants in and around the home. **Directions for Use:** Undo cap and pierce end with pin. Clear up other readily available foodstuffs. Place a few drops of Nippon, preferably in late evening, on a flat piece of plastic, glass, or metal by the ant run. Change bait daily until ant activity ceases, usually 7 to 10 days. Do not disturb feeding ants, which pass Nippon onto the entire colony. Keep out of reach of children. Keep away from food and drink. Keep in a safe place. To avoid risk to man and the environment, comply with all instructions.

After I'd read the instructions once, I read them again. And again. Then I read the suicide note. Then I read the instructions one last time.

Then . . . I can't explain why I did what I did next. I can't explain it because I do not understand myself. I can only tell you what it was.

I put everything down as it had been when I'd entered. I stepped over to the door, and, using the key which Edwin had left in the lock, unlocked and opened the door. I walked out of the room. I walked down the hallway. I stepped into the living

room, and pocketed something I kept under one of the cush-
ions on the sofa. I stepped back into the hallway. I opened the
front door and walked out of the house. I walked away from
the house, down the street. I walked down a flooded alleyway, where there was dried blood on one of the walls. I walked
along the towpath of a disused canal, where records mixed
with algae. I walked past where a shopping trolley once lay,
past The Dying Swan, over a bridge, past an abandoned factory
which was gradually being eaten by nature, past a dozen dog-
walkers with angry dogs — and finally out into the countryside.
I took a footpath which diverged from the canal into a raggedy
copse, and wandered round it till I couldn't distinguish one
clearing, one ant-hill from another.

No longer knowing where I was, no longer knowing the way
back to Edwin, no longer knowing when was now, I lay down
on the ground, taking out of my pocket a photo I had once
stolen of an unknown lad on an unknown quayside . . . and I
stared at the photo . . . and home, Edwin, the landlady, 1997,
the present, all seemed so far away, as if I were losing my grip,
as if I were floating above them, as if . . .

. . . as if I were dreaming a dream, a dream of a past tense I
couldn't find when awake . . .

ENTR'ACTE

*Like ants, the people kept swarming toward the sea as
churches, schools, and orphanages disgorged their inhabit-
ants.*

—Marjorie Housepian Dobkin, Smyrna 1922

There is a girl.

There is a girl hiding.

There is a girl hiding in the grave.

There is a girl hiding in the grave of her great-grandparents.

In the dark of the grave, the girl is lonely.

In the dark of the grave, the lonely girl is cutting.

In the dark of the grave, she is cutting, sawing through her hair with a carving knife.

In the dark of the grave, she is cutting, sawing through her hair with a blunt knife, praying.

In the dark of the grave, she is cutting, sawing through her hair with a blunt knife, praying she might just pass as a man.

In the dark of the grave, she is cutting, sawing through her hair with a blunt knife, praying she might just pass as a man, and avoid what might happen as a woman.

Every hair that falls to the grave is a memory.

Every hair that falls to the grave is a memory of another girl who has done the same in her family's, her people's past.

Every cut, every slice, every hack is also a reminder of now.

Every cut, every slice, every hack is a reminder of now, of the distant gunfire, the muffled screams, the faraway cries of "*Korkma! Korkma!*"

Every cut, every slice, every hack is a reminder of now, of the distant gunfire, the muffled screams, and the faraway cries of "*Korkma! Korkma!*" which creep into the tomb like sunrise through a crack.

The crack has moved.

She is sure the crack has moved.

She is sure it has moved again.

There is a scraping sound, and the crack is widening.

The crack is widening, and there is nothing she can do about it.

She tries to pull the stone back, but she is not strong enough, and the crack keeps widening.

Black and red sky are coming in.

Black and red sky are coming into the grave.

Black and red sky are seeping into the grave, and there is a man's face too.

The man's face is on a soldier's body, dressed in a black uniform with a red crescent and star.

The man's face is on a soldier's body, dressed in a black uniform with a red crescent and star, a pistol in his red sash.

The man's face is on a soldier's body, dressed in a black uniform with a red crescent and star, a pistol in his sash, and he is holding a scimitar in his right hand.

From a long way away, another man is shouting, asking if this man has found anything or anyone.

This man is looking directly down at her, and she — crouching in the grave, her hair in her hands and around her feet — is staring back at him.

She is staring fixedly at his eyes.

She is staring at his eyes, trying not to look at his black uniform with its red crescent and star, not at his pistol or scimitar — in case, by doing so, she might remind him of their existence.

But the soldier in him already knows of their existence.

The soldier in him knows of the pistol in his sash, and particularly of the scimitar in his right hand, which he now grips more tightly.

The scimitar in his right hand is his nation. The scimitar in his right hand is his religion and *jihad*. The scimitar in his right hand is the other soldier, a hundred yards away in the dark, asking him if he has found anything or anyone. The scimitar in his right hand is the whole chain of command, up to Mustafa

Kemal. The scimitar in his right hand is what rumours tell him the enemy has done in Kapakli, Kutchuk Kumlar, Samanly, Akkeui, Usak, Nymphia, Alasehir, Magnesia, Nazilli, Kasaba, Menemen. The scimitar in his right hand is burning villages, murdered men, mutilated women, crucified children, as his enemy retreated from *sandjak* after *sandjak*, district after district.

That is the scimitar in his right hand.

His left hand, meanwhile, is empty.

His left hand, meanwhile, is empty—it is just himself.

He raises his empty left hand.

He raises his empty left hand, and calls back to the other soldier.

He raises his empty left hand, and calls back to the other soldier: "*Yok*. There is nothing, no one here."

And with that, he places the scimitar on the ground, and pulls the stone slab back over the girl's head.

In the darkness, the girl's head is suddenly full of her father's piano playing: the first E-flat-minor Prelude in Bach's *Well-Tempered Clavier*, emerging from a distance and receding again, and then her father's own composition, *Variations and Fugue on an Armenian Folk-Song*: "Bach meets Komitas," one of the priests—she couldn't remember which—had said, and her father had been pleased.

He hadn't been pleased when news of defeat at the Battle of Afyon Karahisar had reached the city, and the Nationalists set their sights on the Mediterranean. The newspapers, their friends, the priests, all had chattered that everything would be fine: the city had escaped the worst in 1915, and would escape now. The retreating army would turn and fight. The Nationalists were too undisciplined to pursue their military advantage. How could a bunch of guerillas defeat the Greeks, those glorious *evzones*? Even if they did, many of the Nationalists had sworn on the Koran not to harm anyone: "*Bir shay olmaya-jack!*" they shouted, "Nothing will happen!" And, well, if the worst came to the worst, the Great Powers had at least twenty-one ships stationed in the harbour—they wouldn't stand by and watch a massacre, would they? Would they? What more reassurance could her father want?

But her father was not reassured. Among friends, he shook his head, and moved his fingers silently over the piano keys, in a mute rendition of Bach's Prelude—a rendition haunted by ghosts of 1915.

"Artists are always Cassandras, always pessimists," one of his friends had said, munching on *sarma*, deaf to the ghosts.

"And pessimists are always right," murmured her father, his Bach carrying on despite the friend, his fingers silently remembering what the Ittihadists had done in 1915 in the name of Union and Progress, what may or may not have happened to his brother in the camp at Deir el-Zor, what General Kazim Karabekir and Nationalist forces had achieved on the Eastern front in Autumn 1920.

"That was Yerevan," said the friend, reaching for the *kete*. "Here the Nationalists are contending with an entirely different kind of enemy."

And her father had stopped miming Bach, and had turned to the speaker: "Yes, an entirely different kind of army, led by a general who is mad, who believes his feet are made of glass."

Thirteen days later, it was her father's wrists which seemed made of glass.

Thirteen days later, it was her father's wrists which seemed made of glass, whilst his daughter watched from upstairs.

Thirteen days later, it was her father's wrists which seemed made of glass, whilst his daughter watched from upstairs, peeping through the floorboards.

It was her father's wrists which seemed made of glass, whilst his daughter watched from upstairs, peeping through the floorboards, as the three soldiers laughed and sliced off his hands, one after the other.

One of the three soldiers picked up his hands and placed them on the piano keys.

One of the laughing soldiers picked up his hands and placed them on the piano keys, asking him to play something.

The Bach Prelude was silent, like before.

The soldiers kicked the father's head and told him he was rude. He had been asked politely to play something, but his hands had refused. So now they would be compelled to bayonet him and burn his *"Giavour"* infidel music, his piano, his hands, in order to cleanse the Haynots quarter of his discourtesy. Perhaps, they said, his hands would relent, and start playing on their own in the flames.

Before the flames came, the girl knew she had to escape. Her own hands shaking, she ransacked her father's wardrobe, and pulled on his boots, a vest, waistcoat, Sunday-best Western suit; and then she tied her hair back in a bun. She balanced her father's old pince-nez on her nose. She glanced in the mirror, and spotted the medal of honour he had been awarded some years ago, glinting from a half-open drawer. She grabbed that, and the golden crescent next to it, and pinned them on the waistcoat. She found a red fez squashed under the wardrobe and smoothed it out. When she put it on it just about covered her hair. She looked in the mirror again to check—yes, it was all a little incongruous, but you never know, it might work. There was no other choice but to try, try and be strong. "You are strong, you will survive," her father had said to her, when defeated Greek soldiers had shuffled, silent as the undead, south of the city towards Chesme, and when their ships had steamed away, abandoning the city and its people. "You are strong, you will survive," her father had said to her, when the victorious Nationalist cavalry had ridden into town, all in black, when planes had buzzed overhead, dropping pictures of Kemal into the streets, when the looting and killing had started. "You are strong, my darling Juliette, you are different to the others, you will survive," her father had said, when the knock came at the door. "It is *them*," he'd whispered, as he hid her upstairs: "Listen to me: you are strong, you will survive, your feet are not made of glass."

With feet made not of glass but of silence, she tiptoed down the back stairway into the kitchen. She tiptoed across the coconut matting, opened a drawer, and took out a carving knife. Turning her back on the body and hands in the salon without saying so much as *"menas parov,"* she peeked out of the sun lattices, tiptoed through the backdoor, and stepped into Ay Paraskevi Street as a man.

There was a cartload of corpses, some still twitching, at one end of the street, alongside a cartload of furniture, jewellery, rugs and silverware collected from the houses. One group of *chettes,* irregular soldiers, was lounging and smoking round the carts, whilst other groups were knocking on doors with their rifle butts: "Why are you hiding like fucking mice?" they shouted. *"Tsikar paragini,* take out your money."

No one shouted at the strange man hurrying by with the expensive suit, the ill-matched fez, the Ottoman medal of honour.

By a fluke, no one noticed him. They were too busy.

They were too busy carrying out orders.

They were too busy to notice him dart past the cartload of corpses.

They were too busy to notice him hesitate for a millionth of a second next to the cart.

They were too busy to notice him touch the limp head of a neighbour, and that of the neighbour's dog—a dog whose grey fur had once been as comfortable as a sofa.

They were too busy to notice the stranger scurrying away, onto Shirin street.

Turning onto Mekteb Street, he almost collided with a lieutenant.

But the lieutenant was too busy to look closely, too busy coordinating operations in the street, too busy with paperwork for the new governor at the *Konak,* too busy admiring his new-old watch. He simply nodded and murmuringly addressed the stranger as *"Bey Effendi"* by mistake. Such politeness.

The stranger carried on, all the way along Mekteb Street. He passed a group of civilians who were huddled on the other side, beating something on the ground with clubs and whips made of barbed wire.

Ahead, at the end of the street, the stranger saw a cordon of soldiers.

The stranger turned away, right onto Suzan Street. St. Stephannos Cathedral was ahead. The doors were closed, and there was chattering, shouting, wailing from within.

The stranger who was really not a man but someone's daughter didn't want to be part of that. He who was really a she didn't want to be asked where her father was.

So she took a detour to the right, into the cemetery-garden, through the cypress and terebinth trees, across the Caravan-Bridge and the Meles River—and into the far corner, where there was a grave she knew.

And now the girl is hiding.

The girl is hiding in the grave.

The girl is hiding in the grave of her great-grandparents.

The girl is hiding in the grave of her great-grandparents, cutting, sawing through the remainder of her hair, so that her disguise might be all the more convincing.

Ten or so hours ago, her disguise didn't fool a soldier.

Ten or so hours ago, her disguise didn't fool a soldier who discovered her.

Ten or so hours ago, a soldier discovered her—and then left her.

Since then, the crack between grave and stone has lightened.

Since then, the scent of jasmine coming through the crack has been replaced by other smells.

Since then, the crack has lightened, whitened.

Since then, the crack has lightened, whitened—and now oranged, reddened.

For a while, she doesn't understand why it should orange, redden. It is too early for sunset.

She thinks about what Archbishop Tourian said once about Revelations and the apocalypse; but surely it is too early for the apocalypse, just as it is too early for sunset.

It is not too early, though, for graves to yield up their contents; and she can hear half a dozen tombstones scraping open around her. It is now too hot in the graves, and those in hiding, those who were not discovered, are creeping back to the open air.

The crack above her is also too red and too hot, and she pulls back the stone.

Outside, the cemetery-garden is full of coughing.

Outside, the cemetery-garden is full of coughing, of smoke, of heat.

The Haynots district is alight. The Church of St. Stephannos, the Church of Aghia Paraskevi, the hospital, Basmahane Station—all are alight.

Her father's hands in a piano in a house on the corner of Shirin and Ay Paraskevi Street are alight.

In front of her, Suzan street is alight. Behind her, Fethieh Boulevard is alight in a sheet of flames. To her right, on Reshidieh Grand Boulevard, soldiers are using hoses to sprinkle buildings — hoses attached to barrels marked 'Petroleum Company.'

Some of the barrels' contents sprinkle on her.

Some of the barrels' contents sprinkle on her, and she decides it is time to leave the cemetery-garden.

She sneaks out of the cemetery-garden, and steps onto Reshidieh Boulevard.

There is fire and heat and fire everywhere.

She runs.

The fire seems to run with her, both she and it blown by a wind from the south-east. Buildings seem to combust spontaneously as she passes them. Houses, flats, churches, cathedrals, palaces, tobacco warehouses, shops, merchants, ammunition stores — all commit *hara-kiri*, falling on their burning swords as she runs past.

She runs down the burning boulevard, past a cordon of infantrymen who are too busy kicking someone else — and then round corners, across burning squares, through burning side-streets.

She runs up wrong turns, down dead-ends, two miles

turning to three, only half-recognising a route she knew well before the fire. All her memories, all her past seem to be going up in smoke. And not only her memories: the whole city seems to be incinerating its three-thousand-year past in a fit of fiery amnesia—until all that is left will be the present tense, nowness, ashes.

Lost in the city's burning past, the girl is still running up wrong turns, down dead-ends, terrified that escape from the labyrinth is an impossible dream.

She runs past three men with photos of Mustafa Kemal on their chests, who are shouting, "*Yasasin!* Long live Kemal Pasha!," and who try and grab her—but catch only her father's fez.

She runs past burning houses and burning shops and burning people and burning everything.

She runs past sights and sounds and odours she will not see, hear or smell, cannot think about.

Instead, she thinks about the colourful flags—the flags which seem to be everywhere: French flags, American flags, British flags, crescent-and-star flags, the tatty sheets hanging over shop awnings, declaring 'ISLAM,' or 'MUSEVI, JEWISH,' the flags which are talismans against war, fire and murder, the flags which are failed talismans because they are already burning.

She runs down Frank Street, where most flags are still waving, not yet burning.

She runs down Frank Street towards the sea, in the direction the flags are waving, in the direction of the wind, in the direction of the spreading fire.

She runs down Frank Street, and finally onto the quay.

The quay is a chaos.

The quay is a chaos of screaming and burning.

Soon, within a few hours, it will be a chaos of half-a-million people, trampled animals and lost possessions, upturned sacks of raisins and figs and pulses, Armenians and Franks and Levantines and Greek *rayahs* and people who didn't know they were any different to anyone else until now—all of them crushed into one fiery sunset.

There will be fire on one side, fire haemorrhaging heat, fire haemorrhaging black smoke, fire two miles long and as high as Mount Pagus, fire engulfing an amphitheatre of thirty thousand homes, dried-fruit warehouses, trading houses, the American Consulate, the Swedish Consulate, the Carpette Orientale, the Sporting Club, the Grand Hotel Kraemer Palace, Passaport, the Théâtre de Smyrne, and the black letters over its arched doorway, advertising the last movie to be shown there: *La Tango de la Mort*.

On another side, there will be sea reflecting fire, a harbour full of corpses and body parts and lads swimming between them, slipping watches and wallets from the dead, a harbour full of scuppered yawls and caiques, and paddles that have been broken to prevent escape to the moored merchant ships, cruisers and warships, unscuppered lighters which carry British, French, American citizens but no one else to safety, twenty-one foreign ships, eleven British, five French, one Italian, the French battleships *Jean Bart, Ernest Renan, Waldeck Rousseau,* the British super-Dreadnought *Iron Duke,* the *King George V, Serapis, Cardiff, Tumult,* the hospital ship *Thalia,* the American *Litchfield,* and the *Winona, Hog Island,* the *Edsall,* the *Sardegna,* the *Bavarian,* which will not get involved, will not intervene, will not help, and many of which, come dusk, will move another 250 yards from the quay to escape the heat—but even from 800 yards away, the girl on the quay will still hear the music played on decks, music from the military bands and the gramophone records, which are there to drown out the half-a-million screams.

On all sides of her will be screams of *"Kaymaste! Kaymaste! We're burning!,"* as volcanic-like ash will pour down on the heads of the refugees, and *chettes* will douse them with benzine and set them alight, and rape women on the burning cobbles, and slice off their breasts and throw them in the sea, and herd the young men off to the *Konak* to be shot, towards the Gediz River near Manisa, or to Pounar Bashi and then the interior, never to be seen again, and cut off noses and bayonet others, telling them that they will finally see "Aya Sophia" in Constantinople, and shouting *"Haide! Haide!* Begone!" as they push, shove and whittle away the 500,000 strong crowd on the quay, spreading out two miles towards Punta, and the crowd will shout, scream for the ships in the harbour to help, or at least to shine their spotlights on them, because the worst things are happening in the shadows, and everyone in the crowd will push and crush not to be in the shadows, on the edges, where the sea, flames, bayonets, benzine and machine-gun posts are, and the press will become so dense — fifteen, twenty deep in places — that the sick balance on the shoulders of the well, the dead remain standing next to the living, and someone will be wailing a long-ago, faraway song called 'Vorskan Akhper' in the girl's ear:

> . . . hunter, alone in the hills,
> Have you seen my son,
> My boy, my little deer?
>
> Yes, I saw him early,
> Heading for a wedding feast.
> On his heart a red poppy I saw.
>
> Tell me, hunter, who is she
> Who took my son away,
> Where does he lie wed with her?
>
> Your son lies on a stone,
> Struck down.
> To a bullet he is wed,
> Not with a doe he lies.
> The swallows fly high,
> The clouds like a mist.
> Quietly the grass whispers
> Over your boy so dear.

And this folk-lament will weave its Armenian harmonies into a chaotic-apocalyptic fugue full of strange dissonances and unexpected consonances never heard before or since, with a distant gramophone record of Caruso singing *Carmen* on one ship, the Overture from Mendelssohn's *Midsummer Night's Dream* on another, the nearby half-million screams, the yells of *"Haide! Haide!,"* the crunching of flames eating the flesh off buildings, and the unheard whimpering of the girl ...

... who will feel she has been divided into two halves—one facing west and the cold breeze from the sea, one facing east and the terrific heat of 100-feet flames, which is scorching her skin off, so she cannot bear it any more, and will have to turn round—like meat on a grill—to cook the other side instead, and then she will have to turn again, and the gaps between turning get shorter and shorter as the night wears on ...

... and the old woman who had been singing 'Vorskan Akhper' will pass out, and the girl will hold her up so she is not trampled, and a Greek with a kind face will hand her a blanket soaked in sea water to cool the woman down, and the girl will whisper to the woman that they will be safe as long as they don't move from this spot, as long as they stay standing on the tramlines which run down the quay road, as though they are enchanted, as though she is playing the game she used to play with her father where she wasn't supposed to tread on the joins in pavements or cobbles ...

... but this time she will lose the game, because a shrieking horse which has been set alight will leap into the crowd near the girl, and she will leap away from it, away from the tramlines, away from the old woman she was helping; and she will be pushed over the harbour wall, and will end up in the reddened water, amongst the bobbing corpses and unseen bullets and rats and dogs and horses and paddles and empty wallets and body parts and ...

... and she will swim, desperately trying to disentangle herself from the flotsam and jetsam, and by the time she has found some space, she will look up and realise she is fifty yards from the quay ...

... and she will look at the quay, and then turn round to look at the foreign ships in the harbour, and then turn round again to look at the quay, the people, the fire, the dead, the living dead ...

... and she will turn round once more and swim towards the ships — the ships that might take her to Chios or Mytilene ...

... and she will swim ...

... and she will swim further than she has swum before, in a sea dyed orange and red with flames, a sea rippled by gun shots ...

... and she will swim until she is so tired she does not know if she is still moving ...

... or if she is going backwards ...

... or down ...

... and she will swim until she suddenly hits her head against steel ...

... and she will go under into weedy, bottomless blackness, and won't know which way is up, and will try and find it in all the wrong directions, and will swallow water and oil, which taste strangely like dirty bathwater, and she will follow a flat-fish downwards, upwards, sideways, and she will eventually come to the surface, and water will explode from her mouth, and the sea, the horizon, reality will foam and crackle and fizz around her ...

... and she will swim back, look up, and see a British warship, and the tiny silhouette of a young sailor's face peering over from twenty-two feet above, pointing a searchlight down at her — and she will remember her father's words: "You are strong, you are different, you will survive," and she will cry and think he must have been right.

In the English taught to her by her father, the girl will say: "Help," believing that the sailor will help her, believing that everything her father had told her about English gentlemen was true. "Help me, English gentleman," she will say, but the words and beliefs will be swallowed by a wave.

273

The silhouette of an English face will shout back at her: "Go away!"

The girl will say: "Help me."

The silhouette of a face will shout back at her: "Go away!"

The silhouette will now also include a right hand, which is holding something over the side of the ship: "Go away!"

The girl will say: "No, help me."

The silhouette of a face with a hand will shout back at her: "Go away! We're under orders not to help Greeks."

The girl will say: "No Greek. Please."

The silhouette of a face with a hand will shout back at her: "Go away! One more warning: go away! Strict orders — no Greeks. Please go away. Please. Please."

The silhouette of a face who wants her to go away will now have two silhouetted hands.

In the right hand will be a metal bucket. The right hand with the metal bucket will be his orders, the other ratings, his new job, his ship, his captain, the whole chain of command. The right hand will be the order from the top not to intervene, not to be seen helping the Greeks. The right hand will be British foreign policy under David Lloyd George, it will be the Allies, the oil industry, the League of Nations. The right hand will be history.

That will be the right hand.

In the left hand, there will be nothing. The left hand will be within reach of a rope ladder.

The left hand will be himself, alone.

"Help me," the girl in the water will say, and the silhouette's left hand will be clenched. "Help me, help me, *imdat, imdat*!"

"For the last time," the silhouette of a face with two hands will cry, "go away. Please. My orders. No Greeks."

"No Greek. No Greek. Armenian. Armenian. Armenian," the girl in the water will say.

But by the time these words reach the silhouette, it will be too late, just as it will be too late when, ten minutes after this, the silhouette will be casually informed that the order to ward off refugees had already been countermanded thirty minutes before, and someone forgot to tell him, someone fucked up.

It will be too late, too late, too late, because the silhouette's right hand will have won, will already have emptied the metal bucket.

The silhouette's right hand will already have emptied the metal bucket of boiling water.

The silhouette's right hand will already have emptied the metal bucket of boiling water onto the girl in the water below — just as he used to pour boiling water onto ants' nests as a boy.

And the girl in the water will look up at the silhouette a moment before the boiling water hits her square in the face, and sends that face under.

And in that moment, as the girl in the water looks up at the silhouette, the silhouette will look down at the girl, and on the promenade, another warehouse will collapse in a hell of sparks, illuminating everything — the bay, the ships, the girl's face, the silhouette's boyish face — and the illuminated silhouette will tremble, and feel that he is losing control of his face, of his mouth, his nose, his eyes, as if the parts are rebelling, all trying to run away from each other, but he will issue strict orders to his face, his mouth, his nose, his eyes not to move, and certainly not to cry, never ever to cry again, and thereafter, something will happen, something will happen to the silhouette's future, and the silhouette's future family's future, and somehow, just as the girl's thereafters will all be cancelled out by the boiling water, so the silhouette's thereafters, and the silhouette's future family's thereafters will also be locked in this moment, in this now, in this present tense, in a girl's dying stare, in a girl's dying dream, thereafter and thereafter and thereafter.

And then the girl will drown.

ACT FIVE

36.

I don't remember. I don't remember waking up. I don't remember staggering my way out of the copse, back onto the footpath, back onto the towpath of the disused canal, past the angry dogs, past the abandoned factory, over a bridge, past The Dying Swan, past a place where old records mixed with algae, and down a flooded alleyway, where there was dried blood on the wall. I don't remember any of this. I just remember getting back to the house.

It came as a bit of a surprise to be back: I hadn't really expected to wake up at all, let alone find my way 'home.' I couldn't help thinking there was a reason for it, and was strangely glad to be back, despite the circumstances.

The landlady had arrived home before me, and had found Edwin. She was kneeling beside him, shaking him, whimpering his name, telling him what a fuckwit he was. I called the ambulance, and brought her a mug of sugary tea. Taking the mug, she looked up at me, and the years and white make-up seemed to fall away from her face. "Will he be all right?" she asked, like a child nursing a favourite pet.

"I don't know," I said, "but the ambulance is coming."

"I'll go with him." Sitting on the bed, trembling, she sipped the tea and looked at me over it. "We need to tell people."

"Who?"

"His wife, his family."

"Oh," I said.

"If I go with him in the ambulance, can you stay here and call them? Tell them to come?"

"I'll try," I said. Somehow, perhaps because of previous conversations, I guessed the image she had in mind: the final scene of *It's A Wonderful Life*, where all of Jimmy Stewart's friends and family turn up to help a desperate man. She wanted that for Edwin. Personally, I didn't hold out much hope of success — but the landlady grabbed my wrist, and wouldn't allow me to be half-hearted about it.

"You must do it, get them to come."

"I will try, honestly."

"It's important," she said, looking straight at me.

"I know that now," I said.

37.

After the ambulance had left—with Edwin, the landlady, and a tube of Nippon Ant Killer to show the doctors—I sat for a while with the phone on my lap. My mind was blank. I didn't know Edwin's ex-wife's number, and for the moment couldn't think of a way of finding it out. I couldn't yet face calling Edwin's mother. So eventually I called the one number I did know and could face: *Encylodial*'s.

After a few rings, an electronic voice started talking to me: "Welcome to *Encyclodial*, the phone-opedia of all human knowledge. Before we continue, please note that this line is charged at £1 a minute." There was a long pause, followed by a different, and strangely hesitant electronic voice: "We are sorry to announce that *Encyclodial* is currently experiencing some technical difficulties, due to extensive restructuring of our services. If you would like to hold, we should still be able to answer your call shortly."

I held. There was no music, just a loud buzzing.

Half an hour passed.

Finally, someone answered. She sounded far away, as if from a long time ago, and terribly young: "Hello, welcome to *Encyclodial*. Sorry for your wait. How can I be of assistance?"

"Can I speak to the manageress, please?"

"I don't know," said the young voice.

There was a silence. "Well, can I?"

"Can you what?"

"Speak to the manageress."

"I don't know," said the young voice again.

I started to lose my temper. "For Christ's sake, just put me through to the manageress."

"Okay," said the voice, meekly.

There was a click, and the loud buzzing returned. I half expected to be cut off. But no: a few minutes later, a clipped voice I recognised replaced the buzzing—the voice of Edwin's ex-boss: "Hello? Team Leader speaking. How can I help?"

I introduced myself—reminded her of the dinner party, which probably wasn't the best move—and explained what had happened to Edwin since he lost his job at her firm. I told her about the suicide, and even about the poisoned ants. I asked her if she'd consider giving Edwin his old job back.

In response, she asked me: "Look, I don't want to be brutal, but how can I give him his job back if he's dead?"

I said I was hoping he wasn't dead. I told her that he'd still been breathing when he was taken away by the ambulance men, so there was every chance. I said that it might help him recover more quickly if he had a job lined up. I asked her again if she'd consider giving him his old job back.

There was a long silence.

"He was very good at it, you know—at least he was when I called him," I said.

There was another long silence.

"Would you at least think about it?" I asked.

"You must be fucking kidding," she said, and hung up.

38.

I found Edwin's ex-wife's phone number in one of the unopened BT bills lying in the hallway. The bill was itemised, and the list of calls for July and early August was dominated by a Stratford number which had clearly been dialled over and over again—sometimes twenty times in ten minutes. I wondered how I hadn't noticed this was going on; Edwin must have done it when the landlady and I were out at work, or at the shops, or in the bathroom.

I dialled the number. The ex-wife's partner, Mr. Open-Top-Bus, answered: "If this is that gay-boy, shirt-lifting fucker again, I'll fucking come round and whip his arse."

I didn't know what to say. I just hoped he didn't answer the phone like that when his mother rang.

"Who the fuck is this?" he demanded. "Is it you? Is it you, gay-boy fucker?"

I tried to say "No," but he talked over me.

"It is you, isn't it? You . . . you . . . you sodomite. Well, I'm not going to put up with this bollocks any more. She's my lover now—she's my fucking shag now. Not yours. I'm not going to put up with these fucking over-and-over-again phone calls any longer. In fact, I tell you fucking what. I'm not going to change our number. I'm not going to call the fucking pigs on you. I'm going to come round there myself to your house and fucking beat you to fucking crap. That'll stop you ringing all the fucking time. That'll fucking stop you. I'll fucking fucking kill you. Do you hear that? Do you fucking hear that?"

"Yes, I hear that," I said.

He hesitated, and the rage hesitated too. "Oh, it's not you. Is it?"

Again, I was unsure how to answer his question: "No, it's not me, I mean you, I mean him."

"Who is it then?" he asked.

"It's Jules."

"Who's Jules?" he asked. He didn't half ask some difficult questions.

Instead of answering, I asked a question myself: "Is Ms. Prince there? I'd like to talk to her."

"Yes, I'll go and get her," he said, suddenly polite. I heard him put the phone down, and then a second later pick it up again. "Look, about just now . . ."

"Yes?"

"I'm sorry if I was a bit . . . abrupt. There's this guy, you see, who keeps ringing . . . or, rather, who kept ringing. He stopped a while ago, but I thought you might be him starting again. So that's why I was a bit—you know."

"Yes," I said. At the other end, I could tell he was waiting for me to say something else, but I didn't, so he put the phone down and went to fetch Edwin's ex.

"What do you want, Jules?" asked the ex's voice, suddenly on the line. I almost jumped.

"I wanted you to know that Edwin is very ill."

"Ill?" Suspicion was everywhere in her voice.

"Yes, ill. He tried to kill himself."

She exhaled through her nose. "For Christ's sake. Is this a joke?"

"It's not. It happened today. He took lots of Nippon Ant Killer."

"Bloody Eddy," she said. "Why couldn't he take paracetamol like anyone else?"

"He didn't," I said, "and he's in hospital. They took him in an ambulance."

Her voice emptied of suspicion for just one moment: "Is he okay?"

"I hope so. He was still breathing, the ambulance people said."

She sighed. "Phew. That's okay then. Gosh, you gave me a shock. Everything's okay."

"We don't know that yet," I said, "not until . . ."

"No," she said, having made up her mind, her tone as definite and imperious as that of a hospital Consultant, "he'll be fine. I know it. Stupid little boy. He can't even do suicide properly."

I tried to ask her if she'd consider coming to the hospital to visit the "stupid little boy," but she interrupted me before I could finish: "You tell me, Jules: what did he do that last night I was there—the night of that crappy dinner party?"

I hadn't expected this question at all. My mouth opened without making any noise. Before I could decide on an appropriate answer, or even form a coherent sound, she said: "Come on, out with it. What did he do? Was he off with some used-up old trollop? Or some young boy? Or someone dressed up in a kinky ant costume? It's bloody obvious from you not saying anything that he did something of the sort." I wanted to tell her that I wasn't saying anything because she wasn't giving me the chance to say anything, but, well, she didn't give me the chance. There were no spaces in her phone interrogation for answers: "Come on, come on—tell me. Bloody well tell me. Tell me. Tell me. Tell me everything now."

Quietly, slowly, I hung up.

I poured myself a Vermouth and sat for a few minutes. Then I called the ex-wife again. She picked up the phone almost immediately, and I opened my mouth to ask her if she'd consider visiting Edwin in hospital. For the second time, my mouth didn't have time to form the words, as she shouted: "He did, didn't he? He did, didn't he? Didn't he? He had some bloody slag on some bloody park bench, whilst I was at home mopping up the mess he'd made of the party. Tell me: am I right? Or am I right? Tell me. Tell me what happened. Tell me. Otherwise, you're involved too—you're all in on it, you, Eddy and that wicked witch of a landlady. God, why did I put up with you bastards for so long? Tell me why, and tell me what happened that night. Tell me. Tell me. Bloody well tell me. Tell me everything."

"I can't do that," I said. "You wouldn't understand everything." And I put down the phone. I didn't pick it up again for half an hour, scared that her voice would still be there, rattling on: "Tell me. Tell me. Tellmetellmebloodywelltellme." She seemed hemmed in by "tellmes," and nothing, not Edwin's illness and suicide, nor the suggestion of her visiting him in hospital, was going to break them down.

I too felt hemmed in, defeated by her "tellmes." I was failing at the task the landlady had set me; and her dream of an *It's A Wonderful Life* finale for Edwin was going up in smoke. The ex-boss wouldn't take Edwin back; the ex-wife wouldn't forgive him; and, as for the Poet Laureate, he was as unreachable on Jura as the past.

There was one last person to try.

39.

"Your son is in hospital," I told Edwin's mother on the phone.

"Oh dear," she said.

I wondered if she had heard me properly. Her voice was directed away from the receiver—as if she were distracted by something happening at the other end. I decided to repeat myself: "Your son. Edwin. He's in hospital. In Leicester, down the road from here."

"Oh dear," she said, this time more directly. "Oh dear." This was followed by a barrage of questions: "Me son? In hospital? Oh God, what should I do? What can I do? What about the cat? I should visit, but how would I get there? Who'd feed that bloody cat? Who'd clean out the litter tray?—I mean, that cat, it's getting on, and shits all over the place, like me dad did when 'e got old. God. Me son, my Ed, in hospital. Everything's in tatters, wrack and bloody ruin. What a shitty life. What do you think I should do? What can I do?" She sounded distressed, though I couldn't help wondering if her distress was more for herself and the potential inconvenience to the cat, than for Edwin.

Or perhaps, underneath all the cat anxieties, what she was really worried about was Edwin's brother: what would he do if she came to visit? On the one hand, how could she leave him in the house alone? On the other, how could she bring him with her? He might do anything if confronted with Edwin; he might do anything if he found out she was visiting Edwin without him.

I don't know whether it was the cat anxieties or worries

287

about her second son's behaviour; but whichever it was, Edwin's mother seemed lost in unanswered questions, inconveniences and difficulties: "What do I do? What should I do? One son mad as an 'atter, one son in . . . in hospital. God help us."

"Edwin's in hospital, yes. He's very ill. He . . . he took some . . . stuff."

"Stuff?"

"Poison."

There was silence on the other end. Despite the seriousness of the news, I still felt uncertain that I had her undivided attention. This was confirmed when she asked me: "What did you say, dear?"

"Poison. Edwin. He took it."

"Oh dear. Oh dear, my dear. I mean, oh dear." She didn't seem to know what to say. I heard a clatter behind her. "Stop that!" she shouted away from the phone: "Bloody well stop that, or it'll be The Rules!" Her voice returned to me: "Carry on, dear," she said, as if we were in the middle of some kind of gossipy chit-chat, not talking about the possible death of her son.

"Your son, he took poison," I said once again; and then to try and gain her full attention: "He might die, you know."

"Oh dear," she said. There was a pause, another crash from behind her, and then she said: "Look, dear, it's rather difficult to talk right now. P'raps you could ring back later?"

And the phone went dead, and I was left staring at it, expecting it to come back to life any moment — expecting to hear Edwin's mother's voice again, reassuring me that the person I'd been talking to wasn't really Edwin's mother, but an uncaring fake, a charlatan. His real mother, of course, would never have hung up, would never have reacted in such an off-hand manner to the news that her son had been rushed to hospital.

But no. His real mother never rang back.

40.

On the other hand, his brother—real or imaginary—did ring back:

"What do you want?" he asked, as if I were the one calling him.

"I want you to know that your brother's ill."

"What do you mean 'my brother'? What do you mean?"

"I mean the person who's your brother. Your mother's other son."

"Don't bring my mother into this. She's not *his* mother. Not *his*. He's . . . different. Leave her out of this."

"I can't."

"You can. I don't want to hear it. I don't want to hear it. Not any more. Not any more." He seemed more desperate than before, like a little boy with his fingers in his ears, whining and squeezing tears from his eyes. "I don't want to hear it. Please. Please. I don'twanttodon'twanttodon'tdon'twantto. I hear it all the time and I don't want to any more. Please make it stop. Tell *him* to leave me alone."

" It's not *him*. It's your brother."

"No it's not. No it's not. It's a trick. You're a trick."

"Listen . . ."

"No, I won't listen. Not any more. Not any more. Please don't make me. Please. Why won't everyone stop? Why won't it go away?" His tone was definitely more childlike than on previous occasions, more pleading, more insistent. "Stop it. Stop it. Stopitstopitstopitstopit. Please make it stop. Why won't it stop?" Gone was the paranoiac violence, gone were the long diatribes about Armenianisation, gone were the specifics of his delusions: here, on the phone, he just seemed scared in a generalised way.

I'd like to say I felt sorry for him, but I'd run out of patience over the course of the afternoon. Five dispiriting phone calls later, I'd had about as much I could take. I'd even begun feeling truly sorry for Edwin. Poor bloke, I thought, with his mother's wrack and ruin on one side, his ex-wife's "tellmes" on another, his brother's Armenian delusions on another, and all around his own manic unhappiness. As if from nowhere, there was suddenly a whispering-whistling-screaming in my head: "*Kaymaste! Kaymaste!*"

Then I heard my own voice, and it too came out as a kind of whispering-whistling-screaming: "For fuck's sake. For fuck's sake. Your brother might be dead. He might be dead now. Dead in hospital. And all you lot are still stuck in your own fucking heads. His ex can't get over a dinner party, your mother's too worried about cat shit, and you . . . You know what? You're fucking wrong, as fucking wrong as it's as fucking possible to be. It's all in your fucking head—no, all in your fucking grandfather's head—this shit you go on about. There are no fucking Armenians in your sink. Edwin's not Aram Catchy-fucking-tunian. Edwin's not Armenian. Edwin's Edwin. He's your fucking brother, for fuck's sake, and he might be fucking dead. For fuck's sake. For fucking fuck's fucking sake fucking fuck . . ." My short-lived fury ground to a halt under the sheer weight of expletives. I couldn't find the words for what I had to say, and "fuck" no longer seemed to cover it.

Edwin's brother didn't seem able to find the right words either, and just said: "Oh," in the quietest, saddest and meekest voice imaginable.

41.

That evening, I felt familiar arms encircle me as I was drifting off to sleep on the sofa: "Are the others coming?" whispered the landlady, "how did you get on with them?"

I told her. I told her about the boss and her "you must be fucking kidding." I told her about the ex and her "tellmes." I told her about the mother and her shitting cat. I told her about the brother and his delusions. The landlady cried and snuffled for a minute or two. "How can things ever get better for him like this?" she asked, and I didn't know what to say to comfort her. Blowing her nose and wiping it and her nose-rings on the sleeve of my jumper, she comforted herself: "Never mind. Never mind. At least Edwin's physically okay. I think he's going to be okay."

And, as if it were a strange lullaby, I drifted asleep to her murmuring everything the doctors had told her, echoing them word for word. She murmured that Edwin had been admitted through Accident and Emergency; that the doctors had taken the tube of Nippon Ant Killer, and called the National Poisons Information Service and Guy's Poisons Unit; that the dangerous substance in the Ant Killer was something called borax; that Edwin probably hadn't been exposed to a large enough dosage to do any real damage — for it to be serious, he would had to have ingested about three tubes for every kilo of his body weight; that he hadn't even drunk enough Vermouth-plus-gin to put him in a coma; that he'd been sick all over her as he started waking up; that he was shaky and disorientated, but nothing worse; that the doctors had transferred him to a medical ward for overnight observation; and that he would be seen by a psychiatric nurse the next day.

Next day, both the landlady and I caught the bus to Leicester and the hospital. In silence, we walked through the murky corridors, past trolleys of the sick, through smelly clouds of hospital food, into a lift of grieving relatives. As the lift ascended, I wondered what I'd say if Edwin asked me about the others — what I'd say if he asked me if his mother, his brother, his ex were coming to visit. To be honest, I had no idea; and by the time the lift pinged and the doors opened, I had given up trying to think of something, anything. There seemed nothing I could say, let alone do, to help. Disconsolately, like defeated soldiers, the landlady and I shuffled out of the lift, were buzzed into the ward, and found the room Edwin was sharing with six other patients.

He was sitting up in bed in loose, silk pyjamas, his chest hair on display. His cheeks looked sunken, and his skin was a mottled grey; but he wasn't still, wasn't relaxing. Rather, his movements seemed jerky, excitable, as he fiddled with something to his left, chatting away.

And he wasn't, or wasn't just, chatting to himself: there were two other people sitting by his bed with their backs to us, one of them half-hidden by the bedside curtains. The one who wasn't half-hidden turned to look at us as we came into the room. It was Edwin's mother. She sat hunched in her chair in an ill-fitting coat, and seemed smaller than I remembered, as though exposure to the world beyond home made her huddle and shrink. She was munching grapes she'd brought along for Edwin, popping them into her mouth one after another in an automatic, nervy way. The rest of her face, above her mouth, was unmoving, fixed, seemingly unaware of the grapes and the munching below. Her eyes were staring wide, and frankly she looked terrified — whether of the hospital, of what had happened to Edwin, or of me, I don't know. Or perhaps she was terrified of what her other son might do, because he was here too, sitting on her right — I recognised that broad back, those slouched shoulders, the greasy hair.

The landlady pulled up a chair on Edwin's mother's other side, and thanked both her and Edwin's brother for coming. "It was 'im," whispered the mother, nodding at her second son, "it was 'im who said we had to — he'd made up his mind." The second son's back remained motionless; he didn't acknowledge either us or his mother's voice. I too stayed still and quiet, standing where I was, feeling like an intruder, not sure what to do, not wanting to break any spell.

Edwin, by contrast, seemed strangely at ease. He was chattering away as though nothing extraordinary had happened — as though he'd seen his mother only the other day, and was accustomed to her dropping by. Back to 'normal,' the suicide attempt seemed forgotten by all but his trembling hands and grey skin; instead, he was engrossed in fiddling with the bedside radio, pushing the buttons and twisting the dial. A dozen radio stations fuzzed in and out, blurring Britpop with drum and bass with a foreign sports bulletin. "Bloody ridiculous," Edwin kept saying, twisting the dial round and round, "bloody ridiculous. Isn't this just typical?"

"What's typical?" asked the landlady.

"This," said Edwin, pointing at the radio, as if it were self-explanatory. He carried on turning the dial, and I couldn't help wondering if he'd been doing this ever since his visitors had arrived. Perhaps he hadn't even said "hello" to them, hadn't even looked up — just carried on messing with the radio and grumbling: "I ask you: why do we get all of these crappy channels, and no proper music? Of all places, you'd have thought hospitals needed a little catharsis from Beethoven or Mahler, or at least a little of what they like to call 'relaxing classics.' But no. We're just subjected to Spice Girls and — heaven save us — twenty-two grown men kicking pig's bladders around. God, it's compulsory philistinism, that's what it is. Institutionalised banality." He spoke these last two sentences loudly, directing them at a passing nurse. The nurse took no notice, and strode past, staring down at her clipboard. "Institutionalised banality, I tell you!"

With one last frustrated flick of his wrist, Edwin spun the radio dial all the way round.

Out of nowhere, it landed on what he'd been searching for: a classical music station. And the classical music station was blaring, of all possible pieces, of all possible coincidences, of all possible worlds, the Adagio from Aram Khachaturian's ballet *Spartacus*.

Edwin looked up at me with wide eyes, and the landlady mouthed "Oh God," and the mother looked confused, and the brother's back straightened, stiffened.

In the brother's right ear, on his right side, was Aram Khachaturian, years of paranoia, a life-time of grandfather's whisperings, a whole unremembered history.

In the brother's left ear, on his left side, was his mother's held breath, the landlady's "Oh God," a kind of silence.

In the brother's clenched right hand, hidden in his pocket, was an ancient 1920s Browning pistol—one of his grandfather's keepsakes from a port he'd visited long ago. I can't tell you how I alone knew what was concealed in the brother's right hand; let's just say it was an unlucky guess.

In the brother's left hand was nothingness, air, himself.

"No," he said, holding up his left hand, "don't worry. Don't worry. Don't. Don't. Please. Please. Don't worry about me. Don'tworrydon'tworrydon'tworry. It's not true. I'm not really hearing that. It'd be too absurd. Too absurd. I'm not really hearing that. It's not really *him*, is it, on the radio? It's not really, is it? I'm just hearing things, aren't I? It's all in my head, isn't it, this conspiracy? Isn't it? There's no conspiracy, is there?" With that, for some reason, Edwin's brother turned round, pulled the curtain out of the way, and directed the questions at me. His face was like Edwin's, but whiter, more thick-set, more rounded, and the features—the eyes, the nose, the wavering mouth—had a streak of boyishness, of childhood, running through them like a scar.

"I'm not hearing that, am I?" he repeated.

In response, I lied. I admit it. I lied, and everyone else there took part in the lie. It was the only way at that moment to overcome the paranoia—the paranoia that was, in this case, also the truth. But I couldn't tell the truth. Surely you can see that? I couldn't. I had to lie, had to shake my head, had to give Edwin's brother the answer he wanted: "No you're not hearing that music."

The music collapsed into quietness, exhausted by its own hyperbolic climaxes, and before Edwin could switch off the radio, a voice-over said: "That was the London Symphony Orchestra. They were playing the theme tune from the hit 1970s TV show *The Onedin Line*."

At that, the brother's right hand came out of his pocket, leaving the pistol behind, and his head jerked up and down with a smile: "You see? I told you. I told you it wasn't him. I told you it wasn't the piece I thought it was. I told you it was in my head and it was really something else. I was right, wasn't I? Wasn't I? Wasn't I? I was rightrightrightrightright, wasn't I?"

I nodded, and he turned back, now triumphant, to his mother and Edwin.

"Hello, Edwin," he said.

EPILOGUE

Better to be an ant's head than a lion's tail.
                                    —Armenian proverb

I'd sat down for a minute on a dog-piss-soaked doorstep in a dog-piss street in a dog-piss town—when the door I was leaning against gave behind me. Through the gin cloud in my head, I'd already guessed what door it was.

It had been days, weeks, months since I'd last been here. I wasn't sure why I was back, and whether I wanted to be back. For a long while, I lay on the threshold, half in, half out, unsure what to do, staring up at the grubby ceiling. My lower half was getting drowned, my upper half drying by the hall radiator. Finally, the shadow of a tall man in a dress passed across my upper body:

"Why, it's you, darling," said the shadow in a dress, puffing at a cigarette.

"Hello, Edwin," I said. "Happy Christmas."

"Talking of Christmas," he said, "you just have to listen to this—one my of my presents," and he bounded back into his bedroom along the corridor. There was no "where have you been all this time?", "why are you here again?", or "would you like to come in and dry off your bottom half as well?"—so my bottom half stayed in the rain, and my top half stayed on the mat.

My top half braced itself, anticipating some kind of Pendereckian-Ligetian-Bergian aural assault from Edwin's stereo. Instead, I was pleasantly surprised by music with a quiet melody—or, rather, music which seemed at first to have a quiet melody—or, rather, music which had a number of quiet melodies—or, rather, music which had fragments of quiet melodies, which couldn't quite coalesce, couldn't quite put themselves together. The music was strangely disconcerting, disorientating, like trying to make out a beautiful landscape through shattered glass.

"Gosh," I said, as Edwin's shadow fell over my head again. "That's a bit different from your usual musical nightmares. What is it?"

"It's post-music for after the end of the world!" Edwin declared. "Isn't it amazing, a post-apocalypse in my own bedroom?" Unexpectedly, he offered his hand to me, and helped me onto my feet. As he did so, he said, "You see, I don't listen to apocalyptic music any more. That was a silly fad, teenagery-meets-thirty-something stuff. No, I've grown out of apocalypse. Now, it's all about post-apocalyptic music."

"Is there such a thing?" I asked.

"You may well ask," said Edwin.

"I *am* asking," I said. He didn't answer, so I repeated the question: "Is there such a thing as post-apocalyptic music?"

"Yes and no," he said. It was coming back to me now, how frustratingly circular conversations with Edwin could be. In the meantime, we'd wandered into the kitchen. He handed me a towel to dry off, and started rummaging in the cupboards. "It's in here somewhere," he said, "silly bitch upstairs has no doubt hidden it from me. Bloody feminists . . . Aha!" With a flourish, he produced a bottle of red Vermouth. He filled three dirty glasses with it, handed one to me, took one for himself, and left one on one side. We clinked glasses, and there was silence for a moment, filled only by the echoes of broken melodies coming from his bedroom.

"The music sounds kind of broken," I said.

"As I say, it's post-apocalyptic," said Edwin. "By definition, things are going to be pretty broken after the end of the world."

"I didn't realise there was such a thing," I said.

"Such a thing as what?"

"Post-apocalyptic music," I said, wondering if our conversation would go round and round in circles forever.

"Again, there is and there isn't, if you understand me."

"I don't."

"Don't what?"

"Don't understand you."

"Of course you do. You must understand that music which is post-apocalyptic—which comes after the end of the world—is *ipso facto* an impossibility."

"How on Earth can you listen to it, then, if it's impossible?"

"That is the question. That is the question, my Dr. Watson: how on *Earth*? How on *Earth*?"

Getting the distinct impression that Edwin was being deliberately cryptic, I decided to change tack: "Look, just tell me who wrote this fucking piece of so-called music. Who writes this post-apocalyptic stuff?"

"The real question you should be asking, though, is: is it written or does it write itself?" asked Edwin. He looked at me, and even he could see he had pushed the subject, and his cryptic comments, far enough: "Okay, okay. It's by Silvestrov, of course."

"Thank you," I said, as if he'd done me a favour telling me—though I had no idea who he was talking about.

"There are other impossibilities I could tell you about as well. Because I only listen to post-apocalyptic music now, I've got to know quite a lot: late Shostakovich, late Schnittke, the end of Vaughan-Williams's Sixth Symphony. And there's another piece I wanted you to hear."

"Oh," I said, following him out of the kitchen and into his bedroom. He turned off the CD that was playing, picked up a tape which was lying on top of the window-sill, and slotted it into the cassette deck on his stereo. Turning the volume all the way up, he opened the window, ushered me out of the room, and then through the back-door into the yard—which was now half-covered by a tatty canopy.

There, underneath the canopy, on the cast iron table, was the old ant-farm. Both the foraging and nesting tanks were as empty, lifeless, desolate as the moon's surface. There was a cardboard plaque stuck on the top of the nest, written in Edwin's best calligraphic hand:

IN MEMORIAM

'It is a greater crime to kill an ant than a man, for when a man dies he becomes reincarnated, while an ant dies forever' (Maximiliano Hernández Martínez).

Here lies a colony of ant-heroes which was betrayed by its capricious God. Its God is very sorry. May you all rest in peace in the Land of Milk and Honeydew. Amen.

By the time I reached 'peace,' I realised that a quietly dissonant guitar adagio was stealing from the stereo, and through the open window of Edwin's bedroom.

"He saw the empty nest, and wrote this piece of music," said Edwin.

"Who?"

"My brother," said Edwin. "He wrote this piece for *them* — the ants. It's called *Threnody to the Victims of Nippon*. My brother wrote it. My brother, my brother," he whispered a few times, each one more quietly.

We stayed still for three or four minutes, not looking at each other, watching the dead soil in the tanks, listening to the piece. It sounded distantly familiar — oddly enough, like a halting guitar memory of the 'Invention' from Khachaturian's *Gayaneh*, impossibly mingled with the sarabandesque melancholy of Bach's E-flat-minor Prelude.

It didn't bring the soil back to life, and when it finished, we wandered back to the kitchen and our drinks. On the way, I caught Edwin's sleeve, and murmured to him: "Promise me you'll never do it again."

"Do what again?"

"Try to . . . hurt yourself."

There was a pause, and for once he looked straight at me, his eyes quivering with seriousness. "I promise," he said, "I promise never to hurt the ants again." There was another pause, as I struggled to find the words for what I wanted to say — but then the moment of seriousness was gone, Edwin turned and stepped into the kitchen, and I knew that was that.

I knew I'd never hear the answers to the questions I wanted to ask him. I knew it was too late, and I felt like sobbing.

I felt like sobbing that I was sorry, that I was always too late, that I always missed the chances of helping him which presented themselves. I felt like sobbing that, after everything that had happened, nothing really seemed to have happened, nothing seemed to have changed, nothing achieved—at least for Edwin himself. I felt like sobbing that he still seemed doomed endlessly to repeat the cycles of depression, isolation, self-destruction. Even his bedroom wall bore witness to these cycles: without looking, I knew that on his wall would now be pinned the wrapper of a Nippon tube, next to the gun with which he'd first (supposedly) tried to kill himself back in 1992. Underneath, there'd be a plaque, reading something like:

Exhibit B:
Nippon used to murder myself, at approximately 10.15 in the morning, on 13th September, 1997, AD.

Somehow, I knew this had joined the gallery of self-murder on Edwin's wall; and I couldn't help wondering when *Exhibit C* would be added to the collection, and *D*, and *E*, and finally *F* for failure, my failure. At that moment, I really felt that I'd failed him, my one and only friend.

But then . . . but then I thought about his whispering "my brother, my brother" to himself in quiet counterpoint with the ants' *Threnody*—a whispering that had seemed part of his brother's music, haunting its other-worldly harmonies as much as Bach and Khachaturian. In a dream-like way, I couldn't help thinking, hoping, believing that the harmonies meant something—that they wouldn't have been possible in Edwin's life, or Edwin's brother's life, a few months before. I wasn't sure why, and I wasn't sure what it all meant.

And I didn't have time to think about any of it, because Edwin had already picked up two glasses, and was leading the way back to the sitting room. There, the landlady was sitting cross-legged on the sofa, reading a book called *Healing With*

Wind Chimes. She put the book down when we came in, and smiled at me, "Hello, stranger."

Edwin gave her one of the drinks, and we all sat, sipping and smiling to ourselves. The sobs had left me, and I felt much calmer now, as I looked round the room. It was noticeably different to before: the floor was still covered in rubbish, but there was a living plant in the corner, Christmas cards on the mantlepiece, tatty pieces of tinsel hanging on drawing pins, and photos on the wall, including one of Edwin and the landlady eating turkey, and drinking Champagne-substitute. One of the photos caught my eye, and I got up to take a closer look. It was the Poet Laureate and his girlfriend, waving from what was presumably Jura. "Look on the back," said the landlady. So I took out the pin and turned the photo over. Scrawled there were the words:

The hawthorns here were hung with may
But still they seem in deader green
The sun e'en seems to lose its way
Nor knows the quarter it is in

I didn't know what the words meant, nor where they came from; but suddenly, I felt bewildered like the sun, having lost my way. Somehow I knew that I didn't belong here or now any more — if I ever did in the first place.

Edwin didn't notice my bewilderment, of course, and carried on chattering at me, showing me things like an excited child with an adult visitor. He'd got up from his chair, and passed me a 'Get Well Soon' card from his mother. "She sent it to me for Christmas," he said.

"For Christmas?"

"Yes, she said they didn't have any Christmas cards left in the corner shop. And 'Get Well' seems kind of apt."

"I suppose so," I said, opening the card. Inside, it just read: 'To our Ed, have a gd Xmas, luv, the old woman xxx.' The sheer concision of the message startled me — I hadn't thought Edwin's mother capable of such brevity. There was no list of woes, no reference to high blood pressure, no wrack and ruin, no emotional blackmail — just the kind of message anyone, any mother, might write. There was, though, one P.S. on the back: 'P.S. gd lock wiv yer book.'

"What book is that?" I asked.

"Ah, you obviously don't know what I've been doing lately," said Edwin.

"Well, no," I said — after all, I had been away for some months.

"In these last few months, I've started writing." He jumped over to the sofa, and reached down the back, behind the land-lady, from where he retrieved some fluff and a chaotic collection of papers and scribbles: "Look."

"What is it?"

"It's a book. I'm writing a book. I've even got a publisher."

"Really?"

"Okay, not really. But I might have, for a book like this. I don't think anyone's ever written it before."

"What is it?"

"I told you — a book."

"I know that. I mean: what's it about, for fuck's sake?"

"It's *A Cultural Encyclopedia of Ants*. That's what it is — an A to Z of ants in music, literature, history, philosophy — what I like to call a work of 'cultural entomology.'" He waved the manuscript in my face. "It's going to be huge. I reckon 3,000 pages, maybe three volumes worth of material. All from here" — he tapped his head — "it's all here. And it's *all* going in — there'll be entries on anything and everything I can think of, from Kropotkin to Nietzsche to Schopenhauer, from operas and symphonies to Adam Ant, from ant-films to ant-paintings, from Darwinian ants to Biblical ants to angelic ants, from ant-farms to ant-cities to ant-superbrains, from ant-technology to ant-apocalypses, from ant-grandfathers to ant-brothers to ant-landladies to . . ." He was getting carried away, and stopped to catch his breath: "You see, it'll be a work of auto-biography too, or should I say '*ant*-obiography'? Everything that's me, everything that's happened is going into it. I've just got to get it down."

"And I'm supporting him while he gets it down — so he better bloody well do it," said the landlady from the sofa.

"I will. I will, darling," said Edwin. He stepped over to her, sat next to her on the sofa, and put his arm round her shoulders. "Honestly, darling. It'll be done soon."

"How far have you got at the moment?" I asked.

"I'm getting through the *A*s as we speak. As we speak. And there are quite a lot of *A*s, given the subject matter. In fact, you might be able to help me with one entry I'm stuck on: 'Armenians.' Don't dare ask my brother."

"Perhaps another time," I said. Looking at them on the sofa, his arm round her, both in matching velvet dresses, I decided it was time to leave. I'd been here long enough, and didn't really think that I'd visit again. It was time to leave this place, this time, and return to the rain, the darkness, the past — whatever it was that awaited me outside the house. At the back of my mind, I thought I could hear distant cries of *"Haide! Haide!"*

No doubt, of course, I'd fallen a bit in love with them both — just a bit. But that didn't change anything, didn't mean anything, didn't mean I'd be back.

I finished my drink and put it down on the mantlepiece, next to the 'Get Well Soon' card. I didn't know how to say "goodbye," so — after some thought — I picked the empty glass up again, and mumbled something about getting the bottle from the kitchen. The landlady said, "Oh," but was suddenly distracted by the phone ringing. We all jumped.

"That'll be mother," said Edwin, in a resigned voice I'd never heard him use before, at least in relation to his family. Both Edwin and landlady got up from the sofa, and scrabbled about on the floor, searching amongst magazines, bottles and dead socks for the telephone.

When she found it, the landlady glanced up at me once more. Before she answered it, she smiled — really beamed — and, for some reason, quoted from *It's A Wonderful Life,* mimicking the voice of a little girl: "'Every time a bells rings, an angel gets its wings.'"

"Yeah, right," I said, and walked out of the room, down the hallway, out of the front door and into the drowning rain.

AFTERWORD, THANKS, ACKNOWLEDGEMENTS

It's March 2001. Whilst my father is in intensive care in Stoke-on-Trent, I've had to come back to Loughborough for a few days to work. Late one night, I'm staggering home, drunk and bent forwards like a Parkinsonian, watching the pavement cracks under my feet, trying to avoid them like I did as a child.

I feel a pressure on my shoulder and hear a voice. The voice is saying: "I'm homeless and I've not eaten in thirty-six hours. Do you have anything on you—anything kebabish?"

I drawl, "No." Then: "Yeah. I mean, no, I don't have anything here. But yeah, why don't you come home and eat our freezer?"

As the voice and I walk together back to my house, I'm saying over and over: "I hope you're not a thief or murderer or rapist or anything. I don't want you to kill me, please."

"I promise I won't kill you," says the voice, who doesn't seem offended at all.

Back at my house, I drunkenly empty the freezer onto the grill—sausages, bacon, chips, even pies. I ask the voice's name, and she tells me: "*Juliet*. It's my favourite play." She doesn't look like the Royal Shakespeare Company's version of Juliet, with her shaved head and khaki jacket.

Whilst Juliet watches the food burn, I drink Vermouth by the pint. I ask her about herself—why is she on the street, where does she come from? Is it a story of 'A pair of star-cross'd lovers' and 'death-mark'd love'?

Loughborough's Juliet, though, won't answer these questions, except to tell me she's been homeless for a couple of weeks, having run away from someone somewhere for somewhy I'll never know. Instead, she prefers to talk about abstractions, domestic violence, debt, and my father.

After Juliet's eaten all the pies, I ask if she wants anything else. She says a bath: "I don't like smelling like this." After her bath, I tell her she should sleep in the house for a night. I offer her my bed. "No. I couldn't possibly take your own bed from you." She thinks for a minute. "Unless we share it." I obviously look shocked, because she adds: "I don't mean like *that*. I promised I wouldn't rape you, didn't I?"

Instead, I make her a bed on my floor. I hide my wallet under my pillow, and feel guilty for doing so afterwards.

Lights off, we settle down. She's already noticed the records in my room, and now she whispers: "Can we listen to something whilst we go to sleep?" She searches through the LPs and CDs scattered everywhere, and retrieves one. "Can we hear this?" she asks. "It's a favourite of mine from long ago. I used to play it." I say yes, and snore off with a homeless woman called Juliet on my floor, crying to Elgar's strange piano miniature 'In Smyrna.'

Early next morning, with a Vermouth hangover, I find Juliet in the kitchen, eating burnt toast. My housemate—a chronic-depressive-dipsomanic-insomniac anarchist—is swigging the remains of the Vermouth and reading out a chapter of his Ph.D to her. The chapter concerns the part played by ants in 1930s literature. Juliet seems quite content, listening and munching away. I whisper to my housemate: "It's not what you think." He says: "I wasn't thinking anything, except about ants." He hasn't even noticed there's a different face in the house. He's just pleased there is a different receptacle for his ant meditations.

And suddenly, Juliet is gone—she says she hopes my father will be okay soon, thanks me for the pies and Elgar, kisses me on the cheek, and whispers that she believes in English gentlemen again. The door slams behind her, and I go back to my room to nurse my hangover and her compliment.

I never saw her again, of course, but this book is at least partly because of her.

It is also partly because of Simon King, and I want to send my thanks to him for being a wonderful friend and ex-housemate. His book *Insect Nations: Visions of Ant Society From Kropotkin to Bergson* (Loughborough: Inkerman Press, 2007) is one of the key sources for this novel.

Thanks also to Kathleen Bell, Simon Perril, Will Buckingham, Phil Cox, and all staff, colleagues and students at De Montfort University for their support and help with the book.

Thanks and acknowledgements to Giles Milton, author of *Paradise Lost: Smyrna, 1922* (London: Sceptre, 2008), Dora Sakayan, author of *An Armenian Doctor in Turkey: Garabed Hatcherian: My Smyrna Ordeal of 1922* (Montreal: Arod Books, 1997), Louis De Bernières, author of *Birds Without Wings* (London: Vintage, 2005), Panos Karnezis, author of *The Maze* (London: Vintage, 2007), Gagik Stepan-Sarkissian and the Armenian Institute, the Brunei Gallery at SOAS for their excellent exhibitions, *My Dear Brother* and *Treasured Objects*, the staff at the National Archives in Kew, Prof. Resat Kasaba at the University of Washington, Michael Pocock (www.maritimequest.com), Levon Ounanian, Richard Lacquiere, and David Senior, Technical Manager at Vitax Ltd., for their essential help and advice.

Thanks to Helen Lingwood for her kind assistance and suggestions, and similarly to Prof. John Schad of Lancaster University.

Thanks to Meg Davis, for her invaluable editorial advice on earlier drafts of the novel. Thanks to Jen and Chris Hamilton-Emery for their unfailing help and support.

And thanks and love, of course, to my mother, Robin, Anna, Sam, Naomi, Erin, Karen, Bruce, Helen, Ben, and my twins, Rosalind and Miranda, who made life mad and fun whilst I was writing the book. Thanks and love to my wife Maria, who, as ever, is responsible for anything that is good about the work; all of the faults are my own.

The quotation from Friedrich Nietzsche in Chapter 2 is from *Daybreak: Thoughts on the Prejudices of Morality*, ed. Maudemarie Clark and Brian Leiter, trans. R. J. Hollingdale (Cambridge: Cambridge University Press, 1997), p.127. The quotation from Alexander Solzhenitsyn in Chapter 3 is taken from 'The Bonfire and the Ants' from *Stories and Prose Poems*, by Alexander Solzhenitsyn, published by The Bodley Head. Reprinted by permission of The Random House Group Limited. The quotation from Arthur Schopenhauer in Chapter 26 is from *The World as Will and Idea*, ed. David Berman, trans. Jill Berman (London: J. M. Dent, an imprint of the Orion Publishing Group, 1995), p.164. The quotation which opens Chapter 31 is taken from Giles Milton, *Paradise Lost*, p.148 (see full reference above). The extract in Chapter 32 from *Atatürk: The Rebirth of a Nation* by Patrick Kinross is reprinted by permission of Peters Fraser & Dunlop (www.petersfraserdunlop.com) on behalf of the Estate of Patrick Kinross. The quotation at the start of the Entr'acte is from Marjorie Housepian Dobkin, *Smyrna 1922: The Destruction of a City* (New York: Newmark, 1998). Extract reprinted by kind permission of Edgar M. Housepian on behalf of the author. The text of 'Vorskan Akhper' in the Entr'acte is from Victor Yuzefovich, *Aram Khachaturyan*, trans. Nicholas Kournokoff and Vladimir Bobrov (New York: Sphinx, 1985), p.165. Extract reprinted by kind permission of Victor Yuzefovich.